Endu

The Lasting Value of the Old Testament for Christians

Pieter J. Lalleman

FAITHBUILDERS

Enduring Treasure: The Lasting Value of the Old Testament for Christians by Pieter J. Lalleman

First Published in Great Britain in 2017. Printed and bound in Great Britain by Marston Book Services Limited, Oxfordshire.

FAITHBUILDERS

An Imprint of Apostolos Publishing Ltd,
3rd Floor, 207 Regent Street,
London W1B 3HH
www.apostolos-publishing.com

British Library Cataloguing-in-Publication Data. A catalogue record for this book is available from the British Library

ISBN: 978-1-910942-76-5

Cover Design by Blitz Media, Pontypool, Torfaen. Cover Images © Clint Cearley | Dreamstime.com

He said to them, 'Therefore every teacher of the law who has become a disciple in the kingdom of heaven is like the owner of a house who brings out of his storeroom new treasures as well as old.' (Matthew 13:52)

Contents

Preface

The keen reader will have noticed that there are some topics in the Old Testament that never, or hardly ever, re-emerge in the New Testament, yet they are still important for us as Christians today. This book argues that the Old Testament is more than a series of predictions about Jesus, as some think; quite a bit more! There are numerous sections of the Old Testament that still have much to say to us in the period after the New Testament. Because of these good and beautiful aspects of the Old Testament, this first part of the Bible is of lasting value for believers. For this reason, my book is an enthusiastic 'yes' to the Old Testament. I want to show what a great book the Old Testament is and how it can play an important role in the churches and in our personal faith.

The introduction first tells something about the Bible and the Old Testament in general. In it I also explain the different ways in which the Old Testament still applies to us, and I show to which persons I owe my inspiration for this book and why I think that the lasting treasure of the Old Testament is an important issue for New Testament believers.

In the chapters which follow I set out these treasures in the Old Testament one by one. These chapters are the core of the book. In the last three chapters I briefly discuss several examples of misreading and misuse of the Old Testament.

Others have done their best to keep the Old Testament free from dust. This book is a supplement to these earlier books. I am focusing on the value of the Old Testament, in the hope that it will be restored to its rightful and valuable place in our personal life of faith and in the communities to which we belong.

I am grateful to the publishers of the Dutch original of this book for their kind permission to translate and edit it for English readers. The translations from other Dutch authors are mine.

Dr Pieter J. Lalleman

London, April 2017

Introduction

Israel

In the past God spoke in many and various ways through the prophets of the Old Testament (Hebrews 1:1). For centuries, the LORD God revealed himself to Israel and this is recorded in the first part of our Bible, the Old Testament (OT). In the beginning, there was not yet a people called Israel; God created the world and made himself known to all humankind (Genesis 1–11). Later on, this same God called Abram to move to a foreign land and made him the father of a new nation (Genesis 12–50). With this people, God made a covenant and he introduced himself to them (Exodus). The rules of the covenant were worked out in detail (Leviticus – Deuteronomy) and so began a long history of falling, getting up, and falling again. We have the ongoing story of God and Israel in the books of Joshua to Kings, and from a different angle, we can read about this in Chronicles, Ezra, Nehemiah, and Esther.

At the end, the story of Israel simply runs into the sand. This happened even though God had sent prophets to reveal the people more of himself, to further clarify his intentions, and to give timely guidelines (Isaiah – Malachi). The people responded to God's revelation by singing hymns, lamentations, and other songs (Psalms). Wise people thought about a good life and about suffering (Job, Proverbs – Song of Songs). Israel collected its holy books and later called this collection Tanakh; Christians call this book the Old Testament. The New Testament (NT) includes a reference to it as 'the Law of Moses, the

Prophets, and the Psalms' (Luke 24:44). At various places in this collection we find the expectation that at some time in the future God would send his people a Saviour.

Jesus Christ

Back to Hebrews chapter 1. After this long period in which God revealed himself to Israel, he did indeed send the promised Redeemer; he revealed himself in a deeper and more definitive way than ever through our Lord Jesus Christ. Although Jesus's outer appearance was that of an ordinary man (Philippians 2:7; Isaiah 53), Christians believe that in him God came to earth. Jesus died for the sins of the world, but rose again from the dead. We will not discuss his person, life, death, and resurrection here, but this event has changed world history for ever. The relationship between God and humans is restored at last. These things are recorded in the New Testament, which contains four biographies of this Jesus of Nazareth (Matthew – John) which show how special he was in many ways.

Upon Jesus's departure from the earth his followers were commissioned to tell the world about him, although that mission only made a slow start (Acts). In the period that followed, leaders among the early Christians wrote letters to churches and individuals in which they reflected on the meaning of the life and ministry of Jesus for time and eternity, and in which they discuss the current situation in the first Christian communities (Romans – Revelation).

Two Parts

So, Israel had collected its holy books and the Christian church not only inherited this collection, but added a second, smaller set of books consisting of the Gospels, Epistles, Acts, and Revelation. From the moment the church began with this second set, the first set became known as the Old Testament, and the second as the New Testament. Because the Lord Jesus is more important than anything in the Old Testament (this superiority of the New in relation to the Old is the subject of the Letter to the Hebrews), the church developed a tendency to depict the Old Testament as secondary and less important. Almost immediately, even before the New Testament was fully established, some people argued that the Old Testament was no longer needed and could better be abandoned. This idea was particularly promoted by the church leader Marcion who lived in the second century CE, though he did not get many followers. The church decided to keep the Old Testament and continued to recognise this book as the first part of the authoritative word of God. Despite this early decision, discussions about the relationship between Old and New Testaments punctuate the later history of the church and continue till the present time. The German liberal theology of the nineteenth century once again tried to throw the Old Testament overboard, but this attempt also failed.

Theory and Practice

Yet even though the church rejected Marcion's proposal and retained the collection of sacred Jewish scriptures next to the New Testament, a huge discrepancy has nevertheless developed between the doctrine and life of the church, between its theory and practice, and this discrepancy is growing in our time. In theory, we confess that God has given us a book in two parts, Old Testament and New Testament. For example, in the Westminster Shorter Catechism question 2 reads:

> What rule has God given to direct us how we may glorify and enjoy him?

And the answer is:

> The word of God, which is contained in the Scriptures of the Old and New Testaments, is the only rule to direct us how we may glorify and enjoy him.

But if we are honest, we know that in practice our attitude to the Old Testament differs to our attitude to the New. We prefer to read from the New Testament – it feels warmer and more familiar to us. We also know the New Testament much better than the Old Testament. We have our doubts about the Old Testament. We may prefer to read an edifying book by a popular author rather than read the Old Testament.

Our ministers and pastors too are setting us a bad example. Sermons and Bible studies deal much more often with the New Testament than with the allegedly difficult and boring Old Testament. The conclusion is inevitable that in practice many Christians have become followers of Marcion, whether we admit it or not.

Purpose

This book is an attempt to dislodge the spirit of Marcion so that the Old Testament once again gets a proper place in our personal faith and in the church communities to which we belong. I will do this by showing some of the good and beautiful aspects of the Old Testament which reveal its lasting value for all Christians.

Primate

This book therefore defends and argues the great and enduring value of the Old Testament, but my intention should not be misinterpreted. It is not a call to become Jewish or to live legalistically! For me, too, the New Testament is more important than the Old Testament because it reveals Jesus to us. He is our Saviour and that of the whole world (1 John 2:2). His coming and especially his victory over death is the decisive event in world history. Because I presuppose knowledge of these things, I will not write about them in any detail here. Rather, I am writing on the basis that the New Testament has the primacy in our life of faith, and that the Old Testament must *primarily* be read in the light of the New Testament.

Yet despite all this, we do not want to give up the Old Testament and there is no need to do so! I want to show some of the elements that make the Old Testament such a great book, and how they can play a role in the faith of the church today.

People of God

But how and why we can say that the Old Testament has lasting value for Christians? What about the things in the Old Testament which were not endorsed by Jesus or the apostles? Are there any criteria that we can use to answer these questions?

Principally, as Christians we have become members of the people of God through faith in Jesus as Lord; we have been grafted into the olive tree of Israel (Romans 11:13–18). The Old Testament contains God's revelation to his people. Just as the Old Testament applied and still applies to the people of Israel, so in principle it now also applies to us as members of God's people who have joined later. The Old Testament tells us who God is, what plans he has for his people and the world, and so on. All these things are still as true, and just as important, as when the Old Testament came into being and when Jesus and the apostles lived by it.

The Scriptures

In our respect for the Old Testament we stand in the tradition of Jesus and his first followers. They only ever spoke positively about the Old Testament; how good and how important it is. They obviously did not call it '*Old* Testament' because in their time there was no New Testament. Like all Jews at that time, they used expressions such as 'the Scriptures', 'the word of God', and the like. It is not difficult to find examples of the positive way in which Jesus and the early Christians treated the Scriptures; here are just three:

- Our Lord Jesus himself speaks positively about the Scriptures; he says that not even a small part of it will be revoked (Matthew 5:17–20).
- 'For the word of God is living and powerful, sharper than any two-edged sword: it penetrates deeply into soul and spirit, joints and marrow, and it is able to judge the thoughts and intentions of the heart.' (Hebrews 4:12)
- The evangelist Matthew repeatedly and emphatically shows how the Scriptures were fulfilled in the ministry of Jesus (e.g. in 1:22–23, 2:15, 17 and 23).

It is therefore fitting for us, as disciples and followers of Jesus, to adopt the same positive attitude toward the Scriptures. The present book is intended as an aid to reading and understanding them.

Fulfilment

We need to reflect on the concept of fulfilment. We believe that the Scriptures were fulfilled in Jesus Christ. In him God has revealed himself in a greater way than ever before. Predictions of the coming of the Messiah have come true and now the Scripture is fulfilled. This means that the status of this ancient book has changed. The idea of fulfilment occurs in texts such as Luke 4:21, 24:26–27, 44–48; John 5:39; Acts 3:18 and James 2:23.

But many people misunderstand this notion of fulfilment: they think that the words which are fulfilled have been crossed out, made inoperative, or set aside. This is a painful misunderstanding. When a promise has been fulfilled in everyday life, it means that we have received what was promised. Our expectation has been fulfilled, we have the promised thing in our hands and we can go on to enjoy it. Likewise, the biblical meaning of fulfilment is not elimination or abolition, but rather becoming full-grown, fully effective or mature. In Jesus, the Old Testament has reached its goal. Therefore, it is of great value to us, next to the New Testament.

The misunderstanding of the concept of fulfilment was bolstered by a mistranslation of Romans 10:4. Here the King James Version reads:

> Christ is the end of the law for righteousness to everyone that believeth.

And even the NRSV has:

> Christ is the end of the law so that there may be righteousness for everyone who believes.

What Paul writes is that Christ is the *telos* of the law; and the Greek word *telos* can mean much more than just 'end'. It often means 'goal' or purpose'; hence the later versions of the NIV correctly have 'culmination':

> Christ is the culmination of the law so that there may be righteousness for everyone who believes.

And the New Living Translation helpfully says:

> Christ has already accomplished the purpose for which the law was given. As a result, all who believe in him are made right with God.

Hebrew Bible

This is perhaps the place to draw attention to another title of the Old Testament. Many theologians today talk about 'the Hebrew Bible' and this is a very meaningful designation. At the very least it helps us to avoid the nasty little word 'old' that has such bad connotations in our time. In the present book, I will normally speak of the Old Testament, as this is the common term in our Bibles and our customary speech, but I will also use 'the Hebrew Bible' from time to time to refocus us.

Groups of Texts

We now come to a tricky point, because when we think about it, we realise that the coming of Jesus Christ – and the New Testament after him – has had a different impact on various parts of the Old Testament. Not all the Old Testament is in the same way affected by its fulfilment in Jesus. We can distinguish at least six groups of texts.

1. Firstly, there are the direct prophecies of the Messiah. About these verses, we can simply say that they have been fulfilled and now help us to understand better who Jesus is. Examples include messianic prophecies such as Micah 5:2 and Zechariah 9:9.

These texts were meant to help Jesus's contemporaries to recognise him, to acknowledge him, and to understand him. For us, they shed light on who Jesus is; conversely, the story of Jesus in the New Testament helps us to better understand these texts within their Old Testament context. To be sure, not all of them are clear. The best-known example of a text which is clearly predictive, but also difficult to understand fully, is Isaiah 52:13–53:12.

2. In the second group we find texts that have unexpectedly become messianic although the original author or the people of Israel never foresaw this. The text did not look messianic and yet it is. One such text is Psalm 22:1: 'My God, my God, why have you forsaken me?' Originally, these words of David (see the Psalm's heading) expressed a hard reality which he encountered at some point in his life: he was persecuted by his enemies and his life was so horrible that he felt abandoned by God. He uttered cries of despair but nothing therein seemed to be prophetic. At least, not until Jesus of Nazareth uttered these same words on the cross. Jesus ended up in the same situation as David and for him these words were more literally true. For whereas David only *felt* alone, the Lord Jesus really *was* abandoned by his Father.

Later in the same Psalm, it says: 'They divide my garments among them and cast lots for my clothing' (verse 18). Nobody who heard David sing these words, and no Israelite who sang them after him, could have foreseen that they would also describe the experience of the Messiah.

Yet Jesus experienced this very situation. Although he did not speak those words himself, the early Christians saw that what happened on Good Friday closely resembled the words of David. It is striking that all four evangelists, who in many respects had their own emphases, quoted these words in their books about Jesus (Matthew 27:35; Mark 15:24; Luke 23:34; John 19:24). Yet only John says that this event was a fulfilment of the Scripture, and he emphasizes it by means of the enigmatic words, 'So this is what the soldiers did' (John 19:24b).

3. A third group of passages from the Old Testament is formed by those laws and regulations which are still relevant for us as Christians. We can think of the Ten Commandments as they are found in Exodus 20 and Deuteronomy 5. The nation of Israel was not allowed to have idols, to steal, commit adultery, or covet what belonged to another person, and this applies to Christians as well. For this group of texts, the coming of Christ therefore makes little difference.

To provide an example: God does not like divorce. We could have long discussions about exceptions to the prohibition of divorce and ask questions such as: 'when is divorce possibly the least bad solution?' Such discussions should certainly take place, but the principle remains intact: God hates divorce (see also Mal 2:16) just as he hates idols, theft, and so on.

4. The fourth group of texts from the Old Testament, however, contains laws and regulations that do not apply to us under the new covenant in the same way as they applied to Israel. There are many laws and rules that belong specifically to the old covenant and which have now got a different status because of the ministry of Jesus. This is, for example, the case with the regulations for the sacrifices, with the laws on unclean animals, and the like. In the Old Testament, this can obviously not yet be seen; we perceive this only in retrospect, in light of the ministry of Jesus and the reflections of Paul and the other authors

of the New Testament. In the later church these issues were much discussed and we can learn much from these discussions.

For us many of the precepts in the books of Exodus to Deuteronomy no longer have the force of commands, but that does not mean that these 'legal' portions of the Old Testament have completely lost their value. Even though the Christian church is not required to obey them literally, we can still learn from them. Many of these rules give clear expression to moral principles that are still generally valid, such as the holiness of God. In this book, however, we will not go into this.[1]

Meanwhile, the difference between the group with still-valid laws (group 3) and the group of 'abolished' rules (group 4) is a major point of dispute in the church and between churches. Anyone who knows something about the different 'flavours' and currents within Christianity knows that there are different views about the question of which laws and regulations are applicable to Christians and which are not. In the terms of this chapter, how can we tell if a particular command belongs in group 3 or group 4? Some believers think for instance that women are not allowed to wear trousers and they invoke Deuteronomy 22:5; others think that this rule does not apply to Christians. Another controversial rule is the commandment to sanctify the Sabbath. We find this briefly in the Ten Commandments (Exodus 20:8–11;

---

[1] See the book by my wife, Hetty Lalleman, *Celebrating the Law? Rethinking Old Testament Ethics* (Carlisle: Paternoster, 2004, 2nd edition Milton Keynes: Authentic Media, 2016).

Deuteronomy 5:12–15) and it is elaborated in Exodus 31:12–17. Some Christians take this commandment literally and – like the Jews – they celebrate the Sabbath (Saturday) as the day of rest and not the Sunday; others may celebrate the Sunday but they avoid as much as possible any work on 'the day of the LORD' because of what it says in the Old Testament; still others handle this commandment more freely and their conduct on Sundays is little different from that of non-believers.

5. The Old Testament contains descriptions of many characters: humans who follow God and humans who turn their backs to him; women and men. It is easy to argue that even several thousand years later many of these cameos and longer stories have much to teach us, their fellow humans. The attention to the narratives of the Old Testament has always been there and Sunday schools have played a great role in disseminating them.

6. In this book I will focus on a sixth group of passages in the Old Testament, a group without laws and regulations, without messianic predictions, and largely non-narrative. The status of this large body of material was hardly changed by the coming of Jesus. We could almost say that these passages are timeless, so that in the Christian dispensation they speak (almost) in the same way to us as they spoke to the people of Israel during the dispensation before Christ. Examples of this material are the Old Testament teaching on the creation and what it tells us about human sexuality.

This group of texts virtually disappears from sight when the Old Testament is only read Christocentrically (that is, in the light of Jesus Christ).

In the chapters that follow, I will examine this material thematically, uncovering the topics about which the Old Testament speaks directly to us today.

'An Enduring Treasure'

I am by no means the first author to suggest that certain parts of the Old Testament are still relevant for Christians in much the same way as they were before Christ; in other words, I am not alone in arguing that there is a 'group 6'.

Two Dutch theologians of the last century specifically raised this issue: Arnold Albert van Ruler and Kornelis Heiko Miskotte. It was the Jewish thinker Martin Buber who allegedly said that, for Jesus, the Hebrew Bible was neither old nor a testament. Van Ruler followed the line of Buber and had much hesitation regarding the expression 'Old Testament'. As a young pastor, he went so far as to call the Old Testament 'the actual Bible' and to refer to the New Testament as 'an explanatory word list at the back'. In his own words, 'that the Old Testament is the actual Bible and the New Testament, so to say, no more than a list of words for explanation at the back.'[2]

We should not reject this provocative statement before we have considered it at some length. Needless to say, I do not fully agree with Van Ruler, but his approach has

---

[2] A.A. van Ruler, 'De waarde van het Oude Testament I' in *Verzameld werk* deel 2 (Zoetermeer: Boekencentrum, 2008) 385.

helped me and many others to find a better perspective. The Old Testament is more than a bunch of prophecies about Jesus!

Some years later, Miskotte wrote that the Old Testament is the actual Scripture and in a subsequent book he used the term 'surplus' or 'excess'.[3] For him this word surplus meant 'moments of the Old Testament that are particularly relevant; they are not surpassed in the New Testament, nor denied, but they are merely in the background'. As elements of this surplus he specifically mentioned scepticism, rebellion, sexuality, and politics.

In what follows I am making careful and nuanced use of the thoughts of Van Ruler and Miskotte. I want to bring the valuable thoughts of these theologians to our attention again, without uncritically repeating their words. As far as I am aware, I am the first to do so in a book at a popular level.

It is possible to show the lasting value of the Old Testament by discussing any of the six groups of texts we have identified. Many books have been written on the first five groups; what makes the present book unique is its focus on group 6, the 'excess' of the Old Testament. It will bring to light the limitations of the Christocentric approach to the Old Testament, viz., that this approach inevitably condemns certain parts of the Old Testament to oblivion.

---

[3] K.H. Miskotte, *Hoofdsom der historie* (Nijkerk: Callenbach, 1945) 13-14; Kornelis H. Miskotte, *When the Gods are Silent* [1956] (London: Collins, 1967) 173-302. The English translation uses 'surplus'.

There is no shortage of books in English which argue the case of the Old Testament (see the list at the end of the book), yet none of them overlaps more than marginally with the present book, despite what their titles might suggest.

Chapter 1: Creation

The Bible begins with two creation stories: the first is found in Genesis 1:1–2:4a and the second in Genesis 2:4b–25. The first story is written in formal language and it has a refrain, so it looks like a solemn song. It emphasises that a few simple words sufficed for God to make the greatest and grandest things; God speaks and things occur. After each act of creation God sees that what he has created is 'good' and after the creation of humankind it is even called 'very good'. Genesis 2 is more a story in which the first humans take central stage. The language of Genesis 2 is also simpler.

What the Old Testament says about creation is supplemented in the New Testament, but not fundamentally altered. The New Testament tells us that Jesus was involved in creation (Colossians 1:15–17), but this does not really change the message of the Old Testament. The Old Testament tells us about one God, without making distinctions between the Father, Son, and Holy Spirit, even though in places like Genesis 1:2 and Job 33:4 we get the impression that God's Spirit – or the breath of God – was involved in the work of creation. The New Testament also contains more about the depth of the influence of sin on creation and how God redeems it (Romans 8, also see Isaiah 11:6–9).

In this chapter I will discuss some aspects of our faith regarding the creation and our faith in God as Creator.

The Creation is Good

Although each has its own emphasis, the two creation stories in Genesis 1 and 2 basically agree: God is the one who created everything in the beginning, and humanity is the crowning glory of his work. It is striking in what a positive way both stories describe the whole creation. Other parts of the Old Testament confirm this positive outlook; for example, the nature Psalms 8, 19, 24, and 104, and Isaiah 40.

Everything God created is beautiful and good. It is also clear that whatever is wrong in the world (sin) does not come from God, but is the fault of humankind. Good food and drink, and sexuality, are in themselves good gifts of God, even though they can be abused; they are then tainted by sin. Refusing to enjoy the good gifts of God is a form of thanklessness.

Sin is not a part of the original creation but it enters the world only in Genesis 3 and 4, when humans reject God's good precepts and regulations because they want to be like God. At that moment, their relationships with each other and their relationship to the earth go astray. Yet notice that when sin enters the world, God does not abandon his creation. He maintains all rights to the earth and everything that lives on it. It makes no difference that these rights are not recognised and indeed challenged by humans.

Some subdivisions of Christianity wrongly see the world as a vale of tears and as a place from which people should try to escape to get to 'heaven'. That the world is indeed a place of suffering and sadness, is the fault of humanity, not the fault of the Creator. Even so, the destiny of humankind is not to escape from the earth, but to receive a new heaven and a new earth from God.

God Made You and Me

Creation is presented as a conscious act of God, carried out according to a well-conceived plan. The element of planning in his work is particularly evident in Genesis 1, where the man and woman are the highest of the creatures. In Genesis 2 the humans are put at the very centre of the creation, in the magnificent central space, the garden, with the rest of creation around them.

We can apply this positive message to our own lives, saying that we too are a conscious creation of God. This means that he loves us and wants to take care of us. Knowing this gives our lives meaning and content.

It would be terrible if our life and this earth were only the result of blind chance. It is great that already on the first page of the Old Testament we discover that God is the Creator of all things and of you and me. Therefore, our value does not depend on what others think of us or on how successful we are, but our value is fixed in God. What he says to Israel in Isaiah 43:1–4 we can surely apply to ourselves:

> But now, this is what the LORD says – he who created you, Jacob, he who formed you, Israel: 'Do not fear, for I have redeemed you; I have summoned you by name; you are mine. When you pass through the waters, I will be with you; and when you pass through the rivers, they will

> not sweep over you. When you walk through the fire, you will not be burned; the flames will not set you ablaze. For I am the LORD your God, the Holy One of Israel, your Saviour; I give Egypt for your ransom, Cush and Seba in your stead. Since you are precious and honoured in my sight, and because I love you, I will give people in exchange for you, nations in exchange for your life.

See also Psalm 139:13–16, which sings about God's involvement in our beginning.

> For you created my inmost being; you knit me together in my mother's womb. I praise you because I am fearfully and wonderfully made; your works are wonderful, I know that full well. My frame was not hidden from you when I was made in the secret place, when I was woven together in the depths of the earth. Your eyes saw my unformed body; all the days ordained for me were written in your book before one of them came to be.

It is true that the creator of an object best knows how it works. Similarly, God knows best what is good for us, his creatures. The Bible contains his 'manual' for us. Psalm 95 is therefore a call to obedience: God created the whole world and that is why we must listen to him:

> Come, let us bow down in worship, kneel before the LORD our Maker, for he is our God and we are the people of his pasture, the flock under his care. Today, if you hear his voice...

Humanity the Crown of Creation

In his *Small Catechism* Martin Luther writes: 'I believe that God created me and all other creatures.' By expressing himself thus, he voiced a profound truth. Humanity is the crowning glory of God's work. I already stated that in Genesis 1 the creation of humans is consciously presented as the culmination of the work of creation, and that Genesis 2 revolves around the first man and woman. On the other hand, we should not overstate this: on the sixth day, the animals were also created, so we do not have a day all to ourselves! Moreover, we should not forget the seventh day, the Sabbath, for it is the actual highlight of the first week. Creation is not about us but about God. To use some difficult words, the creation is not anthropocentric but theocentric.[4]

This tension in the position of humanity becomes visible in Psalm 8:3–5. On the one hand the universe is grand and impressive, and by comparison humans are but tiny creatures; on the other hand, those very humans were made almost divine:

> When I consider your heavens, the work of your fingers, the moon and the stars, which you have set in place, what is man that you are mindful of him, the son of man that you care for him? You made him a little lower than the heavenly beings [that is, almost a god], and crowned him with glory and honour.

---

[4] anthropos = human; theos = God

In God's Image

The value of humanity is also shown in Genesis 1:26, where it says that God made humans in his image. This certainly means that humans are closer to God than the rest of creation. Apart from that, it is a difficult expression which has given rise to many debates. We now know that the fact that we are made in God's image does not refer to a particular aspect of our humanity such as our outer appearance or our mind. It means several things:

1. We are God's representatives on earth and we have received a certain authority from him in relation to the rest of creation. On his behalf we can organise and govern the earth, for example by naming animals and things, as happened in Genesis 2.

2. In the ancient East only the royal family was seen as 'godlike'; only they represented the gods on earth. In Genesis 1, by contrast, Israel says that all humans are equal as image-bearers of God. Not only the king, the priests, and other leaders reflect God – we all do, men, women, and children!

3. Like God, we are creative beings and we can use this creativity. Note that this is said of the first humans and so of all people and nations, not just of the Jews, westerners, or whites! God's word thus challenges the sinful views of racism in all its forms. This characteristic of creativity was not lost when sin entered the world, because in Genesis 9:6 and James 3:9 it is still mentioned.

We can thus see Genesis 1:28–29 as an explanation of the meaning of the image of God mentioned in verse 26: God gives humans authority over the rest of creation:

> God blessed them and said to them, 'Be fruitful and increase in number; fill the earth and subdue it. Rule over the fish in the sea and the birds in the sky and over every living creature that moves on the ground.'
>
> Then God said, 'I give you every seed-bearing plant on the face of the whole earth and every tree that has fruit with seed in it. They will be yours for food.'

These words are often misunderstood. They do not mean that as humans we can do whatever we want with the earth, but that we bear responsibility for the earth as God's stewards. And the term 'responsibility' of course contains the notion of response to God. We are accountable and he will ask us what we have done. Just like a king in Israel could not do what he wanted (see e.g. Deuteronomy 17:14–20), so humans are rulers under God on this earth. This means that we carry a vocation and that we are accountable.

Moreover, Genesis 2 shows that work or labour belongs to creation from the very beginning. Humans are not made to be idle but active in the creation. Both mental and physical work form part of God's good creation. That is because the universe is not only good, but also provides opportunities for further development. And it is our dignity that God involves humanity in that work.

The Other Person is also a Creature

The two creation stories in Genesis 1–2 form the beginning of Genesis 1–11, the part of the Old Testament which is about the world as a whole. Only from Genesis 12 God chooses a particular person, Abraham, for his plan with the world, and then the story narrows down to the ancestors of the people of Israel. Someone has therefore called Genesis 1–11 'the Old Testament of the Old Testament'.[5] It is the earliest history of us all. We were all created by God and therefore all people are basically similar and equal. This means, for instance, that I may not harm another person and that I should treat him or her with respect, because that other person is also the property of God. Even though there are many different races and nations on earth, we are all image-bearers of God.

Creation Shows us God

Article 2 of the Dutch Confession of Faith of 1561 calls the creation 'a beautiful book in which all creatures, great and small, are the letters' that show us God, and in particular his 'eternal power and divinity'. Many people see the overwhelming aspects of nature and the beauty of, for example, flowers as indications that there must be a God. David thinks like this in Psalm 19:1–6. The creation shows us God's power and majesty. The beauty, grandeur, variety, and diversity is evidence of his greatness:

---

[5] It is the title of a book by R. Moberly (Minneapolis: Fortress, 1992).

> The heavens declare the glory of God; the skies proclaim the work of his hands. Day after day they pour forth speech; night after night they reveal knowledge. They have no speech, they use no words; no sound is heard from them. Yet their voice goes out into all the earth, their words to the ends of the world.

The book of Amos contains three beautiful, poetic eulogies which praise God as Creator (Amos 4:13, 5:8–9, and 9:5-6). He is the maker and maintainer of the mountains, the wind, the stars, the heavens, and the sea.

When he wants to encourage Israel to do new things with God, the prophet Isaiah points to the strength and power of God in creation (e.g. 40:12–31, 45:1–13). What Isaiah means is that the God who created and sustains everything is certainly able to deliver his people from the exile in Babylon. The prophet puts God over against the gods of the nations, which have never done anything. Earlier, he had exclaimed that the whole earth is full of God's glory (Isaiah 6:3). Various Psalms, such as 33 and 74, point to the creation as a sign of what God can do for people. By looking at the creation, we gain courage to tackle the things he expects of us!

The LORD himself points to the grandeur and inscrutability of creation for another reason, namely when he tries to silence Job (Job 38–41). A large part of the book of Job consists of the chatter of Job's 'friends' about sins that Job has allegedly done, and Job's stubborn defence that he is innocent. But God does not answer him directly; instead, in chapters 38–41 he points out that he made things which are of no use for humans, except that we can see his greatness in them (cf. Psalm 104:26). Job 38–39 is the longest passage on nature (the creation apart from humanity) in the Bible. Repeatedly God's question returns: 'Were you there, Job?' 'Have you ever performed anything like this?' 'Do you understand how it is done, Job?' God's many questions put Job in his place. God is truly several sizes larger than he. It is absurd to think that people like him should be able to control the world or to call God to account. In our time, we know more than ever about how the creation works, but when it comes to the 'last questions' we know very little more than Job.[6]

Psalm 104 is full of things that the LORD is doing until now to maintain his creation. His concern is not only for humanity, but extends to the animals as well: he provides plenty of water so that they have sufficient (Psalm 104:10–14, 27–28). God's concern for animals is also mentioned in Genesis 9:8–17, Psalm 36:6–7, and Jonah 4:11.

Have such beliefs been made obsolete by modern science? Surely not! We know much about how the world works, much more than the writers of the Old Testament, but there are still many things we cannot explain. And such things will always be there. Here a Christian can see the hand of God. Moreover, by faith we also see the hand of God in things which have a 'natural' explanation. We understand how things work and how we can change them, but that does not take away from our marvel about the fact that they exist in the first place.

---

[6] More on Job in chapters 6 and 7.

A sceptic like the author of Ecclesiastes no longer sees God's loving hand (Ecclesiastes 1–2), and that might also happen to us, but the contribution of Ecclesiastes is by no means typical of the Old Testament as a whole. Normally a believer can see God at work in his creation.

Incidentally, in comparison with other religions it is remarkable that the Bible almost always presents God as active. He rests only on the seventh day of creation. Likewise, humans are busy and active from the beginning. This is completely the opposite of the Greek idea of deity: Greek gods always overslept and they preferred being lazy to being tired – meanwhile leaving humanity to toil. For the Greeks the blessed state meant reaching a situation in which there was no need to do anything because you had a slave doing the work for you.

The Earth is Safe

There is another side to the fact that God the LORD is the Creator: in the world and in the universe we are not confronted with anonymous forces and unpredictable influences, but with the God who has revealed himself to us through his Son, his Word, and his Spirit. This means that the earth and the universe are not unsafe places. God made it all and he has ordered it well. It also implies that the world itself is not in any way divine; the modern talk of 'mother earth' is dangerous because it can give a false impression of the earth. The earth is not a person and certainly not a goddess, and neither are the things that we find on the earth.

This faith in God as Creator of the earth as a safe place for humans enabled Jews and Christians to explore the creation without fear, with the result that modern science could begin. Primitive religions saw the earth as a dangerous place; they believed in ghosts, primordial monsters, forces of nature, and so on. Such a belief obviously does not empower its adherents to investigate and explore the world. Another misconception is that according to some religions the earth itself is divine so that investigation would desecrate it. Jews and Christians are not inhibited by such misconceptions; hence they were and are free to engage in science.

God Owns Creation

As Creator and sustainer, God owns creation, as Psalm 24:1–2 makes clear. We humans live on God's territory and so we are his guests. Some Christians consciously or unconsciously think that God and his opponent have, as it were, divided the territory: the opponent would have gotten the earth and God the heavens. Nothing could be further from the truth! In practice God's adversary may have great power on earth, but that does not diminish God's rights. The fact that God temporarily tolerates sin does not mean that he has given up the earth.

We already see this clearly in the story of the Flood, which tells us that the sins of the people had become intolerable to God. He therefore wanted to punish humanity, but wanted the earth to remain. Sufficient numbers of each animal species were saved that they too could survive.

The above implies that we have to abide by the rules which apply here on earth and that we need to keep matters tidy. Genesis 2:5 NRSV says that initially there were no humans on earth to till the land. (The NIV has 'work'.) In other contexts, the word translated here as 'till' means as much as 'serve'. Humans are not made to exploit the earth but to serve it, to get the best out of it. This is true of everything we do but it is of particular importance in our relationship with animals. Animals are not here to be exploited or eradicated, but for us to enjoy and marvel at.

The Old Testament contains some detailed rules on the preservation of the creation, such as a ban on felling fruit trees in wartime (Deuteronomy 20:19–20). Such rules no longer apply literally to us, but their spirit – preserving the earth – is as relevant as ever. It speaks not just about what happens (or not) in time of war, but more generally about respect for creation.

The Old Testament makes it clear that God punishes people who sin habitually; in Amos 4:6–5:9 this is expressed with words that denote God as Creator; especially note the poetic verses, Amos 4:13 and 5:8.

> He who forms the mountains, who creates the wind, and who reveals his thoughts to mankind, who turns dawn to darkness, and treads on the heights of the earth—the LORD God Almighty is his name. (Amos 4:13)

> He who made the Pleiades and Orion, who turns midnight into dawn and darkens day into night, who calls for the waters of the sea and pours them out over the face of the land—the LORD is his name. (Amos 5:8)

Creation is good and God loves his people, but he does tolerate their sins.

Praise and Enjoyment

Many psalms first refer to the creation and then call us to praise the Creator, such as Psalms 8, 33 and 136:1–9. At the end of describing each day of creation, Genesis 1 states that God saw how good everything was (vs 4, 10, 12, 18, 21, 25, 31), and this comment is there for a reason!

It is striking that not only are humans called to praise God, but so is the whole creation. This is particularly the case in Psalm 148. This does not mean that things in nature have a kind of conscious awareness of God. Nature praises God by just being there, without words. This is what gives nature intrinsic value. Thus the Psalms say that rivers clap their hands and mountains shout for joy (Psalm 98:8; cf. Isaiah 55:12).

Professor Van Ruler, whom I mentioned in the Introduction, emphasised that people may enjoy the creation. Despite his melancholic nature he wrote lyrically about the enjoyment of a juicy peach, and he enjoyed watching football, especially the then famous star Johan Cruyff. He so much believed that this life is the real life and the only life, the life that matters to God, that superficial reading would suggest that he did not believe in life after death. And he wrote that

> God has pleasure in the fact that we exist, and because we are aware of this divine approval, we gradually start enjoying the fact that we exist.[7]

And:

> Our service to the Creator only becomes truly worship once humans enjoy the entire life and each single day as they enjoy a juicy peach.[8]

The World is not Eternal

The Bible testifies that God has always been there, for example in Psalm 90:1–2. This Psalm also says in poetic language that the sea, land, and mountains were 'born' at some point in time, which means that God made them. God is eternal but his creation is not. The present heaven and earth will not always exist, because one day there will be a new heaven and a new earth (Isaiah 65:17, 66:22).

God is eternal – the universe is not. This conviction of Jews, Christians, and Muslims stands in sharp contrast to Eastern thought, for example that of Hindus and Buddhists, who do see the world as eternal. Even Greek philosophers like Aristotle had the same conviction of an eternal world. For other religions and philosophers, the world is a sort of extension of the deity, but the Bible makes clear that God is different from his creation and

---

[7] A.A. van Ruler, *Over de Psalmen* (Nijkerk: Callenbach, 1983) 70.

[8] A.A. van Ruler, *Ik geloof* (Nijkerk: Callenbach, 1968) 40.

goes far beyond it. Therefore, we adore and worship not the creation or any creature in it, but God alone.

The Creator is a person, not an impersonal power. Creation is an act of his love, power, and wisdom (cf. Jeremiah 10:11–12).

Life on Earth is Real Life

Eastern religions such as Hinduism and Buddhism hold that our earthly existence is merely an illusion, whereas they see heaven, the place of the gods, as eternal. These religions also hardly distinguish between God and the world; we call this pantheism. Many philosophers, especially the influential Greek philosopher Plato, merely regarded the earth as a kind of shadow of the world of the gods, or 'heaven'. For them, our world is a pale reflection of a higher reality. Greeks like Plato actually thought it was a mistake of the gods that they made the world because it is so imperfect. Some Christians came under the influence of Plato and thought that the creation of the world was the work of a lower god, not of the Father of Jesus Christ. The best thing a person can do therefore, according to these so-called Gnostics, is striving for the soonest possible reunification with the divine world.

This aversion to the world is totally absent from the Old Testament: heaven is not eternal, but a creation of God in time (Genesis 1:1, 2:4a, 4b). The Old Testament speaks entirely positively about life on earth. That is also why the Old Testament hardly speaks of an afterlife: all attention is focused on this life that is willed by God.

The Jewish-Christian belief in a God who created the world and who does not coincide with it is unique. It also means that we do not believe in an eternal cycle. The world had a beginning and it will have an end.

To finish with the New Testament, in the Apostles' Creed we declare that we believe in the resurrection of the body. This belief is based on faith in creation as a good deed of God. Humans are not just physical beings but also spiritual beings, and that will again be so on the new earth. God will not only renew our spirit but also give us a new, glorified body. Hallelujah!

Chapter 2: The Name and Titles of God

Not so long ago, the minister in my local church wanted to play out a biblical scene and someone was needed to play God. I was called on stage and asked to rub over my beard intermittently. I was not very happy with the task – I don't like to portray God – but because the atmosphere was otherwise respectful, I did as requested anyway. Apparently, as a bald man with a beard, I fit the image of God as most people in the church have it!

Many people have a vague image of God when they think about him without involving Jesus in their thoughts. If people are a bit clearer, two images probably dominate: on the one hand that God would be harsh, demanding, and strict, on the other hand the image of the old man with the beard.

This chapter looks at one of the ways in which God reveals himself in the Old Testament: through the disclosure of his name and his titles. In the New Testament, this aspect of his revelation is hardly present and therefore it remains as one of the enduring riches of the Old Testament.

When we speak or write about God, we usually call him 'God', but the Old Testament has a much richer vocabulary. Especially in the book of Genesis, all kinds of beautiful titles for the God of the Old Testament occur. Of course, he has most fully made himself known to us in Jesus Christ, but this does not mean that the Old Testament titles for God are now obsolete.

I will discuss some of these titles without trying to be complete, in the hope that we might better understand who God is. Even titles that are little used still have a message for us. Each of them reveals an aspect of God's character.

Here I do not discuss titles of God which are carried over from the Old Testament into the New Testament, such as 'shepherd' or 'father' (Deuteronomy 32:6, Psalm 103:13, Isaiah 63:16, 64:7, Jeremiah 3:19–22, Hosea 11:1–3, Malachi 2:10), but those which are only named in the Old Testament. And I merely mention the texts which reveal the motherly aspect of God, without discussing them (Deuteronomy 32:18; Isaiah 42:14, 46:3, 49:15–16, 66:13; Hosea 11:1–4; Psalm 131:2).

We should bear in mind that in the Bible names and titles are much more meaningful than in our western culture. They were meant to explain something or they were symbolic. Often someone's name and their personality coincide. Thus the two sons of Naomi and Elimelech in Ruth 1 are called Mahlon and Kilion, and these names mean 'weak' and 'sick' respectively. The name Nabal means 'fool', as 1 Samuel 25:25 also explains.

A number of times we come across a change of name. For example, God changes the name Abram into Abraham (Genesis 17:5): Abram means 'my father is exalted', but Abraham probably means 'father of many'. Thus his new name testifies to his role as patriarch of the people Israel. On the other hand, Naomi, the mother-in-law of Ruth, no longer wants to be called Naomi but Mara, meaning 'bitter' or 'sad'. Incidentally, the narrator of the book of

Ruth does not comply with her request and quietly continues to call her Naomi, 'the charming one'.

The LORD

Up to now I have used the name LORD to refer to God, although you may not have noticed. The word LORD does not look much like a name, but there certainly is a name behind it. English translators generally use LORD to render the proper name of God, which in Hebrew is Yahweh. They do this to meet the sensitivity of many Jews, who do not want to pronounce or even write down the name of God. This sensitivity largely dates from the centuries after the time of the New Testament. In the New Testament, it is already visible when Matthew uses the term 'kingdom of heaven' where Mark and Luke have 'kingdom of God'.

Out of respect for the Jews, most modern translations replace the name Yahweh with LORD, spelt with a large and three small capital letters. You can see this, for example, in Exodus 15 and Psalm 23.

Exodus 3:13-15a tells us how God first discloses his name to Moses:

> Moses said to God, 'Suppose I go to the Israelites and say to them, "The God of your fathers has sent me to you," and they ask me, "What is his name?" Then what shall I tell them?'
>
> God said to Moses, 'I AM WHO I AM. This is what you are to say to the Israelites: "I AM has sent me to you."'

> God also said to Moses, 'Say to the Israelites, "The LORD, the God of your fathers – the God of Abraham, the God of Isaac and the God of Jacob – has sent me to you."'

By writing 'I AM WHO I AM' and 'I AM' with small capitals, the translators show us the connection between the name of God and the word LORD. The NIV here helpfully imitates the Authorised Version in the use of capitals, as do the NASB, the NRSV, the NLT, and the ESV. On the other hand, the Contemporary English Version has:

> God said to Moses: I am the eternal God. So tell them that the LORD, whose name is "I Am", has sent you.

The words 'I AM' translate the Hebrew word hayah, which means 'to be'. It is not hard to see that the form Yahweh is derived from this verb. God's name is thus a form of the word for 'to be'. This name expresses that God *is.* He is there, he always has been there, and he will be there; he is there for us, but he also *exists* in absolute terms. His name tells us that he is the present one, the totally independent one. That is great to know.

But God does not have a normal 'first name' that we could call at random, because his name is also mysterious. That is in line with the fact that for us humans it is impossible to imagine that God has always been there and that he sustains himself eternally. All we can do is admire him, worship him, and respect his name.

Because of the above I in fact prefer always to write 'the LORD God' and 'Lord Jesus' in full when talking about

God and his Son, as Professor Van Ruler usually does. But because this is uncommon in English, it would distract and I will adhere to the normal use of 'God' and 'Jesus'; yet wherever these words appear, readers can supplement 'the LORD God' and 'Lord Jesus'.

By the way, the name of God is Yahweh, not Yehovah or Jehovah. The latter form originated with Jewish copyists of the Old Testament who were concerned that someone would accidentally pronounce the divine name. To prevent this, they deliberately wrote the wrong vowels between the consonants YHWH. The first western translators did not see through this clever device and were fooled by it: they adopted the wrong vowels. Today we know better and we must therefore stop using the wrong form Jehovah.

'Hallowed be Your Name'

The Old Testament speaks not only about God, but it also often refers to the name of God. The same is true of the New Testament, for example in the Lord's Prayer, in which we pray 'hallowed be your name' (Matthew 6:9). We ask that God will really be honoured in the world and that soon everyone will recognise him as Lord of all. By praying for the sanctification of his name, we also ask that God's promises will be fulfilled. Moreover, praying these words implies that we ourselves are willing to cooperate in this fulfilment.

In Acts 4:12, when Peter speaks about the *name* of Jesus he obviously means Jesus himself: 'for there is no other name under heaven given among mortals by which we must be saved'. Peter's way of speaking makes it clear that Jesus is God. Similarly, God's name and his person correspond. We find this emphasis on the name of God much more frequently in the Old Testament. In Exodus 20:7, Deuteronomy 5:11 and 28:58 God says, for example, that we should not abuse his name. Exodus 20:24 deals with places where God allows his name to be called by humans (cf. Psalm 8:1, 9).

Contemporary Judaism also speaks about the name of God, as for example in the famous Kaddish prayer that begins with the words: 'May his great name be exalted and sanctified.' The *name* is in fact God himself; he is identical with his name, and that is primarily the covenant name Yahweh. Unlike most Jews I am not of the opinion that we can never pronounce this name, but rather that God expects that we will use it very respectfully. And it is good that our Bible translations print the name as LORD.

God Almighty

We now come to the titles of God. The title God Almighty is a rendering of the Hebrew *El Shaddai*, which occurs in Genesis 17:1, 28:3, 35:11, 43:14, 48:3, 49:25, and Exodus 6:2-3. The word *Shaddai* without the word for God is common in Job (e.g. Job 8:3, 5) and also occurs in Psalm 91:1. Strangely enough it is not at all clear what this divine title means. It may indicate that God has power over death, but it can also relate to his loving provision and solace. He is the God who gave two old people, Abraham and Sarah, a son, thereby making them the ancestors of a great nation.

God Most High

The title Most High translates the Hebrew word *Elyon* and occurs for the first time in Genesis 14:19–22. Here and in other places, such as Deuteronomy 32:8, it seems as if there is a silent recognition that other gods also exist, at least in the opinion of non-Israelites. The Israelites seem to use this title to emphasise that they see God as the highest God. The title occurs 28 times, mainly in the Psalms (e.g. Psalm 7:17, 57:2, 78:35). In 2 Samuel 22:14, Psalm 73:11, 107:11, and Daniel 7:18, 22, 25 the word *Elyon* is also used independently. This title stresses God's power, majesty, and sovereignty. No one is equal to him or can even be compared to him. You see that the use of this title differs completely from the use of the name LORD, which is only used in the relationship between God and his people Israel.

The Eternal God

The little word *olam* is common in Hebrew and means 'eternal, everlasting'. The title *El Olam* is only used for God in Genesis 21, but Jeremiah 10:10a expresses the same thought:

> But the LORD is the true God; he is the living God, the eternal King.

In Isaiah 26:4 the word *olam* also refers to the God of Israel: he is 'the Rock eternal', says the NIV. God's perpetual existence means that he can be trusted, that you can build on him, because he is inexhaustible.

The Lord who Provides

Although it only occurs once in the Bible, the title 'the Lord will provide' is rather popular in the English-language songs. In Hebrew, this title is *Yahweh Yireh* and it occurs in the unique story about the sacrifice of Isaac in Genesis 22. Actually, it is not even a real title, but more a confession about God that comes at the end of the story: 'the Lord will provide' (verse 14) is the name which Abraham gives to Mount Moriah, the place where he finds himself with his son Isaac. The Hebrew word here can mean 'see', 'foresee', and 'provide'. This ambiguity is deliberate: Abraham was severely put to the test by God, who had asked him to sacrifice his only son. For a long time, Abraham had no idea how this nightmare would end, but God had *foreseen* that he would *provide* a sacrificial animal that could be sacrificed in place of Isaac. Through the ages, these words have encouraged many people to believe that God will provide what they need at his own appointed time.

This same confession of faith in God's care for people occurs at an earlier point in Genesis as well. After God helps Hagar in the desert, she gives him the title 'God who sees me' (Genesis 16:13), meaning 'You are the God who looks after me, the one who cares'. Again, this is a title which is found only in one place; it translates the Hebrew *El Roi.* We may likewise repeatedly experience that God *sees* us, especially in situations of great need such as that of Hagar.

The writer of Genesis quietly makes a clear and important distinction here: Abraham talks about *Yahweh Yireh* and so speaks the name of God; but the non-Jewish Hagar uses the general word *El* (God), not the covenant name Yahweh. That name is reserved for the Jewish people and people who come to belong to them.

The LORD who Heals You

The reference to God as the one who heals people also only occurs once, namely in Exodus 15:26. In the Hebrew, *Yahweh Rafa* is clearly a title, and although the title itself is rare, the thought that God heals his children is common enough in the Hebrew Bible: for example in Psalm 103:3, Isaiah 30:26, Jeremiah 3:22, 30:17, and Hosea 6:1. Individual believers therefore respectfully ask him for healing (Psalm 6:2, 41:4) and they thank him when their prayers are answered (Psalm 30:1–3, 107:19–22).

The Old Testament also knows of a dark, punishing side of God: texts such as Deuteronomy 32:39 and Hosea 6:1 reveal that God both wounds and heals. But the good news is that he also heals the wounds which have been caused by others. The slavery of the Israelites in Egypt was such a wound, a disease that could have led to death. The exodus from that country is the healing about which Exodus 15:26 speaks, when God says: 'I am the LORD, the one who heals you.' More than most other titles of God, this one points forward to Jesus, the one who healed countless people during his earthly life, and to the actions of the Christians after him, who did the same (e.g. Acts 3:1–8, 8:5–8, 9:32–34). We find a veiled announcement of these things in Isaiah 53:5: 'by his wounds we are healed'.

We may see the healing work of God, Jesus, and his church as healing of spirit, soul, and body. In this aspect of God's work, we as his people are getting involved. Both medical care and miracles of healing show us something of God's goodness.

LORD of Hosts

God's title LORD of hosts, which occurs some 280 times in the Old Testament, tells us that our God is Lord and master over every power that people might fear or revere. Examples of its use are 1 Samuel 1:3, 11, Psalm 84, and Jeremiah 2:19. The title most frequently occurs in Isaiah and Jeremiah, but is missing from the first five books of the Bible.

This title is a rendering of the Hebrew words *Yahweh Tsebaot*. The NIV rather unhelpfully translates them as 'LORD Almighty', which is more a paraphrase, but the KJV and the NRSV do better with 'LORD of hosts'. What is in view here are the (heavenly) armies or powers, the armies of God; in 1 Samuel 17:45 the army of Israel is identified with these powers as well. God's hosts include the stars, the angels, and anything one could conceive as a living force. This does not necessarily mean that the Bible writers actually believed that stars were living beings; it merely indicates that God is Lord and master of everything. The Old Testament makes no clear distinction between earthly and spiritual powers, and so neither can we in our understanding of its teaching.

When God performs his mighty deeds, his angels accompany him, just as an earthly king has a following of courtiers. In Joshua 5:14–15 an angel is presented as the captain of the army of the LORD. While Israel confesses that God is the God of the armies and that he is on their side (Psalm 46:7, 11), it sings at the same time that he will put an end to all wars (Psalm 46:8–10). He is the God of history, who does not rest before the final victory is achieved; but the Old Testament in no way idealises war and violence.

The Jealous God

In the Hebrew Bible, God has also the title *El Qanna* (Exodus 20:5, 34:14, Deuteronomy 4:24, 5:9, 6:15) which means 'the jealous God' or 'the envious God'. It suggests that he does not tolerate any competition and that he acts like a faithful marriage partner. Just as in a marriage, the relationship between God and his people leaves no room for a third person or a third something. God longs for our perfect dedication. He has every right to behave like this, for he created us to take the first place with him; conversely, he expects that he will take first place in our lives. When we give someone or something else the place of honour which belongs to God, he is rightly jealous.

Other things can be beautiful and good in themselves, such as a career, family, or hobby, but they should never be as important to us as God. He does not tolerate any rival. From this point of view his jealousy is a good feature, a real virtue. It has nothing to do with blind revenge: it is a good character trait. In his love for us and all people God is passionate, both for good and for bad. This explains how his anger can target the enemies of his people just as well as his people themselves, when they are unfaithful to him. An example of the former is found in Ezekiel 36:5–6, where NRSV uses the expression 'my hot jealousy' and NIV 'my burning zeal'. Because of this emotion, God punishes the nations around Israel for their attacks on his people. We can also understand Joshua 24:19–20 in this light:

> Joshua said to the people, 'You are not able to serve the LORD. He is a holy God; he is a jealous God. He will not forgive your rebellion and your sins. If you forsake the LORD and serve foreign gods, he will turn and bring disaster on you and make an end of you, after he has been good to you.'

The LORD my Banner

In Exodus 17:15, at the end of the description of a battle between Israel and Amalek, it is reported that Moses builds an altar to God which he calls 'The LORD is my Banner'. In Hebrew it says *Yahweh Nissi.* In this way, Moses expresses that God is the one who gave Israel the victory and that their success in the future will likewise always depend on God's help and blessing. In a traditional war, armies carry banners which serve for identification and act as a sign of encouragement for the army and a warning to frighten the enemy. In our time, it is the black flag of the Islamic State which intimidates their opponents and which has huge symbolic associations.

As New Testament believers, we wage no wars in the name of God and the thought of a flag, a war banner, might therefore be misunderstood. The New Testament points to the spiritual battle in which we take part. The thought that God helps us in that fight is surely very encouraging. In our struggles we must look up to God who is our banner.

As an aside, the Hebrew word *nissi*, my banner, is a form of *nes*, banner. After the creation of the State of Israel in 1948, Christians founded a Christian village in the north of the country which is called Nes Ammim, meaning 'Banner for the Nations'. This name is taken from Isaiah 11:10, where the Messiah is seen as the banner or the standard for all nations. In this text, Isaiah promises on behalf of God permanent peace to all nations on earth. The people of Nes Ammim want to work in this spirit for peace between Jews, Christians, Palestinians, and other Arabs.[9]

History

So far in this chapter we have been looking at the way God reveals his name and his titles in the Old Testament. I hope you no longer see him as an old man with a beard! According to the Old Testament God also revealed himself in history by the mighty deeds that he did for his people, such as the exodus from Egypt, the entry into the promised land, and the return from the exile (cf. Exodus 20:1–2). It is striking how concrete and specific these revelations were. They are not located in the warm, pious feelings of certain people, but in visible and tangible actions which no-one could overlook. If I were to re-tell

[9] See http://nesammim.org/.

all these stories, I could easily fill another book. The fact that God identifies himself as the God of Abraham, Isaac, and Jacob (e.g. Exodus 3:6, 15–16, Acts 3:13) is a reference to these great deeds.

Why Choose Baal?

Why then did the people of Israel so often run away from such a great God to serve other gods, such as the god Baal? Baal was a god of the nations who lived in the promised land before Israel arrived there and he had several attractive aspects:

1. In the land of Israel for your harvest and your cattle you utterly depended on sufficient rainfall. Baal was a fertility god who provided rain so that the cattle had enough to drink, the crops could grow, and there were good harvests. The Canaanites had successfully cultivated the land and it seemed self-evident that their expertise was to be respected.

2. The God of Israel revealed himself first of all in history; in leading and liberating his people. The LORD therefore seemed to be a god of history rather than of nature. As a god of nature, Baal promised that the cycle of summer and winter, of wet and dry periods, would continue. That promise seemed to complement the work of God in a convenient way.

3. The gods of Canaan were tolerant towards other gods – an extra deity was no problem. All those gods were also distant relatives, it was thought.

4. As a follower of Baal there was much that you could do yourself: you could, for example, stimulate his work by

having sex with a temple prostitute, thus influencing the god of fertility. The God of Israel could not be manipulated in this way. People like to keep things in their own hands and they find it hard to trust God.

5. The Canaanites saw little or no connection between everyday life and their religion. If they just occasionally carried out the rituals, they were free to lead whatever kind of life they wanted. The LORD was much stricter, for he expected the sanctification of his people in all aspects of their lives, as can for example be seen in Leviticus 19.

It is worth pointing out that the Old Testament tells us that God is the one who has real control over things such as rain and fertility (e.g. Psalm 65). A highlight is the story in 1 Kings 17–19, where God defeats Baal on his 'home ground' by first sending a drought and later rain through the great prophet Elijah.

Chapter 3: Sexuality

Pretty much everything the Bible says about the origin and the nature of marriage is already present in the Old Testament. The New Testament adds bits to this information and deepens our understanding by comparing marriage to the bond between Christ and the believers, but what God intended for marriage is something we basically find out in the Old Testament. Genesis 1 and 2 are of course important for this subject, but later in the Old Testament substantial things are said about marriage and sexuality as well. The main thought is undoubtedly that marriage and sexuality are good. Miskotte referred to this element of the Old Testament's teaching as 'eroticism' and he wrote that 'without making much fuss about it, married love was for Israel simply taken as a matter of course to be a part of the good gifts of this earth'.[10]

Genesis 1

Genesis 1 was already discussed in the chapter on creation. We saw that humans were created in God's image. Here we pay attention specifically to what this chapter says about men and women and their relationships:

> Then God said, 'Let us make mankind in our image, in our likeness, so that they may rule over the fish in the sea and the birds in the sky, over

[10] Miskotte, *When the Gods are Silent*, 265.

> the livestock and all the wild animals, and over all the creatures that move along the ground.' So God created mankind in his own image, in the image of God he created them; male and female he created them. God blessed them and said to them, 'Be fruitful and increase in number; fill the earth and subdue it.' (Genesis 1:26–28a)

The text suggests that God speaks about himself in the plural: 'Let us make mankind'. God is represented as a compound person. The meaning of this becomes clear in the New Testament, in which he reveals himself as Father, Son, and Holy Spirit. What is at stake in Genesis is the fact that humanity is also created as a compound being: the one 'type' human is made in two varieties, as man and woman. This means that humans are made for relationships. It is also clear that both the man and the woman bear the image of God so that although they are different they are equal.

Verse 28 contains God's command to the first two humans. At that moment in time 'be fruitful and multiply' was meant quite literally. God put the smallest possible number of people on the huge, wide earth, so there was space for large families and it would be some time before the entire earth was populated. Some people today still take this command very literally and regard large families as the will of God. But in our time, when the earth is in danger of getting overcrowded, when animals are squeezed out and commodities are exhausted, we will do well to consider this command as at least partially fulfilled.

Other people tend to spiritualise this command, as if God had said that humans should bring forth many good deeds and numerous good works. It is better to say that one of the intentions of marriage is still that there will be children, if possible, but not in unlimited numbers.

Genesis 2

Chapter 2 pays much attention to the fact that human beings are either male or female. For a short period there was only one person, but verse 18 says that it is not good for a man to be alone. It would, however, be incorrect if we limited this need for company to the need for a marriage partner. Humans are relational beings who do not thrive alone and are intended for regular communion with others. This is how God made us. Verse 18 says that 'the LORD God' thought this while the paradise situation still existed – before the fall. Mutual aid and dependency are therefore not expressions of weakness. They rather express how God intended us humans to be.

God then decides that he will give the man a 'helper' (verse 18). This word 'helper' is often misinterpreted, as if helper meant someone subordinate, a housekeeper or a slave. Nothing is further from the true meaning of this word, which implies that the person to be created will at least be the man's equal. We know this with certainty because God himself is referred to as 'helper' or 'help' of humans in various places, for example in Psalm 33:20, 40:17, 70:5, and 118:7. Sometimes this 'helping' almost has the meaning of 'rescuing'. These words thus in no way suggest a division of labour or inequality. The woman probably got involved in the naming of all animals straight away. It is only in the next chapter that the fall takes place and everything gets corrupted, not least the relationship between men and women. But God's ideal with his creation remains intact.

Genesis 2:21–22 portrays the woman being made from a rib of the man. The meaning of this detail is not immediately obvious because it is not explained in the Bible itself. In any case, it once again suggests the equality of both. A modern saying goes: 'The woman was not created from the head of the man, in order not to be exalted above him; not from his feet, so that he cannot wipe his feet on her; but from his side so that she can be next to him, and close to his heart, to be loved by him.'

Verse 24 contains a sort of definition of marriage: a man and a woman separate themselves from their parents and become one, not only physically but also mentally and hopefully spiritually. This verse is certainly not merely about sexuality. To be really together as a couple, the connections with and commitments to other people must be loosened.

Verse 25 tells about nudity without shame within the marital relationship of the first people. Uninhibited, the two enjoy each other. As I stated earlier, only in the next chapter does the fall take place with the result that everything is corrupted. Not only is the relationship of the humans with God broken, but also between man and woman fights break out about supremacy (Genesis 3:16) and feelings of shame break in (Genesis 3:7, 10–11). Eventually adultery, divorce, and other problems are added to the mix.

In sum, marriage and sexuality were given before the fall and they are therefore good. Human sexuality is both aimed at reproduction and at the unity of man and woman.

Song of Songs

The biblical book Song of Songs can be read as a representation of the relationship between God and the people Israel, between God and the human soul, or between Christ and the Church. Many approaches to this text are possible, but none of these gets close to the original meaning of the Song. Song of Songs was written before Jesus was born and in the New Testament it is hardly cited or mentioned. The non-literal explanation, in which the young man is seen as God or Jesus, arose from shyness about what the book really says. Marginal notes in the Dutch equivalent of the King James Version even explained the two breasts of the woman as the Old and New Testaments – which is ludicrous prudishness.

Song of Songs or 'The Highest Song' is primarily a book about the earthly, physical love between husband and wife. It is about *eros*, erotic love, not about *agape*, disinterested love. The book is a collection of rather loose love songs. A woman, a man, and groups of friends or family speak in turn. God is not or hardly mentioned. It is thus not a 'theological' book, but we can read it as an amplification of God's judgment that the creation was good. Because of its 'earthly', even carnal theme, the rabbis often had prolonged discussions about whether this book belonged in the Hebrew Bible. Every time they decided to keep it in. It is possible that Song was sung at weddings.

Song of Songs uses lots of imagery derived from nature and from war. At the same time, it is quite realistic in identifying the power of erotic love. It contains descriptions of the bodies of man and woman which do not leave much to the imagination. The book is so realistic that in a few places we encounter a warning to be careful. Song of Songs 8:6b–7 describes the power of love and at the same time expresses some concern:

> for love is as strong as death, its jealousy unyielding as the grave. It burns like blazing fire, like a mighty flame. Many waters cannot quench love; rivers cannot sweep it away. If one were to give all the wealth of one's house for love, it would be utterly scorned.

There is a similar warning in 2:7:

> Daughters of Jerusalem, I charge you by the gazelles and by the does of the field: do not arouse or awaken love until it so desires.

The same words are also in Song of Songs 3:5 and 8:4.

The sexuality of this book is characterised by equality and by the absence of coercion. It almost appears as if the situation of the Garden of Eden (Genesis 2) has been recovered. Power struggle and shame are absent. The idea of desire or longing, which had such a negative ring to it in Genesis 3:16 and 4:7, has by Song of Songs 7:10 regained its positive connotation: 'his desire is for me'.

In this way, the book shows that marriage is not merely for having children. In fact, marriage and children are not even mentioned although there is reference to the wedding of King Solomon (Song of Songs 3:11) and the woman is called a 'bride' in chapter 4:8-12 and 5:1 (which is almost exactly in the middle of the book). Whether the two main characters are married remains unclear; on the basis of chapter 2:17 and 4:6 you could think they are not, because these verses suggest that early in the morning they go their separate ways.

In this loose collection of songs, we find distinctly different situations in the life of the two lovers; a logical order seems to be missing. We may assume that the poet or the collector of the songs presumes the usual order of things, namely that marriage precedes sexual intercourse. Yet this is not expressed anywhere, because Song of Songs is poetry and not a guide to 'how it should be done'.

Translations such as NIV and ESV contain headings like 'beloved' and 'lover' (or 'she' and 'he'), but we do well to remember that these have been added by the translators. We can only discern whether it is the woman or the man speaking because the Hebrew language distinguishes between masculine and feminine verb forms.

Psalm and Proverb

A clear contrast with Song of Songs is Psalm 45. This too is a wedding song, which its heading calls a 'love song' (NRSV), but it is a 'baptised' version: God, marriage, and children are mentioned, and it seems that in verse 11 the bride promises the groom obedience.

Unlike Song of Songs, this psalm is cited in the New Testament, namely in Hebrews 1:8–9. The similarities and differences between this psalm and Song of Songs are striking. It is fascinating to see that our Hebrew Bible contains both Song of Songs as the 'worldly' version of a love song next to Psalm 45 as its 'pious' version.

A clear defence of marriage over against adultery occurs in Proverbs 5, especially verses 15–20, in which a father warns his son against contact with the wife of another person, or a prostitute.

Marriage, Family, Community

There have always been people in the church who had difficulty with the body and sexuality. Among other things this is a result of the fact that the early church came under the influence of pagan thinking which regarded physical things as inferior and even as plain wrong. Most Greek and Roman thinkers held that the material world was inferior to the spiritual world. The weak human body had to be conquered and kept under control by the spirit. In the Roman Catholic Church this influence was so strong that it was decided that priests were not allowed to marry. This development could only happen because people had lost sight of the Old Testament.

In certain situations, people choose to remain single or are asked by God not to marry in order to be more available to him (as in 1 Corinthians 7:7, 29–35; 9:5, 12). However, that is a positive decision and has nothing to do with dislike of physicality.

More clearly and more comprehensively than the New Testament, the Old Testament shows us that the true life is not in a different place or a different world; human life is not lived in heaven, but in the good creation of God. Marriage and sexuality are inherent parts of human life. Sexuality is a good gift from God for man and woman, which may be enjoyed within the bounds of the marriage.

Some single people may find the present chapter difficult, so it is important to add the following. The modern form of the family (called the nuclear family and consisting merely of man, woman, and children) is not the biblical form. In biblical times, all the generations of a family lived together, along with the servants (slaves) and the cattle. That was also the case in Europe until some 200 years ago. Old people's homes had not yet been invented and young people did not normally move out to study. One of the adult men was not only the head of the household but also the family's business leader. The existence of such extended families meant that unmarried people, including people with a homosexual orientation, did not have to be lonely or without care.

The Old Testament presents no particular family model as normative, but it teaches us that humans are made for relationships with one another. In our time, in which loneliness is a major problem, the extended family seems a very attractive alternative to the nuclear family. When many people live together as a large family, there is also less pressure on the quality of marriages: married couples depend less on each other and there are always other adults nearby who can compensate for the weaknesses of a marriage partner. It is time that Christians stop the unwarranted idealisation of the nuclear family.

Note that a plea for the large, extended family is not in contradiction with what Genesis 2:24 says about the living together of men and women. It says that 'a man leaves his father and mother and is united to his wife', which means that the priorities of married people change: father and mother used to be the most important people in their lives, but now that position is taken by their marriage partner. The Hebrew word for 'leave', however, does not mean a physical moving away. An extended family is a social and economic unit, but is unrelated to sexuality.

Gods and Goddesses

It is good also to look at what is *not* in the Bible with regard to sexuality. What strikes me most is that God is not sexually active! Most religions have several gods, who are usually sexually active. Gods and goddesses have sex and get children; gods chase and impregnate goddesses as well as human women. The Greek god Zeus is notorious for his many 'conquests'. Many religions combine the worship of their gods with diverse expressions of sexuality, such as by having priests or priestesses who are available for sexual activity in temples. In the eyes of many people, there is a self-evident connection between fertility and religion.

A clear example of the veneration of the gods of nature, in which sex plays a major role, is the worship of the Canaanite god Baal, which was already mentioned in the previous chapter. The Bible refers to him in places such as Judges 2:13, 1 Kings 16:31–32, 1 Kings 18, and Jeremiah 11:13, 17. Baal was a fertility god, who supposedly caused the land to yield a good harvest and the animals to have many young. In order to stimulate or to help the god, in his temples sexual activity took place between priests/priestesses and 'believers'. This made the worship of Baal attractive for certain groups of Israelites.

In relation to the God of Israel we find none of this. Israel has no goddess(es) and the description of the LORD is far from all sexual activity. Yet we hear the context in which the Old Testament was written resounding in the precepts that are given to Israel. For example, Leviticus 15:16–8 states that men and women are unclean after sexual intercourse. Unlike the other provisions for impurity in Leviticus, this rule is not about preventing or containing a contagious disease; it is not about hygiene and it also does not mean that sex is dirty.

The provision that men and women are unclean after sex merely prevents them from becoming active in the worship of God in the tabernacle, temple, or synagogue too soon. The intended consequence is that a priest cannot be sexually active during the discharge of his duties as a priest of God. Leviticus 22:4 repeats this provision in connection with the guidelines for the priests. This was not a prohibition on marriage for priests, but rather a protection against the pagan practices around Israel!

For us these provisions are helpful as they can prevent us from attempting to Christianise our sexuality. Sex is not something supernatural and Christians have no different or better sex than unbelievers, in the same way that Christians are not better at preparing food or at football.

Chapter 4: Politics and the Stranger

The two people who inspired me to write this book, Van Ruler and Miskotte, both had much respect for politics. 'Politics is a holy affair', was a famous statement of Professor Van Ruler, and Professor Miskotte counted politics among the hidden treasures of the Old Testament.[11] Politics is therefore a legitimate subject for a chapter in this book, but we need to keep in mind that my subject is neither law nor precept but rather principles from the Old Testament which have not changed in the New Testament. Given that limitation, I will discuss the governance and the organisation of society based on the Old Testament without getting into the issuing of laws and decrees.

Key Words

The key concepts in politics, for states and governments are: law, justice, and righteousness. It is important to realise that we humans hardly know what these words mean apart from God's revelation.

In addition to these concepts, the books of Proverbs and Ecclesiastes emphasise that it is vital for governments, politicians, and all leaders to work hard, to be diligent, knowledgeable, fair, and honest; see for example Proverbs 16:13; 20:8, 28; 25:2, 5, 15; 28:16; 29:4, 12, 14 and Ecclesiastes 4:13; 5:8–9; 9:13–18; 10:16–18.

---

[11] Miskotte, *When the Gods are Silent*, 170-171, 271-282.

The wisdom in these two books is still relevant thousands of years after they were first written down. It is also not specifically Jewish-Christian, but equally valid in all other cultures.

On the other hand, the way in which we think about the content of the key concepts law, justice, and righteousness must be specifically Jewish-Christian. In what follows, I will confine myself largely to justice and righteousness.

Old Testament and New Testament

In the New Testament, the issue of politics occurs in a way which is very different from the Old Testament. The important practical difference is that in New Testament times the people of Israel and the first Christian communities had little or no influence on politics. The Romans occupied the land of Israel, as they occupied the whole Middle East, including Egypt. The Romans were in control during the first centuries of the church, which remained a small, often oppressed minority.

Meanwhile the New Testament contains quite diverse responses to the Roman government. These different reactions were probably strongly influenced by how government and society treated the Christians at any given moment. The first reaction to the state, in Romans 13:1–7, is rather favourable towards state authority, which is said to be 'God's servant, an agent of wrath to bring punishment to the wrongdoer' (verse 4; cf. also 1 Timothy 2:1–4). On the other hand, the reaction in Revelation 13 portrays the Roman Empire as an anti-

Christian power which threatens to persecute the Christians.[12] More or less in between these two extremes of acceptance and rejection stands the first Epistle of Peter (especially 2:11–25, 3:13–17, and 4:12–19), in which Peter offers the readers help to live in a society that is critical, but not necessarily hostile, towards the Christian faith and the Jewish-Christian lifestyle.

On the other hand, in the Old Testament Israel is a nation state with its own government, territory, army, and borders. It was a church-state not unlike the present-day Vatican State.

A more principled difference is that the community of the followers of Jesus Christ did not belong in any one country or location. The church spread out over all the earth (Matthew 28:19, Acts 1:8) and today the followers of Jesus still live as 'strangers in the world, spread throughout' the entire earth (cf. 1 Peter 1:1). The church does not and should not coincide with any one state; it does not have its own territory and thus it has no army to defend anything.

Because of these two facts, for questions about the organisation and order of the church we turn to the New Testament, but for questions about justice and righteousness in politics and legislation the Old Testament has treasure for us to tap into.

---

[12] See Pieter J. Lalleman, *The Lion and the Lamb* (London: Faithbuilders, 2016).

No Democracy

Whereas believers in New Testament times had no influence on politics, as we saw, this was different in Israel, at least to some extent. In Israel state and people coincided, at least while Israel was an independent state, until the beginning of the exile in 586 BCE. However, the influence of the people was quite limited: Israel was not a democracy in which everyone could have their say. It was rather a theocracy, a state in which God *(theos)* reigned. From the outset, God had established the order of state and society in the legislation he had given, just like he had done with the rules for worship and sacrifices. So, God's laws determined the place and role of the priests, the state officials, and the courts of law.

We find a set of rules for several groups of leaders in Israel in Deuteronomy 16:18–18:22, a section which is a kind of constitution for God's people in their land. Two things stand out immediately. In the first place the fact that responsibility and power are spread over various individuals and groups; this prevents the sole rule of any single person or any small group. The king, the priest, the judge, and the prophet each have their own place in the system. Secondly, the king is only one of the leaders and he is bound to these laws as much as everyone else (Deuteronomy 17:18–20). The king is in no way more or better than his people (verse 20). Israel had to be governed in a different way to other countries, where the will of the king coincided with the will of the (silent) gods, so that the king was effectively the sole ruler.

For our thinking about politics and society, the Old Testament presents us with a variety of themes. In what follows I will deal with the history, the role of the king, the message of the prophets, the view of human beings, poverty and property, and the position of foreigners in Israel.

History

The people of Israel had a clear awareness that God directed their history, and the Old Testament shows God's concrete interventions in world history (e.g. Isaiah 48), in the history of Israel (e.g. Deuteronomy 4:32–40), and in individual people's lives. The Old Testament is the national history book of the people of Israel, who are our ancestors in the faith. The book covers a period of more than a thousand years, in which the political and social situation changed several times. It does not contain one timeless model for the organisation of the state.

The patriarchs, the people who stood at the beginning of Israel, were agro-pastoralists. Later the newly formed nation lived in slavery in Egypt. Their liberation and their exodus from Egypt formed the high point in their history, to which they often looked back. They sang about God's intervention in psalms such as Psalm 78, 105, and 114, because God had shown that he was more powerful than the sacrosanct, divine king of Egypt!

When Israel established itself in the promised land, initially there was no king or other national leader, but Judges 2:6–22, 17:6, and 21:25 make very clear that central leadership was somehow indispensable. The last judge, Samuel, did remarkably well, but at the end of his life the people suddenly wanted a king. Both Samuel and God warned them emphatically against this desire (1 Samuel 8 and 10:17–27), but in vain.

The first king, Saul, was a failure. The second king, David, was a much better leader, although his private life was not equally blessed, as we are told in much detail in 2 Samuel 11–20. In the past, the third king, Solomon, was often seen as the ideal king of Israel, but today we are more aware that the book of Kings is in fact critical of him. Solomon centralised the country's administration, demanding services and heavy taxes from the ordinary people (1 Kings 4, esp. verse 7; 10:14–29). This centralisation resulted in the flow of power and money into the capital city, Jerusalem. In the era of the kings, property became concentrated in the hands of the upper classes and inequality increased, as we also hear in the criticism of the prophets (see below).

So, from the time of Solomon, the kings and the ruling class became increasingly powerful, with the result that many farmers lost their land and other possessions. This was the land which they had inherited from their ancestors. Many became slaves because of debts. This situation was an attack on their place within the people of God, because it was characteristic for Israel that every person had their own piece of land. Israel thus became increasingly like the surrounding nations, where all the land was the property of the king. In 2 Kings 4:13 we see how the king and the commander of the army exert influence on the lives of ordinary people, but also how a peasant woman rejects this, commenting that she is living amid her own tribe and therefore does not appreciate outside intervention.

Because the Israelites usually defied God's precepts, he punished them by sending them into exile: the northern kingdom of ten tribes was whisked away to Assyria (2 Kings 17) and later the southern kingdom of two tribes went to Babylon (2 Kings 25). After a long time, the people from the southern kingdom were allowed to return and to rebuild the city of Jerusalem with the temple (see Ezra), but until the end of the Old Testament era the country around Jerusalem, usually called Judah, never again gained political independence. As a comment on the history of Israel Miskotte correctly states that the books Samuel and Kings present 'an almost complete relativization of the possible forms a state may take'.[13]

The King

The above clearly shows that, unfortunately, Samuel's negative expectations of the kingship came true. When God is not recognised as king, earthly rulers often make the most horrible mistakes. Nevertheless, the Old Testament contains clear instructions for the kings of Israel in at least two places; and if these instructions had been followed, everything would have gone quite differently.

---

[13] Miskotte, *When the Gods are Silent*, 274.

In the first place, there is Deuteronomy 17:14–20, which is also a very relevant text for our time and worth quoting in full:

> When you enter the land the LORD your God is giving you and have taken possession of it and settled in it, and you say, 'Let us set a king over us like all the nations around us,' be sure to appoint over you a king the LORD your God chooses. He must be from among your fellow Israelites. Do not place a foreigner over you, one who is not an Israelite. The king, moreover, must not acquire great numbers of horses for himself or make the people return to Egypt to get more of them, for the LORD has told you, 'You are not to go back that way again.' He must not take many wives, or his heart will be led astray. He must not accumulate large amounts of silver and gold.
>
> When he takes the throne of his kingdom, he is to write for himself on a scroll a copy of this law, taken from that of the Levitical priests. It is to be with him, and he is to read it all the days of his life so that he may learn to revere the LORD his God and follow carefully all the words of this law and these decrees and not consider himself better than his fellow Israelites and turn from the law to the right or to the left. Then he and his descendants will reign a long time over his kingdom in Israel.

Power corrupts, and absolute power corrupts absolutely. This legislation is a precaution against it. The modern version of a horse (verse 16) is a tank or an armoured vehicle. The passage thus means to say that the king may not rely on military power, must not have a harem, and must not be covetous of wealth. It is striking to see the imperative that the king is not to be a legislator, as the kings of the gentiles around Israel were – instead he must have a copy of the law of God. (The NIV and some other translations even say that he must write this copy himself.) God had given the laws through Moses and they were not the king's business. Likewise, justice and the oversight of the worship of God were not part of the king's task; these responsibilities belonged to other people in Israel. The only task left for the king was to ensure that he himself and his people lived close to God. The king was a servant of God and of his people. It is not difficult to see the relevance of this passage for people in positions of power in our time and all times.

The second text about the king is Psalm 72. This psalm has the outer appearance of a prayer for the king and is attributed to Solomon. (However, the New English Translation does not have 'of Solomon' but 'for Solomon', which may well capture the intention.) The psalm is best read as a kind of manual for the kingship; that is, as a manual for people in power past, present, and future. Note that in this psalm the poor are mentioned several times as those who merit the special care of the king. What also strikes us again, as in Deuteronomy 17, is that the fact that the king in Israel is not a demigod. He is not called to be super human – he is merely an exemplary citizen.

The Prophets

The Israelite prophets are best regarded as a kind of political commentators and consultants. They observed what was happening in the country and at the court and provided comments on behalf of God, whether solicited or unsolicited. Their words carried the authority of God himself. Prophets were not part of a system in the way that priests and kings were. Thus, they could be a kind of lice in the fur of kings and other authorities.[14] To see how this worked in practice, it is worth reading what the prophet Nathan did in 2 Samuel 12:1–15 and what Isaiah did in 2 Kings 20.

First Kings 21 tells the story of how King Ahab tried to take possession of the vineyard of the farmer Naboth. When the farmer refused to give way, the king backed off. But his foreign wife Jezebel had a different personality, and she persevered in the attempt to enlarge the king's estate. As a foreigner, she was probably less concerned about the rights of ordinary people in Israel than her husband. Naboth was fully justified in referring to the fact that this piece of land was his God-given inheritance (verse 3), but Jezebel persuaded Ahab to apply the foreign 'principle' which said that the king can get whatever he wants, leading the prophet Elijah to announce God's severe punishment of Ahab and Jezebel.

---

[14] Miskotte, *When the Gods are Silent*, 289.

The prophets spoke out against the smugness of pious people and against any automaticity in the religion. From God's perspective, it is not so relevant that a person brings sacrifices and sings beautiful worship songs; what matters is that they do so deliberately and from the heart (Amos 5:21–24). Besides, Amos, Micah, and Isaiah defend the legal rights of the poor and they speak out against injustice and poverty. Isaiah does this in very eloquent ways; see for example his formal accusation of the wealthy in Isaiah 3:12–15. (Amos 4:1–3 and 5:10–13, and Micah 2:1–2, 9 are also worth reading.) The worst part of the problem was that the injustice against the poor was perpetrated by their own people, not outsiders!

The prophets also spoke clearly about other problems, such as corruption in the administration of justice (e.g. Amos 5:7, 10, 12, Micah 3:9–11, Isaiah 5:23, 10:1–2, and Jeremiah 22:13–17). When we look once more at Deuteronomy 16:18–18:22, the passage about the leaders in Israel, we note a striking contrast: the priesthood is hereditary; the judges and the kings in Israel are selected and appointed by the people; but it is God himself who from time to time calls a person to be a prophet. One does not become a prophet on one's own initiative. We can be grateful to God that during the history of the church even until now, God has repeatedly sent prophets to bring the church back on the right path and to address governments regarding their responsibilities.

Human Nature

Many peoples, such as the Assyrians and the Greeks, saw themselves as superior to other nations; for such people the Greeks used the condescending word 'barbarians'. Other people groups were regarded as stupid and their languages were interpreted as no more than animal sounds.

In Israel this was very different. As we saw in the chapter about creation, the Old Testament first assumes that all peoples are equal before God, regardless of where they live, what language they speak or how they look. In the same way, within Israel itself all people are equal; for example, there is no caste system as there is in India. All people are created in the image of God and all share in caring for the earth. When the land of Israel comes into the picture as the residence of the people of God, we see that in this land all people own a private piece of land (Leviticus 25, cf. 1 Kings 21:3; immediately we also see that this situation often came under threat – we will return to this below). The basic equality of the people is the basis on which the prophets and Bible writers can criticise any corrupt situations in the country.

Secondly, the woman is not the slave of her husband or her in-laws, as was normally the case in the Ancient Near East (ANE). The woman is an image-bearer of God, as we saw in chapter 1.

Thirdly, human life is inviolable. The phrase 'an eye for an eye, a tooth for a tooth' (Exodus 21:23–27, Leviticus 24:20, Deuteronomy 19:21) strikes us as hard and brutal, but in the ANE it was a form of grace because it limited the vicious circle of blood revenge. If someone had damaged your eye, you or your family were not supposed to kill them out of revenge (let alone kill their entire family), but you could only damage their eye. This rule would stop the chain of retaliation before it could even begin. Even the king did not have power over the life and death of his subjects for he, too, was held to the laws (as we saw, for example, in 1 Kings 21).

Fourthly, the Old Testament has a manifest concern for the weak (Deuteronomy 14:28–29, Proverbs 25:21). Even slaves had rights (Exodus 21:2–6, Deuteronomy 5:14–15, Job 31:13–15) and an Israelite could never become a slave permanently (Leviticus 25:39, 42, 46).

Poverty and Property

Professor Miskotte wrote:

> The prophets were always championing the cause of the poor. In the Psalms we hear their laments and in Proverbs the admonitions are often directed specifically to the rich. In the New Testament, apart from several passages in Luke and the Epistle of James, we find little attention devoted to the mystery and the promise which are hidden in poverty.[15]

In my view, Miskotte severely underestimates how much Jesus spoke about poverty, although he is right that the

[15] Miskotte, *When the Gods are Silent*, 249.

Old Testament there is much more about this subject than in the New.

The Old Testament originated at a time when there was yet no old age pension or any social security such as sick pay. The members of a people group or tribe were entirely dependent on each other. Poverty and even hunger were real possibilities. Poverty could have various causes, such as natural disasters or wars, but in the Old Testament the cause is almost always injustice and oppression. Israel was an agrarian society in which possession of one's own piece of land and livestock was vitally important. In such a situation, the sick, widows, and orphans were in a vulnerable position, just like any other persons who did not possess land or could not work it.

On the other hand, the Old Testament looks very critically at the possessions and the alleged property rights of wealthy people. In the very first set of laws in the Old Testament (Exodus 20–23) God sides with the poor in Israel (Exodus 22:24–26). In Leviticus 25:23 and 1 Chronicles 29:15 the LORD is referred to as the owner of all land. The land of Israel is not the property of the people but of God; the Israelites are literally called aliens or strangers who are merely God's guests (Leviticus 25:23). To keep this in mind, they preserved the long lists which show how in the beginning the promised land was divided among them (Numbers 32, 34, and 35; Joshua 13–21). Those lists might be boring for modern readers but for Israel they were essential, since their message was that God had given the land to them, his people, on loan! This is your bit and this mine. The implication is that he might very well take it away from us again if we do not play by his rules, as can be seen in Leviticus 26:30–35, Deuteronomy 28:58–65, Jeremiah 20:3–6, and Amos 9:7–9.

People in the twenty-first century need to be aware that we are all – in the same way as Israel – guests on this earth, which is owned by God, not by us (cf. Psalm 24:1). The consequences of this idea cannot be worked out here, but they are far-reaching. God is on the side of the poor and he expects the same of his people. Psalm 146 offers a wonderful testimonial of who God is: the LORD, the God of Israel, 'upholds the cause of the oppressed and gives food to the hungry' (verse 7). 'The poor man is the real neighbour' and 'The poor man is the representative of the God who humbles himself in order to dwell with us on earth,' writes Miskotte.[16]

The Stranger

In political terms, in the Old Testament we meet three groups of people: foreigners, Israelites, and a group that is often called 'aliens' (NRSV) or 'strangers' (NIV); in Deuteronomy 14:21 the three groups are clearly distinguished. Strangers were not Israelites, but lived in the land of Israel. Foreign nationals may have had different reasons to migrate to Israel, such as famine, poverty, or persecution. Often they had no family, at least not in the country, and they did not possess their own piece of land. This made them as vulnerable a group as the widows and the orphans.

---

[16] Miskotte, *When the Gods are Silent*, 249, 251.

Foreigners and aliens were excluded from participating in the worship of Israel if they had not formally become Israelite or Jew. One could begin to belong to Israel by recognising the God of Israel as the one true God. This possibility of 'conversion' was open to all, but as far as we can see not much use was made of it. Someone who took this step was Ruth. Later, King Solomon prayed that God will also allow foreigners entrance to the new temple (1 Kings 8:41–43).

Other countries did not always pay much attention to foreigners in their midst, but the Old Testament has an open eye for them. (We should, however, not overdo the difference between Israel and the other nations.) In many places, they are mentioned together with the widows and orphans, as people who specifically receive the care of the LORD (Deuteronomy 10:17–18, Psalm 94:3–6, 146:9, and Malachi 3:5).

The words of God in Deuteronomy 10 do supply the reason for this attitude: the Israelites had themselves been slaves in Egypt (verse 19, cf. Exodus 22:20–22; 23:9). For that very reason strangers may not be treated badly in any way (Leviticus 19:33); one must love them (Leviticus 19:34, Deuteronomy 10:19) and treat them in the same way as one's own people (Leviticus 19:34). They too have the right to rest on the Sabbath, the weekly day of rest for humans and animals (Exodus 20:10, 23:12). The prophets defended the cause of these people (e.g. Jeremiah 7:6, 22:3). I refer here only to a limited number of Old Testament texts on this subject, because there are many more. The responsibility for dealing with foreigners is not placed at the door of 'the government' or the king, but in the hands of the society, that is, all individual Israelites acting together.

By the way, the Old Testament also reveals that people in Israel did not always speak positively about foreigners. An example of this behaviour is Rebekah, who clearly expresses her dislike of Hittite women (Genesis 27:46) – and what happens in Judges 19 is completely wrong.

Because this book is not about the rules which applied to Israel or about precepts for us, we merely establish the fact that God's heart and God's people have a special place for foreigners and strangers. In terms of our time, these people include refugees and asylum seekers. The Old Testament condemns the mentality of 'own people first'.

In our time with its hugely increased mobility and globalisation we are confronted with aliens and foreigners in many ways. There are people in our country who did not originally come from here; other people want to come and live here. God taught Israel to adopt a positive attitude towards all such people who would not manage without their help, and he expects us – who have experienced the love of Jesus Christ – to act in the same way.

Chapter 5: Scepticism and Doubt

Many people think that Christians must always be super spiritual, that they must always live 'the victorious life', that doubt is not allowed, and that difficult questions should not be asked. And it is indeed true that many leaders in our churches and communities struggle to cope with hard questions, so that it seems better to keep your mouth shut. But doubt and hard questions are very much present in the Bible. Even Jesus asked his Father shortly before his suffering if it would not be possible for him to avoid that awful cup (Mark 14:36). In the Old Testament, it is no different. People don't hesitate to speak their hearts out and they ask things of God that you perhaps did not know are in the Bible. We will be looking at a few examples which show that God is quite capable of handling such pressure.

Abraham and Sarah

God did not give Abraham and Sarah an easy life. He promised this childless couple a son when they were already at an advanced age (Genesis 12:1, 7; 13:15–16) and then he waited many years before he fulfilled his promise. At a certain moment, Abraham runs out of steam and suggests that a servant can be his heir (Genesis 15:2–3), but God calmly repeats his promise (15:4–5). Sarah in turn thinks that they can help God a little and she gives her slave girl Hagar to Abraham as a second wife (16:1–3); and instead of showing a great faith in the word of God Abraham goes along in this plan (16:4). (The idea as such is not as strange as it seems: in that culture a man could easily take a second wife if the first one remained childless.) Again, God repeats his promise (17:1–8, 15–16), but this time Abraham laughs and proposes to God that the son of Hagar can be regarded as the promised son (17:17–18). Yet God sticks to his original plan (17:19–22). In the next episode, it is Sarah who laughs about God's repeated promise and then denies that she had done so (18:9–15).

At this point – if not sooner – we might have given up on Sarah and Abraham and selected a more faithful, less giggly couple. But God does not. And to be honest, he does try them to the limit by expecting them to wait half a lifetime for their child; most of us would not have held out in such a situation. In any case, it is clear that God accepts the doubt of these two people. Not only does he not punish them, he fulfils his promise and they finally receive what he had promised (21:1–3). Isn't God great?

The Depression of Elijah

The great prophet Elijah comes across as a very modern person, so recognisable and easy to identify with is his depression, which is described in 1 Kings 19. At this moment, he has survived a couple of very difficult years, during which the highlight was his key role in God's great victory over the idol Baal in chapter 18.

What finally brings him down is a woman, queen Jezebel, who threatens him with death (1 Kings 19:1–2). Elijah flees for his life and then says to God: 'I have had enough, LORD. Take my life; I am no better than my ancestors.' (1 Kings 19:4). It is unexpected and strange to hear a great prophet speak like this! But God does not drop him, just as he did not drop Sarah and Abraham. On the contrary, the story ends well: God saves Elijah's life and uses him in his service for many more years, as you can read in 1 and 2 Kings. Again, it is not difficult to see the relevance of this story for us.

Joshua

Here we also mention a person who does not initially speak to God, Joshua. Every time when the fact comes up that he will be the successor of the great leader, Moses, Joshua is told that he must be strong and courageous. So, although we are not explicitly told, Joshua was clearly daunted by his future task as the leader of the people. And a huge task it was, not least because Moses was a formidable predecessor! First it is Moses who encourages him when he appoints Joshua as his successor (Deuteronomy 31:7–8). Then it is God himself who encourages his servant at length (Joshua 1:1-9). Both Moses and God use wonderful words which can also support us when we face a daunting task. And his initial uncertainty did not make Joshua any less effective as a leader.

The Scepticism of Ecclesiastes

In the chapter on creation we saw that life on earth is good in principle because God has made all things well. Although human sin entered later, destroying and corrupting much, life remains worth the living. It is the desire of God the Creator that we exist and this is a cause for joy and gratitude.[17]

It is surprising that this joyful faith has almost been lost in the thoughts of the seeker of the Old Testament, the Teacher in Ecclesiastes. He comes across as a modern man, who thinks, like the majority of our novelists and philosophers, that life is a very bleak experience. In his writing, the author of Ecclesiastes puts question marks against the rest of the Old Testament. Even though in chapter 3:11 he recognises that God has made everything beautiful, in 3:20 he talks about return to dust, which is an allusion to Genesis 3:19. He gets stuck in his disappointing experiences, as we can also see in Ecclesiastes 7:29, where he complements the creation story with the thought that humans are struggling too much.

Because of all these things the trustworthiness of the book of Ecclesiastes was discussed by the rabbis, just like that of Song of Songs: 'Does it fit with our other holy books? Can we hear the voice of God in it?' The conclusion was positive, but with the necessary caveats, and we have similar concerns as well.

Miskotte particularly hears tiredness and fatigue in Ecclesiastes,[18] the same fatigue which he signalled in many people in the church, and that has not improved

---

[17] This is a very frequent theme in the work of A.A. van Ruler, e.g. in *Blij zijn als kinderen. Een boek voor volwassenen* (Kampen: Kok, 1972) 55-56.

[18] Miskotte, *When the Gods are Silent*, 252-253.

much since his time. The Old Testament promises that whoever expects the LORD will receive new power (Psalm 68:35, Isaiah 40:29–31), but this promise eludes the Teacher.

Reading Ecclesiastes

The Jewish author Pinchas Lapide explains that Jews read the book of Ecclesiastes at the Feast of Tabernacles.[19] This is a harvest festival where everyone is happy about the good things which God has given them. Living in a booth, a structure of leaves and branches, so vulnerable and open, reminds the people that they should not put their trust in earthly things such as material property. We are all pilgrims on our way to the promised land (Leviticus 23:42–43). Our faith is not a source of false certainty; it gives us courage for every day. Reading Ecclesiastes strengthens our awareness that nothing on earth is permanent; everything we can see around us, however beautiful, is perishable.

Modern believers may find it good to read Ecclesiastes on New Year's Eve, when we look back on a year in which not everything went as we had expected. Was not much of the year filled with vanity (cf. Ecclesiastes 1:1 NRSV)? God's hand in the world's events is very hard to see. Much in Ecclesiastes could be given a heading such as 'It is hard to track down God's involvement with the world'; see

---

[19] The following pages draw on Pinchas Lapide, *Mit einem Juden die Bibel lesen* (Stuttgart: Calwer Verlag, 1982); Dutch: Pinchas Lapide, *Uit de Bijbel leren leven. Op joodse wijze de Schriften lezen* (Baarn: Ten Have, 1984).

particularly Ecclesiastes 8:10–17. We can read this book as a reflection on themes such as time, temporality, mortality, and transience. The author stresses that in our own power we cannot escape the vanity or emptiness of existence. The only thing we can do is to run to God.

The Scepticism of Ecclesiastes (2)

Ecclesiastes does not use the name of God, Yahweh or the LORD. Instead it always uses the general word 'God'. This suggests that the Teacher feels a certain distance between himself and the God of Israel. He also never mentions God's revelation in the Holy Scriptures and in the worship of his people. He introduces himself as a kind of researcher standing outside the circle of the covenant. This tells us that if we try to understand the meaning of life apart from what we know of the God of Israel, we will not find it. Likewise, philosophy and politics that do not recognise and factor in God can neither help us understand life nor give any meaning to it.

The Teacher does, to his credit, show great respect for God. Even though God is far away, he is righteous and reliable (e.g. Ecclesiastes 2:24–26; 3:12–15; 5:1, 17–19). In this respect the Teacher differs considerably from Job, as we will see in the next chapter.

What is clear is that the Old Testament here calls for an answer which has not yet been given. It only comes in the New Testament: it is Jesus. To him God hands over the judgement over 'the righteous and the wicked' (Ecclesiastes 3:17) that will take place at the end of time.

In our post-Christian culture, it is often impossible to speak directly with people about Jesus, if at all; for many his name is no more than a swearword. Such people perhaps share Ecclesiastes' attitude to life. If so, we can take this as a point of departure to talk about Jesus. What he has done is neither temporary nor fleeting.

Looking around us, it is easy to draw the same conclusion as the Teacher: it is all vanity and emptiness. It seems as if the coming of Jesus has brought little change in the affairs of the world. The creation is in trouble (Romans 8:18–25) and so are we. We are waiting for God's intervention. Meanwhile, we receive the advice to take God seriously while we are young (Ecclesiastes 12:1), to have respect for him, and to keep his commandments (12:13). God does not force himself on us and modestly asks that we should think of him as the Creator while we are still young.

Conclusions of Ecclesiastes

Lapide argues that the Teacher reaches some clear conclusions, which are worthy to be repeated here:

- No-one can discover the meaning of life by good thinking alone; for this God's revelation is indispensable.
- Only God determines the events on earth; he is sovereign.
- There is much injustice in the world and no-one can fully understand what God is doing.
- Humankind is not divine but rather weak and helpless.

These conclusions can act as a splash of cold water on many human pretensions. Much of what Ecclesiastes says is also still true and relevant in the time after the New Testament.

In another respect, I do also understand the Teacher well: he was tired of the large quantities of information that he collected, of his many investigations, and his great knowledge (e.g. 1:13–18, 12:12). We live in the age of information. Someone has said that one major newspaper today contains more information than a medieval person would encounter during their entire life. We have our smartphones and iPads with internet, Facebook, Twitter, and so on. Too much information for most of us, as a result of which we have little or no silence, and barely any good conversations. All that information seems to be super important, but most of it is vanity and emptiness.

This chapter has made it clear that believers may have doubt and that they can be depressed. With the God of Israel there is room for our human feelings. Scepticism does not need to be inconsistent with faith, 'it can even be a legitimate way in which faith exists', as Professor Miskotte writes.[20]

We humans can be disappointed in life. We can lack experience of God's presence. This can depress us much, and then we can say with Ecclesiastes that we have searched intensely but still not found (cf. Ecclesiastes 7:28). The Teacher failed to see God's hand anywhere anymore, and this can be the case for many Christians,

---

[20] Miskotte, *When the Gods are Silent*, 450.

especially if we lose someone dear to us like a child or a partner, if we are attacked by doubt, or suffer from depressive feelings. But hopefully there will also be other, better, times and seasons in your life as a child of God.

Chapter 6: Laments

'Sometimes I behave a bit like David, you know', my hostess said when she told me about her difficult life. I did not immediately understand her and she could see that from my face. So she clarified what she meant by adding, 'Well, David laments to God about his troubles in the Psalms, doesn't he? I simply do the same.'

She was right. In several Psalms David laments about his need to God and the Old Testament contains many more laments of believers who were struggling. In the New Testament, we hardly encounter such laments anymore, so it is fitting that laments are discussed in this book. But isn't lamenting something very negative? According to the Bible it is not, as long as it is directed towards God and respects who he is. In the Bible, a lament is not an act of self-pity, but it is an acceptable form of addressing God. Sometimes all the people of Israel would join in a lament, sometimes an individual would do so. There are laments about God, about other persons (mostly enemies), but especially about an individual's own situation. Let us take a closer look at this enormous diversity.

Laments of the People

At the beginning of the Old Testament, when the people of Israel were just emerging and were living in Egypt as slaves, they lamented to God in their distress. In Exodus 1 and 2 their situation was increasingly hopeless. But then Exodus 2:23–25 tells us that the Israelites began to address God, and this brought a reversal in their fate!

Their laments reminded God of his covenant with the people and immediately we read that he took action by calling Moses to prepare the exodus from Egypt.

After the exodus, the people turned out to be quite an ungrateful bunch and they regularly grumbled against Moses and his brother Aaron (e.g. Exodus 15:24 and 16:2; the translation 'complain' in the NRSV is too positive and can lead to misunderstandings.) Here the people were not lamenting about their need, but rather grumbling. That is not a good thing and it is not what this chapter is about. The laments of the people in Exodus 2:23–25 were productive because they expected something positive of God – the grumbling in Exodus 15 and 16 is selfish.

Among the Psalms we find quite a few laments of the people of Israel, such as in Psalms 44, 60, 74, 79, 80, and 137. At difficult moments in their history God's people knew that they did not have to turn away from him, but could call on him and explain their situation to him. Sometimes one of them did this on behalf of all; thus Nehemiah 9 is a long prayer on behalf of the people of God.

There is even a book named after laments, namely Lamentations. The city of Jerusalem and the magnificent temple of God, built by Solomon, had been destroyed; the nation had experienced terrible things. In Lamentations, various people call to God for salvation and recovery on behalf of the people. It is typical that most of us only really know a few verses from this book, the ones right in the middle, Lamentations 3:22–24, which are positive in tone:

> Because of the LORD's great love we are not consumed, for his compassions never fail. They are new every morning; great is your faithfulness. I say to myself, 'The LORD is my portion; therefore I will wait for him.'

Of course, these are beautiful words, but by taking them out of context we hardly do justice to Lamentations as a whole. I therefore propose that you also read many verses around these well-known verses. You will then encounter emergencies such as desolation (1:4), the mocking of enemies (1:7), hunger (1:11), and consciousness of guilt (1:14). It is clear that God accepted these laments from Israel and took them seriously. The book of Lamentations is not in the Bible by accident.

Laments of Individuals

We now look at some individuals who lament to God about their need. Early in the Old Testament there is Abraham, the man with the great faith. In Genesis 15:1 God speaks to him in an encouraging way and makes him a promise, but Abraham replies that he does not even have a son and that therefore a servant must be his heir (15:2–3). The tone of Abraham's words is not bitter, but he is disappointed because God still has not fulfilled his earlier promise (12:2, 7).

The widow Naomi shows God that she is disappointed in him because she has lost her two sons (Ruth 1:11–13). In her experience the LORD has turned against her. Fortunately, she does not turn away from him, but she rather focuses her lament on him. This gives God the opportunity to go further with her. (We might find it quite common, but note that here a woman speaks to God independently. That was not common in the ancient East.) And not much later, despite – or thanks to – this lament by her mother-in-law, the young widow Ruth from Moab decides to follow the God of Israel (Ruth 1:16).

In the Psalms, we find individual laments in Psalms 3–7, 12–14, and many others. There are laments about danger, enemies, loneliness, despair, disease, and death. The unknown poet of Psalm 130 is very direct: he finds himself in 'the depths' because of his sins. He confesses these sins to God and at the end of the psalm he expresses his expectation that God will forgive not only him but also the whole people of God, Israel.

The prophet Jeremiah does not hold back in his laments. His very individual laments can be found in Jeremiah 11–20 (to be precise, in 11:18–23; 12:1–6; 15:10–21; 17:12–18; 18:18–23 and 20:7–18). Careful reading shows that his words are interspersed with answers from the LORD.

Jeremiah and his people go through a difficult period in their history. God wants to turn his back to them because of their many sins, but he first sends Jeremiah to them as a prophet to warn them. Because they do not listen to Jeremiah, the prophet gets into deep difficulties; he is even charged with treason (Jeremiah 36) and can only turn to God with his need.

The book also contains laments which appear to be sung by the people of Israel (Jeremiah 4:19–21; 8:18–9:1; 10:19–20; 14:17–18 and 23:9). These laments already run ahead of the punishment of God which is becoming ever more inevitable: the destruction of Jerusalem and the temple, and the prolonged exile in Babylon.

The prophet Habakkuk also laments about his need to God. 'Why do you tolerate the sin and why do you not stop the sinner?', the prophet asks. His lament in Habakkuk 1:2–4 contains words like 'how long' and 'why' that also occur in Psalms of lament such as, for example, Psalm 6:3, 10:1, and 13:1–2. Habakkuk 1:5–11 is a response from God, but this does not satisfy the prophet, so that he replies in a more rebellious voice in chapter 1:12–17.

The most famous person to lament in the Bible besides Jeremiah is probably Job. He is initially a rich man with a happy family life, but he loses everything in one day (Job 1:13–19). Initially he reacts very piously to this enormous grief, with the normal signs of mourning: a shaved head and torn clothes (1:20–22). How would we react if we would lose all that was dear to us in one day? Even when his wife forsakes her faith, Job continues to speak positively about God (2:9–10). He does not want to lose his faith and he begins a struggle to preserve it. But when three 'friends' arrive to join and console him in his suffering, after seven days he cannot constrain himself any more (2:11–13) and he curses the day of his birth (3:1). The rest of this chapter is filled with the lament that he brings to God. God accepts this. (More about how Habakkuk and Job contradict God in the next chapter.)

Laments of God

It is quite remarkable that in the Old Testament God himself also occasionally utters a lament. They occur at the beginning of the book of Isaiah (1:2–3) and in Jeremiah 8:4–7, 12:7–13, and 15:5–9. These laments are about the infidelity of the people in whom he had invested so much time and love. God still loves them and he cannot stand the fact that they try to live without him. He must punish them, and for that purpose he uses foreign nations, but he himself suffers under this situation. These laments should not be ignored when we think about who God is according to the Old Testament.

In the New Testament, we hear that Jesus also utters laments. Psalm 22 was at first a lament of David, who used a number of suggestive images to cry out to God about his need. But later this psalm came to play a large role in the narrative about the suffering and death of Jesus in the four Gospels. Jesus used words from this psalm on the cross: 'My God, my God, why have you forsaken me?' He was indeed abandoned by God and felt that deeply – and he gave expression to that horrible feeling! (We know that we will never be left by God in the same way, thanks to the work of Jesus.) Note that Jesus does not say goodbye to God even at this time, as he still speaks about 'my' God. But in his heavy suffering he feels left alone by his father.

Form

The laments which we find in the Bible have many similarities because they usually contain the same elements:

- Description of the emergency.
- Call to God (the actual lament).
- Expression of trust and confidence.
- Request for help.
- Promise to praise God as and when he helps.
- Expression of certainty or reassurance.

Not all of these elements are always present and they may appear in different order. In any case, the actual lament is normally embedded in a longer prayer. What is invisible in translations is that in the original language of the Old Testament most laments have their own peculiar dragging rhythm.

The expression of trust or confidence is of course striking. This shows that the person who utters the lament does expect that God will hear them and intervene to change their situation for the better. Laments in the Bible are uttered with a positive purpose and a positive expectation.

What About Us?

We saw that the people of Israel sometimes murmured or grumbled against God. Such behaviour is nowhere approved of in the Bible. But uttering laments about injustice and suffering is something we are allowed to do. We may speak to God about the injustice and the brokenness in the world, asking him to act. The words 'why' and 'how long' are not out of place in the mouth of a believer. This does not mean that we blame God for what is happening – that would be murmuring. We do not call God to account over what happens, but we lament over what happens. We share our grief, our lack of understanding, our concerns with our heavenly Father. We do so because we believe that he is not a powerless God who cannot do anything about the situation, but because he is our mighty Saviour.

We also believe that he created the world beautiful and good and that it is his desire that we should be happy on earth. He is on our side in the fight against misery, disease, and death. We lament with a positive expectation, even though in this broken world we may perhaps not receive a concrete answer.

If we suffer a heavy loss, questions about the meaning of life come up. For a believer, these are questions to address to God, for he is the one who gives meaning to our lives. He is happy if we speak out these questions to him. We can ask that we may understand, maybe not *why* something happened to us but *what purpose* it can serve. Laments as we find them in the Bible help us in our desperation not to walk away from God, but to move closer to him. In this way, we find a form of consolation without denying or forgetting the reality of our misery.

Church

At a time when many people in our churches like to sing worship songs – and nothing else but worships songs – it would be good to draw renewed attention to laments.

After all, life is not always a bed of roses. We can 'give our hearts to Jesus', but that is sometimes the beginning rather than the end of our problems. All of us always want 'to live in victory', but we inhabit a fallen world which has turned away from God and the consequences of that decision are visible all around us. At the same time our culture finds it difficult to cope with pain, loss, and disaster. In churches and at Christian gatherings we therefore gladly sing our joyful songs, because 'it is hard enough as it is'. We do not sing psalms anyway – and have you ever heard a sermon on Lamentations? (Except, of course, on those positive verses in the middle of the book!)

But can everyone really take part in our sugar-sweet worship or is it only suitable for a limited number of truly happy people? Good, versatile worship has a pastoral role because it can facilitate spiritual recovery and thus contribute to the mental health of the community. It could even work as a preventive measure by helping people to take a realistic position in the world.

Let us also ask ourselves how 'rich' or 'poor' the prayers in our Sunday service are. Do the prayers leave any room for lament? Do we try to keep the world news out or do we scream to God about the injustice around us? About the slaughter of his children and the plight of the poor? Do we refuse to accept evil?

It is particularly necessary to allow space for lament when we are first faced with bad news on a Sunday morning, for example when we hear in the notices that someone is terminally ill, that a murder has been committed, when a case of adultery becomes public, or when we find out that a marriage is otherwise on the rocks. If we hear something like this when we are at home, we can rush to God in our prayers of lament, asking 'why Lord?' and 'How long, Lord?' If we first hear such bad news in the church, it would be foolish (to put it mildly) to follow it with a cheerful worship song. Instead of saying an improvised prayer, the preacher or another leader can, for example, read a psalm of lament.

In the Bible, silence also often belongs to the lament, as we see in Job 2:13 and Lamentations 2:10. The saying goes that a friend is someone with whom you have shared a period of silence. In God's proximity, there is no need always to rattle, and sometimes we just do not know what to say. But whether speaking, shouting or silently, we can utter our lament to God in our need.

Chapter 7: Contradiction

In our modern, empowered age an adult can be contradicted by a child, and a cabinet minister can be cornered by a journalist or an ordinary member of the public. This state of affairs was almost impossible even a century ago, and in the time of the Bible such assertiveness simply did not exist. There were fixed hierarchical relationships in the family, society, state, and religion; anyone who forgot about this was put back in their place with the necessary force.

This makes it all the more striking that in the Old Testament we encounter various people who contradict God. People say, 'This is not fair!' and 'Why me?' to the LORD God. These believers go much further than those who complain to God, whom we met in the previous chapter. And even more remarkable is the fact that these people got away with their behaviour, at least, if they otherwise lived in the right relationship with God.

This phenomenon, the contradicting of God, is limited to the Old Testament. For this reason, it is one of those treasures of the Old Testament Jesus referred to in Matthew 13:52. Our ancestors did of course read about these things in the Old Testament, but they did not appreciate them and preached resignation; Job was regarded as an excellent example of how to accept one's fate. Yet as we study some persons from the Old Testament who contradicted God, we will see that this is not correct.

Cain

The situation of Cain shows that it mattered whether someone who contradicted God lived in the right relationship with him. Immediately after Cain killed his brother Abel, God spoke to him (Genesis 4:9a) and at that moment he would not accept contradiction from Cain. But after God had imposed his sentence on him (Genesis 4:10–12), by which his wrath was tempered, he did allow Cain to contradict him. Here is what Cain said:

> My punishment is more than I can bear. Today you are driving me from the land, and I will be hidden from your presence; I will be a restless wanderer on the earth, and whoever finds me will kill me. (Genesis 4:13–14)

The NLT is even clearer:

> My punishment is too great for me to bear! You have banished me from the land and from your presence; you have made me a homeless wanderer. Anyone who finds me will kill me!

And lo and behold, God acknowledges that he is right: Cain gets the protection of a mark so that no one will kill him (Genesis 4:15)! We could ask all kinds of questions about this story: Who are the other people that could kill Cain? What mark or sign did he get? But that is not the point. What we notice is that Cain does not accept an aspect of God's judgement and contradicts him; and that God accepts this and offers him a solution.

Haggling

In the second half of Genesis 18 God tells Abraham that he intends to destroy the sinful city of Sodom. In his response (verse 23) Abraham does not deny that there are bad, guilty people in Sodom, but he carefully asks God if it is fair that the destruction of the entire city will also kill many innocent people. And when God does not immediately strike him with lightning, but in fact listens patiently, Abraham continues and suggests to the LORD that there might be fifty innocent people living in the city (verse 24). Once again, as a reader you expect that God will now get angry and inflict something on Abraham. But instead the Almighty replies to Abraham that this is actually a reasonable thought! This response gives Abraham the courage to continue with further bold questions: What will you do if there are no more than forty-five or forty good people in the city? (verses 28–29).

If you don't know this story, please read through to the end of Genesis 18, because it is pretty exciting. A modern dictator would have lashed out at Abraham. Two things are amazing. On the one hand Abraham is very courageous to go so far in his questions, haggling all the way down to only ten. On the other hand, God is (unexpectedly?) tolerant of his interlocutor. And at the moment he has had enough, he simply walks away from Abraham – end of story. Abraham is not punished and God does not even reproach him. This outcome gives us the courage that, in all reverence, we can boldly pray for others and ask for the maximum possible. We have nothing to lose.

Unwilling Servants

Moses is another Old Testament character who does not immediately say 'Yes and Amen' to God; we find the story in Exodus 3 and 4. The LORD appears to him and tells him that he must go to the king of Egypt on God's behalf. God wants to use Moses to bring about the release of the people of Israel from Egypt (Exodus 3:10). You and I might immediately have said 'yes', not only for fear of God but also because this was great news for the people of Israel: at last the liberation from slavery was in sight!

Not so Moses. He invents an excuse (Exodus 3:11) and another one (3:13) and another one (4:1) and then two more (4:10, 13). It takes some courage! In this case God does get angry (4:14) – but there is no punishment. Is this because God needs Moses and therefore he cannot inflict anything on him? Of course not, God could easily have called and equipped another person. But he sticks to his resolve that Moses must be his messenger, despite his stubborn opposition. And so it happens.

Later in time another person whom God wants to be a leader – Gideon – is not immediately keen on this assignment as Israel's judge. He starts out by contradicting the Angel of the LORD who had greeted him with: 'The LORD is with you, mighty warrior.' – 'Pardon me, my lord,' replies Gideon, 'but if the LORD is with us, why has all this happened to us?' (Judges 6:12-13) God could find ten others to serve in his place, we would probably have thought. But even after this unfriendly response, God perseveres and still wants Gideon to be the captain of his army. It seems to me that the fact that

Gideon subsequently asks for a sign (6:17–18) is also an attempt to escape, especially since shortly afterwards he demands another sign – and yet another one (6:36–40)! But as with Moses, God carries his plan through with Gideon. God tolerates the contradiction and politely works around it.

Jeremiah

In the book of Jeremiah, we find several cases of the prophet contradicting God. When God first calls him to be a prophet, Jeremiah replies that he is not available. Can you see a pattern emerging? This time the reason given is that he is much too young for the difficult task that God has for him (Jeremiah 1:6). God begs to differ and gives Jeremiah a few encouraging signs. Once again God takes on an unwilling servant.

Jeremiah certainly had a point, because his work turns out to be very heavy indeed and his book contains many complaints about this, as we saw in the previous chapter. But we also find utterances in Jeremiah that go beyond humble complaints:

> Why is my pain unending and my wound grievous and incurable? You are to me like a deceptive brook, like a spring that fails. (15:18)

> You deceived me, LORD, and I was deceived; you overpowered me and prevailed. I am ridiculed all day long; everyone mocks me. (20:7)

Jeremiah feels lured into his role by God, helpless, a pawn between God and the unwilling people to whom he has to speak – and he says so too! His severe accusations are probably on the boundary of what is acceptable, but God does not dismiss him. In the first case he does correct him, though, with the following words:

> If you repent, I will restore you that you may serve me; if you utter worthy, not worthless, words, you will be my spokesman. (Jeremiah 15:19)

This clearly means that by way of his contradiction Jeremiah had effectively resigned from his role as prophet. The next verse (15:20) confirms that God indeed accepts him back in his role. Interestingly, on the other hand, there is no rebuke after Jeremiah's contradicting of God in chapter 20.

Job

The theme of the book of Job seems to be the meaning of suffering and whether God is acting justly. It tells about the suffering of the devout Job and how he responds to it. In the previous chapter, we saw how in this need Job complained to God. In the next part of the story, however, we note that Job subsequently goes further than merely complaining. It was quite something that he cursed the day of his birth, because this meant that preferred death to life (Job 3:1–16). Job 3 seems to be a speech *against* God's good creation. Yet nowhere in the book does God in any way respond to these words.

In the next part of the book, Job is so convinced of his innocence that he accuses God of being dishonest; this thought occurs repeatedly in his long speeches in chapters 6–7, 9–10, 12, 14, 16–17, 19, 23, and 30. Job stages a kind of trial in which God is the accused and is called upon to defend himself (see Job 9:13–20). In his final speech Job swears a kind of oath on his innocence (chapter 31). He accuses God in a way and at a tone that we do not meet anywhere else in the Bible. Thus Job not only defends himself in long chapters against what are three 'friends' claim about him, but also against God. (The storywriter makes Job and his 'friends' rather unsympathetic in our eyes by allowing them to talk for so long, but that is probably a problem of our modern taste.)

Job sees God as the cause of his suffering and calls him to account. Here are some of his hardest words:

> The arrows of the Almighty are in me, my spirit drinks in their poison; God's terrors are marshalled against me. (6:4)

> God assails me and tears me in his anger and gnashes his teeth at me; my opponent fastens on me his piercing eyes. (16:9)

> He has blocked my way so that I cannot pass; he has shrouded my paths in darkness. He has stripped me of my honour and removed the crown from my head. He tears me down on every side till I am gone; he uproots my hope like a tree. His anger burns against me; he counts me among his enemies. His troops advance in force; they

> build a siege ramp against me and encamp around my tent. (19:8–12)

Are these not astonishing words? I would not dare to speak about or against God in this way, and I hope you don't either. But the Dutch theologian Jochem Douma – who refers to God as Yahweh – comments:

> Job deserves praise for the ferocity with which he defends his position. This ferocity can be explained from its strong commitment to Yahweh. Job can simply not imagine that the good relationship which he had with Yahweh is broken. We see that the reciprocity of the covenant between Yahweh and humanity renders the human party all the boldness to bring his cares, his complaints and even his charges to Yahweh. Even if in doing so Job goes too far, we keep in mind that he complains about what for him is most essential in his life, namely his relationship with Yahweh.[21]

Douma adds that Job can be praised because he struggles *with* God and appeals to him directly, whereas his 'friends' merely reason *about* God.

In the book of Job, we learn a lot about who God is – and who he is not. If he had any similarity to the gods of the nations, or indeed if he looked even a bit like your boss or any ordinary person, then Job would not have survived his battle with God. But our God is different! He allows

[21] Jochem Douma, *Job. Psalmen* (Gaan in het spoor van het Oude Testament; Kampen 2005) 16.

Job to complete his speeches. He respects him and even gives him a detailed reply in chapters 38–41. In these chapters, he speaks to Job as a respectable man (38:3; 40:7). He clearly tells Job that he is wrong (38:1–2; 40:1–2) – and Job admits that he was wrong (40:3–5; 42:1–6) – but Job is not punished and he even receives a reward (42:12–17).

Earlier in the Bible someone else was angry at God, namely Moses. In Numbers 11 he was stuck between, on the one hand, the people who were once again complaining, and on the other hand God who did not answer him. He uttered some harsh blame towards God (verses 10–15)! Yet the scene ended well because God tacitly recognised Moses's predicament and gave him the help of seventy elders. Once again, Moses responded in a very assertive way (11:21–22) but God replied quietly (11:23). Apparently, God accepts that, in time of need, his child might pick a fight with him!

The Idols

I just mentioned the gods of the nations. It is characteristic of these pagan gods that they are usually the guarantors of the existing system, of the established order. Pagan religions have a conservative trait, because their gods support the status quo. No wonder it was not thought proper to contradict them.

Our God is completely different! It is the God of Israel who allows the people to oppose the established order; it is this God who even expects his followers to stand up against injustice in the world. To that effect, he sent his prophets as messengers, and their words are relevant to this very day.

Yet our faith in the God of the Bible must at the same time be realistic. There is much in this world that is not good and that should come under criticism in the name of God, but we humans will not be able to achieve Utopia in our own power. The prophet Zechariah (4:6) already knew: it will not happen in our strength, by power or violence, but by the Spirit of the LORD.

Applying the Truth

When our lives pass without too many problems, we are not supposed to speak out against God in the way Job did. But if we are struggling as a result of circumstances outside of our control, we are definitely allowed to say so out loud to God. (Outside of our control, so that it is not our fault, that is the key thought in the book of Job.) In Job's case his bond with God was strong enough. Provided we do it with respect, we can say a lot to God. He has space for our doubts and pain. But is our bond with God as strong as Job's?

In our time many humans are in the habit of asking God why he allows certain things to happen. For example, this happened much with regard to the Holocaust. In so far as we are not personally involved in this tragedy, we do best to remain silent about it. We have other questions, such as why God allows someone in our circle of friends to get cancer, why we did not get the job that we wanted, or why our child is not as brilliant as we had hoped. Just as Job did not receive an answer to his 'why' questions, we will not normally receive answers to such questions. That is something else we learn from Job: we do not usually get answers to 'why' questions.

The Bible

Job's problematic words – and those of his 'friends' – draw our attention to something else. As Christians we acknowledge the Bible as the written word of God that is absolutely reliable and authoritative. But be careful: this applies to such things that the book states positively, to what forms 'the message' of the Bible. We cannot pick and use loose texts at random. And things which are merely described in the Bible but not approved, are not examples for us. It would be hard to preach a sermon based on the words of the 'friends' of Job.

There is a well-known story about someone who was looking for a 'word from the Lord' and who opened their Bible at random. With eyes closed they pointed to a verse and read: '[Judas] went away and hanged himself' (Matthew 27:5). That was not what they were looking for, so they made a new attempt and then read: 'Go and do likewise.' (Luke 10:37)

What I mean is that an isolated verse from Job or from anywhere else in Scripture can sow confusion and do a lot of harm. When we read the words of Job and his interlocutors in their context, which is in this case the book as a whole, it becomes clear that God disapproves of most of them. The Bible is the authoritative word of God, but it is not a grab bag.

Chapter 8: The Message of Esther

You may have never noticed, but in the book of Esther the name of God is not mentioned. He does not appear in the story even once! Of course, the Jews noted this strange situation a long time ago and regularly debated whether Esther really belonged in the Bible. If the Bible is the story of God and the people, can it contain a book which does not even mention him? Yes, said advocates of Esther, because even though God is not mentioned, he is clearly present nonetheless. He is hidden but not absent: his hand is visible in the events. (Pious people later wrote expanded versions of the book in Greek in which God is explicitly mentioned, but these versions are rejected by both the Jews and the Christian church.)

Christians too have sometimes had their questions regarding Esther, not only because of the lack of direct references to God but also because it struck them that the book is not cited in the New Testament. Nowadays these objections are not often heard. We now understand that Esther contains a lot of good theology in the form of an exciting story. Because Esther is absent from the New Testament, it is good to deal with it here.

Storyline

The story is set in Persia, in the fifth century BCE. The Persian Kingdom governs the world and Israel is part of this vast empire. After the exile in Babylon, many Jews have stayed behind in this country and others have moved to Persia, such as Mordecai and his niece Esther. The story tells how someone who hates the Jews, Haman, is trying to wipe out all the Jews and how this is prevented by the courage of a handsome, young, Jewish woman. As the new queen she has a strong position at court and she manages to get the King on her side. Her uncle and protector Mordecai is correct when he says to her that she has become queen 'for such a time as this' (Esther 4:14). This is of course a thinly-veiled reference to God's hand in the events. The fact that Esther and many others fasted for a day (Esther 4:16) undoubtedly means that they were dedicated to God and prayed to him on that day, so here too he is present in the background.

Message

What can we learn from this book?

The book of Esther gives us insight into the terrible consequences of ethnic conflicts and of the hatred between peoples (especially Esther 3:1–8). It shows us that in this respect there is nothing new under the sun and it tells us to be on our guard against anti-Semitism.

God does not abandon his people. In the difficult period caused by the plans of Haman he is not absent, but he saves them. He will do so also in the future, for he is faithful to his promises to them, which are later repeated by Paul in Romans 11. In this history, salvation comes not because the Jews faithfully keep the law or because of their return to the promised land or the coming of the Messiah, but through God's active, hidden presence. Esther calls us to trust God as the Saviour of those who seek him, and to live in faith and trust.

It strikes us how hard it is to get access to the king of Persia: you have to wait and see if his mental state is fit (Esther 4:11; 5:1–2; 8:1–4). That is an entirely different situation than with the kings of Israel, where everyone could simply walk in (2 Samuel 12:1–10; 14:1–5; 1 Kings 3:16; 2 Kings 8:3–6). In this respect the king of Israel resembles God, to whom we humans always enjoy free access.

God uses people. God in particular uses people who help themselves. He saves the Jewish people, but he makes himself dependent on the initiatives and perseverance of Esther and Mordecai. If these people had not done their duty, if they had not understood that this was their duty, then the story might not have ended happily. Consider whether you are expecting too much of God's direct intervention, while he might be waiting for you to act yourself. Maybe he will only act – indirectly – by means of your intervention. As someone said: 'We act as if all depends on us. Then we rely on God because we know that everything depends on him.'

God uses people who are not perfect: Esther had kept her Jewish identity hidden and that was wrong (Esther 2:10, 20); the way in which she was chosen to be queen was morally repugnant: she and all her competitors were first robbed of their virginity before the king made his choice. At the end the Jews take bloody revenge on their enemies (8:11; 9:5–6, 16), but even then God is on their side.

God also works through circumstances. The book of Esther is full of seemingly random events such as the presence of Esther as a candidate for the role of queen

(2:8), the insomnia of the king (6:1), the fact that the king reads exactly the section about Mordecai in the chronicles (6:2), and the fact that Haman enters the palace at that very moment (6:4). Not everything in life is 'spiritual' and we must be careful that we do not spiritualise ordinary life. Yet even when he is invisible, God is active on our behalf. He can work in spectacular events such as the exodus from Egypt and the crossing the Sea (Exodus 12–14), but he can also unobtrusively support Esther and Mordecai. While he appears to be absent, he is powerfully at work!

Esther and Mordecai serve God in a secular environment, and even in the service of a pagan government. Other biblical persons such as Joseph, Daniel, and Nehemiah also had important positions in the palace of a pagan king, and because of their pious way of life and their wise advice, they had great influence for good. There are several parallels between the story of Joseph (Genesis 37–50) and Esther: both main characters get their important role at the court of the king with the intention that they can save their people, that is, God's people. Christians too can serve non-Christian employers and even governments.

We often ask for the guidance of God in our lives. Many Christians do not undertake any great things without a sign, a vision, or a word from God. Esther and Mordecai, on the other hand, knew well what to do without such supernatural guidance. They just did it. They were guided by their conscience which told them to do so. When we live close to God, we too can prayerfully trust our conscience and do what is expected of us. We do no need a sign or prophecy to know this, because the Holy Spirit works in our hearts.

Esther's action is not rushed but well thought-out. She uses the weak spot of the king by first offering him a few good meals. When she finally says what she wants to say, she begins not with an accusation, but by pleading for her own life (Esther 7:3–4).

When we receive a blessing, we should welcome it and celebrate it, just as the Jews instigated and annually celebrated the festival of Purim (Esther 9:24–26). Evil had been overcome and that was a reason for exuberant gratitude.

Do What You Can

An old fable tells of three frogs. One day three frogs fell into a bucket of milk. They splattered around in the milk and were wondering how they would ever get out of that bucket. The walls were too smooth to climb up and they had nothing to use as a jumping point. The first frog said: 'This situation is hopeless.' He lost courage, shrugged – and drowned. The second frog said, 'God will certainly help us. We just have to wait.' He folded his front legs – and drowned. But the third one, although he had as yet no clue what might happen, was keen to stay above milk, hoping that external help would somehow come. As he kept trampling the milk, the milk gradually became butter on which he could stand! He did not drown and could eventually jump out of the bucket.

Many of our contemporaries have great experiences which they ascribe to the activity of the Holy Spirit. On the other hand, there are many religious people who have little or no experience of God. They know and believe that he exists and that he loves them, but they do not feel this every day. The book of Esther is an encouragement for this second group of believers. It shows us that God works in inconspicuous details and through people who simply do their duty without deep emotions or powerful experiences. Esther's willingness to venture her life for her people (Esther 4:16) is a great example for all of us to be faithful and brave in the place that God has given us, and to do what he expects of us.

Chapter 9: The Jewish Canon

This chapter differs from the others in that it does not discuss specific things within the Old Testament, but the Old Testament as a collection of books. It is worthwhile to reflect on the order in which the Jewish people have organised the books of the Hebrew Scriptures because this differs from the order in Christian translations.

The Christian Bible is originally not one book, but a collection of 66 books. For long time, these books were written and transmitted separately. For the 39 books of the Old Testament, God inspired all kinds of different people to be authors and collators. These people often did not know each other because they lived in very different times. Authorship was not very important in the Ancient Near East and copyright was unknown.

As a result, for many books we do not know who the author was. The printing press had not yet been invented – let alone the word processor or the iPad. Each book was therefore written by hand on a scroll. When the Jews later gathered their sacred books and recognised them as canonical – that is, authoritative and normative – these books were not yet in any particular order. As long as they were written on separate scrolls, such order did not matter. In the temple and in the synagogues people simply had two arms full of scrolls.

In the first or second century CE, the book was invented, and people gradually moved over from texts written on scrolls to texts in book-form, that is, a cover with pages in between. Bound books can hold much more text than scrolls, so that all kinds of texts now fit together in one cover. These books also took much less space, which was a big step ahead. At that moment the question presented itself, in which order the books of the Hebrew Bible had to appear within that one cover.

Greek Order

As I said above, for the books of the Old Testament two different orders exist. In all modern translations they appear in the order that is derived from the Greek translation of the Old Testament. When you look at the table of contents of the Old Testament, you can distinguish four groups.

The first group is formed by Genesis to Deuteronomy; these five books have several different names: they are called the Books of Moses, the Torah (= 'instruction') or the Pentateuch (= 'group of five').

This group is followed by a second group, the books from Joshua to Esther, which are seen as historical books. They tell the history of the people of Israel both in their country and in exile.

The third group consists of Job through to Song of Songs; to these books we can refer as wisdom books or poetic books.

Finally, there are the books of the prophets, Isaiah to Malachi.

LAW
Genesis, Exodus, Leviticus, Numbers, Deuteronomy
HISTORY
Joshua, Judges, Ruth, 1&2 Samuel, 1&2 Kings, 1&2 Chronicles, Ezra, Nehemiah, Esther
WISDOM
Job, Psalms, Proverbs, Ecclesiastes, Song of Solomon
PROPHETS
Isaiah, Jeremiah, Lamentations, Ezekiel, Daniel, Hosea, Joel, Amos, Obadiah, Jonah, Micah, Nahum, Habakkuk, Zephaniah, Haggai, Zechariah, Malachi

This division into four groups has associations with a time line: the first two groups tell the story of God and the people from the oldest history of the world and of Israel (in Genesis) to the most recent history at the time of writing (in Chronicles and Esther). With the third group people take a break, as it were, to sing the praises of God (Psalms) and to reflect on life (wisdom books such as Job and Proverbs). Finally, there is the last group, that of the prophets, who ostensibly speak about the future.

But when we think of the prophets only in this way, we do them no justice. As we saw especially in chapter 4, prophets in Israel were no fortune tellers and they did not major on distant eras; they were messengers of God who commented on the contemporary situation. Observing the people of Israel, the land, the king, the worship. and so on, they addressed these on behalf of God. Often their tone was critical because Israel did not keep God's precepts.

The prophets called the people to change, to repent and convert. Sometimes they indicated what the future would be like if Israel listened or did not listen, but that is something other than predicting the future. We conclude that the order of the books in our Old Testament, based on the Greek translation, is open to misunderstandings.

Hebrew Order

In the Hebrew Bible (which we call the Old Testament) the books have a different order: they are not on a kind of time line, but there is a heart, a core, surrounded by two circles. So there are only three groups in total: the Law, the Prophets, and the Writings. (In Hebrew, these words are Torah, Nebiim and Chetubim respectively; from the first letters of these words, T N Ch, the Jews derive the name Tanach for the entire collection.)

The Law, the core of the Old Testament, consists of Genesis, Exodus, Leviticus, Numbers, and Deuteronomy; these are the Books of Moses, the Torah or Pentateuch. They form God's original revelation to his people, in which he tells them who he is and through which he forms them as a nation. Later, he makes a covenant with this people, a covenant that comes with guidelines for the right lifestyle.

The first circle around this core is formed by the Prophets. First of all, there are the so-called Early Prophets: Joshua, Judges, Samuel, and Kings. This means that in Israel these books are not seen as 'historical books' but as prophetic books. The thought behind this is that their authors do not just tell us a bunch of facts but that they shine God's prophetic light on the history of his people. That is why these books are so selective in their presentations. They pay much attention to the great king David and to the important prophets Elijah and Elisha (and so to king Ahab, Elijah's opponent), but much less to most other characters in the story. An eloquent example of this selectivity is the fact that according to the Assyrians king Omri of Israel was an important ruler – but the prophetic author of Kings needs only a few verses to characterise him (1 Kings 16:23–28). The leading question in the descriptions is always: do the rulers and the people keep the commandments of the Lord? Compared to this, military and political successes are hardly relevant.

In this first circle we also find the Later Prophets, also known as the writing prophets: among these are the three major prophets Isaiah, Jeremiah, and Ezekiel, and the twelve minor prophets, Hosea to Malachi.

The books in this first circle around the Torah form God's ongoing revelation to his people: the prophets use and develop God's revelation in the Books of Moses and apply its teachings to the current situation of the people and the world.

The second, outer circle of the Hebrew Bible consists of the so-called Writings – not a very original name! In these books the people of God respond to the revelation which was given in the first two groups (the Torah and the Prophets) and to the road that God is travelling with them. At the head of the Writings we always find the Psalms with their multi-faceted human response to God's actions. Then there are the wisdom books Proverbs, Job, Song of Songs, and Ecclesiastes. Furthermore, in this group we meet a few books that we had expected somewhere else, namely Ruth, Lamentations, Esther, Ezra, and Nehemiah. And here Daniel also finds a place, a book which for unclear reasons is not among the Prophets. The last book of this second circle and thus of the entire Jewish Bible is usually Chronicles, which scholars suggest was originally written specifically to stand at the end of the canon. Chronicles tells the entire history of the world and of Israel once again, but this time from the perspective of the lineage of king David.

This Jewish arrangement of Law (Torah), Prophets, and Writings is very old, as it is already mentioned in the second century BCE in an apocryphal book entitled *Wisdom of Jesus Sirach.* (The name Jesus was a common name at the time.) Its prologue reads in the NRSV:

> Many great teachings have been given to us through the Law and the Prophets and the other books that followed them, and for these we should praise Israel for instruction and wisdom. Now, those who read the scriptures must not only themselves understand them, but must also as lovers of learning be able through the spoken and written word to help the outsiders. So my grandfather Jesus, who had devoted himself especially to the reading of the Law and the Prophets and the other books of our ancestors, and had acquired considerable proficiency in

> them, was himself also led to write something pertaining to instruction and wisdom, so that by becoming familiar also with his book those who love learning might make even greater progress in living according to the law.

The same tripartite division is also reflected in the words of Jesus in Luke 24:44, 'everything must be fulfilled that is written about me in the Law of Moses, the Prophets, and the Psalms'. Jesus here refers to the third group of books, the Writings, with the title of its first and most important component, the Psalms.

Number

You may have noticed that I am referring to Samuel, Kings, and Chronicles as one book instead of two. When you look at these books, in particular at the transition between the two parts, it is easy to see why I do this: each of these books was originally one work. They were only split in two much later, perhaps because they were considered a bit long. This splitting happened in the Greek tradition of the church, but in the Hebrew Bible these books are still one, as their original authors intended. The Jews also treat Ezra and Nehemiah as one book, as well as the books of the twelve minor prophets. Hence the total number of books in the Hebrew Bible (Tanach) is 24, while we in the church distribute the same amount of text over 39 books. Thus the content of the Hebrew Bible is the same as that of our Old Testament, but it is divided over fewer books.

The Five Scrolls

Many Jews call five books of the group of the Writings – Esther, Lamentations, Song of Songs, Ecclesiastes, and Ruth – by the title Megillot, which simply means Scrolls or Festive Scrolls, because they are read at specific events. There are obvious, strong connections between Esther and the Festival of Purim (see Ester 9), so Esther is read at that feast. Similarly, Lamentations is read during the commemoration of the destruction of the temple. More tentative connections consist between Song of Songs and the Jewish Passover, between Ecclesiastes and the Feast of Tabernacles (Sukkot), and between Ruth and the Feast of Weeks (Shavuot).

Perspective

We have seen that there are two ways in which the contents of the Hebrew Bible are organised. Neither of these is best as a matter of principle, but I prefer the Jewish order for several reasons. First of all, it is a refreshing alternative to the order in our Bibles.

Secondly, in this arrangement the distinct character of many books comes out better. This applies in the first place to the big picture. By recognising the three groups, we see better how some books speak about things more from God's perspective and how others rather contain the responses of the people. The Early Prophets are released from the label 'historical books', so that we no longer need to be surprised at the selectivity of their writers, who were inspired by the Holy Spirit to show God's perspective on the history of his people. The Later Prophets can no longer be seen as foretellers of the future and can be recognised as political and religious lice in the fur of those in power in Israel and Judah.

Finally, at the level of the individual books, we can appreciate the Psalms more as the answer of the faithful to God's word and God's guidance in their lives. Lamentations is no longer an appendix to Jeremiah, but a text in its own right with its own voice. And as a reader you can probably see further new perspectives!

The New Testament

The same question about the ordering of the books also came up when the New Testament was formed. Although the church accepted a certain group of books and called them the 'Bible', they never decided over the internal order of the collection. Old manuscripts show that the sequence of the 27 books was not always the same. In the beginning, for example, versions of the Gospels circulated in which the order was Matthew – John – Mark – Luke. This probably reflects the fact that Matthew and John were attributed to apostles, whereas Mark and Luke stem from friends and companions of apostles. Acts was often followed by the 'General (or Catholic) Epistles' (James to Jude), which were in turn followed by the letters of Paul, including Hebrews, which was attributed to Paul at that time. These alternative lists might also bring modern readers some new perspectives.

Chapter 10: Mixed Mistakes

So far I have presented the treasures of the Old Testament in a positive way and shown their relevance for our lives as Christians. But in the Introduction I argued that it is not always easy to distinguish which things in the Old Testament are still relevant for us and which are not. We also know that in this respect the followers of Jesus sometimes make different choices. For this reason, here in the final chapters I am going to reverse the approach: instead of the lasting meaning of the Hebrew Bible, I will now look at some misuses of it; and instead of elements of the Old Testament that are of lasting value for us, I shall focus on elements that are no longer relevant, but which are nevertheless maintained by some Christians, Jews, or Muslims. I will discuss usage of the Old Testament which is wrong in my opinion because it is does not – or not sufficiently – take account of the New Testament and of the fulfilment of the Scriptures in Jesus.

The order of the topics in this chapter is random and the next two chapters (on the Jewish festivals and the prosperity Gospel) are only separate chapters because these topics require more attention.

Rebuilding the Temple

Some Christian groups, especially in the United States and in the Netherlands, expect that in the future the Jews will rebuild the temple in Jerusalem. Not only that, they think that this reconstruction is a good thing which evangelical Christians should support. I do not agree.

The expectation that there will be a new temple in Jerusalem is based on the Old Testament, in particular on the visions of the prophet Ezekiel in chapters 40–48. In these visions the prophet, who lives in exile in Babylon and who has heard that the city of Jerusalem has been destroyed (Ezekiel 33:21–29), gives a detailed picture of a future new temple. It would seem reasonable to expect that this prophecy, which so far has not been fulfilled, will be fulfilled in the future.

After the exile the Jews did build a new temple (see Ezra 6), but that one did not resemble the temple which Ezekiel describes. Shortly after King Herod had extended and embellished it (see John 2:20), the Romans destroyed this temple in the year CE 70. Consequently, the Jews are again without a temple and cannot bring the sacrifices prescribed in the Old Testament.

In the New Testament, the situation is very different because the coming of Jesus makes the existence of the temple unnecessary, surplus to requirements. This is the conclusion drawn in the Epistle to the Hebrews. Jesus himself suggests this in John 2:13–22, and Revelation 21:22 explicitly states that there will be no temple in the new Jerusalem.

This situation leads us to ask what the function of a temple is. Temples are places where people can meet a god. In the faith of Israel, the temple is the place where the LORD is close to his people. Well, such a special place is no longer needed after God's revelation in Jesus Christ. It is now Jesus in whom we encounter God, in whom God has come close to us. John 1:14 states that the Word, that is Jesus, lived among us. The Greek word that is used here for 'live' is not the usual word, but one that specifically means 'to pitch a tent'. Choosing this word, John alludes to the fact that Jesus lived among us as in a tent, a tabernacle, as God did in the time when Israel travelled through the desert (Exodus 33:7–11, 40:34–38). Jesus was as present among us as God ever was. And John 1:18 declares that Jesus has made God known to us. After Jesus's ascension, God's presence continues by means of the Holy Spirit who lives as God in our hearts (e.g. John 14:15–21). As Christians, we have therefore no need for a temple.

The New Testament also tells us that the believers, each individually but also together, are the temple of God and of the Holy Spirit. That the body of each individual believer is such a temple is stated in 1 Corinthians 6:19; that the faithful together constitute a spiritual temple, is a thought shared by Paul (1 Corinthians 3:16–17; Ephesians 2:21) and Peter (1 Peter 2:5).

To build a new temple of stone would thus be an outright denial of God's New Testament revelation in Jesus, in the Spirit, and in the believers. It would mean a return to the situation before the coming of Jesus, which is of course impossible.

For Jews who do not believe in Jesus as their Messiah the situation is obviously different. From their perspective they actually need a temple to approach God and to bring the sacrifices that God has prescribed. It is therefore not impossible that Jews will try to rebuild the temple in Jerusalem. Such an attempt would be logical and we could have respect for it; but as Christians, such a temple would have no meaning for us and we could not support its building.

The Sabbath

When it comes to keeping the Sabbath, or celebrating the Sunday, we are in the area of God's commandments. There are some groups (such as Seventh Day Adventists) who suggest that believers in Jesus Christ should keep the Jewish Sabbath (Saturday) rather than the Christian Sunday. Yet in such *theological* matters, we must be guided by the New Testament and not the Old. Paul's firm conviction was that Christians from gentile backgrounds do not need to keep the whole law.

The members of the Church of the Seventh-day Adventists claim that they adhere to the Ten Commandments.[22] The most conspicuous element of this practice is the fact that they keep the Sabbath. Unlike other Christians, they do not celebrate the Sunday. I think they are wrong in this respect.

Seventh-day Adventists do have a point: initially the first Christians were all Jews and they stuck to the rules about the Sabbath, like all good Jews. It is also true that the New Testament contains no command to observe the Sunday, the first day of the week, as a Christian holiday. It is evident, however, that very early on the believers began to meet on Sundays; this can be seen in such diverse texts

---

[22] See for example www.adventist.org/en/beliefs/living/the-law-of-god/ [accessed 13 October 2016].

as 1 Corinthians 16:1–3, Acts 20:7–12, and Revelation 1:10. According to John 20:19–26, this habit started immediately after the resurrection of Jesus, which took place on a Sunday. It is thus very likely that the meetings on Sunday began as a celebration of the resurrection of the Lord Jesus.

These facts imply that for a while Jewish Christians probably attended meetings both on the Sabbath and on the Sunday, and for some messianic Jews this might still be true today. But what matters for us is that believers from gentile backgrounds never celebrated the Sabbath. In the second century, the church officially abolished the Sabbath; later still, the Sunday was officially introduced and made mandatory.

As I understand Paul in his letter to the Galatians, he has no problem with the fact that Jewish Christians continued the practice of circumcision, keeping the food laws and also observing the Sabbath. Yet on the other hand he expected that gentile believers would *not* keep these precepts. Indeed, Paul wrote to the Galatians in anger and frustration because legalistic people wanted to impose these rules also on Christians from a gentile background. For this reason alone, keeping the Sabbath is wrong for gentile Christians. We are not Jews and we must not try to behave as if we were.

Tithing

In the Old Testament God commanded Israel to tithe of their harvest to him (Numbers 18:21, 24, 26; Deuteronomy 26:12; Nehemiah 10:38–39). For those who don't know, the expression 'tithing' means giving a tenth of your income; a ten percent tax, in modern terms. In practice these gifts were not received by God himself, but they were for the priests and the Levites, the people who worked full-time in the service of God and who therefore could not earn their own income. In this way the priest and the Levites, and the entire system of the public worship of God, were maintained.

In the New Testament the rule regarding tithing is not repeated, hence it is one of the many laws which do not apply literally to us as believers from the Gentiles. In the Introduction to this book, I have classified these laws in group 4. Nonetheless, it is quite common for Christians in certain churches in England to speak about the obligation to tithe, and many churches in other parts of the world expect their members to give tithes. I think this is not correct.

It is clear that believers are jointly responsible for the salary (stipend) of their minister(s), if they have any, and for the wages of anyone else employed by the church, such as the caretaker. No-one else will give money for such purposes, least of all the state. This means that the members of the congregation bear these costs directly or indirectly (e.g. through a national organisation). If a congregation owns or rents a building, money will be needed for that purpose as well; and there are still further items of expenditure. However, I do not believe that the church can require that its members strictly donate ten percent of their income for any purpose. That would be legalistic and it would fail to take into account the transition from the Old Testament to the New Testament dispensation.

Tithing never happens in the New Testament. Paul writes at length to the Corinthians on the issue of giving money and he puts considerable pressure on them in 2 Corinthians 8–9, but he does not mention an obligation to tithe. This silence is eloquent. Again, Paul writes a thank-you letter to the Philippians in which he discusses their support of him at the end (4:10–19), but they clearly have not given him tithes.

So how does the church receive its income? If at all possible, everyone – that is, all members – are expected to contribute. Some believers are so rich that they can easily donate 20% or even more of their income for 'the work of the Lord'; certain people should even be ashamed if they do not give (much) more than 10%. But it is the role of the Holy Spirit to convince them that they should do so. The Spirit may well use a solid sermon or Bible study, but in my view the church cannot impose anything as mandatory. For people on an average income, whatever that may be, giving away some ten percent of it seems to me a good rule of thumb. But this is a guideline, not a divine commandment. For people at the lower end of the income scale, ten percent is normally too much. Hopefully such people can also contribute something, varying from a token amount to a few percent of their income, but probably not ten percent. Jesus praises a poor woman who gave her last two coins to the temple (Luke 21:1–4), but someone who has so little might well give less. In any case, the words of Paul apply to all of us:

> Remember this: whoever sows sparingly will also reap sparingly; and whoever sows generously will also reap generously. Each of you should give what you have decided in your heart to give, not reluctantly or under compulsion, for God loves a cheerful giver. (2 Corinthians 9:6–7)

Priesthood

In the Old Testament God appointed priests to mediate between him and the people of Israel (Exodus 28:1; 29:1; Leviticus 8). The priests largely worked in the tabernacle and later in the temple, the places where God was present. Other nations also had priests, who had similar roles. The New Testament tells about the priests and their leaders when it comes to the Jewish people, but not in connection with the church of Jesus. Jesus called twelve persons to be his disciples, who became the twelve apostles. In turn they later appointed elders and deacons, but never priests (e.g. Acts 14:23; 15:6; 20:17). Likewise, the different lists of spiritual gifts (Romans 12:1–8; 1 Corinthians 12:8–10, 28–30; Ephesians 4:11) include gifts of leadership, but priests are emphatically not mentioned. On the contrary, Peter writes to the believers that they are *all* priests (1 Peter 2:9); later in the same letter it is evident that there are leaders in the local churches (1 Peter 5:1–4), but once again the word priests is notable for its absence. We conclude that the church of Christ has no priesthood.

It is therefore a mystery to me how so many churches, such as the Roman Catholics, all Orthodox churches, and the Anglican Church, can still have priests. This is a clear case of maintaining an Old Testament institution, which according to the New Testament should no longer exist. As believers we all receive the Holy Spirit. In worship and prayer we all have free access to God through Jesus Christ. Under the new covenant there is no need for a human mediator such as a priest anymore.

Islam and the Old Testament

Islam is a religion that has borrowed much from the Christian faith and from the Bible. This is possible because it began with Muhammad who lived centuries after Jesus (c. CE 570–632), when the Bible was in wide circulation. At the same time, we must say that he and his people understood very little of the Bible. I shall confine myself here to the Old Testament:

1. In order to be saved a Muslim is expected to do good works. At first sight that idea seems to come from the Old Testament, for many Christians also think that in Old Testament times God expected the people to perform good works. Yet it is a misunderstanding. Abraham was accepted by God on account of his faith, not because of his works (Genesis 15:6; Romans 4). And God accepts Israel as his people and liberates them from Egypt, *before* he gives them the rules and precepts that belong to life as his children. That is the order of things in Exodus and not the other way around; it is also the gist of Deuteronomy 5–9. Consequently, the Old Testament teaches that faith, redemption, and salvation precede the issuing and

keeping of regulations, which serve to help people live a life of gratitude. This means that good works play no role anywhere in the Bible in earning God's approval.

2. Islam holds on to the belief in one god and therefore it denies the divinity of Jesus Christ. Again, this *seems* to be a form of faithfulness to the Old Testament, but it shows that Muhammad did not understand that Christians believe in one God who reveals himself in three persons. If all is well, no Christian believes in three gods. Jesus is not a second God, but he is one with the Father (John 10:30). This conviction is clearly implied in the book of Revelation. In Revelation 11:15 John speaks about God and the Messiah, and then continues in the singular: 'He will reign for ever and ever.' That is a clear expression of the unity of Father and Son. And in Revelation 22:1–3 God and the Lamb (= Jesus) are sitting on the same throne. It does not go against the confession of God's unity to believe that the Father, the Son, and the Holy Spirit are God. It is also not contrary to the Old Testament, because it teaches us that God is one, but it does not rule out the possibility that he is a more 'complicated' being. (See my comments on Genesis 1:26 in chapter 3.)

3. Islam recognises many prophets from the Old Testament, such as Abraham, Moses, and Jeremiah, yet denies that any prophet of God ever suffered whilst carrying out his ministry. Muslims allege that God always protects his servants so that they are always successful. Therefore, according to Islam, it is impossible that Jesus, who is regarded as one of the prophets, suffered any harm while on earth.

For us as Christians, this is a strange premise, because the Bible is not a simple success story. Yet for this reason Muslims deny that Jesus died on the cross, and consequently they also deny the resurrection and the reconciliation with God. And as for the Old Testament, this means that – according to Islam – prophets like Jeremiah and Hosea cannot have suffered, which is clearly in contrast to what we read, for example, in Jeremiah 37–38 and Hosea 1. The ministry of many prophets, like that of Jesus, was inextricably bound up with suffering.[23]

Diets

Over the years, all kinds of diets come in and out of fashion; many that were famous in my lifetime are now long forgotten; dieting gurus come and go. Without wanting to offend anyone, I think especially female readers will remember some diets in which they themselves may or may not have participated.

I discuss this issue here because some of these diets are allegedly based on the Bible, and then always – as far as I know – on the Old Testament. In the eyes of certain believing people this sometimes gives them a kind of divine authority. I myself know the names of the Genesis

---

[23] More on Islam in the following books: Colin Chapman, *Cross and Crescent,* rev. edn. (Nottingham: IVP, 2007); Bill A. Musk, *Kissing Cousins? Christians and Muslims Face to Face* (Oxford: Monarch, 2005); James R. White, *What Every Christian Needs to Know About the Qur'an* (Grand Rapids: Bethany House, 2013).

diet and the Daniel fast.[24] Go on the internet for the latest!

To my mind this is an inappropriate and unhealthy use of the Old Testament. Of course the Bible contains principles for our lives. Occasionally it also gives details of what people were eating in a given time period. But nowhere do we find a general rule in which certain foods are promoted or rejected. The closest we come to such a thing are the dietary laws in Leviticus 11 and Deuteronomy 14, but the church has always known that these laws do not apply to New Testament believers. In terms of the groups of texts in the Introduction of this book, the dietary laws decidedly come in group 4, the rules which are no longer literally applicable after the coming of Christ.[25]

Modern claims that we can derive any health advice or diet from the Bible are surely only made in a selective, random manner. The fact that a certain biblical character was or was not eating a particular food item is merely historical information for us; no sound dietary advice can be derived from it.

---

[24] See e.g. https://en.wikipedia.org/wiki/Bible_Diet [accessed 26 November 2016].

[25] On the dietary laws in Leviticus and Deuteronomy, see Hetty Lalleman, *Celebrating the Law?*, 62-76.

New Truths

I end this chapter with a much more general point. The Christian church does not believe that anyone in our time, however inspired or learned they might be, can suddenly discover something important in the Bible which no one else had ever seen before. We can surely *re*discover things which had been forgotten, such as happened, for example, with the Reformation in the sixteenth century and at the beginning of the Pentecostal movement early in the twentieth century, but we are not to expect that entirely new truths will yet be discovered. All that God wanted to reveal to us is already known and has been amply scrutinised in the course of the history of the church. The finding of entirely new 'truths' is a sure characteristic of false teachers, heretics, and cults. It also ties in with the individualism of our time and the populist suspicion against establishments which allegedly withhold information. We would do well to heed the advice of John, and have no desire to add anything to the Gospel that we have received:

> Anyone who does not stay with the teaching of Christ, but goes beyond it, does not have God. Whoever does stay with the teaching has both the Father and the Son. So then, if some come to you who do not bring this teaching, do not welcome them in your homes; do not even say, 'Peace be with you.'. (2 John 9–11, GNT)

You might wish to respond to the above by saying that it is the Holy Spirit who reveals new things to us and that we should not obstruct the work of the Spirit. My answer would be that we receive the Spirit so that he can refer us to Jesus and glorify him (John 16:13–15). The Spirit leads us personally and he can give us guidance for our own lives, showing us God's intentions for us, but such revelations are always personal and they do not have universal value.

Chapter 11: The Prosperity Gospel

'If you believe, you can rich and prosperous.' 'God does not want his children to be sick. You should just pray, and he will give you health.' These are some of the ideas we hear from preachers and adherents of the prosperity gospel.[26] You see them on alternative television channels and you hear them at conferences. But their teaching is not true!

What is The 'Prosperity Gospel'?

People who proclaim or believe the prosperity gospel think that every Christian has a God-given right to wealth and health. They say that Christians who are not healthy and wealthy have only themselves to blame. According to this 'gospel', the keys to health and prosperity are faith and obedience; so whoever lack anything has little faith, or is disobedient, or both.

In this 'gospel', the requirement of faith says that you should already begin to live as if you were rich and healthy before this is actually the case. Buy attractive, expensive clothes, and stop going to doctors or hospitals, because that behaviour would be an expression of disbelief. Driving a small or second hand car is also an expression of lack of faith, so the thing to do is buying a big, expensive car.

---

[26] More on this subject in Roger Olson, *Counterfeit Christianity* (Nashville: Abingdon Press, 2015).

A person's obedience, according to the preachers of prosperity, can be seen in their adherence to the 'principle of sowing'. This principle says that believers must sow their possessions, which means give them away, in order to receive more in return. In practice, this means that one should give a lot of money to 'the work of the Lord' in order to become rich in return. The 'seed' is handed over to the pastor or the church leadership. Church members give tithes or even more of their income on the promise that there will guaranteed be rich fruit, even hundredfold (derived from Mark 4:8; 10:29–30). Some people also call this 'the law of compensation'.

In practice it happens rarely, if ever, that someone sows in this way and recoups even what they have given, let alone that they receive it back manifold. Yet the faithful who dare to ask questions of their leader are told that this lack of success is the result of their own errors: their faith is too weak or there is an unconfessed sin in their life. 'Go and sow much more, and then the promised results will follow.' Such answers can throw people into an abyss of deep poverty and distress.

Social disruption, crises of faith, and the abandonment of church allegiance are some of the consequences of the prosperity gospel. Pastors, preachers, and 'prophets' are living in luxury and sometimes even own private aircraft, while most church members just get poorer.

Unlike what you might think, the prosperity gospel did not originate in a poor part of the world but in the United States. It has now spread globally, including to countries like South Korea. Over time, some people give all they have to the church or to the minister; many incur debt in order to be able to give, of course without ever receiving back a hundredfold. Conversely, such churches do not care for the poor and needy because that would be a form of unbelief. The poor are, after all, the people with weak faith!

The New Testament

The preachers of the gospel of prosperity appeal to texts from both parts of the Bible. From the New Testament, they use especially Mark 10:28–30:

> Peter said to [Jesus], 'We have left everything to follow you!' 'I tell you the truth,' Jesus replied, 'no-one who has left home brothers or sisters or mother or father or children or fields for me and the gospel will fail to receive a hundred times as much in this present age (homes, brothers, sisters, mothers, children and fields – and with them persecutions) and in the age to come, eternal life.'

Here Jesus promises his followers compensation for all that they left behind when they decided to follow him. (Peter still possessed a home and a boat – see Mark 1:29 and Luke 5:3 – but he now shared these things with Jesus and the other followers.) The question is how literally we have to take Jesus's words. Being given a hundred mothers or sisters is probably too much of a good thing! We conclude that Jesus meant in general terms that Peter and the others would not be worse off as a result of their decision to follow him. Jesus's followers will be each other's relatives in the community that he is founding. In the church we have hundreds of brothers and sisters. However, in these very verses Jesus also speaks about dangers and persecution, as he had previously done in Mark 8:34–38! Discipleship is clearly a *mixed blessing*, not a guarantee of an easy life. The preachers of the prosperity gospel conveniently ignore these things.

Another variant of the prosperity gospel assumes that because of the finished work of Jesus, all of God's blessings are already available to us. While the New Testament clearly says that the perfect state will only come at the second coming of Christ, prosperity preachers believe that all of us can already be rich, healthy, and prosperous. They suggest that all consequences of sin are already cancelled out this side of eternity, arguing as if Paul did not write clearly that perfection has not yet come (Romans 8) and that the cross of Christ puts our human ambitions to shame (1 Corinthians 1–2).

Elsewhere in the New Testament, we also find the realisation that our lives here on earth, especially as believers, can be difficult, and that many things will only get better on the new earth, 'the home of righteousness' (2 Peter 3:13). Jesus blesses the poor (Luke 6:20–23) but warns the rich (Luke 6:24–26). He also tells his followers that he himself does not even have a place to stay, let alone great wealth (Matthew 8:18–22), which undoubtedly means that his followers are to expect a similar fate.

The apostle Paul prays for healing but he does not receive it, and he learns to accept the situation as it is (2 Corinthians 12:5–10). And it was Paul who wrote about

> people of corrupt mind, who have been robbed of the truth and who think that godliness is a means to financial gain. ... Those who want to get rich fall into temptation and a trap and into many foolish and harmful desires that plunge people into ruin and destruction. For the love of money is a root of all kinds of evil. Some people, eager for money, have wandered from the faith and pierced themselves with many griefs. (From 1 Timothy 6:5–10)

In short, from the New Testament you can derive no prosperity gospel.

The Old Testament

I discuss the prosperity gospel here because it is also partly based on the Old Testament. It seems indeed as if in the Old Testament the promises of God's blessings are more focused on this earth than in the New Testament. To the extent that this is correct, we must conclude that the Old Testament has been overtaken by the New Testament and that we cannot go back to the previous dispensation. With reference to the Introduction, the Old Testament texts about prosperity belong to those texts that are no longer in force unchanged. In the Hebrew Bible the blessing of God was in particular expected here on Earth, during the life before death, probably because there was no clear expectation of life after death. But careful reading makes clear that even in Israel prosperity was not automatic; it was not something one could claim in faith. Here is some evidence for this thesis:

1. Prosperity preachers appeal to God's word to Adam in Genesis 1:28, 'be fruitful and increase in number', and explain this as a promise of material prosperity, which it is not. Also do not forget that the breaking in of sin (Genesis 3–4) has driven the history of humanity off course, so that not everything which would have been possible in creation is realised.

2. Many followers of the prosperity gospel are obsessed with Abraham. Now here is a rich man! God made a covenant with him and promised prosperity to him and his descendants (for example in Genesis 17:1–8), but of course not that only: Abraham is blessed in order to be a blessing for all peoples. God does not grant him the right to claim anything his heart desires. God retains his freedom and is not subordinate to human desires. Abraham and the other patriarchs were rich, but this is not a major theme in the stories about them and the Bible never makes their wealth an example for us, as it does with their faith!

We Christians are children of Abraham and as such we are heirs to God's promises, but in the spiritual sense; the blessings that flow from this covenant relationship must be understood spiritually: we receive peace with God, our friend, and we are commanded to be a blessing for the world. In Galatians 3:14 Paul says that all people can share in the blessings of Abraham. When he unpacks this promise, it turns out not to be about wealth, but about receiving the Holy Spirit!

3. In Deuteronomy 7:12–16 God promises the people Israel prosperity:

> If you pay attention to these laws and are careful to follow them, then the LORD your God will keep his covenant of love with you, as he swore to your ancestors. He will love you and bless you and increase your numbers. He will bless the fruit of your womb, the crops of your land – your corn, new wine and olive oil – the calves of your herds and the lambs of your flocks in the land that he swore to your ancestors to give you. You will be blessed more than any other people; none of your men or women will be childless, nor any of your livestock without young. The LORD will keep you free from every disease. He will not inflict on you the horrible diseases you knew in Egypt, but he will inflict them on all who hate you.

But this is not the prosperity which is claimed by a strong faith; it is God's response to the *obedience* of the people to the regulations he has given them. And whereas this promise was valid for Israel, it is not automatically valid for us. It tells us that prosperity is not an end in itself – in fact, not an end at all – but the result of living in the covenant relationship with God. The intention of Deuteronomy is similar to the words of Jesus:

> Seek first the Kingdom of God and his righteousness, then you will get other things as well (Matthew 6:33).

4. Some stories in the Old Testament are about concrete material blessings, like the story of the widow in Zarephath in 1 Kings 17:8–16. She first had to use her last remaining meal and oil to feed the prophet Elijah, before she was allowed to provide for herself. Yet this story, and others like it, is certainly not an example for all of us to follow. God's prophet performed a unique miracle which was not repeated in following generations.

5. However, there are a lot of promises of prosperity in the Old Testament, such as Psalm 25:13 (NRSV): 'They will abide in prosperity, and their children shall possess the land.' But the preachers of this 'gospel' conveniently forget that the next verse says: 'The friendship of the LORD is for those who fear him, and he makes his covenant known to them.' The words 'the fear of the LORD' signify respect and awe for him, not 'being afraid of him'. It is an expression for the right relationship between the believer and the God of Israel. For prosperity preachers belief in God is, above all, a business contract, not a warm, personal relationship. That cannot be correct.

6. Another Bible text that is used to propagate the prosperity Gospel is Malachi 3:10:

> 'Test me in this,' says the LORD Almighty, 'and see if I will not throw open the floodgates of heaven and pour out so much blessing that there will not be room enough to store it.'

This verse is completely taken out of context, however, because it is not a general promise of prosperity. It is about a specific situation of conflict between God and the people of Israel: the leaders of the people are sinning against God and he shows them the road to return to him. (On tithing see the previous chapter.)

7. Psalms 49 and 73 make clear that faith and prosperity do not always go together, even though it may seem so. Initially the poet of Psalm 73 marvels at the prosperity of certain people, but then he sees that their end is quite bad (73:16–20, cf. 49:12–14). These are not cases of automatic prosperity, in the same way that the bad outcome does not follow automatically. Both psalms merely show us that life is not logical or predictable, let alone that we could get a grip on it.

8. Wealth and prosperity are not always positively valued, as we see for example in Psalm 37:16; 52:6–7, Proverbs 8:10–11; 11:4, 7, 28; 28:20, and Ecclesiastes 5:9–13. Several prophets, especially Amos, criticise the wealthy in the land of Israel because their wealth is ill-gotten and because they do not care for the poor.

9. Deuteronomy 15 is typical of the variety in what the Old Testament says; this chapter contains three statements that seem to contradict each other and that keep each other in balance:

> There will, however, be no one in need among you (verse 4 NRSV)
>
> If there is among you anyone in need (verse 7)

> Since there will never cease to be some in need on the earth (verse 11)

The Old Testament asks that believers be zealous and use the opportunities they are given, to give a good testimony to the world around them. Concern for the poor, the orphan, and the widow is a natural part of this. We saw in chapter 4 above that God is on their side.

10. Ecclesiastes pours a bucket of cold water over anyone's ambitions to become wealthy by pointing out that this, too, is meaningless (5:8–20). Here is part of it in the words of The Message:

> The one who loves money is never satisfied with money, nor the one who loves wealth with big profits. More smoke. The more loot you get, the more looters show up. And what fun is that – to be robbed in broad daylight? Hard and honest work earns a good night's sleep, whether supper is beans or steak. But a rich man's belly gives him insomnia. Here's a piece of bad luck I've seen happen: A man hoards far more wealth than is good for him and then loses it all in a bad business deal. He fathered a child but hasn't a cent left to give him. He arrived naked from the womb of his mother; he'll leave in the same condition – with nothing. This is bad luck, for sure – naked he came, naked he went. So what was the point of working for a salary of smoke? All for a miserable life spent in the dark?

To sum up: the Old Testament expects that God will bless the faithful, but it also knows that this is not always happening in material terms. In this respect it is in line with the New Testament, in which Jesus commands his followers to trust God to supply his children's material needs (for example Matthew 6:25–34), but not in a way which implies wealth or rewards greed (Matthew 6:19–21, 24).

Principles

We have seen that the prosperity gospel goes against both the New Testament and the Old Testament. What is wrong with this doctrine theologically? Its fundamental flaw is that it makes our relationship with God a matter in which we humans take centre stage, at the expense of God and his honour. Although God promises his children his forgiveness through Jesus Christ and his presence by the Holy Spirit, he gives no guarantees for wealth and health. We may respectfully ask for health and for our daily bread, but we cannot claim any of these things.

In the prosperity gospel, on the other hand, prayer, faith, and the giving of tithes (or more) are construed as things which work automatically. Like a coffee machine which gives you coffee if you throw in the right coins, so God is supposed to bless you with money and good health if you comply with a few rules. This thinking is in line with the culture of our time, but entirely at odds with what the Bible tells us about God. Our God is not an impersonal organisation that owes you certain things.

In the prosperity gospel the church has become a kind of company that exists to deliver certain services and goods on demand. Such worldliness runs counter to the values of the kingdom of God.

It is worth noting that almost always when the Bible promises prosperity, this is a promise for the people of God, the church as a whole. Whereas the prosperity gospel is a form of thinly-veiled selfishness, the Bible never puts people against each other. The Torah rather contains numerous rules for the distribution and redistribution of property, such as the Sabbath year and the Jubilee (Leviticus 25, see also chapter 4).

Chapter 12: Jewish Festivals

For a generation or so now, certain Christians have been in the habit of celebrating Jewish festivals. Usually, they do so in the absence of Jews, unless they travel to Israel for the occasion. Among the Old Testament festivals which are celebrated by Christians in this way are the Passover meal and the Feast of Tabernacles (*Sukkot*), but not – as far as I know – the Day of Atonement, Purim, or Hanukkah, the Feast of the Dedication of the temple. So far, the practice is less well known in England than in the USA and in continental Europe. I will expound why I am not a great advocate of this practice.

Arguments in Favour

Various reasons are given why Christians are allowed or even obliged to celebrate Jewish festivals. One of these is that it is good to go back to our Jewish roots – which is definitely a sympathetic argument. In this book I am in fact doing something similar. The Jewish roots of our faith are, of course, primarily in the Hebrew Bible, and we cannot read enough in this book.

For others, celebrating Jewish festivals is a sign of solidarity with 'our Jewish brothers and sisters'. This too is in itself a good intention and I would like to see Christians in general showing more solidarity with Jews.

However, I want to question the celebration of Jewish festivals by followers of Jesus, especially when this is merely yet another 'experience', in addition to the many other festivals and praise services which we already attend and which mainly serve to make us feel good.

Jewish Feelings

My first argument is that most Jews are not at all happy with the fact that Christians are 'hugging' them in this way. They have not asked for these expressions of friendship and various rabbis do not hide their unhappiness with this practice. These rabbis are all too well aware of the differences which exist between Jews and Christians, in addition to the many similarities. They may feel threatened by a form of solidarity for which they have not asked.

Jews do sometimes demonstrate to outsiders what is involved in a Passover celebration, but this happens for people who express an interest in Judaism as such, not for Christians whose motives they regard as impure. Religious Jews find it extra painful when Christians celebrate a Jewish festival and then add a Christian element at the end. It feels as if in this way the Jewish festival is given a Christian makeover. This Jewish objection is understandable: imagine if Muslims adopted a Christian festival and at the end also read some passages from the Koran...

Jesus Did It

A common argument to celebrate Jewish festivals is that these are the feasts in which Jesus took part. As his followers, we therefore have to do the same.

It is indeed true that Jesus celebrated an earlier version of these festivals, but are we therefore supposed to follow him in this respect? I do not believe so. Jesus of Nazareth lived as a faithful, law-abiding Jew in the land of Israel. He visited the synagogue, paid the temple tax (Matthew 17:24–27) and kept the dietary laws. As a child he was circumcised at the request of his parents (Luke 2:21) and a sacrifice was made for him (Luke 2:22–24, 39). We live in a different dispensation and we are not expected to live as Jews. Our imitation of the Lord must be spiritual. That is exactly what Paul points out in his letter to the Galatians: believers from the Gentiles do not need to become Jews in any way.

Besides, the form of the Jewish festivals – in particular the Passover meal – has gradually changed in the course of the centuries; how Jesus celebrated this meal is not fully known, but it was most likely different from what Jews usually do nowadays.

Fulfilled

Another argument for why Christians should celebrate Jewish festivals is that these feasts are prescribed in the Old Testament. This argument is erroneous and I as I have pointed out in the Introduction, not everything that we find in the Old Testament is still normative for us as Christians. In my view, the festivals, as ordained by God in Exodus to Deuteronomy, belong to the group of precepts which no longer apply in the same way to us as Christians. They were good and necessary for the Jewish people up to the time of John the Baptist and Jesus, but according to the New Testament their meaning must necessarily change due to the coming of Jesus.

This point is best understood by reading John's Gospel chapters 5–10 in their entirety. The evangelist here systematically shows how Jesus attends all kinds of Jewish festivals in Jerusalem and how he always points to himself as the fulfilment of the meaning of those events. For his audience at that time, and also for his hearers today, he wants to be the living bread, the living water, the light of the world, the door of the sheep, and the good shepherd. Seen in the light of the finished work of Christ, the Old Testament festivals were no more than a foreshadowing (type) of him and his work. After the death and resurrection of the Messiah it is definitely impossible for a Christian to celebrate those festivals from the Old Testament which represent the work of reconciliation, such as the Passover and the Day of Atonement. The Feast of Weeks has got its fulfilment in the outpouring of the Holy Spirit during the annual celebration of this festival fifty days after the resurrection of the Lord Jesus. (You see that my arguments are similar to the ones used with regards to the temple and priests in chapter 10.)

Feast of Tabernacles

But how about the Feast of Tabernacles? Is that also fulfilled? This feast was on the one hand a harvest festival, at which God was given thanks for the past harvest and during which the people also prayed for rain for the next season of planting and harvesting. In New Testament times, the last day of the feast saw a procession to the pool of Siloam in Jerusalem to fetch water, which was brought to the temple with much rejoicing. The high priest then poured the water symbolically over the altar. John 7 tells how Jesus attends this festival and makes the stunning claim that he is God's final and deepest revelation (John 7:28–31). John adds that on the last day of the Festival Jesus again drew all attention to himself:

> On the last and greatest day of the festival, Jesus stood and said in a loud voice, 'Let anyone who is thirsty come to me and drink. Whoever believes in me, as Scripture has said, rivers of living water will flow from within them.' By this he meant the Spirit, whom those who believed in him were later to receive. Up to that time the Spirit had not been given, since Jesus had not yet been glorified. (John 7:37–39)

These words led to a sharp division among the Jews (John 7:40–53). For us as Christians it is clear that the coming of the Holy Spirit fulfils the Feast of Tabernacles in this regard.

On the other hand, the Feast of Tabernacles was a week of remembrance of the exodus from Egypt and of the period the people of Israel had spent in the desert (see Leviticus 23:33–43). For Jews their booth symbolised God's faithful protection and guidance. For us as Christians, this aspect of the feast is less relevant because we have neither been in slavery in Egypt nor travelled through the desert. Once we begin to spiritualise these things to involve ourselves in the history of the people of God, we cannot ignore the fact that our salvation was completed through Jesus – which we celebrate on Good Friday and at Easter.

Not Jewish

This rejection of the celebration of Jewish festivals does not mean that I find knowledge of Judaism irrelevant; but you do not need to get closely involved in order to get to know something. I would by no means deny or ignore the Jewish roots of our faith, as the present book has hopefully made clear! But in my view both the new covenant that Jesus brought, and the fact that the temple in Jerusalem no longer exists, imply that we are not called to celebrate Jewish festivals. These events found their fulfilment in the coming of the Messiah and of the Holy Spirit. Nobody requires that we become half Jewish; neither our Jewish friends and neighbours, nor our Saviour. We can express our solidarity with Jews in other ways than by celebrating their festivals, for example by clearly speaking out against modern anti-Semitism.

Jewish Christians

One final remark, about Jewish Christians, also called Messianic Jews.[27] These brothers and sisters of ours live – as it were – in two worlds: they profess Jesus as their Messiah, their Saviour, and their Lord, but in many ways they live like the other Jews, adhering to many of the Old Testament rules. They thus celebrate the Sabbath and

---

[27] For more see Evert van de Poll, *Messianic Jews and their Holiday Practice: History, Analysis and Gentile Christian Interest* (Frankfurt am Main: Peter Lang, 2015).

most Old Testament festivals. (They are divided about which ones should be celebrated.)

It would be correct to celebrate with these sisters and brothers as and when the opportunity would present itself. In this way we would be like a Jew with the Jews (1 Corinthians 9:20). But most of us do not know any Jewish Christians, and this chapter was directed at the majority.

In Conclusion

Here ends our trek through the Old Testament. I am grateful for the inspiration which I received from the Professors Miskotte and Van Ruler to look at the Old Testament from the perspective of its continued relevance for our lives as followers of Jesus Christ. I sincerely hope that by means of this book you too have got more of an eye for the permanent value of the Hebrew Bible, and that you can now make better use its enduring treasure.

Let us finally silence old Marcion by giving the Old Testament, including those portions not repeated in the New Testament, its legitimate position in our life of faith, in our churches, and in society.

Bibliography

Bauckham, Richard, *Living with Other Creatures* (Milton Keynes: Paternoster, 2012)

Brueggemann, Walter, *Theology of the Old Testament* (Minneapolis: Fortress Press, 1997)

Carr, G. Lloyd, *The Song of Solomon* (Tyndale Old Testament Commentary; Leicester: IVP, 1984)

Douma, Jochem, *Job. Psalmen* (Gaan in het spoor van het Oude Testament; Kampen: Kok, 2005)

Lalleman, Hetty (ed.), *Ongemakkelijke teksten van het Oude Testament* (Amsterdam: Buijten en Schipperheijn, 2014)

Lalleman, Hetty, *Celebrating the Law? Rethinking Old Testament Ethics* (Carlisle: Paternoster, 2004, 2nd edn Milton Keynes: Authentic Media, 2016)

Lapide, Pinchas, *Mit einem Juden die Bibel lesen* (Stuttgart: Calwer Verlag, 1982)

Miskotte, Kornelis H., *Hoofdsom der historie* (Nijkerk: Callenbach, 1945)

Miskotte, Kornelis H., *When the Gods are Silent* [1956] (London: Collins, 1967)

Parry, Robin, *Lamentations* (The Two Horizons Old Testament Commentary; Grand Rapids & Cambridge: Eerdmans, 2010)

Provan, Iain, *Seriously Dangerous Religion: What the Old Testament Really Says and Why it Matters* (Waco: Baylor University Press, 2014)

Ruler, A. A. van, 'De waarde van het Oude Testament I' [1940] in *Verzameld werk* [Collected Works] 2 (Zoetermeer: Boekencentrum, 2008) 385-393.

Ruler, A. A. van, *Over de Psalmen* (2nd edn, Nijkerk: Callenbach, 1983)

Ruler, A. A. van, *Ik geloof* (Nijkerk: Callenbach, 1968)

Wright, Christopher J. H., *Old Testament Ethics for the People of God* (Leicester: IVP, 2004)

Questions for Group Meetings

Introduction

The first two paragraphs provide a brief overview of the whole Bible. Do you think this is reasonably complete or would you like to add anything?

Have you ever been in a discussion about the place of the Old Testament in the church? How did that go?

How have you handled the Old Testament until now? How much of Marcion is there in you? What feelings come up?

Discuss what it means that the Christian church has been grafted on the old olive tree, Israel.

Do people around you speak about 'the Hebrew Bible'? Would this parlance have disadvantages?

1. Creation

How can you tell that the first creation story extends to Genesis 2:4a?

Do you experience a sense of strangeness or alienation in this world? Has this chapter helped you to deal with it?

Does Psalm 139 make you feel happy? Why (not)?

What does it mean for you personally that you were created in God's image?

In which things around you, if any, do you see God? Which songs do you know about this?

How do you experience the creation? Is it a safe place?

What are the tasks of God's stewards?

'God is eternal, but his creation is not.' What does this phrase mean and what kind of feeling does it give you?

2. The Name and the Titles of God

Some people think of God as an old man with a beard. How do you see God?

Which name(s) or title(s) do you use to speak *about* God? And how do you address him? Has this chapter encouraged you to change anything or has it rather confirmed your practice?

Explain to someone else what the name 'The LORD' means.

Why is the form Jehovah wrong?

Is it possible that God would be jealous?

3. Sexuality

'The command to fill the earth has largely been fulfilled.' Would you agree?

If you have a partner, how do you help each other, if at all? If not, do you have any other help?

Whose helper are you?

How would you describe the biblical view of marriage? Can it be maintained in our time? Why (not)?

Talk about Song of Songs. What do you actually think about it?

Have you been affected by the idea that sexuality is bad? If so, how?

Would you be able to do something with the concept of the extended family?

4. Politics and the Stranger

Try to describe your view of human beings.

What are for you key concepts when it comes to good politics?

What does it mean that the Christian community does not belong to a particular country?

How can Deuteronomy 17:14–20 be applied in our situation?

What do you think prophecy is? Do you know any modern prophets?

Does your church act on behalf of people who need it? Who are they?

5. Scepticism and Doubt

Do you ever have doubts regarding your faith? How do you deal with that?

Explain what was the problem with Elijah. What helped him?

What are attractive and less attractive sides of Ecclesiastes? Do you agree with Miskotte and/or Lapide?

How do you as a Christian handle any feelings of disappointment?

6. Laments

Do you ever complain to God? If so, about what for example?

Is your own church open to your laments about God?

Would it be good to organise a meeting at which people can lament?

Read a psalm of lament (from Psalms 3–7 and 12–14) and talk about it.

Why was Jeremiah's position so difficult?

What do you think about the fact that God also utters laments?

7. Contradiction

Describe in your own words what Abraham does in Genesis 18.

What do you think of the reaction of the 'friends' of Job?

Why does God so often have unwilling servants, do you think?

Look closely at a few other texts in which Job blames God. What does he mean?

Has your view of God changed as a result of reading this chapter?

'The Bible is the authoritative word of God but not a grab bag.' What does this mean to you?

8. The Message of Esther

Why is the book of Esther in the Bible?

Which of the 'learning points' from Esther speaks to you most?

Has God ever guided you by means of 'accidental' events?

Do you ever pray for people in important positions in public life? Do it now.

9. The Jewish Canon

What impact – in general – has the order in which the books of the Bible are placed?

What is the core of the Old Testament for you?

Did this chapter give you a new view on the Pentateuch? And on the prophets?

Discuss what it says under the heading 'Perspective'.

10. Mixed Mistakes

Do you know any church leaders who adopt the status of a priest? How do you handle this?

Is the place where your local church meets a temple or not? What does this imply?

What is your view of tithing?

Explain that the Old Testament is not about good works.

Do you always do justice to the fact that there is only one God?

What does the Sunday mean for you and those around you?

How do you react when someone presents something completely new from the Bible or from a prophecy?

11. The Prosperity Gospel

Do you hear the prosperity gospel around you? What impact does it have on the lives of people who believe in it?

If you already knew the prosperity gospel: which arguments were used for it? And how do you evaluate them?

How is it possible that after Jesus the world is still not perfect? Are his promises unreliable?

Why do you love God? What happens if he does not give you what you asked for?

12. Jewish Festivals

Do you celebrate the feast of Tabernacles or do you know others who do this? Has your opinion changed after reading this chapter?

Do you feel any solidarity with Jews?

Read (part of) John 5–10 and discuss how Jesus fulfils the Scriptures.

Do you know Jewish Christians? What do you know of their habits? Could you get to know them better?

Suggested Further Reading

Goldingay, John, *Do We Need the New Testament? Letting the Old Testament Speak for Itself* (Downers Grove: Inter-Varsity Press, 2015)

Holladay, William L., *Long Ago God Spoke. How Christians may hear the Old Testament today* (Minneapolis: Fortress 1995)

Lalleman, Hetty, *Celebrating the Law? Rethinking Old Testament Ethics* (Carlisle: Paternoster, 2004; 2nd edn Milton Keynes: Authentic Media, 2016)

Motyer, J. Alec, *Roots: Let the Old Testament speak* (Fern, Ross-shire: Christian Focus, 2009)

Motyer, J. Alec, *A Christian's Pocket Guide to Loving the Old Testament* (Fern, Ross-shire: Christian Focus, 2015)

Provan, Iain, *Seriously Dangerous Religion: What the Old Testament Really Says and Why It Matters* (Waco: Baylor University Press, 2014)

Schlimm, Matthew R., *This Strange and Sacred Scripture: Wrestling with the Old Testament and Its Oddities* (Grand Rapids: Baker Academic, 2015)

Schreiner, Thomas R., *40 Questions about Christians and Biblical Law* (Grand Rapids: Kregel, 2010)

SPREAD SHEETS *and* BEDSHEETS

GRAFTON CARTER

ISBN: 9798311639477
Independently Published

DEDICATION

To my husband, thank you for loving me.

To my children, thank you for pushing me.

To my dogs, thank you for the cuddles.

CONTENTS

ACKNOWLEDGMENTS

I want to acknowledge the wonderful world of LGBTQ+ Romance writers everywhere. Thank you for your wonderful work to recognize and celebrate queer love, queer sex, and queer life. I am proud to be one of you.

"Without order nothing can exist-without chaos nothing can evolve.
Nowadays people know the price of everything and the value of nothing."
~ Oscar Wilde ~

1

JULES

Early spring in Havenwood was a sensory ambush. The breeze carried faint hints of lavender, cinnamon, and freshly baked bread, mingled with the earthy tang of newly turned soil from garden beds. The sunlight filtered through the budding trees, dappling the cobblestones in soft, golden light. It was the kind of idyllic, picturesque scene you'd expect from a small-town postcard, or the opening act of a Disney musical.

Mid-March in Havenwood brought a cautious but welcomed shift toward spring. The air was still crisp, with a faint chill that lingered from the cooler-than-normal winter, but the sun broke through more often, coaxing people outdoors. Street vendors were set up along the cobblestone paths, their tables ladened with baked goods, handcrafted jewelry, and early spring produce.

Locals strolled by in light jackets and scarves, clutching steaming cups of coffee or hot cider as they browsed the stalls. Children darted between tables, their laughter blended with the hum of conversation. The trees were just beginning to bud; tiny hints of green peeked out, while a soft breeze carried the scent of fresh bread and the earthy promise of the season ahead. It was not quite warm, but it was enough to make people linger, grateful for the sunshine and the hint of brighter days to come.

I adjusted the strap of my tote bag. A sunflower I couldn't resist buying from a vendor twirled idly in my hand, its bright yellow petals caught the sunlight as I walked. The Rivermere District hummed with

life, just as I remembered it, yet somehow more vibrant now, like the years away have sharpened my view of it.

Children darted between stalls, laughed as they chased shimmering bubbles that floated lazily on the breeze. Street musicians strummed a jaunty tune near the corner café, their melody woven seamlessly into the sounds of the market, vendors chatted, the occasional clink of a cash register, footsteps on stone. The whole scene was so storybook-perfect that I couldn't help but grin.

"This place is so... *Beauty and the Beast*," I muttered under my breath, spinning the sunflower. "Any second now, someone's going to burst into song."

I hummed a few bars of "*Bonjour*!" quietly, half-expecting the townsfolk to start harmonizing as they bustled about. It was ridiculous, but the thought made me laugh softly to myself. And maybe it's the absurdity of it all, but a part of me felt strangely like Belle, too, a queer protagonist returning home after years away, navigating the simultaneous familiarity and alienness of it all.

The Rivermere District felt unchanged in so many ways. Sweet Haven Bakery still smelled like cinnamon and sugar; its window filled with pastries that looked too perfect to eat. Bright Horizons Bookstore stood like a beacon on the corner, its teal-and-gold facade glowed in the morning light. The cobblestones beneath my feet were still slightly uneven, just enough to remind you to watch your step. And yet, I can't help but wonder if I've changed too much to belong here anymore.

I paused near a trio of musicians whose violinist caught my eye and winked as I passed. I winked back, letting the rhythm of their song tug at my feet for a moment before moving on. Everywhere I turned, Havenwood felt alive, impossibly bright, impossibly perfect, like a painting that might dissolve if I looked too closely. Nestled just a few towns away from its more famous twin sister, Asheville, NC, Havenwood hummed with its own quiet Appalachian charm, even if it's often overshadowed by the grandeur of Biltmore.

"Still as cute as I remembered," I said to myself, the sunflower spinning lazily between my fingers. "Good job, Havenwood. You're holding up."

As I wandered further, a mural on the side of the bookstore pulled me in. It's massive. It stretched across the entire wall in bold, sweeping strokes of color. A fantastical forest filled the scene, trees that morphed into dancers, rivers curled into laughing faces. Near the bottom, a burst of red and orange caught my eye. A fox, maybe? Or

flames? The longer I looked, the more details emerged, like the mural was alive, constantly shifting.

"Whoever painted this?" I said aloud, my voice filled with admiration. "Brilliant. The energy, the colors, the vibe! Havenwood's really stepping up its art game."

A chuckle interrupted my musings. I turned to see a honey vendor leaning on the counter of his stall, his apron streaked with golden smudges of beeswax. He looked like he belonged in a Norman Rockwell painting, weathered but warm, with eyes that seemed to know all the town's secrets.

"You sound like someone who knows a thing or two about art," he said, his smile easy and knowing.

I shrugged, walking over with the sunflower still twirling in my hand. "I dabble," I replied. "Just moved back to town. Figured I'd trade airport terminals and activist rallies for a little small-town charm."

"Well, welcome home," he said, picking up a jar of honey and setting it in front of me. "If you're looking for charm, you should check out The Green Bean Café. Best coffee and people-watching in town."

I picked up the jar, holding it to the light as if it might reveal some hidden truth. The honey inside glowed like liquid sunlight, warm and rich. "Local honey and good coffee? You're really trying to sell me on this place."

"Not selling, just stating facts," he said with a wink.

I laughed and handed him a few bills, slipping the jar into my tote bag. "Alright, you've convinced me. The Green Bean Café it is."

As I stepped back into the flow of the market, the sunflower bobbing with every step, I let my gaze wander across the Rivermere District. Everything here felt impossibly neat, like it had been arranged to make me nostalgic. The colors, the sounds, the scents, they swirled together in a way that felt magical, but also a little overwhelming.

And yet, beneath all the perfection, there was a quiet hum of something real. Something honest. Maybe it's in the way the kids laughed as they stumbled over uneven cobblestones, or the way the musicians' notes sometimes faltered before coming together again. It reminded me that perfection wasn't the point, it was the life, the messiness, the way the story kept unfolding.

I inhaled deeply, the scent of lavender and cinnamon filling my lungs, and for the first time in years, I felt like I might be able to belong. Havenwood wasn't just holding up, it was thriving. And if this place can thrive, maybe I can, too.

Spring afternoons in Havenwood had a way of slowing time, and as I stepped into The Green Bean Café, it felt like the rest of the world melted away. The door's bell jingled overhead, its cheerful chime as much a greeting as the hum of voices and the hiss of a milk steamer behind the counter. The café smelled like heaven, freshly brewed coffee, buttery pastries, and something floral I couldn't quite place. Lavender, maybe? It was cozy and chaotic all at once, a perfect reflection of the Rivermere District.

The place felt alive. Every table and chair were mismatched, like someone raided a dozen garage sales and brought back the most eccentric pieces they could find. There was a round table with peeling yellow paint in one corner, surrounded by metal chairs, while a plush armchair with faded floral upholstery claimed the coziest spot by the window. A cluster of dangling light bulbs cast a warm glow over the room, and the walls were an explosion of personality. Local art, bold abstracts, delicate watercolors, black-and-white photos of Havenwood, covered nearly every inch, giving the space a patchwork charm that felt both curated and entirely accidental.

Behind the counter stood Morgan, the barista, with a bright yellow bandana tied loosely around their curls and a black apron that looked like it had been through a hundred busy mornings. Their name tag, written in colorful sharpie, read Morgan (they/them), and their easy smile was instantly disarming.

"You've got that 'new to town' look," they said, leaning on the counter as I approach.

I laughed, dropping my tote bag at my feet. "Technically, I'm an old-timer making a comeback. Born and raised here, left to explore the world, find myself, yadda yadda, insert cliché here. Now I'm back, and I need coffee to make sense of it all. Suggestions?"

Morgan tilted their head toward the chalkboard menu hanging on the wall behind them. It was handwritten in looping, colorful chalk, complete with little doodles of coffee cups and croissants. "Lavender Honey Latte," they said confidently. "Smooth, creative, and just the right amount of kick. Kinda like you, I'm guessing."

I leaned forward, resting my elbows on the counter. "You get me. One Lavender Honey Latte, please, and maybe a muffin. You know, for balance."

Morgan grinned, grabbing a mug. "Coming right up."

While they worked, I wandered toward a crowded bulletin board near the entrance, scanning the kaleidoscope of flyers and notes. There was a lost pet poster with a blurry photo of a cat named Tinkerbell, a

yoga class schedule with a hand-drawn lotus flower in the corner, and a flyer for a knitting circle promising "craft and community." But it was a bold orange flyer that caught my eye: Havenwood Playhouse presents *A Midsummer Night's Dream*! The text was surrounded by whimsical doodles of fairies, stars, and a crescent moon.

My fingers brushed the edge of the flyer as I pulled it closer for a better look. Beneath the title, there was a line that read: Seeking volunteers for all roles, onstage and off!

"Caught your eye?" Morgan's voice drew me back. I turned to see them setting a steaming mug and a muffin on the counter, their expression one of amused curiosity.

"Big time," I admitted, walking back with the flyer in hand. "Theatre's kinda my thing, well, one of my things. Directed a few shows, painted some sets, wrote a couple of weird plays no one understood. What's the vibe over there?"

Morgan leaned on the counter, chin resting on their hand. "They do great work. You'd fit right in. They're always looking for people to help out. Are you thinking about jumping in?"

I shrugged, though my grin gave me away. "I mean, I just got here, but why not? This town's not gonna know what hit it."

Morgan chuckled, sliding the mug toward me. "That's the spirit. Good luck shaking things up."

Later that afternoon, the Havenwood Playhouse stood before me like a relic of another time, charming in its modesty. Ivy crept up the brick exterior, curling around the windows and framing the small marquee that read: *COMING SOON: A MIDSUMMER NIGHT'S DREAM.* The lettering wasn't perfect, some letters leaned a little too far left or right, but that just added to the place's character.

I hesitated for a moment at the entrance, inhaling deeply. There was something sacred about places like this, small community theaters where art was made not for money or prestige but for love. I ran my fingers lightly over the worn brass handle before stepping inside. Immediately, the familiar scent of sawdust and fresh paint washed over me, wrapping me in a strange sense of nostalgia.

The theater's interior was small but brimming with potential, its worn wooden floors and patchwork curtains spoke to decades of passion and creativity. A small group of staff and actors milled about on the stage, their voices overlapped as they debated lighting cues and blocking. Ladders were propped against the walls, half-painted set pieces stood like unfinished thoughts, and scraps of fabric were scattered over the seats, organized chaos, the way all theaters seemed to live and breathe.

A rush of longing pressed against my ribs. It had been too long since I've felt this, the energy of a space mid-creation. My fingers itched to take hold of something, to sketch a set piece, tweak a monologue, adjust a light cue. To belong to it.

"Can I help you?"

The voice belonged to a man in a slightly rumpled cardigan that draped over his tall, lean frame. His dark curls were speckled with silver, and his round glasses sat slightly askew on his nose, giving him an air of effortless charm. His friendly smile immediately put me at ease.

"You look like someone with ideas," he added, his rich, warm voice carrying a hint of amusement as he approached with an outstretched hand. The faint scent of coffee lingered around him, and a clipboard tucked under his arm suggested he was already juggling a dozen tasks.

I laughed, shaking it. "Guilty. Jules Moreno. Just moved back to town, saw the flyer, and figured, 'Why not?' Theater's been my life for as long as I can remember. I'd love to help out, directing, painting, random creative chaos. You name it."

"Creative chaos, huh?" he said, his grin widening. "I'm Darnell, the manager here. And chaos is exactly what we need. Welcome to the team."

Before I knew it, I was swept into the energy of the Playhouse. Someone handed me a stack of costume sketches, and I pulled out my own sketchpad to throw out bolder, more daring ideas. Titania in shimmering silvers and greens, Oberon in moody indigo with sharp, modern accents. I pitched tweaks to Shakespeare's dialogue, modernizing it just enough to make the humor land harder and the drama cut deeper.

Darnell glanced over my shoulder at the sketches. "You've got an eye for this."

"I like to think so," I admitted, flipping the page to start another concept. "I used to direct back in Chicago. Community and semi-pro. Then life happened, and…" I trailed off, but Darnell didn't push. Instead, he nodded like he understood more than I was saying.

The team picked up on my energy, and soon, the room felt like it was crackling with possibility. Despite the playful chaos, I felt something settle deep inside me, a quiet determination, a need to prove to myself that my spark hasn't dimmed.

The hours flew by in a blur of ideas and laughter, the kind that left you breathless but buzzing with purpose. Sketches were passed around, notes scribbled, and bold suggestions tossed into the air like confetti. Every now and then, someone paused to question an idea, only for another to leap in with a way to make it work. It was messy, exhilarating, and exactly what I didn't realize I needed.

"You're good at this," one of the younger actors, a girl with cropped pink hair, told me as she sorted through fabric swatches. "You sure you're not already running this thing?"

I smirked. "Not quite. Just lending a hand."

By the time we called it a day, my fingers were smudged with pencil marks, my bag was bursting with papers and fabric swatches, and my heart felt… lighter. Fulfilled, even. It was not just the work, it was the people, the shared excitement, the spark of something new being created together.

Then, as we were packing up, the unexpected news landed like a thunderbolt: the director originally hired had quit on the spot after a heated disagreement with the board president.

Darnell sighed, rubbing his temples. "Well, that's a disaster."

"What happened?" I asked, my heart already hammering.

He exhaled sharply. "Creative differences, allegedly. But honestly? It's a miracle she lasted this long."

A silence fell over the group, uncertain and heavy. Then, Darnell turned to me, eyes thoughtful. "Jules… you ever thought about taking this on?"

My breath caught. "Wait, you mean…"

"Directing," he clarified. "You clearly know your stuff. And we need someone now."

I stared at him, at the expectant faces around me. This wasn't the plan. I was just easing back in, testing the waters. But then, wasn't that what I always did? Held back, hesitated?

The answer was already there, thrumming beneath my ribs. "Yes."

By the end of the day, the offer came: *Jules Moreno, the new director.*

And with that spark still glowing inside me, I stepped out into the evening, the world quieting as the sun began its descent. As I walked home through the Rivermere District, the sky was painted in streaks of

orange and pink, the warm light softened the edges of the ivy-covered cottages I pass.

Outside my small studio apartment, I paused, catching my reflection in the window. My grin faded into a softer, more thoughtful smile. This place wasn't much, but it was affordable and exactly what I needed to get back on my feet after moving back.

"Alright, Havenwood," I said, my voice barely audible above the evening breeze. "Let's make some magic."

For the first time in years, I felt like I just might.

2

ELLIOTT

The hum of fluorescent lights buzzed faintly in my ears as I stood at the front of my classroom. The rhythmic scratching of pencils filled the air, each sound deliberate and steady. This room was my sanctuary, a reflection of who I was, meticulous, intentional, and quietly welcoming. Maps of historical trade routes adorned one wall; their edges precisely pinned to avoid curling. On the opposite wall, portraits of underrepresented historical figures stood as silent sentinels: Audre Lorde's gaze brimming with resolve, Harvey Milk's infectious grin radiating optimism, and James Baldwin's penetrating eyes challenging anyone to dig deeper, think harder, and never settle.

At the center of it all was me, glasses perched on my nose, hands clasped loosely in front of me. The students leaned forward slightly in their chairs, a small but telling sign. They were listening.

"Now," I began, my voice calm but deliberate, "let's talk about Bayard Rustin." I turned to the whiteboard, where the words Intersectionality in the Civil Rights Movement stood in neat, precise handwriting. Below them, bullet points charted our discussion: Rustin's critical role in organizing the March on Washington, his lifelong advocacy for nonviolence, and the unique challenges he faced as an openly gay Black man in a time of widespread prejudice, even within his own movement.

"Most people know about the March on Washington," I said, letting my voice rise slightly, "but what they don't realize is that Rustin was the mastermind behind its logistics. He was openly gay at a time when that alone could make him a target, not just from outside forces, but within his own community."

The weight of those words hung in the air. I scanned the room, gauging the students' reactions. Amelia, always the first to dive in, shot her hand into the air. I nodded in her direction.

"Why didn't we learn about him before?" she asked, her voice tinged with frustration and wonder. "This is so important!"

A faint smile tugged at the corners of my mouth. "That's a good question," I replied, pausing to let the thought settle. "History isn't just about what happened, it's about who gets to tell the story. Too often, those in power decide which voices are heard and which are silenced. That's why it's our job to dig deeper, to make sure voices like Rustin's aren't forgotten."

The bell rang, jolting us from the moment. Backpacks zipped, chairs scraped, and the students began filing out. A few lingered, as they often did, eager to ask follow-up questions or share their thoughts. I answered each one carefully, appreciating their curiosity. For a brief moment, the room buzzed with energy, and I felt a flicker of satisfaction.

But when the last student left and the door clicked shut behind them, silence filled the space. I stood at the front of the room for a long moment, staring at the whiteboard. Slowly, methodically, I picked up the eraser and wiped away the lesson. The words disappeared, one by one, leaving behind a blank slate.

It was mid-March, that grueling stretch between winter break and spring break when both teachers and students felt like they were crawling toward the finish line. The days seemed longer, the energy in the classroom thinner, and even the most vibrant lessons struggled to cut through the collective drain. I felt it too, the heavy pull of exhaustion, the relentless countdown in the back of my mind to those few precious days off.

"Another day," I murmured to myself, my voice barely audible. The weight of the week pressed down on my shoulders, a familiar exhaustion that had become routine. I ran a hand through my hair, staring at the blank whiteboard like it might offer some profound insight, but all it reflected back was the same restless energy I couldn't shake.

Before I could fully retreat into my thoughts, the door creaked open again. I turned to see Sam Ortiz leaning against the doorframe, his trademark mischievous grin in place. Sam was a fellow teacher and one

of my closest friends, a rare bright spot in the sometimes-isolating world of high school education.

"Well, don't you look introspective," he teased, stepping into the room and plopping down into a student desk near the front. He stretched his legs out, tapping his fingers against the desk in an uneven rhythm. "What's up, Brooks? Deep in thought, or just zoning out?"

I chuckled, setting the eraser back on the tray. "A little of both. The existential crisis that comes with grading a hundred essays will do that to you."

Sam whistled. "Brutal. Any diamonds in the rough?"

I shrugged. "A couple. But mostly, it's just a lot of 'the symbolism of the green light in *The Great Gatsby* represents dreams' kind of analysis. It's like they all read the same SparkNotes summary."

Sam snorted. "Gotta love it. Maybe you should give them an assignment on something more exciting. *Die Hard*, perhaps? 'Analyze the use of holiday cheer as an ironic counterpoint to violence.'"

I laughed, shaking my head. "Yeah, somehow I don't think the department head would go for that."

Sam leaned back, crossing his arms. "Just thought I'd check in. See how you're holding up. Also, we're grabbing drinks this weekend, and you're coming. No excuses."

I smirked. "Oh, am I? Didn't realize my social calendar was already filled."

"Filled with what? More grading? Staring at your ceiling and contemplating your life choices?" Sam arched an eyebrow. "Come on, man. One night won't kill you."

I sighed, leaning against the desk. "You know, I could use a break."

Sam grinned triumphantly. "Now you're talking. I'll even let you pick the spot."

I pretended to consider. "Anywhere that won't involve you challenging strangers to dance-offs this time."

Sam gasped in mock offense. "I stand by that. I won."

"You absolutely did not."

He shrugged. "Debatable. Anyway, it's settled. You, me, drinks. I'll text you details."

I laughed, shaking my head. "Fine, I'll be there. Someone has to make sure you don't get us kicked out of wherever we go."

Sam grinned as he stood, pointing at me. "You're not just the voice of reason, my friend. You're the life of the party; you just don't know it yet."

As he left, the silence returned, but it felt a little lighter now. I glanced back at the blank whiteboard, then at the empty desk Sam had occupied, a faint smile tugging at my lips. Maybe this weekend will be a good break after all.

The sun dipped low over Havenwood as I pulled into the driveway of my small, single-story home on the edge of town. The clapboard siding gleamed faintly in the fading light, freshly washed just last weekend. Potted marigolds flanked the porch steps, their vibrant orange blooms standing like cheerful sentinels. Above, the branches of the old oak tree swayed gently in the evening breeze, its budding leaves hinting at the spring's promise of renewal.

I lingered for a moment, taking in the serenity of the street. The occasional bark of a dog or the distant hum of a car punctuated the stillness. This, at least, was familiar, predictable. After gathering my leather messenger bag and coat, I climbed the steps and unlocked the front door.

Inside, the house greeted me with its usual quiet. The faint scent of lavender lingered in the air from the candle I'd lit earlier that morning. Everything was as I'd left it, neat, orderly, intentional. I hung my coat on the hook near the door, placed my bag on the hall table, and bent to straighten a pair of shoes that had shifted slightly out of place.

In the living room, my gaze settled on the mantle, where a row of carefully arranged frames captured fragments of my life. Caleb's photo always stood out first, a candid shot of him grinning at the camera, his gap-toothed smile brimming with mischief and joy. The boy's energy had a way of filling every corner of the house when he was here, but in his absence, the quiet felt heavier. Beside his picture was a more formal photo of me and my ex-wife on our wedding day, our smiles cautious but kind, the weight of our shared history etched in the space between us. A black-and-white portrait of my late parents rounded out the collection, their faces serene and timeless. But it was always Caleb's photo that held my attention the longest, a vivid reminder of warmth and vitality in a house that often felt too still.

I sighed, running a hand through my hair, the weight of the day settling into my shoulders. The house was quiet, but not the comforting

kind of quiet, more like an emptiness that stretched through the rooms. I thought about calling Caleb, just to hear his voice, but I knew it was close to his bedtime. Instead, I stepped into the kitchen, the soft pad of my footsteps the only sound accompanying me.

In the kitchen, my windowsill herbs thrived in neat terra-cotta pots, basil, thyme, rosemary. I brushed my fingers over the basil's leaves, the sharp, clean fragrance grounding me in the moment. The act of tending to them was small, but it gave me something to focus on, something alive and growing in my space.

"You're growing well," I said to the plants, my tone soft and conversational. "Better than I expected this season."

Filling the kettle, I set it on the stove and waited for it to heat. The ritual of making tea had always been a small anchor for me, a way to transition from the structured demands of the day to the solitude of the evening. I leaned against the counter as I waited, letting my gaze wander to the small window above the sink. Outside, the night had fully taken hold, the sky a deep indigo with scattered stars beginning to emerge. A porch light flickered on across the street, momentarily illuminating the figure of my neighbor, Mrs. Tate, as she watered the row of daisies along her walkway. She did that every evening, rain or shine, a routine as steadfast as the ticking clock in my living room.

When the whistle sounded, I poured the water over loose leaves, steeping the tea just long enough to coax out its full flavor. Carrying the mug to the living room, I settled into my favorite armchair, the leather creaking softly beneath me. The warmth of the cup seeped into my hands, a welcome contrast to the coolness of the room. On the side table lay Queer History in America, its pages dog-eared from use. I flipped to a section on the Stonewall riots, underlining passages and jotting meticulous notes in a small leather-bound journal. But my focus wavered, my gaze drifting to Caleb's photo on the mantle, then to the garden outside.

I sighed, tapping my pen against the open journal. The words in the book blurred together as my mind drifted. I thought about the last time Caleb had been here, his laughter echoing through the house as he built a pillow fort in the living room. He had declared it his "castle" and insisted I be his loyal knight, wielding a foam sword with exaggerated bravado. That kind of joy was infectious, the kind that lingered long after he had gone.

The house felt different when he was here, alive, filled with a kind of lightness I hadn't realized I needed until it was gone. My ex-wife, Anna, and I had managed to navigate co-parenting amicably, but the

distance between my time with Caleb and the long stretches of solitude in this house still felt jarring. I reached for my phone before stopping myself. Another call might disrupt his bedtime routine, and I didn't want to intrude. Instead, I let out a slow breath and turned my attention back to the book in my lap, willing myself to focus.

I sighed, tapping my pen against the open journal. My mind kept drifting back to the library earlier this week. Havenwood Public Library had always been a refuge for me, a place where polished wood shelves and the comforting scent of aged books greeted me like an old friend. It was orderly, quiet, predictable, everything I needed it to be. But, as was often the case, Aggie had disrupted the stillness in her usual fashion.

"Elliott Brooks," she'd said, standing at my table with her hands firmly on her hips. Her tone was teasing, but there was warmth in it, the kind you only hear from someone who's known you for years. "Let me guess, another deep dive into queer history? You're single-handedly keeping our nonfiction section in business."

I hadn't looked up right away, choosing instead to underline a particularly striking passage. "I like to stay informed," I replied evenly, the response as measured as she'd likely expected.

Aggie had chuckled, pulling out the chair across from me and lowering herself into it. "You're too young to be spending every evening in a library," she quipped. "Ever thought about trying something a little more… social?"

I sighed, finally meeting her gaze. "Aggie, you know I'm not exactly a social butterfly."

Her grin widened, undeterred. "No," she admitted, leaning back in the chair. "But even caterpillars leave the cocoon eventually. There's more to life than books and basil, you know."

She'd left me with that parting shot, patting the table as she rose to walk away. I remember watching her go, the sound of her low heels fading against the polished floors, her words hanging in the still air.

Now, back at home, they lingered still. I closed the book on my lap, the weight of its cover pressing lightly against my thighs, and stared at it for a moment. Aggie had a point, though I wasn't ready to admit it, not even to myself. She always had a way of challenging me without being confrontational, just enough to unsettle the stillness I so carefully cultivated.

The ticking of the wall clock marked the time with precision, the rhythm both soothing and unnerving. Outside, the stars had begun to punctuate the indigo sky, their faint glow casting a soft light through the

windows. I set the book and journal aside and closed my eyes, exhaling deeply.

Somewhere in the back of my mind, Aggie's words echoed again. *There's more to life than books and basil.* Was there? The thought felt foreign, almost intrusive. But it lingered, stubborn and insistent, as I sat there in the stillness, contemplating what might come next.

I glanced at the unopened text on my phone. Aggie had sent an address for a community event at a local café tomorrow night, an open mic night, she'd said. Something fun, something different. Something outside my usual carefully structured routine.

I closed my eyes, letting out a slow, measured breath. The faces of my students flickered to life behind my eyelids, Amelia, with her eyes lighting up when she made a connection during class, and Anthony, who always stayed behind to ask about the figures left out of the textbook, his questions quiet but determined. I could hear their voices, their eager curiosity breaking through the structured lessons, the way Amelia would practically bounce in her seat when she had an idea, the way Anthony's forehead creased in concentration as he considered a difficult question.

For all my reserved tendencies, I knew I mattered in that classroom. It was my sanctuary, a place where curiosity could thrive, where I could guide inquiry and challenge the narratives most people never questioned. It felt good to make an impact there, to feel useful, but even that wasn't enough to fill the gaps. There were parts of me, parts that teaching couldn't reach, parts I wasn't sure how to tend, that felt persistently untended.

The ticking clock on the wall seemed louder in the silence, each second an unrelenting reminder of time slipping by. Outside, the sky had deepened to a velvety indigo, the stars beginning to dot the darkness, their light faint but steady. I glanced down at the cup of tea on the side table, untouched and cold now. I didn't move to warm it. Instead, I stared out the window at the garden below, its familiar lines softened by the silvery glow of the moon. The mint I'd planted last spring had spread more than I expected, its green leaves a stubborn reminder that things could grow even when left alone.

Havenwood buzzed faintly in the background, the distant hum of voices, a car pulling into a driveway, the gentle trickle of Rivermere Creek weaving its way through the quiet. The town had a way of settling into the edges of my solitude, a presence both comforting and suffocating.

Aggie's words from the library came back to me, uninvited but insistent. *There's more to life than books and basil.* I thought of Caleb, his

laughter echoing in my memory from our last visit, his grin so full of life it was impossible not to smile back. I could almost hear him now, the way he called my name excitedly when I picked him up, the way his small hands had tugged at my sleeve when he wanted my attention.

It had been two years since my divorce after coming out to Anna, and while the separation had been amicable, the adjustment to shared custody still caught me off guard at times. Caleb spent most of the school year with Anna for the sake of consistency, and though I knew it was best for him, the quiet moments without him still felt hollow. My thoughts drifted further, to my past, the years I spent trying to fit into a life that never quite felt like mine. I'd taken slow, cautious steps toward something more honest, more authentic, but it still felt halting, incomplete.

I opened my eyes, the question rising unbidden in the stillness: *What's next?* It lingered, pressing against the boundaries of my carefully constructed world, seeking an answer I wasn't sure I could give. My fingers traced the rim of my mug, the ceramic smooth and cool under my touch. A soft breeze filtered through the open window, carrying with it the scent of damp earth and blooming jasmine.

Maybe Aggie was right. Maybe there was more. But the idea of stepping beyond what I knew, beyond the carefully built walls of my solitude, made my pulse quicken. Change was slow, but it was coming, whether I was ready for it or not.

My gaze fell back to the garden, serene under the moonlight. It was thriving, but I knew it needed tending, just like the parts of me I'd ignored for too long. The rosemary had grown wild, stretching past its neat borders, and the basil was beginning to flower. I made a mental note to trim it back before it lost its potency. With a quiet sigh, I stood, the cold mug still in my hand. The deliberate sound of running water filled the room as I rinsed it out, my movements steady and methodical. The rhythmic motion was comforting, an act of control in an otherwise unpredictable world.

Tomorrow, I thought, setting the mug upside down to dry. Tomorrow, I'll refill the bird feeder. Spend more time outside. Maybe even take Aggie's advice… or at least consider it. The idea of change still unsettled me, but maybe small steps were enough for now.

The house exhaled into silence as I returned to the living room. My eyes drifted to the mantle, settling on Caleb's photo. His smile had the same effect now as it did when he was in the room, filling the space with a kind of warmth no other presence could match. I traced the edge of the frame with my fingers, as if that simple touch could bring me

closer to him. I smiled softly, then glanced one last time at the garden before turning out the lights.

As I moved toward the bedroom, a thought struck me, and I paused. I needed to write my weekly letter to Caleb and get it in the mail tomorrow. It had become our tradition; a small but meaningful connection that helped bridge the days we spent apart. I didn't want to let the routine slip, not even for a week.

Making a mental note, I added another task to my list: pick up some stickers tomorrow. Caleb loved it when I decorated the envelope, dinosaurs last week, maybe space rockets this time. He'd once joked that he could always spot my letters in the pile of mail because they were the most colorful. I chuckled softly at the memory, imagining him sorting through the envelopes, his eyes lighting up at the sight of mine.

I reached for my notepad on the nightstand and jotted down a reminder. It felt good to have something to look forward to, even something as small as picking out stickers. Maybe, I thought, it was the little things that kept loneliness at bay.

With a faint smile, I headed down the hallway, the quiet weight of the day settling around me. The thought of Caleb opening his letter and laughing at the stickers made the lingering quiet in the house feel just a little less lonely. I pulled the blanket up around my shoulders as I sat on the edge of my bed for a moment, letting the stillness wash over me.

The night air was cool and steady, wrapping around the promise of another day waiting just beyond the horizon. Change might be slow, but maybe, just maybe, I was ready to take a step toward it.

3

JULES

A light rain pattered intermittently against the windows of Bright Horizons Bookstore, the kind of March drizzle that hinted at the season's unpredictability. The gentle rhythm paired perfectly with the warm, inviting hum of the shop, offering a cozy escape from the still-cool March air outside. It was the kind of place that wrapped you up like an old blanket, rows of overstuffed shelves, a faint whiff of aged paper mingling with the aroma of espresso drifting from the café tucked in the back. Perfect for a rainy grey Saturday. I hadn't stepped foot in this bookstore in years, but it felt like no time had passed. The posters advertising local events and author readings plastered across the entryway were new, but the cozy reading nooks and mismatched chairs were the same, down to the faded fabric on my favorite armchair near the fiction section.

I set my umbrella by the door and shook the rain off my jacket, glancing around with a grin. Bright Horizons had always been one of my favorite spots in Havenwood. Even now, years later, it felt like a time capsule of the life I'd left behind. The creak of the wooden floorboards under my feet was familiar, grounding me in a way that nothing else quite did.

"Still the same old Jules," Callie Nguyen's voice called from somewhere near the queer lit table. "Late as usual."

I rolled my eyes as I weaved through the aisles toward them. "I'm not late," I countered. "I'm just… unpredictably on time."

Callie was leaning casually against the table stacked high with books, their petite but athletic frame draped in one of their signature jackets, a bold patchwork of fabrics that shouldn't have worked together but somehow did. Their chin-length black bob gleamed under the soft bookstore lights, the precision of the cut accentuating the sharp angles of their jaw. A constellation of freckles dusted their nose and cheeks, softening the striking intensity of their dark, almond-shaped eyes, which were lined with their trademark winged eyeliner. As always, their look was effortlessly pulled together, with high-waisted jeans giving them an air of playful but polished confidence.

Their grin widened as they saw me. "Uh-huh," Callie said, handing me a book without even looking at the title. "Here. Something for your *Midsummer* research."

I glanced at the cover and snorted. "A How-to Guide for Fairy Gardens? Very helpful. Thanks."

"You're welcome." They winked, unbothered by my sarcasm. "So, what are we fighting about today?"

I grinned, knowing exactly where this was going. Callie and I never needed much to spark a debate, and this table, with its mix of old classics and glossy contemporary covers, was practically a battleground waiting to happen. I picked up a brightly colored novel and held it out for emphasis.

"Queer lit," I declared. "I'm just saying, we need more of this. Messy, unapologetic queer protagonists. Not everything has to be a coming-out story or some tragic drama."

Callie folded their arms, their grin turning playful as they glanced at the stack. "Oh, so you're just erasing the classics now? What about the stories that paved the way for all your chaotic, joyful space pirate fantasies?"

The ribbing stung just enough to make me laugh. "First of all, space pirates deserve their due." I clutched the book dramatically to my chest. "Secondly, you're just mad because I'm right."

"Mad? Never. Entertained? Always." Callie's laugh rang out, their voice smooth and filled with easy confidence, earning us a few side-eyes from nearby browsers. But they didn't care, and honestly, neither did I.

This was Callie to a T: unapologetically bold, effortlessly charming, and always ready to dive headfirst into a spirited argument. They'd been like this in high school too, dragging me into thrift stores when I was too stuck in my head or convincing me to join an impromptu

poetry reading in the park. Even now, after years apart, falling back into this rhythm felt like coming home.

"Okay, fine," Callie conceded with a dramatic sigh, holding up their hands. "I'll allow the space pirates. But only if they have fabulous hair."

"Obviously," I said, rolling my eyes. "Have you met me?"

Their quick, disarming smile flashed as they reached into their crossbody bag, likely filled with an assortment of sketch pads and fabric swatches. The way Callie could mix banter with affection always made conversations with them feel like sparring with a sibling, equal parts challenge and camaraderie.

The debate was playful, sure, but I couldn't help feeling a deeper connection to the books on the table, and to the argument itself. After spending years away, working on activist projects and constantly moving, returning to Havenwood to direct *A Midsummer Night's Dream* at the Playhouse had felt like both a homecoming and a challenge. The play was a dream, literally, an excuse to reimagine familiar material and inject it with queer joy, bold visuals, and unapologetic individuality. But my creativity felt… rusty. Hence the stacks of books.

"Honestly, I could use some inspiration," I admitted, gesturing to the table. "The costumes, the energy, the fairies, I want it all to feel fresh. Joyful, messy, magical. Like these stories."

Callie arched an eyebrow. "You're putting a lot of pressure on one play, Jules."

"Because it matters," I said simply. "Queer stories, on stage, on the page, anywhere, they matter. They deserve to be as big and loud and colorful as everyone else's."

Callie's smirk softened into something warmer. "And that's why you're the one directing. You'll make it brilliant, Jules. You always do."

Before I could thank them, or deflect with a snarky comment, a quiet voice interrupted.

"I think Baldwin would agree with you," the voice said, steady and soft. "He once said that artists have to bear witness to the truth."

Callie and I turned toward the voice in unison. A man stood a few shelves away, holding a book about queer figures from the Harlem Renaissance. His neatly cropped sandy brown hair, streaked faintly with grey at the temples, complemented the quiet intelligence in his hazel eyes. The tailored jacket he wore, subtly checkered in muted green, fit well over his solid, slightly broad frame, giving him a polished, academic air. Yet, there was an endearing softness in the way he adjusted his rectangular glasses, as if unsure he belonged in this moment.

"Baldwin, huh?" I said, tilting my head, a slow smile creeping across my face. "Not a bad choice."

Callie, always quick to pick up on a shift in energy, grinned and took a step back, but unashamed of being heard said, "Well, this just got interesting. I'm grabbing coffee before the sparks start flying. Don't burn the place down, you two."

I barely noticed Callie leaving. My focus had locked onto the man who looked like he might regret speaking up. His grip on the book tightened, knuckles brushing against the edge of a simple but classic wristwatch. There was something striking about the way he held himself, like he was both perfectly put together and on the verge of disappearing into the background. I cleared my throat and took a step closer, my curiosity piqued. "You always quote Baldwin to strangers in bookstores?" I asked, tilting my head slightly.

He crossed his arms and smiled. "Oh, absolutely. Quoting Baldwin in bookstores is part of my personal brand. Right between alphabetizing my spice rack and debating the queer subtext in *Frankenstein* with unsuspecting strangers."

I blinked, then let out a short laugh. "Wow. That might be the most curated personality I've ever heard. Do you have a business card, or do I just follow the scent of well-organized existential crisis?"

He chuckled to himself as he began to walk on. "So," I said, taking a step closer and letting curiosity soften my tone, "what's your story? You don't exactly give off 'jump into debates with strangers' vibes. I'm Jules. Jules Moreno."

He hesitated, his brow furrowing slightly. For a moment, I thought he might retreat entirely, but then he spoke, his voice measured and calm. "I'm… a history teacher. Here in town."

A local. That was interesting. The quiet, bookish type wasn't exactly common in Havenwood, or at least, not the part of Havenwood I remembered. "No kidding," I said, leaning casually against the table and crossing my arms. "I grew up here too. Just moved back after a long stint of… adventuring."

"Adventuring?" His eyebrow arched slightly, the faintest hint of a smile tugging at the corner of his mouth. It was subtle, restrained, like he didn't want to give too much away.

"It was," I said with a shrug, as if my life could be summed up in two words. "But there's something nice about being back. Familiar faces, new ones… like yours."

That seemed to catch him off guard. His posture shifted, just a fraction, his shoulders straightened like he was trying to decide whether

to meet the moment or retreat from it. His eyes flicked briefly toward the café counter where Callie was no doubt watching us, grinning like a cat with a secret. I softened my tone, taking a step back to ease the tension.

"You're not used to this kind of thing, huh?" I asked, keeping my voice light.

He shook his head, his faint smile returning as if it had been coaxed out of hiding. "Not exactly."

The silence between us stretched, just long enough to brush against awkwardness without quite falling into it. It felt like the moment was tipping toward goodbye before he nodded slightly. "I should… get going."

"Sure," I said, my smile turning playful to lighten the weight of his exit. "But don't be a stranger, Teach."

His polite smile lingered for a moment, a hint of something thoughtful in his expression, before he turned and walked toward the register. I watched him go, my gaze inevitably dropping to the way his perfectly pressed pants fitted snugly over his amazing ass as he moved, deliberate and purposeful, like he calculated every step. My chest buzzed faintly, curiosity mixing with a touch of something I didn't care to name.

As he passed a pair of teens in the corner giggling over their iced coffees, they perked up and waved enthusiastically. "Hi, Mr. Brooks!" one of them called, grinning. He returned the greeting with a quick nod and that same understated warmth in his voice. Mr. Brooks, I repeated silently, filing the name away, though it gave me no real insight into the man who'd already made quite an impression.

"You're staring," Callie said, appearing suddenly at my side with a steaming cup of coffee in hand. Their grin, as always, was infuriatingly self-satisfied.

"I am not," I shot back, though I felt the heat rising to my cheeks.

"Uh-huh." They leaned against the table, stirring their coffee lazily. "So? What's the deal with Mr. History Teacher?"

I rolled my eyes but couldn't quite stop the smirk that crept onto my face. "Quiet, thoughtful, definitely doesn't know what to do with someone like me."

Callie laughed, loud enough to turn a few heads. "Sounds like a project. You gonna see him again?"

"Who knows?" I said with a shrug, turning my attention back to the stack of books. But as I ran my fingers over the spines, my mind wandered back to the man with the tailored jacket and the Baldwin quote. "I wouldn't mind."

Callie grinned knowingly. "Might be good for you, you know. Somebody to balance out all your chaos."

I shot them a look but didn't argue. Callie had been my grounding force for years, ever since we'd spent our high school days tearing through thrift stores and crashing every open mic night within driving distance. They knew me better than most, knew how easily I got restless, how often I left without looking back. But they also knew when to push me, and I could see that glint in their eye now.

Through the rain-speckled window, I caught one last glimpse of him stepping into the street, his book tucked under his arm. His silhouette blurred slightly against the grey afternoon, but something about him stuck in my mind. A quiet spark, unexpected but intriguing, in the familiar streets of Havenwood.

"Well," Callie said, breaking the moment, "if this turns into something, I call dibs on officiating the wedding."

I shoved them playfully, laughing despite myself. "You're ridiculous."

"And you love it."

They weren't wrong.

Before I could retort, two teens appeared at the end of the aisle, whispering and glancing in my direction like they'd just stumbled upon a unicorn. Callie turned to follow my gaze, instantly catching on. "Oh, great. Your adoring fans," they muttered, crossing their arms with an exaggerated sigh.

The braver of the two stepped forward, a wiry teen with teal-tipped jet-black hair styled in a short, tapered cut. Their slim frame moved with restless energy, hands fidgeting with the hem of their oversized graphic tee, which bore an abstract design in bold colors. A silver hoop glinted in their left ear, catching the bookstore's soft lighting. "Um, excuse me," they started, their voice cracking slightly with nerves. "Are you Jules Moreno?"

I blinked, caught off guard, but managed a smile. "I am. And you are…?"

"I'm Jayden!" they said quickly, motioning to their shorter friend, who was wearing a hoodie covered in enamel pins. "This is Maya. We're huge fans. Like, huge fans. Your videos on design and storytelling are, like, everything to us."

"Oh my gosh," Maya gushed, gripping the edges of her hoodie. "I can't believe you're here. In Havenwood. At this bookstore."

Callie, leaning against a nearby shelf, pretended to stifle a yawn. "It's Jules. He's just a person," they teased, smirking at me. "Don't let it go to your head, superstar."

Ignoring Callie, I focused on the teens, feeling a genuine warmth spread through me. "Thank you. That's really sweet of you both to say. Do you live here?"

Jayden nodded eagerly. "Yeah, we're students at Havenwood High. We're in the GSA, Maya's the president, and I'm the VP."

"Would you mind," Maya started, holding up her phone sheepishly, "could we get a selfie with you? It would mean so much."

"Of course," I said, grinning. The kids scrambled to position themselves, and I crouched slightly to fit into the frame. Maya snapped a photo, then another "just in case," her hands trembling slightly with excitement.

"Thank you so much!" Jayden said, tucking their phone away. Their dark, thoughtful eyes gleamed with excitement as they added, "Actually, we were wondering… Would you ever consider coming to speak to our GSA? It's a small group, but we'd love to hear about your work and your journey. You're such an inspiration."

I didn't even hesitate. "I'd love to. Let me give you my number so we can set it up."

I reached into my bag, rummaging for a moment before pulling out a small notepad and pen. With a quick, fluid motion, I scribbled down my number, tore off the sheet, and handed it to Jayden with a grin.

"Here you go," I said. "Shoot me a text, and we'll figure out a time that works. I'm excited to meet everyone."

Jayden hesitated for a beat before glancing down at the paper, then back up at Jules. "Would it be okay if I passed this on to our teacher? He's the one organizing things, so he can help set it up."

My smile widened. "That's perfect. I look forward to talking with him."

"You're seriously the best," Maya said, clutching her phone like it was a golden ticket. "Thank you!"

The two thanked me about three more times before dashing out of the bookstore, their excited chatter echoing as the door swung shut behind them. Callie let out a low whistle, pushing off the shelf. "Well, well, aren't you the local celebrity? You'd better watch out, or they'll start naming streets after you."

I rolled my eyes, but I couldn't help smiling. "They were sweet. And they're doing important work with their GSA."

Callie smirked, patting me on the shoulder. "Yeah, yeah. Keep that humility act going. But don't forget, I knew you before you were a big deal."

"Noted," I said dryly, though the glow of the moment lingered as we returned to browsing.

Callie reached for a book on the shelf, flipping through the pages absently. "You know, it's kinda cool," they said, their voice more thoughtful now. "Seeing kids look up to you like that. It's not just about the work you do, Jules. It's about who you are."

I paused, glancing at them. "You're getting sentimental on me, Nguyen."

"Don't get used to it," they shot back, smirking. "But seriously. They see something in you that resonates. And that's worth something."

I exhaled, considering that. The idea that my work, my voice, could mean something real to people beyond a stage. That it could help kids like Jayden and Maya see themselves more clearly, more confidently. It was humbling. And terrifying. And exhilarating all at once.

"Yeah," I finally said, my voice softer. "I hope so."

Callie grinned. "Well, if you ever need a reminder, I'm happy to keep your ego in check."

I laughed, shaking my head. "Good to know."

We fell back into browsing, but the bookstore felt a little different now, warmer, more alive. Maybe, just maybe, this homecoming was exactly what I needed.

4

ELLIOTT

Wednesday morning, the GSA meeting room at Havenwood High was alive with energy, even in the soft drizzle of late spring. Pride flags and student artwork decorated the space, an explosion of color and creativity that felt both defiant and welcoming. Inspirational quotes, many from queer figures throughout history, lined the walls, and in the center of it all, Maya perched on the edge of her chair like she might combust from excitement.

"We need someone big for the Pride Month event in June," Maya declared, gesturing with her hands as though she were already directing a stage production. "Someone who's not just going to give a boring speech, but someone who can actually get people fired up!"

Jayden, seated next to her, adjusted his glasses and nodded thoughtfully. "What about Jules Moreno?" he asked.

His tone was calm, but there was a glimmer of excitement behind his measured words. "He's kind of a big deal. I mean, his social media has tons of followers, and he's done activism work all over the place, protests, marches, even a queer youth theatre program in Chicago."

Maya's eyes lit up. "Yes! Jules is perfect! And he's back in town now! We saw him at the bookstore last week, and he's got this energy, you know? Like, he walks in, and everyone just notices him."

Jayden smirked. "Didn't Mr. Brooks meet him? At Bright Horizons?"

I froze mid-note, my hand hovering over the whiteboard as Jayden's comment hit me squarely. The students' voices buzzed around me, their energy crackling like static electricity. My gaze flickered to Jayden and Maya, both practically glowing with excitement.

My mind raced. Jules Moreno. His name had carried an unexpected weight in the room, almost like a spark igniting a fuse. I hadn't mentioned my brief encounter with Jules at the bookstore to anyone, least of all my students.

But now that I thought about it, I had seen a few of them at Bright Horizons that day, as I left the store. They must have caught the exchange.

Still, why were they so worked up about it? Students loved any glimpse into their teachers' personal lives, tiny revelations that reminded them we were human, but this felt different. There was a buzz to their enthusiasm, as if Jules wasn't just a person but an event. Like he was some kind of local celebrity I hadn't realized I'd met.

Maya's eyes practically danced as she leaned forward in her chair, while Jayden's usually calm demeanor betrayed a flicker of amusement, like he knew something I didn't.

What was it about Jules that had them so captivated? And why did it feel like I was walking into a conversation where everyone else already knew the ending?

Maya leaned forward, her face breaking into a mischievous grin. "Oh yeah! You totally met him, right?"

I straightened, adjusting my glasses in a futile attempt to buy time. "I… might have met him briefly," I admitted.

"Perfect!" Maya exclaimed, clapping her hands. "Then you have to ask him!"

Jayden, ever the quiet voice of reason, added, "I got his number at the bookstore last week and asked if he'd be okay with me passing it on. He seemed cool with it." He slid a small piece of paper across the table.

I hesitated, the weight of the moment settling on me. Jules Moreno wasn't just a name; he was a presence. The kind of person who seemed to carry the room with him wherever he went.

But Maya's hopeful expression, paired with Jayden's quiet nod of encouragement, left me little choice. "Alright," I said finally, tucking the paper into my pocket. "I'll reach out."

The students cheered, their excitement spilling into the room. I gave them a small, polite smile, but inside, my nerves were already building.

The students' excitement buzzed like electricity. Their enthusiasm was contagious, filling the space with energy that felt almost tangible. My gaze lingered on the event flyer pinned neatly to the board: *Pride Month: Stories That Change Us*. The words seemed to pulse with their own importance, a reminder of just how significant this event could be.

As the students launched into a flurry of suggestions, streamers, music playlists, guest introductions, I found myself scribbling furiously on the whiteboard, breaking down tasks, timelines, and backup plans with a level of detail that even I recognized was excessive. My notes sprawled across the board in perfect rows, each bullet point meticulously underlined. My mind raced ahead, mapping every possible contingency as if I were planning a historical reenactment rather than a Pride Month speaker.

"Okay," I said, tapping the marker against the board. "If Jules agrees to come, we'll need to finalize reserving the library, the seating arrangement, test the sound system, and…" I stopped mid-sentence, realizing I'd written Jules Moreno in block letters at the top of the board, underlined twice. My ears burned, though I wasn't sure why.

"Mr. Brooks," Maya interrupted, her grin both amused and concerned. "You're seriously overthinking this."

Jayden nodded; his expression calm but pointed. "It's Jules, Mr. Brooks. He's not going to need, like, a red carpet. He'll just show up and be awesome."

I turned to face them, the marker still in my hand. "I'm just trying to make sure everything's ready," I said, a bit more defensively than I intended. "He deserves to feel welcomed, especially if he's taking time out of his schedule to do this."

The students exchanged a look that I couldn't quite decipher, somewhere between amusement and sympathy. Maya leaned forward, resting her chin in her palm. "We get it. You want everything to be perfect. But you don't have to try so hard. Jules is cool. Like, really cool. He'll probably be happy just being here."

I pressed the marker against the board harder than necessary, the squeak of it grating. They were right. I was overthinking. I'd been spiraling into logistics since the suggestion came up, and deep down, I knew it wasn't just about the event. There was something about Jules, something about his energy at the bookstore, his easy smile, the way he'd mentioned James Baldwin like he was a mutual friend, that had me tying myself into knots.

The thought crossed my mind before I could stop it: Jules was attractive. And not just in a physical sense, though his effortless charisma

had made him impossible to ignore. It was more than that, something about his presence had lingered with me, a kind of magnetism I didn't entirely understand. I shook the thought away, focusing back on the students, who were now eyeing me with barely concealed amusement.

Maya tilted her head, her grin widening. "You're nervous, aren't you?"

"Nervous?" I repeated, too quickly. "Of course not. Why would I be nervous?"

Jayden raised an eyebrow, his tone measured. "Because he's kind of a big deal. Everyone in town is talking about how Jules Moreno is back. He's got that whole social media thing, the activism stuff, oh, and he's super talented. People love him."

"Plus, he's, like, stupidly charming," Maya added with a smirk. "But, you know, no pressure."

I let out a small sigh, leaning against the desk and trying to regain my composure. "It's not about me," I said, more to myself than to them. "This is for all of you."

"Right," Maya said, her grin softening. "But it's okay if you're a little freaked out. Jules is cool, but so are you. And you're good at this stuff, Mr. Brooks. We'll figure it out."

Jayden nodded. "Just don't overthink it. He'll probably appreciate whatever you plan."

Their reassurance settled something in me, though the nerves didn't completely fade. I glanced back at the whiteboard, at Jules' name standing out amid the flurry of notes.

The meeting wrapped up with their usual buzz of excitement, but as I erased the board and capped the marker, I couldn't shake the weight of my hesitation. The thought of calling Jules felt monumental in a way I couldn't quite explain. He'd seemed perfectly nice at the bookstore, welcoming, even. So why did the idea of reaching out tie my stomach into knots?

As the students filtered out, Maya called over her shoulder, "Just breathe, Mr. Brooks. It's going to be fine."

I nodded, offering her a faint smile. Breathe, I thought to myself. It's just a phone call. What's the worst that could happen?

But the knot in my chest remained as I packed up for the day, their voices echoing in my mind. "He'll light up the room no matter what."

The steady ticking of the clock on my office wall seemed louder than usual that afternoon, a metronome to my restless thoughts. I sat at my desk, staring at the small slip of paper with Jules Moreno's number

scribbled in a bold, flowing hand. My desk, as always, was an orderly reflection of me, stacks of graded essays on one side, a row of pens lined up in perfect symmetry, and a steaming mug of chamomile tea on the other. But today, the anticipation coiled in my chest made the usually familiar space feel foreign, almost claustrophobic.

I couldn't help but admit that Jules had been on my mind more than I was comfortable acknowledging. His unruly, slightly shaggy hair had caught my attention right away, the streaks of vibrant color woven through it making him look like he belonged to another world entirely, one far more alive than my carefully ordered one. His expressive dark eyes, warm and lively, had a way of making you feel like you were the only person in the room when he focused on you. And his hands, lean and capable, with faint smudges of ink or paint along his fingertips, spoke of someone who was constantly creating, constantly moving. Jules wasn't the type of person I'd typically find myself drawn to, too unpredictable, too bold, but those traits only made it harder to stop thinking about him. His confidence wasn't just magnetic; it was impossible to ignore, and I found myself wondering if I could ever match that kind of energy.

I picked up the phone, then set it down again, my hand hovering as if the weight of the decision was too much. It wasn't like me to hesitate over something as simple as a phone call. But this wasn't just a phone call, it was a bridge to someone who exudes charisma and creativity, traits that had lingered in my mind since our brief meeting at bright Horizons. I took a deep breath, picked up the phone again, and finally dialed, the sound ringing on the other end both too fast and agonizingly slow.

"Hello?" The voice that answered was warm, curious, and unmistakably Jules.

"Hi, is this Jules Moreno?" I asked, sitting up straighter, as if he could see me through the phone.

"That depends," he replied, his tone playful but tinged with caution. "Who's asking?"

"It's Elliott Brooks," I said, clearing my throat as if that would smooth over my nerves. "We met briefly at Bright Horizons. I, uh, mentioned Baldwin."

"Oh!" His voice brightened instantly, as if a light had been switched on. "History Teacher! Got it. What's up?"

His enthusiasm caught me slightly off guard, but I pressed on. "I'm the faculty advisor for the Gay-Straight Alliance at Havenwood High," I began, trying to keep my tone steady. "We're organizing a Pride Month event, and the students suggested inviting you as a guest speaker. They, uh, seem to think quite highly of you."

"Well, they sound like smart kids," Jules said, his voice laced with humor. "What's the event?"

Encouraged by his interest, I explained the details. But as I spoke, I realized my words were coming out more formally than I intended, stiff and rehearsed, as if I were presenting a thesis rather than extending an invitation. I wondered if Jules could sense the nerves in my voice.

"Sounds amazing," he said without hesitation, his reply as effortless as his demeanor. "I'd love to."

I blinked, the ease of his agreement catching me off guard. "Really?"

"Of course," he said warmly, and I could almost hear the smile in his voice. "It sounds like a great way to connect. And I'm all about hyping up the next generation of queer leaders."

His enthusiasm was so genuine, so confident, that I found myself momentarily speechless. I cleared my throat again, finally managing, "The students will be thrilled."

"Good," Jules said, his voice softening, carrying a warmth that felt almost personal. "And you, Teach? Are you excited?"

The question caught me by surprise, a small but pointed shift in the conversation. I hesitated, not sure how to answer. "I… think it's a wonderful opportunity for them," I said carefully, my voice quieter.

"Alright," he said, his tone turning lighter again, like he was letting me off the hook. "Just send me the details. I'm in."

We scheduled a time for him to come meet the group at one of our afterschool meetings. The call ended with an easy, "Talk soon," from Jules, but his presence lingered in the room long after the line went dead. I leaned back in my chair, exhaling a breath I hadn't realized I was holding. The tension in my chest began to ease, replaced by a strange mixture of relief and curiosity. Jules' confidence, his immediate willingness to say yes, stood in stark contrast to my own hesitations.

I glanced at the flyer for the event, now tacked to the corner of my desk. *Pride Month: Stories That Change Us.* For the first time all day, a small, genuine smile tugged at the corners of my mouth.

My phone buzzed on the desk, pulling me from my thoughts. Caleb's name lit up the screen, and a grin spread across my face as I opened the message.

Caleb: *Hey Dad! Just saw the new Deadpool movie with Mom. Have you seen it yet? It's hilarious. Also… very inappropriate lol.*

I chuckled softly, typing back a quick response.

Elliott: *Not yet, but it's on my list. I'm sure it's completely inappropriate if you loved it. I'll let you know when I watch it, and we can compare notes.*

Caleb's reply came almost instantly.

Caleb: *Deal! Miss you, Dad.*

My heart squeezed in that familiar way, and I typed back,

Elliott: *Miss you too, buddy. Love you.*

A warm sense of anticipation settled over me, Spring Break was just a few weeks away, and I'd finally get to see him again.

I set my phone down, but my thoughts didn't settle as easily. My mind drifted back to Jules, his laughter, his energy, the effortless way he had agreed to the invitation. I wasn't used to people like him, people who jumped in without hesitation. And yet, there was something about it that felt oddly… refreshing.

5

JULES

The late afternoon sun hung low in the sky, casting long shadows across the weathered brick facade of Havenwood High. The crisp March air carried the faintest hints of warmth, teasing the arrival of spring. Daffodils and early blooming tulips dotted the edges of the school's walkway, while the trees, still bare from winter, showed the first signs of budding leaves against a pale blue sky streaked with wisps of cloud. The school was just as I remembered it, though it seemed smaller now, its edges softened by the years and my own nostalgia. Kids were sprawled out on the front steps, laughing and chattering, backpacks flung haphazardly around them. Their carefree energy was infectious, and for a moment, I let myself imagine what it would've been like to have a space like this back when I was in high school.

As I stepped through the school's double doors, the familiar smell of pencil shavings and old textbooks hit me, a strange blend of comforting and sterile. It had been a week since the call from Elliott inviting me here, and we'd texted a couple of times to set up today's meeting with the GSA. The hallways were quieter this time of day, save for the occasional echo of footsteps or a locker slamming shut. But the library? The library was alive.

The moment I pushed the door open, it felt like I'd stepped into a different world. Pride flags draped proudly across the tall windows, catching the golden light streaming in and casting faint rainbows across

the floor. Hand-painted posters adorned every available wall space, boasting slogans like *Love is Love* and *Be Proud of Who You Are.* A display table near the entrance held a mix of queer literature, rainbow stickers, and information about the upcoming Pride Month event. The tables, arranged in a welcoming semi-circle, were already occupied by a lively group of students.

Before I could fully take in the scene, two figures darted toward me, practically skipping across the room with notepads in hand.

"You're here!" Maya exclaimed, her voice a mix of excitement and relief, like she'd been worried I might bail at the last minute.

"Jules Moreno," she said, holding out her hand as if we were meeting for the first time. "I'm Maya, and I'm, like, the unofficial president of the GSA, or maybe the very official one. Still waiting for confirmation on that."

I laughed, taking her hand and shaking it firmly. "Nice to meet you, Madame President."

Jayden, standing slightly behind her, offered a shy smile. "I'm Jayden," he said softly. "Thanks for coming. Everyone's been really excited about this."

"Yes, we met before. Nice to see you again. Well, I hope I live up to the hype," I replied, flashing them both a grin.

"Oh, you will," Maya said confidently, looping her arm through mine like we were already old friends. "Come on, we've got the best seat in the house for you. And wait till you see the room, it's fabulous. We went all out."

As they led me further inside, I took in the details. Pride flags weren't just hanging from the windows; they were everywhere, miniature versions taped to the backs of chairs, larger ones draped across bookcases. A corner of the library had been turned into a photo booth, complete with glittery props and a makeshift backdrop that read, Proud and Fearless. The students had poured their hearts into this space, and it showed.

By the time we reached the tables, the room had quieted, all eyes turning toward me. There was a moment, a heartbeat where everyone seemed to hold their breath.

"Alright," I said, throwing my arms open wide and letting my voice fill the room. "Who's ready to make some queer history today?"

The silence broke in an instant. Laughter rippled through the group as Maya let go of my arm and practically launched herself into the air.

"That would be us!" she said, her enthusiasm bouncing off the walls.

"Good answer," I replied, laughing as I made my way toward the tables. "You're already my favorite."

I took my time greeting the students, making a point to connect with each one. High-fives for some, fist bumps for others, and quick compliments that earned bright smiles. "Rainbow sneakers? Iconic. Love the flair." One kid's denim jacket was covered in pins, and I couldn't help but gush over it. "Okay, where did you get that 'Bi-Furious' button? I need it in my life."

The tension melted quickly, replaced by easy laughter and chatter. It always amazed me how these moments played out, people hesitating for just a second, unsure of me, and then opening like flowers as soon as I made the first move.

Out of the corner of my eye, I caught sight of a familiar figure standing near the back of the room. Elliott Brooks. Mr. Baldwin himself. Clipboard in hand, glasses perched neatly on his nose, watching the room like he wasn't sure where he fit into the scene. His expression was unreadable, but I could sense the nerves beneath the surface.

I gave him a quick nod and a smile, hoping to ease whatever tension he was feeling. Something about him always seemed just slightly out of step with the chaos around him, like he was trying to map everything out before he made a move. It was… endearing, in a way.

Maya leaned toward me, her voice dropping to a stage whisper. "That's Mr. Brooks. He's the one who reached out to you."

"I know," I whispered back, my grin widening. "We've met. He's the reason I'm here."

"Well," she said, crossing her arms and smirking, "he doesn't know what he's in for."

"Neither do you," I teased, before stepping forward to take my place at the head of the room.

I moved to the front of the room, letting my stride slow as I reached the table. I leaned against its edge, keeping my posture relaxed but grounded. My grin softened into something warmer, something inviting, as I took in the faces staring back at me. The semi-circle of students seemed a mix of eager and unsure, their energy buzzing just under the surface.

"So," I began, my voice cutting through the hum of the library, "let me tell you something about this person standing in front of you. I didn't always look or feel this confident. Growing up, I didn't even have the words to describe who I was. But that's the thing about being queer,

you're constantly discovering new pieces of yourself. It's like the world hands you a puzzle with no picture on the box."

The room shifted, the students leaning forward slightly in their chairs, their expressions sharpening with curiosity. I felt the weight of their attention and took a deep breath, letting the moment settle before continuing.

"I get it," I said, pacing a step or two in front of the table. "It's messy. It's confusing. There were moments when I felt like I'd never figure it out, like I was fumbling around in the dark trying to find something, anything, that felt real. But every time I found a piece of the puzzle, it felt like coming home to myself. And let me tell you," I added, letting a grin curl onto my lips as I perched on the edge of the table, "protesting in six-inch heels? A choice I will never make again."

That got the laugh I was hoping for, a big, wonderful laugh that rippled across the room. Even Elliott, standing near the back, let the faintest smile tug at his lips. It was subtle, but it was there, and for some reason, it felt like a tiny personal victory.

"But here's the thing," I said, letting the laughter fade naturally as I adjusted my tone. "Being queer isn't just about surviving, it's about thriving. It's about finding your people, your purpose, and your power."

The words hung in the air for a moment, and I could see the way they landed, the little nods, the quiet shifts in posture, the way some of them seemed to straighten their spines like they were holding onto the idea with both hands.

The room had settled into a quiet hum of reflection when, from near the middle of the semi-circle, a hand hesitantly rose. I straightened slightly, making sure to keep my expression warm and inviting. "Yes, friend," I said, nodding toward them, "what's your name?"

The student hesitated, their face partially hidden by their bangs as they glanced around the room. "Alex," they muttered, their voice barely audible.

"Hi, Alex," I said gently, crouching slightly to meet their gaze better. "What's on your mind?"

They shifted in their seat, their arms folding protectively across their chest. "But... what if you can't find your people?" Alex asked, their voice quiet but weighted with vulnerability. "What if you always feel like you don't belong?"

The question struck me in the chest, its weight sinking in immediately. I pushed away from the table and crouched down to their level, making sure to meet their gaze directly. Their uncertainty was

mirrored in the way they sat, arms folded tight, eyes darting between me and the floor.

"Belonging isn't about fitting in," I said softly, my voice steady and measured. "It's about finding people who celebrate you exactly as you are. And trust me, those people are out there. Sometimes it takes time, and sometimes it feels like forever. But I promise you, you're not alone in this. Not now, not ever."

The room went completely still. For a moment, all I could hear was the faint rustle of the Pride flags by the windows, the hum of the library's fluorescent lights, and the sound of my own heartbeat pounding in my ears. I stayed crouched, waiting, not wanting to rush the moment.

Maya, ever the natural leader, broke the silence with a clap that quickly turned into a round of applause. It wasn't polite or perfunctory, it was genuine, loud, and full of warmth. The rest of the students joined in, their clapping filling the room as Alex's expression shifted from uncertainty to something softer, something lighter.

"Thank you," Alex said, their voice just audible over the applause.

Maya beamed, turning to me with an expression that said, this is exactly what we needed. "You're amazing, Jules," she said, grinning so wide it looked like her cheeks might burst.

I stood, giving Alex a reassuring pat on the shoulder before facing the rest of the group with a playful grin. "Alright," I said, gesturing to the circle of students. "Who's ready to take over the world? Or at least make some noise while trying?"

Their cheers and laughter filled the room, and I felt a surge of pride, not just for them, but for the community they were building together. Out of the corner of my eye, I saw Elliott watching, his expression still guarded but noticeably softer. I didn't need to catch his eye to feel the weight of his presence; it was steady, quiet, and there all the same.

When the meeting ended, the library burst into a whirlwind of energy. Students crowded around me, their excitement filling every corner of the room. Questions came rapid-fire, about activism, identity, and everything in between, and I did my best to answer each one with humor and heart. Phones were handed to me for selfies, their owners chattering happily about how inspiring the talk had been.

"You're going to be such a hit at the event," Maya gushed, practically vibrating with enthusiasm as she clutched her phone.

"That's the plan," I replied, laughing as I handed her phone back after yet another selfie, this time with her throwing up peace signs while I pulled a dramatic face.

I thrived in moments like this, moments where I could connect, inspire, and feel the pulse of a shared experience. Each student's story, each hopeful or hesitant question, only fed my energy. It was the kind of chaos I lived for; the kind that made everything I'd been through feel worth it. And yet, amid the buzz of it all, my gaze kept flicking toward the back of the room, where Elliott stood like a quiet sentinel.

He was a stark contrast to the rest of the space, still, composed, and unobtrusive, his hands clasped neatly behind his back. His presence grounded the room, even from the edges, and I found myself wondering what he thought of it all.

As the last student lingered for a quick goodbye, the crowd finally began to thin. The library grew quieter, the echoes of chatter fading into the hum of the fluorescent lights. Slinging my tote bag over my shoulder, I made my way to Elliott. He straightened slightly as I approached, his expression as reserved as ever.

"Ah, Mr. Baldwin himself," I said, grinning as I stopped in front of him. "What'd you think?"

For a moment, he hesitated, his gaze flicking to the now-empty room. It felt like he was carefully choosing his words, weighing them as though they mattered more than I'd expected. "That was… impressive," he said finally, his voice softer than I anticipated.

"High praise from the man of few words," I teased, though something in his sincerity caught me off guard. "Thanks, Teach."

We stood there, a strange quiet settling between us. The air felt charged, humming with something I couldn't quite name. His gaze was steady, though his expression remained unreadable. I felt a flicker of curiosity about what might be going on behind those neat glasses and that composed demeanor.

"You know," I said, tilting my head with a playful smile, "you're not as scary as you look."

That earned me a raised eyebrow. "I wasn't aware I looked scary," he replied, his tone as dry as a textbook.

I laughed, the sound breaking the stillness of the empty library. "You know, the whole stoic history teacher vibe. It's a lot."

To my surprise, a small smile tugged at the corners of his mouth. It wasn't much, but it was enough to make me wonder what else was hidden under that reserved exterior. For someone who seemed so

buttoned-up, there was an undeniable warmth lurking beneath the surface, waiting to be uncovered.

"Well," I said, stepping back toward the door, "I'll see you around, Teach."

He gave a small nod, his gaze following me as I turned to leave. The evening light filtered in through the library windows as I stepped outside, painting the school grounds in hues of gold and pink. The breeze was a welcome relief after the buzzing energy inside.

As I walked away, I couldn't shake the feeling that there was more to Elliott Brooks than met the eye. Behind that quiet demeanor and carefully structured exterior, I sensed a depth that made me wonder what it would take to unravel the layers.

6

ELLIOTT

The Green Bean Café buzzed with its usual morning rhythm, soft chatter, the faint hum of indie music playing overhead, and the steady sounds of the espresso machine hissing and whirring in the background. The scent of fresh coffee mingled with the earthy remnants of an earlier spring rain, creating a warmth that contrasted with the crispness of the air outside. The sunlight filtered through the large front windows, casting warm streaks of golden light across the mismatched furniture and the eclectic art decorating the walls, making the whole space feel like something out of a cozy novel.

Outside, the cobblestone streets of the Rivermere District reflected the kind of spring awakening only Havenwood could offer in early April, with cherry blossoms and dogwoods beginning to bloom along the sidewalks. People strolled by in light hoodies and jeans, some carrying umbrellas just in case, as the occasional gust of cool breeze stirred the air. It was the kind of morning that made you want to linger, to take in the world at a slower pace.

I had no such luxury.

My corner table by the window was perfectly positioned to watch the world come alive, the vibrant atmosphere providing a sharp contrast to the meticulous order of my open notebook. My black coffee sat untouched beside it, steam curling lazily above the rim, forgotten as I focused on the carefully organized bullet points outlining potential

collaborations for the GSA. My pen tapped idly against the page, my fingers twitching with impatience.

Jules was late.

Surprise, surprise.

I checked my watch again, exhaling through my nose. This wasn't new, Jules moved through life on his own timeline, a whirlwind of enthusiasm and spontaneity that seemed to function entirely independent of clocks and schedules. And yet, despite myself, I found my anticipation settling into something sharper, more pointed. Curious, and, I admitted to myself, a little nervous. He'd been impossible to ignore at the GSA meeting: bold, charismatic, and effortlessly captivating. He had a way of drawing people in, of making every conversation feel like the most exciting thing happening in the world at that moment.

The question was, would that energy translate into actual collaboration?

Or would I spend the entire meeting trying to rein him in?

The door swung open with a cheerful jingle, and there he was.

Jules breezed into the café with the kind of presence that turned heads without trying. His vibrant scarf trailed behind him like a banner, his tote bag slung over one shoulder and looking ready to burst at the seams with its overabundance of contents. His curls were slightly damp from the lingering mist outside, a few stray strands sticking to his forehead. He radiated the same energy I'd seen at the meeting, alive, electric, like he was always one thought ahead of the world and moving too fast to explain it.

His eyes scanned the room until they landed on me, and his grin widened.

"Ten minutes late!" Jules called, making a beeline for the counter. "But in my defense, I had a costume brainstorm for *Midsummer* that just couldn't wait. The muse doesn't care about punctuality."

I arched an eyebrow, tapping my pen against my notebook. "Does the muse also make coffee runs?"

He gasped theatrically. "Excuse you, this is fuel."

Jules waved to the barista, rattling off his latte order with the ease of someone who had done this a hundred times before. Then, as if remembering I existed, he turned briefly toward me and pointed to the counter, his expression conspiratorial. I'll be right over.

I just shook my head and turned my attention back to my notes, though my ears still picked up his conversation with the barista.

"I'll have a honey lavender latte extra hot with an extra shot, and, of course, oat milk. We're not savages," he was saying, his voice carrying easily.

The barista chuckled. "Long night?"

Jules sighed dramatically. "Oh, you know, just the usual, revolutionizing community theatre one costume at a time."

I watched as he leaned casually on the counter while waiting for the barista to call his order. His outfit was its own kind of statement, a tailored jacket over a graphic T-shirt, bold jewelry that caught the light, and his ever-present scarf adding a splash of chaotic charm. He exuded a vibrancy that felt both effortless and deliberate, like he'd stepped out of some artist's vivid daydream.

I smiled despite myself.

When the barista called his order, Jules pushed off the counter with a small bounce. Turning to retrieve his latte, he grabbed it with both hands as if it were the most precious thing in the world. As he turned back toward me, I caught myself watching him again, the way his movements were purposeful yet unhurried, like he lived in a different rhythm than the rest of us. Like he was always one step ahead of the world and enjoying the chase. His smile lit up his face as he thanked the barista and headed my way.

I shifted in my seat as he made his way over, latte in hand, the steam curling above it in soft wisps. By the time he reached the table, I had composed myself.

"Okay," Jules announced, dropping his tote onto the chair opposite me. "Now I'm ready. No brainstorming interruptions this time, promise."

"I'll believe it when I see it," I said, lips twitching into a small, reluctant smile.

Jules laughed as he settled into his chair, his notebook already in hand. "See, this is why we work well together. You bring the skepticism; I bring the chaos. It's perfect balance."

He dove into the conversation with his usual energy, flipping open his notebook and gesturing animatedly. "Alright, so here's what I'm thinking for the GSA: something interactive, like an improv workshop. We can get the kids up and moving, help them find their confidence, their voices. It's creative, fun, and totally my jam."

I nodded, jotting down notes in my own meticulous fashion. "That could work. We'd need to arrange a space big enough for

movement, coordinate with the drama department, and make sure we have an outline of activities."

I nodded thoughtfully, picturing my students and the way their eyes sparkled with understanding when a lesson truly resonated with them. "That's why I plan the way I do," I said after a pause, my voice filled with conviction. "Because they deserve that effort. Every detail, every contingency, it's the least I can do for them."

Jules tilted his head slightly, observing me with a look of genuine admiration. His laughter suddenly broke the moment, bright and unrestrained, drawing a few amused glances from nearby patrons who momentarily looked up from their conversations. "You're incredible," he said, shaking his head with a smile that reached his eyes. "No wonder the kids adore you."

"I wouldn't say 'adore,'" I replied, arching an eyebrow playfully. "Appreciate, maybe."

"They adore you," Jules insisted, taking a sip of his steaming latte. "And honestly, so do I. Even if you do need to loosen up."

I bristled slightly at that. "Loosen up?"

"Yeah," he said, reclining with a twinkle of mischief dancing in his eyes. "When's the last time you did something completely unplanned? Like, oh, I don't know, took a spontaneous road trip just because the idea popped into your head?"

"A road trip?" I echoed; my voice tinged with disbelief. "I plan my trips weeks in advance, routes, stops, the whole itinerary. Without that, it's pure chaos."

"That's exactly the point," he replied, his grin widening as if he'd just unveiled a hidden truth. "Tell you what, let's make it simple. You pick a direction, no map, no itinerary, and just see where you end up. One day, one trip. You can even document it in your precious spreadsheet."

I raised an eyebrow, skeptical. "You're suggesting I add 'unplanned chaos' to my to-do list?"

"Absolutely," he responded without a moment's hesitation. "Think of it as an experiment. Let your heart be the compass for the adventure, and I trust you to actually follow through."

I sighed, shaking my head slowly. "One day. But if it turns into a disaster, I'm holding you personally responsible."

He laughed, a sound that was warm and rich, resonating from deep within his chest. "Deal," he said, his grin stretching even wider. "You might even have fun. Who knows? Stranger things have happened."

By the time our drinks were empty, the sunlight outside had shifted, casting a warm glow over the cobblestone streets of Rivermere District. Jules slung his bag over one shoulder as we stepped outside, the café door jingling softly behind us.

"This was fun," he remarked, offering his hand with an exaggerated flourish. "We should do it again sometime, preferably when you're not treating me like one of your spreadsheets."

I paused, then took his hand. "I'll see what I can do."

As he walked away, his vibrant energy seemed to illuminate the entire street. I stood there a moment longer than necessary, watching his scarf trail behind him like a vivid banner. For the first time in a long while, I felt something unexpected, perhaps a lightness, or maybe curiosity. Whatever it was, it lingered with me as I turned back to my meticulously planned day, the memory of his laughter hanging in the air like the subtle, comforting aroma of coffee.

7

JULES

The cool, crisp April night escorted me to The Rainbow Taproom, Havenwood's liveliest queer haven. Outside, the earthy scent of recent rain, and the sidewalks shimmered faintly under the streetlights, reflecting the lingering moisture. The temperature hovered at that perfect in-between where a light jacket was enough. I pushed open the door and the hum of conversation mixed with the faint clink of glasses and the lively crackle of laughter joined Robyn's Dancing on My Own playing over the speakers. Strings of rainbow fairy lights hung in lazy loops across the ceiling, their soft glow bouncing off the colorful artwork that adorned every wall.

Maxie Glam, the queen of Havenwood's Trivia Nights, adjusted her mic stand on the small stage, rhinestones glittering under the overhead lights. Standing at an impressive 7' 2" in her signature towering heels and enormous wig, she commanded the room with an effortless blend of humor and glamor. Her cascading platinum blonde wig shimmered like spun gold, framing her flawlessly made-up face, dramatic winged eyeliner, glittering eyeshadow that caught every beam of light, and bold, ruby-red lips that curved into a mischievous smile. Her dazzling sequined bodysuit hugged her statuesque figure, complemented by oversized rhinestone necklaces and bracelets that sparkled with every gesture. Maxie was, as always, a force of nature wrapped in confidence, charisma, and just the right amount of chaos.

I spotted Callie immediately at a table near the center of the bustling room, their cocktail already in hand. The drink was a riot of colors, an obnoxiously bright concoction topped with a tiny paper umbrella and a slice of lime perched on the rim. Callie was impossible to miss, their vibrant presence commanding attention effortlessly, like a lighthouse cutting through a foggy night.

But what truly made me grin was the sight of Elliott sitting at the edge of the table. His posture was textbook straight, like a soldier at attention, and his hands were clasped tightly on the table in front of him, as if he were bracing himself for an unexpected pop quiz. He looked completely out of place amidst the lively scene, yet somehow… perfect, like a puzzle piece that, against all odds, fit.

Getting him here had been no small task; it took a feat of persistence. Earlier that week, I'd texted him the invite, determined to coax him out of his usual routine.

Jules: *Trivia Night at The Rainbow Taproom. 7 PM. Be there or be tragically unhip.*

I fully expected Elliott to decline. Sure enough, his reply buzzed back almost instantly:

Elliott: *Thanks, but I have papers to grade.*

I rolled my eyes, fingers flying over the keyboard.

Jules: *Don't care. There's a history round, Teach. You're basically required to show up.*

He didn't budge, of course.

Elliott: *I'm sure you'll manage without me,*

Like hell I would let him off that easily.

Jules: *Manage? Without my secret weapon? Absolutely not. 7 PM. No excuses,*

I typed, smirking at the screen. He might think he could out stubborn me, but I wasn't about to back down. This was going to be fun.

He hadn't replied after that, and I'd chalked it up as a loss until I spotted him sitting there, looking simultaneously resigned and bemused. He was already nursing a glass of water, appearing as though he'd accidentally stumbled into a party where he didn't know a soul. A grin spread across my face as I navigated through the bustling crowd toward him.

"Elliott!" I called out, throwing my arms wide with enthusiasm. He turned toward me, his expression hovering somewhere between apprehension and amusement. "You made it!"

"I was coerced," he replied dryly, though a faint twitch at the corner of his mouth betrayed his attempt at seriousness.

"Coerced or not, you're here," I replied, dropping into the seat beside him with a playful bounce. "And just in time. We're about to dominate."

Callie grinned, twirling her ridiculous cocktail umbrella with a flourish. "Only because you dragged in Mr. History Teacher."

Elliott adjusted his glasses, his tone perfectly measured. "Happy to be used for my knowledge."

"That's the spirit," I said, giving him a friendly pat on the back. His shoulders were tense, yet I caught the flicker of amusement dancing in his eyes.

Maxie Glam's voice boomed over the speakers, drawing the room's attention. "Alright, my fabulous friends! It's Trivia Night, and I hope you came prepared. Remember, no phones, no cheating, and if you lose, no crying. Let's get started!"

The rounds began with pop culture, geography, and music, and the table quickly fell into a steady rhythm, answers being thrown out, groans rumbling over mistakes, and triumphant cheers erupting with each correct guess. I dove into every pop culture question with an almost comical surge of overconfidence, even when it was typically unwarranted.

"Titanic came out in 1998," I declared as if unveiling a monumental secret, my pen dancing confidently across the sheet of paper.

"1997," Elliott said softly, his eyes still fixed on his own writing.

I crossed out my answer with a mischievous grin, giving him a gentle nudge with my elbow. "This is why I brought you," I teased.

In that moment, our closeness shifted subtly, the fabric of our clothes and the heat of our bodies aligning as my knee brushed softly against his under the table. I began to ease away, but hesitated when he didn't pull back. That simple inaction took me by surprise. A tingling warmth spread wherever our skin had met, and suddenly, I found it impossible to focus on anything else. My heart thumped wildly in my chest as I deliberately pressed my knee closer against his. Still, he remained motionless, completely at ease.

I stole a glance at him from the corner of my eye. There he was, scribbling away on his answer sheet with quiet determination, his expression calm and focused. My pulse raced, and a wave of heat rolled through me, a heat so intense it had nothing to do with the muggy air outside or the vibrant chatter filling the Taproom. This newfound awareness left me questioning: What was it about him? The proximity alone was sending my world spinning, and, quite unnervingly,

And God was I turned on!

Shifting uneasily in my seat, I tried to adjust myself discreetly, though the rush of arousal left me feeling embarrassingly like an adolescent grappling with uncontrollable hormones. I couldn't believe the moment unfolding, there was something magnetic about his quiet confidence, the way he met my teasing without retreating but without completely embracing it either. Whatever the reason, I was irrevocably hooked.

In a bold gesture, I allowed my foot to slide just a bit under the table until it brushed against his. He looked up then, his brow tilting slightly in silent inquiry, but his eyes revealed no discomfort. I offered him a playful grin, and the faint lift of his lips hinted at a smile, his version of amusement. Buoyed by his reaction, I let my foot linger there, each gentle touch unleashing tiny shocks of electricity along my skin.

By the time the history round commenced, Elliott had blossomed into his element, rattling off answers with a confident ease that filled the space between us. I cheered enthusiastically every time Maxie announced a correct response, leaning into him with exuberance as my shoulder brushed against his in celebration.

"You're a trivia wizard," I remarked in a conspiratorial tone while Maxie tallied our scores. "Why hide such a talent?"

"It's not exactly something that comes up in everyday conversation," he replied lightly, though his focused expression suggested otherwise.

"Well, consider yourself my secret weapon then," I teased with a playful punch of his shoulder. Delight sparkled in my eyes as he didn't recoil from the contact.

When Maxie finally announced our victory, the entire table erupted in jubilant cheers. Callie swept up the glittering tiara Maxie handed over and placed it atop their head with an exaggerated, theatrical bow. I turned to Elliott, raising my hand for a celebratory high-five. He hesitated for a split second before his warm palm met mine.

"See?" I said, grinning broadly. "You're far more fun than you give yourself credit for."

He ducked his head modestly. "Thanks," he said, and I swear, just for an instant, a faint blush colored his cheeks.

"Well, consider you officially promoted to team MVP," I declared, deliberately letting my knee bump his once more. This time, with a satisfying reciprocity, he bumped mine back.

The crowd began to thin as the night wound down, and the warm buzz of camaraderie lingered as Elliott, and I stepped outside. The crisp

night air was quiet, a stark contrast to the Taproom, and the distant chirping of crickets blended with the sound of Rivermere Creek.

"You have to admit," I said, bumping his arm playfully, "you had fun."

He glanced at me, a small smile playing at his lips. "It was… better than grading papers."

"High praise," I teased, laughing softly.

The silence between us was easy as we reached the point where our paths diverged. I turned to him, my grin softening. "Thanks for coming tonight," I said. "I know this isn't really your scene, but… I'm glad you were there."

"I am too," he said, his voice carrying a sincerity that made my chest ache in the best way.

"Next time," I said, letting the moment linger, "karaoke."

He raised an eyebrow, his lips twitching in amusement. "Don't push your luck."

I laughed, giving him a mock salute as I turned toward my street. But as I walked away, I couldn't help glancing back. He stood there for a moment, his hands in his pockets, watching me go. I glanced back once, catching him standing under the streetlight, his expression thoughtful as he watched me go. For a man so reserved, his presence lingered, leaving me with a flicker of curiosity that I couldn't quite shake.

8

ELLIOTT

The early April evening was cool and crisp, the golden light of the setting sun casting a glow over Havenwood as I arrived at the Havenwood Playhouse. The cobblestone sidewalks gleamed faintly under the warm amber of the streetlights. Jules had mentioned I could stop by to pick up the event poster mock-ups he had promised for the GSA's Pride Month event. I hadn't originally planned to come tonight, Sundays were usually my quiet reset days, but Jules' breezy text earlier in the afternoon had included a casual invitation that made me feel like declining would be more trouble than showing up.

Jules: *Come grab the posters tonight! I'll be at the Playhouse. Besides, you've got to see the glittery chaos I'm herding for Midsummer. You might even get inspired.*

I'd stared at the message for too long before replying tentatively.

Elliott: *I'll stop by after dinner.*

And now, standing just outside the open doors, I realized I had no idea what I was walking into.

The brick facade buzzed with vigorous activity, the grand, arched doors thrown open wide as if they were a portal to another vibrant world. Actors, crew members, and the occasional befuddled volunteer flitted in and out, their arms laden with scripts, set pieces, and, on one memorable occasion, a stray cat that darted mischievously between their hurried legs.

I hesitated at the threshold, momentarily entranced by the swirling energy before summoning the courage to step inside.

Standing just inside the threshold, I found myself overwhelmed by the sensory overload and the rich mosaic of sound and motion. My gaze was then drawn to Jules, positioned at the epicenter of the commotion. Balancing a clipboard as if it were an extension of himself, he radiated a frenetic energy that somehow managed to anchor the storm of creativity surrounding him. With expressive hand gestures and impassioned tones, he directed an actor clad in a glittering costume, his voice rising just enough to slice through the ambient noise with a blend of authority and contagious enthusiasm.

"No, no, no! Oberon needs to command the stage!" Jules exclaimed, his fervor echoing against the walls. "You're not just a fairy king; you're THE fairy king. Own it!"

In that charged moment, the actor straightened, adopting a regal bearing, and delivered their lines with newfound boldness. Jules clapped his hands together, his grin broadening into an expression of triumph as he nodded in approval. It was at that precise moment that his gaze swept over to me, where I stood awkwardly by the wall, a silent observer amidst the vibrant, living tableau.

Jules' smile widened like the spreading of a sunrise, and he bounded over with an infectious energy that seemed to ignite every corner of the room. "Look at you, Teach," he said, his voice dropping into a conspiratorial, hushed whisper that felt like a secret shared just between us. "Welcome to the glittery chaos."

I raised an eyebrow, feeling a reluctant smile tug at my lips as I absorbed the vibrant scene around us. "It's… a lot," I admitted, my voice tinged with awe.

He laughed, a sound so rich and resonant that it filled the space like warm sunlight. Nudging my arm with his clipboard, he declared, "Controlled chaos, thank you very much. There's a method to this madness." His words danced in the air, as if sprinkled with stardust.

I followed him as he gracefully weaved through the bustling space, his focus switching with a mesmerizing agility from one task to the next. Amidst the hectic demands of his role, Jules managed to find moments for everyone, a quick note scribbled on a notepad here, a sincere compliment there, a playful scolding that invariably drew bursts of laughter from the recipient. Watching him at work was like witnessing a conductor masterfully orchestrate a symphony of energy and creativity.

After a while, Jules plopped down beside me on an old, battered theater seat, its surface worn by countless performances, during a brief

lull in the whirlwind. With his clipboard precariously balanced on his knees, he turned to face me, his eyes bright and endlessly curious. "So, what do you think? Controlled chaos or just chaos?" he asked, his tone inviting me into his world.

I glanced around at the scene in all its glory: costumes spilled haphazardly from creased racks, wires tangled across the floor like reckless vines, and the half-painted set loomed in the background with an almost theatrical drama. "It's… impressive," I confessed. "You thrive in this."

Grinning wider, he reclined further into the timeworn seat. "You should try it sometime, step onstage and let loose," he urged, his voice brimming with mischief and encouragement.

I shook my head, releasing a soft, amused laugh. "I think I'll leave the herding of glittery cats to you."

His laughter rang out, unabashed and joyful, drawing indulgent smiles and fleeting glances from nearby crew members who soon returned to their tasks. Before I could add another word, a frantic stage manager appeared at Jules' elbow, relaying a hurried list of pressing issues that demanded immediate attention.

With a resigned sigh that mingled exasperation with amusement, Jules stood, casting me one last quick, infectious grin. "Hold that thought, Teach. Don't go running off," he said, disappearing back into the vibrant fray.

I lingered, watching him move with an effortless grace through the luminous chaos. This world, the noise, the glitter, the beautifully disorganized energy, was entirely foreign to me, yet Jules navigated it as if he were born from its very essence. It was utterly captivating, and I couldn't shake the sense that coming here tonight was more than just a matter of picking up posters. It was like receiving an invitation to step deeper into Jules' dazzling world, one brilliant, enchanted fragment at a time.

The first days of spring had arrived like a gentle exhale of relief. With the soft patter of April showers and the emergence of radiant sunshine and milder breezes, I found solace in the quiet moments spent among my garden beds. The late afternoon light slanted in, bathing every leaf and

petal in a warm, golden glow, its beams casting long, delicate shadows across the carefully ordered rows of aromatic herbs and vibrant flowers. A whispering breeze stirred the foliage as I knelt beside the basil bed, its verdant leaves glowing with dew as I trimmed a few sprigs and gathered them into a neat, fragrant bundle.

The rhythmic snip of the shears and the gentle rustling of leaves was meditative, turning a simple task into a cherished ritual that softened the chaotic cadence of the outside world. I had begun to weave an internal tapestry of recipes, imaginative dishes featuring the herbs, perhaps pesto, roasted potatoes, or even a daring experiment with infused oils. The garden's tranquility enveloped me like a comforting cloak, a welcome counterpoint to the ceaseless pace of the school year. In a spontaneous moment of connection, I pulled out my phone and captured the scene, sending the image off to Caleb with a lighthearted note.

Elliott: *Looking forward to you visiting for Spring Break next week and helping me with the garden!*

A sudden creak of the gate shattered the silence of my reverie. I rose, wiping the garden's fragrant traces from my hands on worn jeans, and turned toward the sound. There, framed in the rustic embrace of the weathered wooden gate, stood Jules, his ever-present tote bag casually slung over one shoulder. His outfit, a brightly colored, lively shirt paired with artfully distressed jeans, spoke of effortless vivacity, as though he carried a piece of the day's vibrancy with him.

"Wow," Jules exclaimed as he stepped gracefully through the entrance, his tone imbued with reverence. His eyes, wide with wonder, swept slowly over the garden, absorbing every meticulously arranged row of plants and the vine-draped trellis that arched gracefully above. "Okay, Teach. This is… incredible. It's like stepping into a Monet painting."

A flush of unexpected pride warmed my cheeks, and I replied modestly, "It's just a garden," though my tone betrayed the delight burrowed within me.

Jules, hardly one to miss a detail, crouched next to a lavender bush, letting his fingers gently brush the delicate purple blooms. "Don't sell yourself short. This is the very antithesis of chaos. It's… peaceful."

After a brief moment of quiet admiration, he rose and allowed his hand to linger on the lavender, as if to capture its ephemeral scent, before moving deeper into the garden. There was a deliberate calmness in his movements now, softer and more measured than usual. Watching him wander, I noted how his gaze lingered on each plant with an

unspoken reverence, contrasting strikingly with the theatrical exuberance I was used to.

"So, what brings you here?" I finally asked, breaking the silence that had settled like a soft mist.

Jules turned back at me with a playful grin, lifting his tote bag as if unveiling a secret. "I was dropping off the finalized poster designs for the Pride event, and I thought I'd deliver them in person. Callie mentioned you were the type who savors the outdoors, so I took a chance. She might have let slip where your home is." He paused, raising an eyebrow in teasing challenge. "You're lucky I'm not some unhinged superfan!"

With a raised brow, I teased in return, "Callie casually keeps tabs on where I live?"

"Not exactly," he replied with a mischievous lilt. "Apparently, you mentioned your house was near the park during one of your post-GSA meetings, and Callie, with her mind like a steel trap, didn't let that detail vanish. One offhand comment, and boom, I had your address. Honestly, you should be impressed by our teamwork."

I chuckled softly and said, "Well, welcome to my quiet little corner of the world." Just then, my phone buzzed in my pocket. Drawing it out, I couldn't help but grin as I read Caleb's text.

Caleb: *Looking good! Can't wait to see you, Dad!*

It was accompanied by a selfie of him pulling a goofy face, his tongue comically outstretched. A warm glow spread through my chest as I lingered on the image a moment longer than necessary, my smile softening with affection.

Jules resumed his wander, his fingers brushing lightly against the emerald leaves as he strolled. Upon reaching the vine-laden trellis, he leaned casually, his gaze roaming over the tranquil space. "You're really good at this," he said, his voice now soft and reflective. "It suits you."

Glancing down at the bundle of basil in my hand, I adjusted a few leaves absentmindedly. "It helps me focus. Keeps things… grounded."

He plucked a sprig of rosemary from a nearby bush and twirled it thoughtfully between his fingers. "And here I thought you were all spreadsheets and bullet points. Turns out, you're quite the plant whisperer."

Another blush unfurled across my cheeks as I looked away, a small, genuine smile tugging at my lips. "I wouldn't go that far. But I do cherish something tangible, something I can nurture and see grow."

His gaze softened further, his usually sharp, impish expression melting into something unexpectedly tender. "You know," he said, his voice lowering to an intimate whisper, "you surprise me, Elliott Brooks."

Meeting his eyes, I responded quietly, "I hope they're good surprises."

"The best kind," he replied, his smile warm and unforced, his tone imbued with a sincerity that took me aback.

For a suspended moment, neither of us moved. The garden, usually a haven of quiet routine, seemed to pulsate with a newly charged intimacy, as if the very air had woven us together in a delicate dance of connection. Then Jules straightened, breaking the fragile spell as he raised his tote bag once again. "Where do you want these posters?"

I gestured toward the sunlit porch, a bittersweet reminder of the return to routine. As Jules followed me along the winding garden path, his rich presence hovered in the air, his words echoing softly in my mind. The late afternoon sun dipped lower, streaking the sky with hues of amber and rose, and I found myself saying, "Why don't you come inside for a bit? I should wash up, and I can get us something to drink."

JULES

The invitation to step inside caught me off guard, yet it stirred an immediate eagerness. "Lead the way, Teach," I replied, my voice mingling with the aromatic tendrils of basil and rosemary that danced in the warm air. As we ascended the stone steps, an inquisitive spark flickered within me, wondering about the secrets his space might hold. His garden, arranged with meticulous care, hinted that the rest of his home might boast the same refined attention to detail.

Elliott swung the door open and beckoned me in with a graceful gesture. "Make yourself comfortable," he offered.

"Sure," I said, stepping over the threshold and instantly absorbing the interior. The cool, conditioned air provided a refreshing contrast to the lingering embrace of the day's warmth outside. Every element of the décor revealed a crisp, pristine order, the walls flaunted subtle hues of soft greys and warm beiges that lent an air of effortless composure to the home. The furniture, elegant in its understatement and clearly of the highest quality, sat purposefully arranged, each item

contributing to a tableau of calm and order. In stark opposition to the vibrant chaos of my own space, every gleaming hardwood floorboard mirrored the meticulous care taken, and not a speck of dust disturbed the symmetrical display of carefully arranged books on the shelves.

"Wow," I whispered under my breath as I trailed my fingertips along the back of the spotless sofa. "This is… very you."

A slight, amused smile played on his lips as he glanced over his shoulder. "What's that supposed to mean?"

"Clean, calm, controlled," I teased, returning his smile with a playful glimmer in my eyes. "It's like walking into the physical manifestation of your spreadsheets."

Elliott chuckled, a sound full of gentle mirth, as he made his quiet departure toward what I presumed to be the kitchen.

I drifted deeper into the living room, drawn magnetically toward a mantle resting above a softly crackling fireplace. There, a curated row of photographs in silver and black frames commanded my attention, each frame perfectly aligned like pieces of a well-told tale. The arrangement was far from the sterile precision of a catalog display, there was life in it, a warmth laden with memories waiting to be discovered. One image depicted Elliott standing beside a woman whose soft auburn hair cascaded around a cautious smile. They stood near enough to share intimacy yet maintained a respectful, deliberate distance, as though their relationship was forged with equal parts tenderness and decorum. It was not a casual snapshot; it was a carefully chosen moment.

Adjacent to it, a striking black-and-white portrait captured an older couple, their faces etched with kind lines and gentle laughter. The woman's eyes twinkled with a secret joy, and the man's subtle smile spoke of decades spent in silent understanding. But it was the photo of a boy, no more than nine or ten with light brown hair and a mischievous grin, that held me captive. His smile was wide, his front tooth endearingly crooked, and his bright expression radiated the spirit of a little rebel chasing adventures.

"Find something interesting?" Elliott's voice gently broke through my reverie, pulling me back to the present.

I turned swiftly, a blush of mild embarrassment mingling with delight. "Just admiring," I replied, nodding in the direction of the mantel. "You've got a good eye for… balance."

He shifted his gaze over the photographs, his expression unreadable yet not unkind. "I guess I like things to feel grounded," he said in a tone as measured and steady as the composed interior.

I stored away the image of that joyful boy and the tender couple, along with a growing curiosity about the lives captured in those frames. Who was the boy? Who was the couple? And what of the woman beside Elliott? I decided these questions would wait, tucked away for another time.

Elliott then reappeared with a tall glass of lemonade, condensation beading along its surface like tiny jewels. "Thanks," I said gratefully as I accepted the drink.

The first sip carried a burst of tart sweetness that sliced through the lingering heat of the day, invigorating my senses.

"You've got a nice place," I remarked, gesturing around the immaculately arranged living space. "Definitely not like my apartment."

"I can imagine," he said, his smile broadening mischievously. "Decorating isn't exactly my forte."

"Yet functionality looks pretty damn good on you," I countered, and that spark of connection returned, subtle and undeniable. I let the silence linger for a moment, savoring the interplay of cool lemonade and warm conversation while gazing out the window at the garden we had just left behind. The gentle hum of the space, combined with the steadfast calm of Elliott himself, left me with an inexplicable feeling that I was on the brink of something transformative.

Breaking the comfortable silence, Elliott gestured toward the porch. "Shall we sit outside? The light is fantastic at this time of day."

I nodded eagerly, already drawn to the serene allure of the garden. "Lead the way, Teach."

We stepped back into the embrace of the evening air, settling onto wooden chairs placed under a soft cascade of string lights that framed the roof's edge. The transition from the pristine interior to the intimate garden felt like a seamless merging of two worlds, each reflecting elements of his character: structured precision softened by inviting tranquility.

"This is really nice," I observed, reclining slightly as the cool glass rested warmly in my palm. "Do you spend much time out here?"

"As much as I can," he admitted, his voice imbued with the simple pleasure of the moment as his eyes swept across the garden. "It's... peaceful. A perfect way to end the day."

I nodded, absorbing the quiet comfort that wrapped around us like a soft blanket. The rhythmic chirping of crickets filled the spaces between our words, and for once, I found solace in that silence rather than an urge to fill it. Elliott exuded a calm steadiness, a contrast to the

vibrant, ceaseless energy that surged within me. Yet, sitting beside him, I discovered an unexpected ease.

"So," I ventured lightly, "how does a history teacher become so adept at gardening?"

A faint smile curved Elliott's lips. "Trial and error, lots of research, and," he added with a playful glint in his eye, "a spreadsheet or two."

I laughed, the sound ringing clear amid the quiet symphony of the night. "Of course. The spreadsheets. I should've guessed."

As we continued our conversation, the day yielded to night. The stars began to scatter like diamonds across the deepening sky, and the evening air grew cool and inviting. There was something in this unhurried moment, a simplicity that felt almost sacred. Although the path of our evolving connection was uncertain, I knew in my heart that I was eager to explore it further.

"You've created something really special here," I said, gesturing towards the lush garden. "It's like the mirror opposite of the Playhouse."

Elliott nodded, his eyes thoughtful as he considered my words. "I suppose that's why it works. The theater, it's vibrant, alive. Your world surges with movement. Mine... thrives on stillness."

I turned my gaze toward him, admiring the depths of his reflection in the gentle glow. "And yet, here we are, carving out a sort of unexpected middle ground."

With a tender smile, he declared, "Maybe chaos and order aren't so incompatible after all."

We lingered in silence for a while, a silence rich with unspoken understanding. I tilted my head back, letting my eyes wander to the sparkling stars above, and softly said, "Thanks for sharing this space with me, Elliott."

He regarded me with a quiet humility, the lines of his face softened by the dim light. "Thank you for reminding me there's more to life than quiet gardens." His words hung between us, a delicate truth acknowledged without fanfare.

I exhaled slowly, savoring the moment as he fixated on the stars a moment longer before shifting beside me to catch my eye. "I should probably be going," I said quietly yet firmly. "I wouldn't want to keep you from your night."

He nodded, though his hesitant pause betrayed that he wasn't entirely ready to dissolve the warm cocoon of our shared evening. Reaching for my now-empty glass, his fingertips brushed mine briefly, a touch that sent a soft, electric impulse through me. Before I could dwell

on it, he rose gracefully and motioned toward the house. "Come on, I'll walk you out."

I followed him through the softly lit kitchen, where the atmosphere had grown even cozier, as if the walls had absorbed the ease of our conversation. Approaching the front door, Elliott hesitated, rubbing the back of his neck as if weighing his words.

"Would you like to have dinner sometime?" he asked, his tone tentative and careful, clearly uncertain of my reaction.

I blinked in surprised delight, warmth spreading through me. "Yeah," I replied, the unexpectedness softening into genuine warmth. "I'd love that."

A small, content smile curved his lips. "How about Friday? Seven o'clock at Rivermere Bistro?"

"That sounds perfect," I answered, my response flowing with an ease that delighted me.

Stepping out onto the porch, I was met by an evening sky awash in deep purples and gentle pinks, the first stars delicately emerging as night took hold. I began ascending the path toward the sidewalk but couldn't help glancing back.

Elliott stood in the doorway, his thoughtful eyes following me, his gaze a quiet promise brimming with anticipation. As I turned forward again, an uncanny feeling stirred within me, an intuition that tonight had subtly altered the course of our connection.

9

ELLIOTT

The soft, honeyed glow of an April evening spilled through the expansive windows of Rivermere Bistro, bathing the room in a warm, golden radiance that danced over polished surfaces and rustic wooden accents alike. Every detail of the establishment exuded an air of refined yet effortless sophistication; dark wood and smooth marble blended with plush seating in a way that invited both quiet reflection and friendly conversation. Outside, delicate string lights crisscrossed the patio like celestial threads, their gentle luminescence framing an unobstructed view of Rivermere Creek, whose water meandered lazily as if whispering secrets to the night. In the background, soft jazz notes floated like hums in the air, mingling seamlessly with the subtle clink of glassware and the low hum of intimate chatter.

I was seated at a small table illuminated by the soft flicker of a single candle near the window, where I idly swirled the cubed ice in my water glass, watching it spin slowly as if measuring time in transient reflections. The memory of the previous evening, charged with an exhilarating and almost otherworldly lightness brought on by Jules, played over in my mind. His laugh, a sound that held both warmth and mischief, his extravagant but expressive gestures, and the way his voice had transformed my once quiet porch into a stage for possibility, all of it repeated on a continuous loop behind closed eyelids.

When I finally drifted off, my dreams betrayed my thoughts in vivid, carnal detail.

In the dream, Jules' laugh had morphed into soft moans, his touch electric, his body pressed against mine in a way that felt too real. I woke up tangled in my sheets, my erection aching and persistent. The memory of the dream made my chest tighten with equal parts longing and shame. Should I be thinking this way about Jules? Should I want him this much? My dick certainly didn't seem interested in waiting for answers, it pulsed insistently as I lay there, fighting the temptation to… relieve myself.

Not usually a morning sex guy, I let out a frustrated sigh and gave in to the need that had been building up inside me. My hand wrapped around my cock, feeling its warmth and hardness as I began to stroke it slowly. The thought of Jules' soft moans and electric touch flooded my mind, sending shivers down my spine and straight to my groin. I closed my eyes and let myself get lost in the fantasy, imagining what it would be like to have Jules' hands on me, his lips on mine.

As I jerked off, my mind wandered to all the things I wanted to do with Jules; the way I wanted to kiss him, touch him, feel him against me. My cock leaked precum while my strokes grew faster and more urgent as the images played out in my head. I gripped my cock tighter as I could almost smell Jules' scent, feel his warm breath on my skin. My cock throbbed in response, begging for release.

I bit back a groan as I came closer to climax, trying not to make too much noise as I worked myself over. But it was no use. The tension built up inside me until it finally burst free, spilling out first in a shot that hit my face then more onto my chest and stomach as I let out a stifled cry of pleasure. For a moment, all other thoughts disappeared, replaced by pure sensation and relief.

As the aftershocks subsided and reality began to creep back in, I felt a twinge of guilt for fantasizing so easily. But another part of me just lay there feeling spent but calm knowing that for now at least that need was taken care of. I got up and went to the bathroom to shower and begin my day.

The small mercy of spring break starting today when school ended was that I wouldn't have to get up for work for a week. With just a couple of days left until Caleb arrives, I'd napped in the afternoon, hoping to clear my head, but now, sitting here at the bistro, waiting for Jules, the memory of that dream and my early morning lingered like an uninvited guest. I adjusted my glasses, taking a calming breath just as the front door swung open.

Jules' presence filled the space with an unmistakable energy even before his face emerged from the twilight haze. He carried himself effortlessly in a breezy button-up shirt adorned with a bold, vibrant floral print that perfectly mirrored the spark of his personality. His eyes, playful and instantly inviting, scanned the room until they found mine. With a graceful wave and an apologetic grin that softened the impact of his tardiness, he glided through the maze of tables straight towards me.

"Sorry, sorry," Jules mumbled, sliding seamlessly into the chair opposite me with the kind of casual ease that belied his evident haste. Thankful I didn't have to stand up to greet him with my cock still at attention from my thoughts before his arrival. "Traffic on Rivermere Drive was a nightmare. I mean, who knew this many people craved overpriced cocktails on a Monday?" he continued, his tone light despite the familiar frustration in his eyes.

I met his apology with a soft smile that warmed the space between us. "No need to apologize," I assured him, my words gentle as I allowed myself to absorb the sight of him in full, radiant presence. "I just arrived a little early."

Jules' gaze roamed appreciatively over the intimate interior, absorbing the interplay of warm lighting and rustic decor. "This place is gorgeous. Do they really think that the phrase 'farm-to-table' is some sort of incantation that magically elevates everything?" he remarked with an amused tilt of his head.

I chuckled, shaking my head lightly. "Possibly," I teased, "but trust me, the food truly is out of this world."

Leaning forward, Jules rested his chin casually on his hand as he perused the menu with genuine curiosity. "You're really setting the bar, Teach. A candlelit dinner at a fancy bistro, it's definitely a far cry from the Green Bean Cafe. Are you trying to impress me?" His question hung in the air, playful yet laced with an undercurrent of inquiry.

Caught slightly off guard by his candid tone, I managed a teasing smile. "Is it working?" I asked, my voice light even as my heart pounded a bit faster.

His smile deepened in response. "I'll let you know after dessert," he replied, a promise of further intrigue lingering in his words.

It was at that moment that our waiter approached; a figure of impeccable service with an easy, professional smile that seemed to brighten even more the effervescent ambiance of the bistro. "Good evening," he greeted in a crisp tone. "I'm Evan, and I'll be taking care of you tonight. Have you had a chance to peer over the menu, or would you like a few extra moments?" His black uniform, pressed to perfection, and

the white apron tied snugly at his waist, spoke of a meticulous professionalism that was as appealing as his neatly styled dark hair and warm, inviting smile.

Jules exchanged a glance with me, then set his menu aside with a confident air. "I think we're ready. What would you recommend?" he inquired, his voice carrying the quiet ease of someone who enjoyed life's well-planned surprises.

Evan's eyes lit up as he launched into an engaging description of the night's specials. His tone was equal parts conversational and refined as he spoke of salmon brushed with a delicate lemon and dill glaze, a summer salad brimming with heirloom tomatoes, and a cocktail artfully crafted from fresh basil and muddled strawberries. Jules ordered the salmon with an unmistakable gleam of anticipation, while I settled on the timeless comfort of a steak frites, classic, secure, and as dependable as the sunset.

As Evan retreated with promises of a seamless service, his confident stride and attentive demeanor left an indelible impression, a subtle dance of glances ensuring every guest felt valued. Jules leaned back, his eyes settling on me with an earnest warmth that sent delightful shivers along my skin. "Well, Evan is a real cutie, isn't he?" I laughed, the comment light and genuine. "So, how excited are you for spring break?"

"You have no idea," I replied, though the phrase carried a double meaning, mirroring not just the anticipated break from routine but also the whirlwind of thoughts and emotions that Jules stirred within me.

Jules, his fingers idly toying with the edge of his napkin, remarked thoughtfully, "Your garden is magical, Teach, like something plucked from a dream." His words, imbued with tenderness, drew a rush of unwanted recollections of that steamy, vivid vision from my sleep. "Thank you," I muttered softly, the compliment a fragile shield against the storm of conflicted feelings. "It's my way of keeping everything grounded."

He chuckled gently, his eyes flicking to mine. "You use that word so much, 'grounded.' Maybe it's something I could use more of in my own chaotic life."

His candid observation hung between us, a delicate bridge over our shared silences. My fingers absentmindedly adjusted my glasses as I inhaled deeply, the musty aroma of candle wax and the faint citrus of my water blending with the ambient perfume of the bistro. Just then, our drinks arrived. Jules' cocktail shimmered like summer captured in a glass, a vivid red elixir kissed with basil, while my water, clear and unassuming, sat almost sorrowfully beside it.

"This," Jules said, holding his glass aloft in a quiet toast, "is why I forgive all that pretentious farm-to-table marketing." The clink of our glasses, water to cocktail, resonated warmly as Jules leaned in, his knee accidentally, or perhaps deliberately, brushing softly against mine under the table. The contact was subtle yet insistent, a quiet reminder of our decreasing distance that sent a spark cascading up my leg, tightening both my focus and my attire. I wondered, with a mix of bemusement and innocence, if I were regressing to that adolescent state when even the gentlest breeze had the power to awaken longing.

Jules' gaze lingered on me, softening from a playful smirk into something tender and unguarded. "I'm truly glad you invited me tonight, Elliott," he said sincerely.

"I'm glad you came," I responded, my words earnest despite the lingering echoes of the earlier dream and physical desire. For just a moment, the tumult of the bistro fell away, leaving only our private bubble of intimacy.

Jules stirred his cocktail, the vivid red liquid swirling around the basil sprig that bobbed delicately at its surface. His wildflower-print shirt, usually bursting with restless energy, seemed to have adopted a more reflective tone against the warm hues of the evening. He rested his chin on one hand as he regarded me, his eyes making a quiet, teasing proposal. "You've got that contemplative look, Teach," he observed, his tone playful yet imbued with a perceptive curiosity. "As if there's a profound history lesson waiting to be unlocked in that head of yours. Spill."

I couldn't help but laugh softly, shaking my head as I met his expectant gaze. "Not a history lesson," I began, my voice dropping to a more confidential register, "more like something personal."

His eyes softened further, and he leaned in just a fraction, the space between us charged with a silent promise of understanding. "I'm all ears," he said, his voice a steady harbor in the sea of emotion.

I paused, gathering the scattered pieces of my narrative like carefully chosen words on a precipice. Earlier that evening, while Jules had visited my space, I had caught the way his eyes lingered on cherished family photos, one featuring Caleb's infectious, gap-toothed grin alongside another of me and my ex-wife, both smiling with cautious hope. Jules' quiet curiosity had spoken volumes without a single inquiry. Now, I felt compelled to unveil that part of my story. I lowered my eyes to the condensation gathering on my water glass and, with a steadying breath, began, "I didn't come out until my late thirties. For most of my life, I lived as everyone expected, a dutiful husband to my college sweetheart, building a life that from the outside appeared flawless."

Jules listened intently, his brow furrowing ever so slightly as if absorbing every weighty syllable without judgment. His presence in that moment made my confession feel less burdensome. "It wasn't fair to her," I continued, my voice tightening around the raw memories. "I thought I could become the person everyone wanted me to be. But as the days passed, my true self began to suffocate under the relentless pressure of expectations."

The silence that followed was heavy and resonant with unspoken regret, fragile from years of hidden truths. My fingers tightened their grip on the glass as I admitted, "When I finally told her the truth, it felt as if I was shattering both our worlds. The guilt still clings to me, and sometimes I wonder whether I waited too long, or if in trying to be someone else, I betrayed both of us."

Jules reached out gently, his hand hovering above mine on the table, a warm, silent reassurance that bridged the space between our vulnerabilities. "Hey," he said softly, his words a gentle caress, "you're not a failure, Elliott. We're all just pieces in the process of becoming who we're meant to be."

His affirmation soaked into me like a soothing balm. I locked eyes with him, his gaze reflecting understanding and an acceptance that mirrored my own fragility. "You did what you could with what you knew then," Jules continued, "and now you're here, brave enough to show up. That takes courage."

With a slow nod, I swallowed the lump in my throat and whispered, "Thank you." The intimacy of our shared honesty mingled with the evolving flavors of the evening, softening the edges of past regrets. After a measured pause, I ventured further, "One of the hardest parts wasn't just ending my marriage. It was navigating the most important relationship of my life."

Jules tilted his head, his voice gentle as he probed, "Who's that?"

"My son, Caleb," I said quietly, my tone brimming with both love and trepidation. "He's twelve now, and he's the greatest gift I've ever received. When I came out, I feared the changes it would bring, worried about the way it might alter the way he looked at me."

Jules' eyes widened slightly in recognition, his gaze softening as he pieced together the hints from the cherished photos. "The boy in the picture, with that infectious grin," he remarked gently.

A tender smile crept onto my face as I affirmed, "That's him. Caleb is full of life, his curiosity boundless, and he's been my anchor through every storm. I see him one weekend a month during the school year, and we share daily conversations. With spring break around the

corner, he'll be joining me soon. The longer summer stretches when he stays with me… those moments truly make every sacrifice worthwhile."

Jules' expression glowed with admiration. "It sounds like you've cultivated something incredibly special," he said. "An unbreakable bond."

"I can only hope so," I confessed softly. "Caleb's happiness means everything to me. While I'm still traversing the uncertain terrain of my own life, being his dad is one certainty I'll never regret."

His hand still hovered close, and with comforting sincerity, Jules said, "You're an amazing dad, Elliott." The conviction in his voice struck a deep chord within me, easing some of the weight of my own self-doubt.

As our conversation deepened, the bustling bistro seemed to recede into a gentle blur until only the shared cadence of our words and the soft jazz in the background remained. Jules eventually shifted the focus back to his own journey. "So, what about you, Jules? What brought you back to Havenwood after all those years?" I inquired, my attention fully anchored in his vulnerability.

He took a moment, tracing his finger along the rim of his cocktail glass, the sound of its gentle clink blending with a quiet sigh. "I burned out in the relentless rhythm of the city," he admitted softly. "The protests, the relentless organizing, the ceaseless battles, they were devouring me from within. I kept pushing, tormented by the belief that pausing meant betraying everyone counting on me."

A pause stretched between us before he continued, "Then I hit a wall. One day, I awoke unable to rise from bed, gripped by a fear so raw it scared me to my core. I ran back here, to Havenwood, hoping to rediscover a version of myself I'd almost lost."

I nodded in a palpable silence. "And?" I prompted gently.

A wry smile played on his lips as he confessed, "I'm still figuring it out. I've always been a whirlwind, leaping from one passion to the next. It's part of my nature, but sometimes I wonder if it's merely a way to keep true intimacy at bay."

"You're afraid of losing who you are," I said, the observation slipping out before I could refine it further.

"Yeah," he replied quietly, a brief flash of vulnerability in his eyes. "Exactly."

In that shared silence, the air between us thickened with our intertwined secrets and unspoken hopes. Jules broke the tension with a disarming laugh. "Well, that got deep fast," he quipped, his smile returning with a spark of mischief. "Is there a tipping scale for emotional oversharing, or should I simply add it to the tab?"

I managed a smirk, replying, "Probably, but tonight feels like one of those rare nights where vulnerability is perfectly acceptable."

His laughter filled the moment with warmth as he said, "Thanks for listening, Teach. And thanks for sharing. I think we're both pretty good at this whole vulnerability thing."

As our entrees arrived, our conversation flowed effortlessly between light-hearted banter and reflective musings, a delicate rhythm of connection that seemed to make the world around us recede into a gentle, comforting hum. After lingering over dessert and a few more drinks, the natural finale of the evening approached. Despite Jules' playful protests against paying for everything, I insisted on taking care of the bill. Evan, our attentive waiter, wished us goodnight with a wink and promised that next time we'd be on his priority list.

Stepping out of the bistro into the velvety embrace of the night, we were greeted by a world transformed, the creek's soft babble intermingled with the distant hum of the town, each cobblestone path and string of fairy lights painting the scene with magic. "I think Evan might have been part of the family," I remarked quietly.

Jules laughed, the sound light and teasing with sarcasm. "You think so?"

We ambled along the cobblestone pathways lining the riverfront district, our conversation softening as if the night itself encouraged a more measured pace. Occasional couples drifted by, their laughter mingling with the rustle of leaves in the gentle breeze, as if sharing our private delight in the enchantment of the evening.

I found it hard to believe the night would surrender to its end, and by the way Jules kept naturally leaning closer as we walked side by side, it was clear he felt the same. Our voices fell into a comfortable cadence, a rhythmic blend of quiet observations and reflective silences. "This place feels utterly magical at night," Jules said softly, his voice carrying an intimacy that made my heart flutter. Bathed in the warm glow of a nearby streetlamp, his profile took on an almost ethereal quality. "I'm really glad you invited me tonight, Teach."

A genuine smile tugged at my lips as I slowly shoved my hands into my pockets. "Me too. It's been so long since I've felt this relaxed, so unburdened."

With a playful tilt of his head and a mischievous smirk, Jules teased, "You mean to say you don't get a thrill from grading essays?"

I chuckled, shaking my head in amusement. "Not quite that kind of thrill."

Our meandering eventually brought us to a small lookout where the river expanded gracefully, its surface mirroring the crescent moon and a scatter of twinkling stars overhead. Jules leaned against the railing, his arms folded loosely, his vibrant scarf fluttering lightly in the cool, nocturnal breeze. I stood beside him, close enough to share his warmth yet careful to respect the delicate balance of our space.

For a suspended moment, the world fell into stillness, and as if guided by an unspoken understanding, Jules turned towards me. His expression was open, his eyes filled with the sort of tender inquiry that made my pulse quicken. "Elliott," he said softly, his voice carrying a weight both gentle and profound, "I've been trying to figure out how to say this better, but… tonight was really nice. You are really nice."

I swallowed hard, meeting his searching gaze with equal vulnerability. "I feel the same," I admitted, the quiet truth tumbling out in a whisper that vibrated with sincerity.

The charged silence thickened, making the air between us vibrate with unspoken possibilities. In a heartbeat, Jules closed the remaining distance between us, his hand brushing tenderly against my arm. His eyes searched mine, a momentary flash of hesitance mingling with desire. And then, in that incandescent moment, he kissed me.

It began as a soft, tentative meeting of lips, a gentle press that sent a shiver spiraling down my spine. I stood frozen for a heartbeat, overwhelmed by the delicate sweetness of his gesture, until instinct took over. My hand lifted to cradle his jaw as I returned the kiss, a deepening passion that transformed the gentle encounter into a more intense communion of desire. Jules leaned into me, his body melding close, the warmth radiating through our layers of clothing, igniting every fiber of my being. The mingling heat, the barely concealed arousal that pulsed between us, and the shared breath created an atmosphere densely charged with longing.

Then, with a sudden, deliberate inhale, I forced myself to pull back, the abrupt break punctuated by a sigh of both surprise and reflection. My hands rested softly on his shoulders as I gently reestablished a tentative distance. Jules blinked, his parted lips and quickening breath betraying the intensity of the moment.

"Jules," I managed, my voice uneven as I gathered myself, "I…I…"

He stepped back slightly, his cheeks flushing with a mix of embarrassment and desire. "I'm sorry," he said quickly, regret tinting his tone. "I didn't mean to…"

"No, don't apologize," I interjected, letting my hands fall to my sides as I steadied my racing thoughts. "I liked it. A lot. I just…" I ran a hand through my hair, pausing to look into his eyes, "I don't want to rush this. I don't want to screw something up by diving in headfirst."

Jules' expression softened into an understanding smile that radiated warmth. "You're a good man, Elliott Brooks," he said, his voice imbued with care and certainty. "I get it. Slow is good."

I exhaled deeply, releasing the tension that had built up, and replied, "Thank you. And just so you know…" I hesitated just a moment longer before a small smile broke through the uncertainty. "That kiss was incredible."

He laughed, a sound that melted away the lingering tension, his eyes twinkling with relief. "Good to know," he replied, playfully readjusting his scarf as if to reassert the lightness of our banter.

We both subtly shifted, adjusting the tightness in our pants while avoiding eye contact, and the shared awkwardness brought a hint of levity back to the moment. We both laughed.

"I guess we should call it a night," I mused, though the thought of parting from him was unexpectedly cruel.

Jules nodded, his face still holding that familiar gentle expression. "Yeah. But this was... something," he said, his tone redolent with gratitude and hope.

"It was," I agreed, the truth palpable between us.

As we eventually strolled back to the edge of the district, our hands brushed intermittently, a fleeting tactile conversation that hinted at closeness without overstepping boundaries. At the crossroads where our separate paths would diverge, Jules hesitated, then offered a warm, lingering smile. "Goodnight, Teach," he said softly, his voice a gentle benediction in the cool night air.

"Goodnight, Jules," I replied, watching his figure slowly meld into the night as his colorful scarf caught the silver gleam of the moonlight.

Walking home later, my lips still tingling with the memory of that kiss, a furtive storm of emotions churned within me, a delicate mixture of warmth, exhilaration, and a trembling undercurrent of fear. Something indefinable had shifted between us, a promise of something real and untamed that both thrilled and terrified me in equal measure. The prospect of surrendering to that possibility felt as daring as stepping onto a precarious bridge, uncertain whether it could bear the weight of my hopes. Part of me yearned to let go completely, to fall into the embrace of this burgeoning connection, while another part trembled at the

thought of ruining what little magic had begun to blossom between us.

10

JULES

The Green Bean Café pulsed with its usual Saturday midday rhythm, a delectable symphony of sounds that danced through the air. Baristas called out orders in a smooth, practiced cadence over the buzz of animated conversation, accompanied by the delicate hiss of the espresso machine and the sporadic clink of mugs and saucers. Sunlight poured through the expansive windows, splashing warm, golden patterns onto the polished hardwood floor, while the inviting aroma of freshly ground coffee wove a gentle spell around every patron. I thrived in environments like this, where energy swirled in vibrant, unpredictable patterns, as if life itself were performing a spontaneous dance full of promise. Before me lay an open sketchbook, its pages a riotous collection of rough costume designs and hastily scrawled notes from an early morning brainstorm.

An iced latte, its glass slowly beaded with condensation, rested alluringly within reach, droplets lazily trickling down its sides before pooling on the table like tiny mirrors. My leg tapped restlessly against the chair as I added another intricate flourish to Titania's gown, the scratch of my pencil on paper keeping perfect time with the upbeat ambience of the café.

The soft jingle of the door snapped my focus back to my sketch, and instinctively, I looked up. There he was, Elliott, a presence that filled the doorway with quiet intensity. With his book neatly tucked under one arm and a sharp gaze that measured every detail of the controlled

commotion around him, he exuded a relaxed confidence that made him seem entirely at home. Today, he wore a casual navy polo paired with khaki shorts that subtly accentuated lean, strong legs I hadn't noticed before, and his glasses sat perfectly on his nose. His effortless style sent a flutter racing through my chest.

"Hey, Teach!" I called cheerfully, waving him over with an exuberant smile that widened as his lips curved into the faintest, knowing smile. "Just in time."

Navigating gracefully through the bustling café, Elliott approached with his customary calm, setting his book down with deliberation before seating himself across from me. "In time for what?" he inquired in a measured tone, though a twitch of curiosity danced at the corner of his mouth.

I closed my sketchbook with a flourish, leaning forward as excitement bubbled up. "An adventure," I said, my eyes sparkling. "Havenwood Hills, gorgeous weather, breathtaking views, and a trail that leads to the perfect spot to watch the sunset."

Elliott's eyebrow arched skeptically as he glanced at the book he'd just placed on the table. His lips pressed together in thought, and I could almost hear the silent workings of his mind. "Today?" he asked, the word laced with an uncertain edge.

"Yes, today!" I insisted, practically dancing in my seat. "Right now, actually."

He hesitated, glancing at his watch as though it offered an escape from spontaneity. "I had… plans," he began carefully, his tone tinged with a sincere apology. "Caleb arrives tomorrow, there's cleaning, errands to run. What about our planning meeting"

"Oh, come on," I interrupted with a dismissive wave of my hand. "Cleaning can wait and we can chat on the trails. Trust me. You won't regret it." His shoulders tensed and his eyes dropped to his hands still resting on the table, a silent debate playing out in soft flickers. My smile never wavered as I radiated the kind of infectious optimism that I hoped might draw him into my orbit. Slowly, his gaze softened; it wasn't just logistics he was weighing, but whether to be swept up in my world.

He sighed, a sound heavy with reluctant resignation. "One hike," he conceded at last, his words wrapped in soft reluctance yet warmer than moments before.

I clapped my hands together in triumph and leaned back with a playful flourish. "That's the spirit!"

As I scrambled to tuck my sketches back into my tote bag, a surge of adrenaline electrified me at the thought of dragging Elliott into a

spontaneous escapade. Sure, our dynamic had been a bit off since that lingering kiss, with occasional awkward pauses hanging between us, but I wasn't about to let that dampen the day. If anything, it made me want to double down on the joy of stepping out of routine, to remind him how exhilarating life could be when you abandoned the script.

Stepping outside, we were immediately greeted by the Mid-April day, a blast of warmth that enveloped us like a tangible wall. The sun reigned overhead, its rays shimmering off the sun-warmed pavement and transforming the distant, cool refuge of the café into a fading memory. I tilted my head back, relishing the warmth as it spread over me, while Elliott, ever the picture of composure, adjusted his glasses and ran a hand through his hair.

"Alright, Teach," I said with a wide grin as I fell into step beside him, "prepare to have your mind blown. Havenwood Hills awaits."

It seemed as if any lingering doubts in his eyes were melting away as the trail and the sunset beckoned, demanding we seize the moment and etch this day into memory.

The sun hung high in the sky, speckling the dense canopy of trees in Havenwood Hills with dappled, golden light as I bounded forward along the rugged trail. Every step crunched rhythmically on uneven gravel, a natural beat to accompany the lively hum of spring, a delicate rustling of leaves stirred by a playful breeze, the varied trill of birds exchanging enchanting melodies, and the distant, soothing trickle of a hidden creek. It was a day that seemed to insist on being lived fully, in all its unguarded, imperfect glory.

Mid-stride, I spun around, my boots skidding slightly as I faced Elliott. The trail behind me rose gently, bathed in soft, light filtered through the trees. A few paces behind, Elliott moved with his usual deliberate caution, each step calculated as though he were meticulously assessing every patch of uneven ground. His hands were buried deep in the pockets of his practical jeans, and his lips were drawn tight in a firm, unreadable line.

"See?" I called out, throwing my arms wide to encompass the boundless, evergreen expanse around us. "Isn't this better than being cooped up indoors?"

Elliott turned his gaze toward me, his face a study in ambivalence with only a subtle furrow forming between his brows. His eyes then shifted back to the trail ahead, and his shoulders tensed slightly. "It's nice," he admitted after a measured pause, his tone clipped, "but I wish I'd known about this sooner. I could've planned for it."

A laugh bubbled from my lips, echoing warmly off the trees as I tried to bridge the sudden silence. "Where's the fun in that?" I teased playfully, spinning to face forward once more. "The best moments in life are the ones that catch you off guard."

For me, the truth of those words was unmistakable. But when I glanced back over my shoulder, I saw that Elliott's pace had slowed until he stood rooted in the middle of the trail. The space between us felt charged with unspoken tension, the sunlight seemed dimmer now, filtered through a canopy of conflicted emotions.

"Not everything can be spur-of-the-moment, Jules," he said, his words deliberate and carefully considered. His hands emerged from his pockets as if to anchor himself in our rapidly shifting dynamic.

"It's just a hike," I replied softly, uncertainty creeping into my tone as I struggled to understand the sudden shift in mood, the sharp undercurrent in his voice.

"It's not… just that," he hesitated, weighing each word. "I'm trying, but these last-minute plans throw me off. I need to know what I'm stepping into."

His words struck me not with cruelty, but with a deliberate precision that stung. I crossed my arms defensively, bristling at the distance that now seemed to stretch between us. "Sorry for trying to have fun," I snapped, my voice hardening. "Not everything requires a neatly penciled-in plan, you know."

"And not everything is simple to jump into," he replied, his tone steady yet still cutting enough to leave a mark. "I didn't say no, I came, Jules. I'm here."

In that moment, the gap between us felt cavernous, a chasm formed by clashing worlds and the weight of unmet expectations. I turned away, staring up the trail as a tightening in my chest reminded me of our differences. The once harmonious symphony of birds and rustling leaves now filled the silence with an almost overwhelming intensity.

"I didn't realize this would be such a chore for you," I mumbled finally, my voice soft with hurt.

A pause stretched behind me, thick with the heavy residue of unspoken words. When Elliott finally spoke, his tone was gentler, imbued with a quiet regret. "It's not a chore. I just… need a moment to catch up, that's all."

"Let's just finish the hike," I said flatly, swallowing the lump of emotion rising in my throat as I resumed my pace along the trail.

Every crunch of gravel beneath my boots drowned out any attempt at further dialogue. My mind whirled with a medley of emotions,

hurt, frustration, and stubborn hope, as I forced myself to focus on the path ahead, each step a determined rebellion against the heaviness in my chest.

At the hill's summit, the clearing unfurled before me like a vivid dream. The valley below was bathed in the molten gold of a setting sun, its rays stretching lazily across the landscape as if painting an impressionist masterpiece. Shadows of trees danced gently with the breeze, and the rich, earthy aroma of pine and damp soil mingled perfectly with the cooling air. The soft, enveloping light wrapped the world in a serene glow, yet I found myself barely registering its beauty, my thoughts still tangled in the ache of Elliott's words.

I lowered myself onto a flat rock near the clearing's edge, drawing my knees close in a gesture that tried to shield me from the internal storm raging within. The view before me begged for awe, yet all I could feel was an inward heaviness that made breathing seem oddly difficult.

Behind me, the restrained crunch of Elliott's footsteps on the trail grew steadily nearer. He moved deliberately, each step intentional and cautious. Eventually, he halted a few feet away, and for a long moment, I feared he might choose to remain distant. Instead, his gentle voice cut through the silence.

"You're not a burden, Jules."

I kept my gaze fixed on the far horizon, the words hanging in the air like a fragile promise. "Sometimes it feels like I am," I confessed softly, the steady cadence of my voice belying the tightness in my chest. "Like my… spontaneity is too overwhelming for some people. Like I am too much."

I sensed him stepping closer, the sound of his boots on the soft dirt grounding my swirling emotions. He settled onto the rock beside me, his presence a tentative solace despite the palpable tension still between us.

"It's not too much," he said quietly, his voice gentle and sincere. "It's just… different from what I'm used to."

I finally turned to him, my frustration bubbling over unexpectedly. "And your need to control every little detail?" I challenged, the edge in my tone sharper than I had intended. "Sometimes it feels suffocating."

His jaw clenched slightly, and for a heartbeat, an array of emotions, anger, guilt, longing, flashed across his face before he diverted his gaze downward. "I don't mean to make you feel that way," he explained, his voice softening into genuine contrition. "I'm trying to understand… but it's hard."

A bitter laugh escaped me, shaking my head as I looked back toward the breathtaking view. "And maybe I need someone to slow me down," I admitted, my voice softening to a confessional tone. "But I don't want to feel like I'm being judged for who I am."

He turned fully to face me, his steady, earnest eyes searching mine. "I'm not judging you," he said firmly yet gently, "I'm just… trying to find my footing. You are not too much."

The sincerity in his words loosened some of the tension coiled tight inside me. Though the discord between us had not vanished entirely, it shifted now, a quieter, more vulnerable connection emerging from the shared moment.

I glanced back at the horizon, where the colors deepened into sumptuous shades of orange and pink. "We're not so bad at this whole compromising thing, are we?" I ventured lightly, teasing as if to test the balance of our fragile truce.

A small, tentative smile tugged at the corners of his lips, and he exhaled a long, soft breath. "Maybe we're just a work in progress," he admitted.

Moving closer, he settled beside me on the sun-warmed rock. In that intimate moment, for the first time since the hike began, I felt as though we were in synchrony, a fragile alliance mending the fissures of our differences.

"I can live with that," I replied, my tone lightening as it carried a quiet honesty that resonated between us.

Silence fell for a spell, but it was not oppressive; rather, it was warm and complete, much like the golden light that embraced the hills around us. For a while, it was simply us and the mesmerizing view, a temporary reprieve from the chaos of our conflicting worlds and the uncertainties that loomed ahead.

Then, softly, I felt the brush of his hand against mine, a tentative, cautious touch that carried the weight of unspoken understanding. When his fingers gently wrapped around mine, the contact was comforting, a silent testament to the bond that persisted despite our differences. I glanced over, catching the profile of his face bathed in the molten glow of the falling sun, and I needed no words; the moment spoke volumes.

As the sun sank lower, its last rays stretching languidly across the valley and drawing long shadows from the trees, I finally exhaled a small, contented sigh. "We should head back before darkness fully settles in."

He nodded softly, releasing my hand gradually as we prepared to stand. The walk back down the trail was quieter, the vibrant tension replaced by a tentative calm. The rhythmic crunch of our boots on the

earth and the occasional whisper of rustling leaves created a soothing cadence that seemed to ease the weight of all that had been unsaid.

For all our differences and the occasional clashes, something indefinable about Elliott steadied me, perhaps even as much as I was beginning to ground him. And in that delicate interplay of strengths and flaws, I felt hopeful that, in some intricate way, we were each slowly finding our footing.

11

ELLIOTT

The morning air was cool and crisp, carrying a subtle hint of dewy dampness as I stood on the front porch. The smell of freshly turned earth mingled with the delicate aroma of early spring as I waited, every breath filled with an undercurrent of hopeful anticipation. A small, brisk breeze toyed with the collar of my jacket, its fleeting caresses unable to quell the bubbling excitement within me. For the last two years, Spring break with Caleb has been a burst of brilliance in my otherwise routine academic year, a full week of uninterrupted closeness with my son, free from the constraints of school, lesson plans, and the endless interruptions of everyday life.

The past week had been tense, Jules and I had barely spoken since the fight during our hike, exchanging only the most functional and curt texts about the playhouse production. My phone buzzed in my pocket occasionally, but it wasn't him. Not that I was expecting it. I think we were giving each other space as we navigated his demands at work and my preparations for my week with Caleb.

I spotted Anna's car turning as it rounded the corner and turning onto my quiet street. I straightened up instinctively, tucking my hands into my pockets as I watched it pull gently into the driveway. The familiar blue sedan was a welcome sight as it pulled into the driveway. Even before the car had come to a complete stop, Caleb had already burst forth from it, his energy causing him to practically leap out as he ran towards

me with an exuberant grin that stretched wide across his face, making him seem even taller than I remembered.

"Dad!" he called out joyfully, his voice carrying both warmth and eagerness as he jogged over. I met him halfway and wrapped him in a quick, firm hug, inhaling a faint mix of peppermint gum and the fresh, earthy scent of the outdoors with the faintest hint of fabric softener, a reminder of his endless energy and restless spirit.

Caleb stepped back, adjusting the strap of his duffle bag with a conspiratorial smile. "You ready for the best spring break ever?"

"Always," I replied with a smile that mirrored his own. "Go on inside and settle in. I'll be right behind you."

As he bounded up the front steps and vanished into the house, Anna emerged from the car. Her auburn hair cascaded in a loose ponytail, and her soft, knowing smile was complemented by her casual posture as she rested one hand in the pocket of her cozy coat.

"He's been looking forward to this all month," she observed with a gentle, almost wistful tone, leaning against the car as if it were an old friend.

"Same here," I admitted, my eyes following Caleb's retreat through the front door. Then, gesturing toward the welcoming entrance, I added, "Do you want to come in for a minute? You're welcome to."
Anna hesitated, her smile softening into a tender yet apologetic expression. "Thanks, but I really should get going. I don't want to take up your time with Caleb."

I nodded, though a part of me silently wished she would linger a little longer. Anna had the remarkable ability to pierce through my muddled thoughts, her presence always a consoling force I rarely allowed myself to acknowledge. Respecting her boundaries and our shared focus on Caleb, I let the moment pass. She studied me with her sharp, kind eyes, which narrowed slightly as if trying to read the hidden layers behind my tired gaze.

"You look… tired. Is work wearing you down or is it something else?" she asked softly.

I paused, my internal debate waging over how much to reveal. Anna and I had carefully rebuilt our friendship after the divorce; though the embers of romance had long since cooled, there remained a deep-seated trust and care between us. Yet, certain subjects, like Jules, remained locked away, my heart still gripped by lingering guilt and memories I wasn't ready to share. "It's a mix," I finally said. "School's been fine, and the GSA is really thriving, but… there have been some other things. Complicated stuff."

"Complicated," she echoed as she tilted her head, eyes inquisitive. "Would that have anything to do with a particular friend of yours? The one Caleb briefly mentioned at dinner the other night? Jules?"

Her unexpected question caught me off guard. "Caleb mentioned Jules?"

Anna nodded, her tone both casual and curious. "He said you had a friend from the theatre you were working with. You know, he's pretty perceptive, Elliott. He notices more than you think."

I exhaled slowly, crossing my arms against the cool morning air. "Jules and I… it's been rocky. We're collaborating on the GSA project, and we haven't been seeing eye to eye on a lot of things. But this week isn't about that, it's about Caleb."

Her expression softened further, an unspoken understanding shining in her eyes despite the fleeting hint of concern. "If anyone can compartmentalize, it's you. Just don't shut out everything else, okay? You deserve more than just work and co-parenting."

Her words lingered in the crisp air as she straightened and glanced up at the house. "He's happy, you know. He really loves spending time with you."

"And I love my time with him," I replied quietly.

She smiled, delivering a quick hug before turning back to her car. "Have fun, Elliott. And tell Caleb I'll call him midweek to check in."

I nodded and waved as her car melted away down the street, the faint hum of its engine gradually fading into silence. I lingered on the porch a moment longer, attuned to the soft, rustling sound of Caleb rummaging through his belongings inside.

Soon after, Caleb emerged again, his goofy grin still plastered on his face as he greeted me. "So, what's the plan?" he asked brightly as I stepped into the house behind him.

Locking the door behind us, I replied, "Well, you've got two options: we can go camping for a few days, hiking, fishing, and sleeping under the stars, or we can head over to that amusement park two towns away. It's your call."

He grinned mischievously, sprawling dramatically onto the couch as if he were the ruler of our little kingdom. "Why not both?"

I laughed, tousling his hair affectionately as I passed him. "We'll see how ambitious you're feeling after the first day."

I brushed aside the residual worries of my earlier conversation with Jules and Anna, stepping deeper into the comforting order of our home. This week was Caleb's, and that thought alone was enough to anchor me firmly in the present.

Our first two days took us deep into the heart of Rivermere Woods, a sprawling, verdant park crisscrossed by winding trails, dotted with towering pines, and centered around a crystal-clear lake that shimmered under the radiant mid-spring sun. Caleb practically bounced out of the car the moment we arrived, his anticipation tangible as he snatched his gear and dashed toward the trailhead without waiting for my signal.

"Hold on, buddy. Let's set up camp first," I called out, hefting the heavy tent bag over my shoulder.

He groaned theatrically but quickly doubled back, his enthusiasm still blazing. "Okay, fine, but can we please set up camp right by the lake?"

"Deal," I said with a smile, knowing full well that Caleb's heart had always been drawn to water, whether he was splashing enthusiastically in puddles as a young child or racing eagerly to the beach.

We eventually found the perfect clearing just off the main trail, a sunlit patch of grass close enough to the lake that we could hear the gentle, rhythmic lapping of water softly kissing the shore. The tent setup quickly turned into a comedy of errors: Caleb, stubborn as ever, insisted he didn't need my help, only to spend several minutes wrestling with a recalcitrant tent pole before finally conceding and handing it over with a dramatic sigh.

"Fine," he declared with exaggerated flair as he sprawled onto the dewy grass. "You can handle the boring stuff while I go gather wood for our epic fire."

I smiled fondly as he dashed off into the nearby trees. A few minutes later, he returned with an armful of sticks, most of them far too slender for any practical use but perfect for kindling, his face alight with pride at his efforts even if I refrained from any teasing criticism.

Once camp was set up, we spent a languid afternoon by the lakeside. Caleb embraced nature with an unquenchable zeal reminiscent of his younger days, laughing heartily as he skipped flat stones across the water and insisting he could catch a fish with nothing more than a discarded stick and a length of string. He darted along the shoreline like a wild creature, his erratic yet joyous movements mirroring the playful dance of birds overhead.

"You're not exactly Puck from *A Midsummer Night's Dream*," I teased, amused as he attempted to fashion a makeshift fishing rod from a crooked branch he'd scavenged.

He furrowed his brow, his small fingers fumbling with the string as he tried to secure it in place. "Shakespeare? You've clearly been spending too much time at the Playhouse."

I laughed, settling back onto the soft grass as the warm sun caressed my face. "Fair enough."

"Good. That guy's a troublemaker," Caleb shot back, grinning as he tied an elaborate knot that immediately came undone.

"Pretty sure you've got him beat," I said. "Puck never tried to catch a fish with a branch."

"Yet," Caleb countered, tossing his failed creation aside and plopping down beside me. He skipped another rock, this one sinking after just two bounces. "Fine. You win. I'm not Puck. But at least I'm outside. How long do you think you'd last without your coffee?"

"Longer than you'd last without Wi-Fi," I retorted, nudging him with my shoulder.

He gasped in mock offense. "Rude. I could go without Wi-Fi. I just don't want to."

That evening, the campfire's glow illuminated our faces as the air filled with the rich scents of pine and smoky wood. Caleb, with the precision of a seasoned chef, skewered hot dogs onto sticks and declared himself "Hot Dog King" as he carefully balanced his charred creation over the dancing flames.

"You're way too interested in this theatre stuff," he teased at one point, stuffing a sticky marshmallow into his mouth and grinning dauntlessly despite the sugary mess on his face.

"Not enough to bring work along on this trip," I replied, reaching over to tousle his unruly hair affectionately.

"Thank goodness," he said dramatically. "I don't need any more stories about battles or ancient civilizations tonight, Dad."

I chuckled softly, prodding the fire with a slender stick as the flames crackled and danced. "I'm more interested in hearing about your day. What's new at school?"

Caleb launched into a rapid, animated recount of teacher antics, favorite classes, and the elaborate prank he and his best friend had orchestrated in science class. His words tumbled out one after another, each story laced with infectious enthusiasm, even as I feigned mock horror at the idea of a frog puppet being flung across the room.

"Did you get in trouble for that?" I asked, trying to sound stern but unable to hide my amusement.

"Nah," he replied with a mischievous smirk. "Mr. Thompson thought it was hilarious, even if it meant extra homework for us later."

As the stars began to reclaim the night sky and the fire dwindled to soft embers, we slipped into a peaceful rhythm, roasting marshmallows, sharing whispered stories against the backdrop of nature's quiet symphony. Despite the lingering thoughts of Jules and the unresolved tension with him, I managed to push those worries aside. This time belonged solely to Caleb, and I was devoted to preserving every fleeting moment of his laughter and wonder.

When the fire's warmth finally faded, Caleb leaned his head gently against me, his energy finally ebbing. "This is nice," he said, his voice barely audible against the crackle of dying embers.

"It really is," I agreed, feeling my heart swell with gratitude and quiet contentment.

The amusement park two towns over was alive with a riot of color and sound. The air buzzed with the melodic whir of rides, the cheerful hum of lively music, and the exuberant screams of thrill-seekers. The intoxicating aroma of popcorn, hot dogs, and sugary cotton candy intertwined with the faint tang of grease from the rides, creating a sensory feast. Caleb's excitement was almost tangible as he eagerly tugged my hand and practically dragged me toward a towering roller coaster, its steel frame looping and twisting like an adrenaline-fueled serpent.

"Dad, look, this one has three loops!" he shouted, pointing excitedly at the roller coaster whose cars spun rapidly along its intricate track.

"Three loops? Are you trying to kill me?" I teased, though I was already in line beside him.

"C'mon, you can handle it. You're tougher than you look," he said, grinning up at me.

I feigned hurt. "What's that supposed to mean?"

Caleb just laughed it off, nudging him playfully. "Relax, history nerd. It's a compliment."

While we waited in line, Caleb filled the air with animated chatter, stories of his best friend Cooper, who he claimed would chicken out on this ride, his vivid imaginings of the breathtaking views from the top, and his confident assertion that this roller coaster was destined to be the highlight of the day. When our turn finally came, he bolted forward,

positioning himself at the front row with all the impetuous energy of youth, leaving me no choice but to follow suit.

As the ride steadily ascended, the clanking of the track punctuating our anticipation, Caleb leaned forward, eyes wide with exhilaration. "This is gonna be awesome!"

Then came the drop, sudden and heart-stopping. My stomach did a flip as we hurtled downward at a breathtaking speed, the world blurring around us. Caleb's unrestrained laughter rang out, pure and unfiltered, and soon enough, I found myself laughing along with him. By the time the ride finally screeched to a halt, I was breathless, my hair dancing wildly in the wind, my heart pounding in a symphony of adrenaline and joy.

"Let's do it again!" Caleb exclaimed, practically bouncing off his feet as we stumbled off the ride.

"You're relentless," I laughed, shaking my head as his infectious enthusiasm continued to lift my spirits throughout the rest of the afternoon. We hit every ride Caleb deemed a "must-do" from the dizzying spins of the Mind-Bender to the soaking thrills of the Log Flume. Between rides, we meandered through the bustling midway. There, Caleb became fixated on winning a giant stuffed animal from a ring toss booth.

"You're going to blow all our cash trying to win that thing," I teased, watching him line up his shot with serious, determined focus.

"Not a chance," he replied, tongue peeking out in concentration.

After several humorous misfires and plenty of good-natured ribbing from me, he finally achieved a perfect toss. The booth attendant presented him with a neon green bear nearly as tall as he was, and Caleb held it up over his head as if it were a prized trophy.

"This bear's coming home with me!" he declared triumphantly, his smile broad enough to light up his entire face.

"That bear better earn its keep," I quipped, examining it jokingly. "Does it know how to do laundry?"

Caleb rolled his eyes, a playful glimmer in them. "He's a bear, Dad. He's here for moral support."

The day gradually mellowed into evening, the sun dipping low and setting the sky ablaze in brilliant pinks and oranges. Strings of whimsical lights flickered to life throughout the park, casting a warm, magical glow over the lingering crowds. We shared a funnel cake at a small picnic table, powdered sugar dusting our noses and fingertips. Caleb burst into laughter as I attempted to brush the sugary mess off his face, only for him to smear a bit more onto mine.

"Really, you're worse than a toddler," I teased amid our laughter, wiping at my cheek.

"Yeah, but I'm a toddler with a giant bear," he retorted, clutching his new companion as if it were a shield against the soft evening gloom.

As the park's lights grew brighter against the encroaching darkness and the crowd slowly thinned, we wandered over to the carousel. Caleb insisted on climbing onto one of the wooden horses, inviting me to take the one right beside him. As the carousel spun slowly, the soft strains of classic carnival music mingled with the distant echoes of roller coaster screams.

"This is a perfect day," Caleb said quietly, his usual exuberance subdued into a tender moment of reflection.

I glanced at him, feeling a subtle tightening in my chest. "Yeah, it really is."

For a few blissful hours, all else melted away, no lingering thoughts of school, no underlying tension with Jules, no worries about the days ahead. It was just Caleb and me, laughing, sharing funnel cake, and absorbing every magical moment beneath the kaleidoscopic amusement park lights. Yet, as night deepened, a bittersweet sadness crept in; I knew that this week with him was ephemeral, its sweetness destined to become a cherished memory.

"You know," Caleb said as we made our way back to the parking lot, clutching his neon green bear like a personal talisman, "we should do this every year."

I smiled, tousling his hair once more. "We already do."

"Then let's keep it that way," he said, his tone turning serious for a fleeting moment before breaking into a carefree grin. "Next time, I'm picking the rides again."

"Deal," I agreed, wrapping an arm around his shoulders as we walked towards the car. The night air was cool and crisp, a perfect close to a nearly perfect day, even as it reminded me all too clearly of the impending goodbye.

Saturday morning arrived with an invigorating crispness that hinted at the full bloom of spring, though the lingering dampness of melting earth still clung to the air. Caleb's week with me had swept by like a vibrant, cherished dream, a dazzling week filled with laughter, adventure, and those quiet, intimate moments that filled my heart. Now it was time to help him pack his belongings, a task that I approached with both practicality and an undeniable sting of reluctance.

Caleb darted down the hallway, his hair disheveled in the charming way of sleep and the neon green bear clutched tightly under

one arm. "Dad, do we really have to pack already?" he whined dramatically.

I couldn't help but smile at his theatrics. "Unless you intend to wear the same clothes for the rest of the year, yes."

He flopped onto his bed with a melodramatic sigh, his bear landing softly beside him as I began folding a neat pile of his t-shirts.

"Okay, but can we at least make pancakes first? Packing always tastes better with pancakes," he bargained.

I chuckled warmly, shaking my head. "Deal. You start gathering your stuff while I whip up breakfast."

Soon, the kitchen was filled with the homely, comforting aroma of pancakes sizzling on the griddle. Caleb appeared in the doorway, his duffle bag already half-packed, and began excitedly recounting his favorite moments of the week while he carefully buttered his first pancake.

"The roller coaster with the loops? That was the GOAT," he declared between mouthfuls, his voice muffled by the sweet treat. "And fishing was awesome, even if I didn't exactly catch anything."

I teased him gently. "You nearly caught that tree branch once."

He grinned conspiratorially, syrup slowly dripping down his chin. "That was skill, Dad. Pure, unadulterated skill."

By mid-morning, we were back in his room, folding shirts, stuffing his favorite books into his bag, and ensuring the neon green bear was placed safely by his duffle, far too big to be crammed in with his clothes. Caleb insisted that the bear ride shotgun for the journey home, and I didn't have the heart to argue.

Just as I zipped up his duffle bag, a horn honked sharply outside, signaling Anna's arrival. Caleb rushed to the window, waving with unbridled enthusiasm, and I couldn't help but feel a pinch of bittersweet emotion as I followed his gaze outside.

"Alright, buddy," I said, giving him a light, affectionate nudge. "Let's get your stuff out to the car."

Anna stepped gracefully out of the blue sedan, her auburn ponytail swinging as she approached. Her warm smile was tinged with the same quiet sadness I felt. "Ready to go, kiddo?" she asked kindly, gently ruffling Caleb's hair as he hefted his duffle toward the car.

"Almost!" he called back, darting inside one last time to retrieve his cherished bear.

Anna turned toward me, her eyes softening as they lingered on my face. "Looks like you two had a wonderful week."

"We did," I replied, leaning against the worn yet familiar porch railing. "The best."

Her gaze searched mine for a moment longer. "You look lighter, Elliott. Happier."

I hesitated, trying to decide just how much to reveal. The pressing tension with Jules had been a constant undercurrent in my life, yet this week with Caleb had provided a serene escape. "It's been good to focus on him," I said finally. "To just… be a dad for a while."

Anna nodded in silent understanding, her expression a mix of empathy and hope. "He talks about it all the time. He loves his time with you. And his letters!"

"That means everything to me," I replied quietly.

Before she could say another word, Caleb reappeared, the bright neon green bear slung over his shoulder like an honorary companion. "Ready!"

Anna grinned broadly. "Alright, let's hit the road. Thanks, Elliott."

"Always," I responded, pulling Caleb into a quick, heartfelt hug. He held on tightly for a moment, his lanky arms wrapping around me as if to squeeze every ounce of affection possible, before he stepped back with an exuberant grin and climbed into the car.

As the car pulled away and disappeared around the corner, Caleb leaned out the window, waving energetically. "Bye, Dad! I'll call you about the Marvel marathon!"

I waved back, standing on the quiet porch until the car was nothing more than a speck on the horizon.

Once inside, the house felt achingly empty, the joyful echoes of Caleb's laughter replaced by a reverberating silence. I wandered from room to room, tidying up subtle remnants of our week together: an empty soda can perched on the coffee table, a lone sock peeking out from under the couch, and the lingering, familiar scent of campfire that still clung to the jackets by the door.

Every small reminder brought a bittersweet smile to my face: memories of Caleb's laughter on the roller coasters, his determined attempts to fish with a makeshift rod, the dusting of powdered sugar from our shared funnel cake. I refused to burden him with the intricacies of the tension with Jules or the unresolved emotions that simmered quietly in my mind. What mattered was that I had been present, that we had given each other a week bursting with love and adventure. And I vowed, in the quiet solitude of the empty house, that I would do it all again whenever the chance arose.

I settled at the dining table, reaching for the stationery I kept in the drawer. A fresh letter to Caleb was already forming in my thoughts, a cherished habit we had maintained since the divorce, a small ritual to bridge the distance when our daily lives diverged. Even though Caleb didn't write back as often as I'd wish, I now knew the letters held a special place in his heart.

My phone buzzed on the table, breaking the silence. It was a text from Jules.

Jules: *Hope you and Caleb had a great week. Should we meet tomorrow to go over plans for the GSA event?*

I stared at the message, feeling a tightening in my chest. Jules' words came across as careful, neutral, as though he was treading lightly, not wishing to intrude. I typed back succinctly.

Elliott: *Thanks. We had a great time. Tomorrow works.*

Though my response was terse and almost mechanical, I wasn't ready to face more complications, not yet. Jules would have to wait, just as I would wait eagerly for the next summer, for the next stretch of blissful, uninterrupted time with Caleb. Until then, I would write my letters, make my calls, and hold these vivid memories close.

In that quiet moment, as the soft hum of the day faded into memory, I acknowledged that despite the challenges and unresolved threads in my life, the time with Caleb had rekindled something within me, a reminder that sometimes, the simplest moments of genuine connection were enough to fill even the deepest voids.

12

JULES

Sunlight poured in through the mismatched curtains of my tiny studio apartment, illuminating every corner with a warm, golden glow that revealed the vibrant edge of fabrics draped artfully over a worn armchair. The sunlight bounced off these colorful textiles, scattering a mesmerizing collection of hues across the eclectic, cluttered floor. My studio wasn't so much messy as it was a carefully orchestrated chaos, a symphony of stacked books, scattered sketches, and a collection of mismatched dishes, all arranged with an odd, intuitive rhythm.

Callie had commandeered the sturdiest chair available, sitting with their legs crossed in relaxed defiance while holding a bagel aloft as if proclaiming a royal edict. Their eyes, sharp and playful, locked onto mine with a teasing intensity.

"You're impossible, you know that?" Callie teased, gesturing with a bite-marked piece of bagel pointed directly at me. "I told you not to text him. Let the man spend his spring break with his kid. And what do you do?"

A mischievous grin spread across my face as I took a deliberate sip from one of my many coffee mugs, a chipped relic with a crack tracing its handle, still reliable despite the wear. "I texted him. And guess what? He replied. So, problem solved. Everything's under control."

Callie exhaled dramatically, leaning back as they rested their chin in their palm. "Under control? You call a series of curt texts 'under

control'? Jules, you're like a golden retriever, achingly enthusiastic over a bouncing tennis ball. You can't simply sit and wait."

"I'm more like a border collie," I retorted, reaching for another bite of my bagel as if bolstering my argument. "Focused, diligent, and driven. Loyal to a fault."

"Needy," Callie shot back with a playful sneer. "Tirelessly insistent. But sure, we'll stick with 'loyal.'"

I crumpled a napkin into a loose ball and tossed it in their direction, watching with a wry smile as they deftly dodged it with a practiced flick. "Anyway," I deflected, barely acknowledging the sneer tugging at their lips, "we have a meeting now. We're back on track. I can't wait to share some of these ideas I've been brewing."

Callie groaned and ran a hand down their face, exasperation lining every gesture. "Oh my god, you're not even listening. Jules, the man barely bothered to reply. You're acting like he just popped the question."

"Why are you like this?" I countered deadpan, leaning back in my chair and gesturing vaguely at the whirlwind of their presence.

"Why are YOU like this?" Callie fired back. "You can't just bulldoze through every moment because you crave a morsel of attention."

"It's not just a morsel," I insisted, straightening up as I tried to project confidence. "It's communication. We have a plan here. He said he'd meet me to discuss the GSA event."

"Right," Callie replied dryly, absently picking at the edge of their bagel with a touch of cynicism. "Because nothing promises 'emotional resolution' quite like a purely logistical meeting."

I waved off their skepticism, reaching for my notebook that rested on the cluttered table. "Listen, I've got an idea for an interactive timeline display that we could…"

"Jules," Callie interjected sharply, their tone slicing through my excitement. "Just stop."

I paused, notebook still half-open, blinking in surprise. "What?"

"Stop bulldozing," they commanded firmly, placing their coffee cup down with a resonant thud. Their eyes narrowed as if drilling into my very thoughts. "You're distracting yourself with grand plans and elaborate ideas instead of really addressing the situation."

"I'm not bulldozing," I said, though my voice wavered slightly. "I'm simply planning."

Callie snorted, folding their arms as if shielding themselves from my fervor. "Planning, my ass. You're trying to fix everything at once,

exactly like you always do. And you're ignoring the fact that Elliott is still untangling his own thoughts. You can't force him to be on the same page as you, Jules. It doesn't work that way."

I rolled my eyes and flipped open my notebook regardless of their admonition. "It's not as if I'm suggesting we elope. This is just about organizing an event for the GSA, not mapping out our future."

Leaning forward, Callie's piercing gaze softened my resolve even as they pressed on. "One: do you know that? And, two: You really think he's oblivious to the connection between you two? That he doesn't sense the pressure you're putting on every conversation?"

I opened my mouth to argue, but Callie raised a hand to silence me. "No, don't. Just listen."

Their voice mellowed, though their expression retained its earnest seriousness. "I know how much you care about him, Jules. You don't need to spell it out, the way you throw everything into the people you love is both your strength and sometimes your downfall. It's one of the things I admire most about you, but it can overwhelm."

I caught my breath and looked away, the weight of their words settling around me like a heavy fog. The notebook on my lap suddenly felt far weightier than before.

Callie reached across the table, their hand gently resting on mine. "I'm not saying stop caring. I'm saying be patient. Let him come to you. If you push too hard, too fast, you're going to frighten him away."

I nodded slowly, the adrenaline of my earlier excitement slowly draining away as a soft sigh escaped me. "I just… I don't want to lose him."

"And you won't," Callie whispered, their tone gentle yet insistent. "You need to meet him where he is, not where you want him to be. He's not going anywhere, Jules. Not if you give him the time and space to figure things out."

For a long moment, only the ambient hum of distant traffic and the soft rustle of fabric punctuated the silence. I drew a deep breath, striving to let Callie's measured words permeate my hurried thoughts. They were right, as they invariably were, but patience was hardly one of my natural virtues.

"I hate it when you're right," I mumbled, a faint smile tugging unbidden at my lips.

"I know," Callie replied with a warming grin, reclining back in their chair with an air of self-assured mischief. "But you love me anyway."

I chuckled, shaking my head in playful disbelief. "Debatable."

Callie raised their coffee cup in a mock toast, the clink of ceramic echoing softly in the sunlit room. "To not fucking this up."

"To not fucking this up," I echoed, our mugs clinking together like a pact sealed in the quiet morning light.

As the sun's rays continued to dance artfully through the sheer curtains and the lingering aroma of coffee merged with the early day, a quiet flicker of hope kindled within me. Maybe, just maybe, Callie was right. If I could learn to balance the impulsiveness of my heart with the calm of my thoughts, there might still be a chance for Elliott and me to harmonize our lives. But first, I had a rehearsal to conquer, a long, intricate evening of blocking, notes, and creative energy, before I could face Elliott tomorrow.

13

ELLIOTT

Later in the day I balanced the cardboard coffee tray in one hand, carefully weaving between parked cars in the lot. I hadn't planned to come, not really. The idea had struck me while I was running errands. I'd ordered his favorite lavender honey latte with oat milk and found myself driving toward the playhouse without much thought. Maybe it was the memory of our hike, still raw and unresolved. Or maybe it was the way I couldn't stop thinking about the kiss, unbidden moments of warmth catching me off guard throughout my day. Whatever the reason, I was here, standing in the shadowed entryway with a coffee tray and a growing sense of unease.

As I approached the building, muffled voices reached me, a vibrant hum that seemed to vibrate through the walls. The moment I pushed open the heavy double doors, the energy of the space hit me like a wave. Actors' voices overlapped as they rehearsed lines, punctuated by bursts of laughter. Crew members darted about, clutching props or adjusting lighting rigs. Onstage, someone stood with fairy wings askew, gesturing animatedly at another actor.

The late afternoon sun streamed down through high, slender windows of the Havenwood Playhouse, scattering long, golden streaks of light over time-worn floorboards. The air was thick with a rich mixture, a blend of sawdust and weathered wood, softened further by the fresh tang of lingering paint, an aroma that perfectly encapsulated

chaos interwoven with raw creativity. I paused at the doorway, momentarily overwhelmed, until my gaze finally found Jules.

There he stood center stage, a living nucleus of the performance, clipboard gripped tightly in his hand as he guided the actors with a blend of animated grace and theatrical exaggeration. Every gesture he made radiated energy that seemed to electrify every corner of the theatre. His commanding yet playful voice soared above the clamor, compelling everyone to focus as if his tone alone could transform the soundscape. In that tumult, Jules was the unwavering anchor, a vibrant, magnetic presence impossible to ignore. My chest constricted as I absorbed his passionate energy, every thought of our kiss flooding back: the memory of his warm lips and the gentle pull that had drawn me close, an image that haunted me throughout the day.

Before I could drown in my spiraling thoughts, Jules's eyes caught mine and his face blossomed into a radiant smile, making the surrounding din fade into a blurry background. With effortless grace, he leaped from the stage, weaving through the bustling activity as if the chaos were an extension of him. "Well, look who decided to grace us with his presence!" he announced with a teasing lilt as he made his way toward me. Suddenly aware of every detail, the slight tremor in my hand, the weight of his gaze, I extended the coffee tray, murmuring, "Figured you could use a little fuel," attempting to keep a casual tone despite my heartbeat drumming rapidly against my ribs.

Jules accepted the cup with an exaggerated gasp, his eyes twinkling with amusement as he theatrically placed a hand over his heart. "A lavender honey latte with oat milk?" he said, and with a dramatic sip that made him close his eyes in momentary rapture, he declared, "You're spoiling me, Teach." His warm, genuine laughter echoed in that space, melting some of the tension.

I couldn't help but softly retort, "You say that like it's a bad thing," a small smile tugging at the edge of my usually reserved expression.

As his grin broadened, there was a noticeable shift in his demeanor, a softness that spoke of sincerity. "Stick around," he urged, already pulling me toward the farthest rows of seats in the dimly lit auditorium. "I need your second set of eyes." I tried to form a protest with a simple "Jules," but his movement swept me away until I found myself seated in the back row, cradling the warming coffee cup. Almost immediately, Jules bounded back to the stage with an air of renewed zest.

"Alright, everyone, let's run it again!" he called out crisply, clapping his hands to rally the cast. His instructions flowed with theatrical

precision: "John, remember you're the Fairy King, each word must sound as if it were etched in stone. Jill, Titania must match his intensity, be his equal, and make him believe every syllable." The actors nodded, slipping back into their positions as Jules perched boldly on the stage's edge, clipboard ready for another round of notes. I tried to focus on the scene unfolding before me, but my attention drifted repeatedly to the mesmerizing presence of Jules. His quick, graceful scribbles and timely calls for adjustments amidst the controlled chaos pulled me in, even as my mind was haunted by that electric kiss. Every so often, his eyes would wander back to where I sat, sending my heart into a flutter as the tender memory resurfaced with relentless persistence. I forced myself to sip the now slightly bitter coffee, as if the taste might ground the weight of my emotions.

"Hey, Teach!" Jules's voice rang out, snapping me back with its exuberance. I blinked in surprise as he turned, his eyes sparkling from in front of the stage. "What do you think?" he inquired, his tone imbued with both mischief and genuine curiosity.

All eyes in the room pivoted toward me, and I felt an uneasy warmth bloom across my face. Clearing my throat, I rose with reluctance and managed, "The energy is good. The... intentions are clear," carefully choosing words that resonated with honesty and restraint.

Jules raised an inquisitive eyebrow, his playful brightness faltering just a touch. "Okay, but what about the delivery? The pacing? The staging?" he pressed.

For a long, weighted moment, I searched for the right words; then, with a hesitant decision, I said, "It works. It's... effective."

His expression hardened momentarily, the light-hearted banter giving way to a sharper critique. "Effective? Really? That's all you've got?" he challenged, his tone cool yet cutting, making each word slice through the charged air.

I straightened my shoulders defensively, insisting, "What's wrong with it being effective?"

His hands shot up in an expression of exasperation. "It's safe. Diplomatic. Noncommittal."

Those words sank into me, pricking deeper than I cared to acknowledge. I responded, my voice cooling to match the sudden chill, "And not everything has to be a grand performance." The room seemed to pause, heavy with the tension between us, as if the very air was holding its breath.

"This isn't about a grand performance," Jules said quietly, his frustration threading through his words, "It's about honesty, about caring enough to push people to be better."

I countered softly, "And sometimes, people don't need to be pushed. Sometimes, good enough is enough." My tone held both a plea and a challenge, and Jules's eyes briefly darted toward the cup in my hand.

After a brief moment of silence, he took it, his clipped "Thanks," ringing in a way that stung more than I anticipated.

Caught off guard, I stammered, "I just thought…" I hesitated, trying to wrap the unfinished sentence in fragile sincerity. "I wanted to see you."

He exhaled sharply, shoulders tensing in a mix of exasperation and something unspoken. "Well, now you have," he replied curtly.

Before I could respond, a stage manager approached, clipboard clutched under one arm, asking Jules about a lighting issue. With a quick dismissal, "Give me a minute", Jules moved away, and with that interruption, the fragile thread of our conversation unraveled further. Running a hand through his disheveled hair, he muttered, "Look, I'm in the middle of a lot right now. I don't have time to… entertain visitors."

His words cut through the lingering hope in my chest, and with a quiet, edged retort, I asked, "Is that what you're doing? Entertaining me?"

Immediately, his gaze snapped coldly toward mine, eyes narrowing as tension thickened the air. "You tell me, Elliott. What are you doing here?" he demanded, the question hanging in the space between us like a sharpened shard.

I found myself unable to muster a satisfactory reply, and my grip on the now-empty coffee tray tightened instinctively. "I thought…" I began, then shook my head in resignation. "Never mind."

Jules's expression remained inscrutable as he held my gaze for what felt like an eternity. Finally, he stepped back, gesturing toward the exit with a motion that felt like a final verdict. "Maybe you should go," he said, his voice heavy with a mix of disappointment and resolve.

The words hit me like a sudden blow, but I nodded slowly, swallowing the metallic lump in my throat, "Right," I agreed with a steadiness that belied the chaos within. "I'll let you get back to it."

Turning away, I walked out as the sound of the heavy doors closing reverberated through the quiet parking lot. The summer air, warm yet strangely indifferent, enveloped me, while I felt an inner chill as the tense vibrations of that interaction trailed behind like an

inescapable shadow. "What the fuck just happened?" I whispered into the solitude of that fading afternoon.

Sitting in my car, fingers gripping the steering wheel as if to hold on to some semblance of control, I realized just how vast the gulf between Jules and me had become. The tender kiss, the intimate moments of our shared hike, even the fleeting instances where we seemed to be unraveling our tangled feelings, all now felt like distant, bittersweet memories overshadowed by an ever-growing chasm. I drove away with the coffee tray forgotten on the passenger seat, a silent testament to lost connection, and my thoughts were heavy and unresolvable. The tension between us had thickened, lingering like a relentless storm cloud that I couldn't shake, and with the GSA event meeting looming on the horizon, that unease deepened further. Conflict had never been my preference, yet something was stirring between us, a brewing turbulence that was as unpredictable as it was unsettling.

14

JULES

The late afternoon sun poured through the towering windows of Harmony Concert Hall's modest meeting room, its golden beams spilling across the space yet doing little to dissolve the icy tension that clung to us like a stubborn mist. I stood at the whiteboard, a marker poised in one hand while the other gripped my clipboard as if it were a lifeline in a turbulent sea. The unresolved tension from yesterday's Playhouse event still hovered at the peripheries of my thoughts, unspoken yet profoundly present, like a gathering storm threatening an imminent downpour.

Elliott sat across the table, every inch his posture exuding rigidity, his laptop aglow and papers arrayed with the meticulous order of a crafted catalogue. He remained detached, his eyes fixed on a neatly printed timeline rather than meeting mine, igniting within me a roar of frustration that begged for an outburst. For a moment, the urge to scream, or even hurl the marker in his direction, was overwhelming. Instead, I distilled that raw emotion into the fervor of my pitch.

"This isn't just another event!" I declared, my voice slicing sharply through the thick silence before I even recognized its intensity. My hand flew towards the whiteboard, punctuating my words with wild gestures that animated a chaotic mural of sketches, notes, and arrows, each line colliding and intermingling with the next. The vivid hues of neon pink, electric blue, and lime green burst from my markers, a stark rebellion against the room's sterile, bland professionalism. It was as if my

very ideas had erupted from my mind, colliding on the board in an unrestrained flurry of creative passion, messy, vibrant, and defiantly alive.

"This is about immersing people in queer history," I continued, speaking so rapidly that the words tumbled out in a rush, barely pausing to form coherent sentences. "Not merely reading or hearing it, but feeling it, letting it seep into their bones." I turned to face Elliott, waving the marker like a conductor's baton as I painted a dynamic scene with my words. "Imagine interactive displays, touchscreens that aren't just glass and pixels, but actual portals that pull you into the stories. Audio snippets playing with real voices, stirring interviews, layered soundscapes, even background music that morphs with every section. And live storytelling sessions! And theatrical performances! We can interlace them into a living story so that it's not a static list of events but a breathtaking experience, dynamic, immersive, and utterly unforgettable!"

With a dramatic pivot back to the whiteboard, I pointed emphatically at a scribbled circle encircled by a flurry of frantic notes. "Right here," I said, "this spot could be the transition from narrative to performance, imagine the magic of theatrical storytelling enhanced with light projections. Or, oh my God, what if we dared to include holograms? Too far-fetched?" I spun back toward Elliott, barely pausing for a breath. "Okay, scratch the holograms, but think big, bold, unrestrained! People need to leave this with goosebumps, as if they've been jolted awake into a new reality."

In my fervor, the marker slipped from my grasp and clattered against the table, but I barely missed a beat. I quickly scavenged another from the chaotic cluster on the desk and circled a section of the board with a flourish. "This part? It could serve as the timeline, but not in the tedious way you're used to, imagine it moving, fluid as you swipe along, coming to vibrant life! Pictures, videos, quotes, all intermingled to show history not as static, but as living, breathing, and utterly in-your-face."

Breathless, I turned back to Elliott, my heart pounding as I searched his stoic face for even the faintest reaction. My grip on the marker was desperate, as if it anchored me to a reality that was rapidly blurring. "Do you see it?" I pleaded. "This is extraordinary. This is the future!"

I paused, the charged silence hanging between us until it felt unbearable. "Well?" I prodded, the word slicing sharply into the air.

At last, Elliott glanced up. His face was a mask of unreadable calculation as he responded in a voice as even and measured as ever. "It's ambitious," he said calmly, "but have you fully considered the logistics?

Those interactive displays alone? They could swamp our budget and throw off the entire timeline."

His measured tone grated on me, its pragmatism a cold slap against my flushed excitement. "We'll figure it out," I retorted dismissively with a wave of the marker. "This isn't about ticking boxes on a project plan, it's about making a monumental impact, Elliott."

Elliott leaned back slightly, his shoulders still drawn taut. "Impact doesn't materialize if it's executed poorly," he countered. "If we overreach and fail to deliver, the entire message is lost. Also, you aren't working with some big New York non-profit with tens of thousands of dollars to make this happen. This is a high school afterschool club with no funding from the district. These kids raise money with bake sales and car washes."

His words struck me like a well-aimed dart, a precise, painful critique. I let out a short, bitter laugh devoid of humor. "Must everything be about potential pitfalls with you?" I snapped, turning fully to confront him. "God forbid we actually take a risk!"

His jaw tensed, a flicker of irritation darkening his eyes. "It's not about what might go wrong," he said in a firmer tone, "it's about ensuring that what we do actually makes the impact you're chasing. You can't ignite inspiration with a half-baked idea on a $50,000.00 budget!"

Stepping closer, the marker still clutched tightly in my hand, I replied heatedly, "This isn't half-baked, it's a vision, a blueprint for something extraordinary. But sure, if you prefer to retreat into your safe, sterilized PowerPoint, then by all means, do it."

Abruptly, he rose from his seat, the screech of his chair scraping the floor and cutting through the charged atmosphere like a blade. "This isn't about dialing it down," he said sharply, his voice taut and cutting. "It's about respecting the realm of possibility. You can't just scatter a thousand ideas onto a wall and hope one sticks."

"And you can't see beyond your damn checklist!" I fired back, words lashing out like cracks of lightning. My voice climbed relentlessly, the intensity building like a gathering storm. "You're so obsessed with dodging failure that you're choking the life out of creativity, eclipsing the fire needed to inspire."

Elliott's voice rose in response, his tone crisp as his hand sliced the air between us, as if carving a physical gap. "It's not stifling creativity to want this to actually work," he retorted. "Not every wild idea you spew is going to land, Jules."

"Oh, so now they're just *wild ideas*?" I shot back, stepping even closer, each word dripping with sarcastic disdain. "Maybe you're too

frightened to dream bigger. Perhaps the terror of failure has chained you to a safe and boring path instead of daring to create something breathtaking!"

"Safe and boring? At least I'm not setting us up for an inevitable crash and burn!" he countered, his voice echoing off the walls as he jabbed a finger at the vibrant whiteboard. "You really believe that by slapping together a hundred disparate concepts, you create vision? It's chaos, Jules, it's a shambles."

"It's called ambition!" I roared, sweeping my hand at the explosion of colors and chaos on the board. "It's having an unyielding passion for something! But fine, let's reduce it to a bland, sanitized presentation and play it safe."

"You think I don't care?" he shot back, his voice slicing through the thick air. "Just because I don't scream every few seconds doesn't mean I'm not equally invested."

"Could've fooled me," I lashed out, bitterness spilling over before I could contain it.

With his jaw set and a frustrated hand combing through his hair with visible aggression, Elliott spat, "You don't get to measure my investment by comparing it to your theatrics."

"And you don't have the right to silence me simply because my approach makes you uneasy," I countered as I stepped forward once more, the space between us crackling with unresolved tension. "You're so entrenched in what you deem 'possible' that you're blind to what could truly be."

"And you're so enraptured by your idealism that reality eludes you," he replied coldly, each word sharper than the last. "Not everything flourishes in your beautifully orchestrated chaos."

The word "chaos" fell over me like a heavy blow. I froze, chest heaving, as I stared hard at him. "Chaos?" I repeated quietly, yet with venom. "Is that all you see? Just... noise?"

"You said it yourself, you thrive on it," he countered, his tone transitioning into something distant and almost unrecognizable. "But not everyone can ride your tumultuous wave, Jules. Not everyone can keep up."

"Keep up?" I laughed bitterly, the sound hollow and humorless. "You mean obediently follow your color-coded, meticulously structured plans? Newsflash, Elliott: you can't orchestrate magic through a checklist."

"And you can't depend on disorder to fabricate it!" he shot back, frustration spilling over in his increasingly raised voice.

"God, why do I even bother?" I muttered, more to myself than to him, though he caught every syllable.

"What is that supposed to mean?" he demanded, stepping even closer, his expression taut with suppressed tension.

"It means I'm done fighting for something you clearly don't believe in," I snapped, my voice cracking just a little as I gripped my bag with trembling hands. "If you want your prim, sanitized version of this event, then by all means, have at it."

"Jules…" he began, and I cut him off with a sharp, dismissive gesture.

"Don't," I said, my tone icy and irrevocable. "Just don't."

I turned and strode to the door, every step laden with purpose and a seething tightness along my jaw as I fought back tears and the heat that threatened to spill over. Behind me, I heard him start to speak, only to falter as silence swallowed his words whole. The door slammed shut, its sound reverberating in the room, leaving him isolated in the oppressive glare of the afternoon sun.

I pivoted on my heel, my boots clicking emphatically against the polished floor, each step echoing as if marking a final farewell. The air between us seemed as fragile as spun glass, one slightest touch would shatter it into oblivion. My fingers tightened around the strap of my bag as I reached the door once more, forcing it open with more urgency than necessary. The hinges groaned in protest before the door swung shut behind me, its heavy thud resonating in the quiescent hallway like the final gavel of a court.

The hallway was cloaked in an almost mocking stillness. Every breath I took seemed to carry the weight of the heated words that had just been hurled between us. I quickened my pace, my vision narrowing as I focused on the vibrant exit sign glowing steadfastly at the corridor's end. Overhead, the fluorescent lights hummed a faint, monotonous tune, a stark contrast to the emotional tempest I had just escaped. My legs forced me onward, even as my mind pleaded to turn back, to cry out, to undo the damage, but I heeded no such summons.

Stepping outside, the world engulfed me. The late afternoon sun was glaringly bright, the sky a piercing blue, and the cacophony of honking traffic mixed with the vibrant chatter of passersby was almost overwhelming. It was as if the universe, in all its vast indifferent splendor, had moved on, unaware of the small implosion that had just shattered that stifling room. The heaviness in my chest persisted, the sting of his words settling over me like an inescapable weight.

I wandered without destination until my feet led me toward Rivermere Creek. The soothing sound of water cascading gently over smooth rocks reached my ears before I could even see it, a lullaby of nature inviting me to pause and heal. Leaning against the weathered railing of a narrow footbridge, I allowed my fingers to curl tightly around the cool metal, gazing downward at the shimmering creek beneath. In the dying light of day, the water rippled and danced in the golden hue of the setting sun, each chaotic movement imbued with an unforeseen purpose.

A shaky breath escaped me, too large for my lungs to contain. My jaw burned as the bitter argument replayed in endless loops, every cutting remark sharp and echoing in the silence that followed. His voice, colder and more detached than ever, rang in my ears, melding painfully with my own raw, jagged retorts, leaving me exposed and vulnerable in ways I wished I could forget.

Why did I even believe this vision could work? The relentless question churned in my mind. Why did I think we could actually succeed together?

With my eyes squeezed shut, I tried to banish the thought, but it clung stubbornly. My grip on the railing tightened until my knuckles throbbed with pain. Below, the creek paid no heed to my spiraling doubts, its waters flowed steadily, a compelling insistence on progress and calm that contrasted starkly with the turbulent storm raging within me.

In a flash of thought, I envisioned Elliott back in the sterile meeting room: his papers and timelines arranged methodically, his face set in that familiar, guarded expression as if protecting a well of hidden frustrations. The memory twisted my stomach into knots. For a fleeting moment, I wanted to believe that he, too, felt the acute sting of our tug-of-war, an internal battle where words cut both ways. Yet another, harsher part of me whispered that perhaps he never truly cared, that the very heart of his passion remained locked behind his orderly facade. And at what point did that argument become less about the Pride event and more about 'us'?"

15

ELLIOTT

The classroom carried a subtle aroma of cleaning supplies mixed with the crisp scent of freshly printed paper, a quiet herald of the school year's imminent close. The open windows allowed a flood of late-spring sunbeams to dance across the meticulously polished floors, stretching long, drowsy shadows over rows of unoccupied desks. Outside, the humid May air in Havenwood shimmered with the promise of an impending rainstorm, its moisture clinging to every surface as if suspended in a dream. I sat at my desk, deeply bent over a pile of loose papers, a vibrant red pen clutched in my hand, while the warm sunlight bathed the room in a gentle glow that contrasted with the cool whisper of the persistent air conditioner humming in the background.

The stillness of the room should have been a balm, yet my concentration was fractured. Every few moments, I caught myself drifting into a vacant stare, watching as the neat words on the page blurred into an indistinct haze. My restless mind repeatedly circled back to the bitter argument with Jules, the piercing sharpness of his tone and the unmistakable hurt glimmering in his eyes. It was a relentless loop that I couldn’t seem to escape no matter how many times I tried to force the thoughts away.

A heavy sigh escaped me as I set my red pen aside and reclined slightly in my chair. The slow, rhythmic creak of the wooden hinges reverberated in the solitude of the room, serving as an audible reminder

of how much I cherished this quiet isolation over the turbulent chaos raging in my own thoughts.

A sudden knock at the classroom door jolted me from my thoughts. I straightened up, my heart giving a small, unexpected leap. For a fleeting second, I allowed my mind to wander, hoping that maybe it was Jules returning, though deep down I knew such a reunion was not in the cards.

In stepped Sam, his short dark hair slightly tousled from the breeze and with a grin as radiant as the spring day outside. His presence was a burst of contagious energy that seemed to illuminate every room he entered and today was no exception.

"Mind if I interrupt?" he asked, his voice bubbling with warmth and a hint of playful teasing.

I made a small gesture toward the empty chair across from me. "Please, have a seat."

Sam approached with a small, neatly wrapped box in one hand. With an almost theatrical flourish, he placed it on my desk, releasing the sweet, inviting aroma of chocolate that seemed to promise delight with every sniff.

"Bribery," he declared lightly, reclining into the chair with an easy grace. "Chocolate chip, your favorite, if my memory serves me right."

A gentle smile tugged at the corners of my lips, softening the lingering heaviness in my chest. "Thanks," I said softly.

For a moment, Sam studied my expression, his keen eyes narrowing just enough to suggest genuine concern. "Alright, Elliott," he began, one leg casually draped over the other. "Spill it. You've been sporting that somber, 'something's definitely wrong but I won't say a word' look for weeks now. I figured I'd give you some space, but it seems you're still immersed in it, so here I am."

My hands clutched the edge of the desk a little tighter as I hesitated. I wasn't ready to unfold the story, yet the silence between us had grown too cumbersome to bear alone. Eventually, surrendering to the weight of the moment, I exhaled deeply and leaned back.

"Jules and I had an argument," I confessed, the words tasting bitter as they left my lips.

With a raised eyebrow, Sam quipped, "The theatre whirlwind?"

I nodded, the vivid recollection of Jules' animated gestures and the acerbic edge to his words flashing unbidden in my mind. "We were planning the GSA Pride event, and… things escalated. Since then, we haven't spoken."

Sam regarded me thoughtfully, his expression weaving together curiosity and concern. "Let me guess, you craved clarity and structure, but he revels in chaos?"

A small, rueful grin played on my lips. "Something like that."

Leaning forward, Sam rested his elbows deliberately on the desk. "Listen, Elliott. You've got something special with Jules. Sure, he's unpredictable, a whirlwind of chaos, literally, but sometimes that chaos is exactly what sparks growth. Maybe you're the grounding force he needs, and that's not such a bad thing at all. Differences challenge us to evolve."

I looked down at the open box of cookies before me, the gesture of sweetness almost dissolving the edges of my frustration. My fingers hovered over one, its chocolate chips beginning to soften as they met the gentle warmth of my skin.

"I just…" My voice faded into a whisper, laden with uncertainty. "I don't know how to fix it."

Sam's expression softened further, and a gentle smile spread across his face. "Start by showing up," he advised calmly. "The rest will follow naturally."

I lingered on his words, letting them permeate the quiet that enveloped me. Showing up, such a simple act, yet amidst the stirring complexities of my heart, it felt incredibly profound. Jules was like an unpredictable storm, both beautiful and tumultuous, and I worried about how I could endure its force without losing myself in the process.

"Thanks, Sam," I said at last, my voice steady yet hushed.

As he stood, Sam reached over and patted my arm in a friendly gesture before turning to leave, his grin reappearing as brightly as the spring day outside. "Anytime, Brooks. And seriously, eat more cookies, they do wonders on stubborn brain fog!"

I chuckled softly, watching the sound of his footsteps fade away down the hallway. Left once more in the gentle stillness of the classroom, the late-summer sun inched its way slowly across the floor, casting growing shadows as it moved. I stared thoughtfully at the cookie in my hand, my thoughts once again drifting unbidden to Jules.

Perhaps showing up wouldn't mend everything, but it was a beginning, a tentative step toward untangling the storm within, and maybe, just maybe, that could be enough.

JULES

The early evening sun poured through the towering windows of the Havenwood Playhouse, its golden light slicing through the hazy air like a focused beam illuminating a secret stage. Dust motes danced in the shafts of sunlight while the familiar scent of sawdust and weathered wood intermingled with a whisper of old paint, supporting me in the only place that ever truly felt like home.

There I stood in the center of the stage, clutching a well-worn clipboard that felt both steady and reassuring in my grasp. Its weight was a tangible reminder of purpose, a constant anchor amid the dull throb of an ache that had rooted deep in my chest. My voice rang out, crisp and clear, echoing off the cavernous walls as I tried to convince myself it was full of focus and drive, anything but tinged with desperation.

"Alright, John," I called out, my hands coming together in a sharp clap that cut through the noise, commanding every pair of eyes. "From the top. Make your gestures larger, more commanding. Oberon is not just a fairy king…' John repeated back to me, "... I'm THE Fairy King. I know, I know." And Jill," I swept my gaze over to the actress portraying Titania, her eyes meeting mine with a hint of apprehension, "match his energy with defiant strength. She is every bit his equal in strength. This is a clash of wills, make us feel every bit of it."

The actors exchanged brief, weary glances, their tired expressions hinting at countless hours spent in rehearsal, yet none dared voice any resistance. They straightened their postures, stepping boldly into their roles as I paced along the stage's edge. The steady click of my boot heels against the worn wooden floor punctuated the silent rhythm of our performance. My clipboard, meanwhile, was a chaotic collage of scribbled notes and half-formed ideas, its pages forever dog-eared from my constant flipping through plans and revisions.

My usual vibrant, frenetic enthusiasm felt replaced by a sharper, almost frantic energy. I could sense it in every slightly stilted movement, in the way the raw edge of my voice made the younger cast members flinch ever so slightly.

At the back of the house, Callie sat comfortably in an old theatre seat under the balcony near the booth, the worn velvet cushion giving just a little beneath them, arms crossed, a knowing smirk playing at the

corners of their lips. Their gaze was fixed on me, not on the rehearsal or the actors, but solely on me. I pretended not to notice, my focus remaining solely on the stage and the unfolding scene.

"Again!" I shouted, hastily scribbling a few illegible instructions on my clipboard as the scene resumed. The actors dove into their lines, their voices rising in a river of Shakespearean grandeur that filled every corner of the cavernous space. Yet even then, my gaze drifted, catching a glimpse of my own reflection in one of the darkened windows high above the stage, a worn, drawn face tightened by unspoken burdens.

By the time rehearsal drew to a close, my voice had grown hoarse, and the cast shuffled off in a flurry of hurried farewells. The theater slowly emptied, the faint hum of activity dissipating until it was just Callie and me in the quiet shell of the playhouse. I sank into a battered chair near the stage's edge, my clipboard slipping from my exhausted grip and meeting the floor with a dull, disgruntled thud.

"If you pace any harder, you're going to wear a trench into the stage," Callie teased as they approached, balancing a steaming cup of coffee in one hand. Their tone carried a light, teasing quality, yet their eyes were sharp and discerning, missing nothing in the weariness etched on my face.

"Just trying to keep things moving," I replied, managing a forced smile that didn't quite reach the depths of my eyes. Callie handed over the coffee and settled beside me in the chair, their legs crossed casually as they fixed me with a look that seemed capable of peeling back every layer I guarded.

"Or maybe you're just running away from something," they observed quietly, tilting their head with a hint of concern.

I shot them a warning glance but said nothing; Callie was a relentless seeker of emotional truths, and there was no use in trying to mask mine. I took a languid sip of the coffee, the warmth seeping into my chest as I let the weight of the past few weeks press down even harder on my ribcage. I exhaled slowly, the tension in me ebbing in the steady rhythm of my breath.

"I screwed up, Cal," I admitted in a quiet, raw tone that barely rose above a whisper.

"Let me guess," Callie said, their smirk softening into an expression of genuine sympathy. "You and Mr. History Teacher?"

A subtle nod was all I offered, my fingertips tightening around the now slightly warm coffee cup. "We had this ridiculous fight about the GSA event. I don't even know if it's going to happen now."

After a moment of thoughtful silence, Callie reached into their bag and produced a small, well-used notebook, extending it toward me. "Then fix it," they said simply, their voice imbued with unwavering confidence. "Channel your drama into something productive. You have a knack for turning chaos into brilliance, use it."

I studied the notebook for a long, silent moment before accepting it, its frayed edges attesting to the many ideas that had been poured into its pages over time. It felt comforting in my hands, as if it carried not just blank sheets but the promise of new beginnings.

"Thanks," I said softly, the faintest curve gracing my lips as a tentative smile broke through. "I'll try."

Callie gave my shoulder an affirming, playful nudge, a silent vow that they'd always be there, come what may. As they sauntered off up the aisle, I opened the notebook. The blank page stared back at me like an open challenge, a silent invitation to craft something new. Although the ache in my chest lingered, for the first time in weeks I felt a small, glimmering spark of hope.

ELLIOTT

While visiting Caleb at his mom's house for the weekend, we spent a lazy afternoon at his favorite park, a place where time seemed to slow beneath the gentle May sun. The golden light hung heavy and warm in the sky, casting elongated, intricate shadows that danced across the park's lush carpet of green as the trees swayed ever so slowly in the summer breeze. As much as I cherished Havenwood with all its tangled memories and familiar comforts, escaping to this sunlit haven for a couple of days felt like inhaling fresh air after a long confinement. Here, watching Caleb dart about with boundless energy and that immense, infectious grin lighting up his face, was a poignant reminder to pause, breathe deeply, and savor the simple, fleeting beauty of life.

Caleb and I settled onto a weathered, timeworn bench tucked away near the playground. A chocolate ice cream cone, its surface already beginning to betray the heat with sticky drips, melted steadily in his small, eager hands, leaving caramel trails down his fingers. In contrast, I cradled a steaming cup of coffee, a soothing weight in my hand that anchored

me as I watched him with a bittersweet mix of pride and longing out of the corner of my eye.

"Why do trees grow so tall?" Caleb suddenly asked, his clear voice interrupting the comforting quiet that enveloped us, as if he were pondering the mysteries of the universe.

I couldn't help but smile at his innocent curiosity, a quality that always caught me off guard. "So, they can reach the sunlight they need to grow," I explained, taking a mindful sip of my coffee as if tasting wisdom.

His head tilted ever so slightly as he squinted upward to absorb the intricate canopy of leaves above. "Do they take all the sunlight?"

"No," I replied gently, shaking my head while my eyes traced the delicate interplay of light and shadow. "They take just what they need. And the rest filters down to nurture the plants below."

He nodded slowly, a small frown of concentration creasing his little face as he mulled over my words. "So, they share?"

"In a way, yes," I said while leaning back against the familiar bench, its surface rough with age. "They all work together so that they can survive and thrive."

Then Caleb turned to face me, his eyes filled with a seriousness that belied his tender age, making me pause in thoughtful reflection. "Is that how people work too?"

I raised an eyebrow, both amused and taken aback by the unexpected shift in his inquiry. "What do you mean?"

"You know… like sharing stuff," he explained, shrugging his tiny shoulders in a manner that felt both natural and profoundly wise. "Like hugs, talking, and…" he paused with a mischievous glimmer in his eye, "ice cream."

I laughed softly, the sound mingling with the distant playful shouts and laughter of other children. "Yeah, I guess people are supposed to share, too."

His little feet started swinging faster as his sneakers made soft scuffing sounds against the gravel beneath. "Do you share with Jules?" he asked suddenly, his voice as innocent as the gentle breeze, yet the question struck me with unexpected weight.

I hesitated, the grip on my coffee tightening as a lump formed in my throat. "What makes you think that?"

With a casual shrug that belied the depth of his thought, he said, "I dunno. You said you like him. When you like someone, you share stuff with them. That's how it works."

"Something like that," came my quiet, tentative reply, unsure of how to navigate the fragile conversation unfolding with my son.

Caleb turned his attention back to his ice cream, methodically licking around the edges before any drips could stain his shirt. "You just have to make sure it's fair, though," he stated matter-of-factly, a tone that resonated with the clarity of youth. "If one person takes all the sunlight, the other person can't grow."

I froze, his words slicing through me like a finely sharpened blade. I thought about Jules, his vibrant energy, his fiery spirit, the dazzling chaos that animated him. And then I reflected on myself, my constant efforts to organize, plan, and corral life's chaotic currents into neat little boxes. Had I been hoarding too much sunlight for myself? Or had I been withholding the brightness altogether, too afraid to share in Jules's radiant, unpredictable chaos?

"You're pretty smart, you know that?" I said gently, reaching out to tousle his soft hair, hair the color of warm mahogany, slightly disarrayed from a recent romp on the playground.

He grinned broadly, a smear of ice cream decorating his cheek like a badge of honor. "Mom says I'm an old soul."

"She's not wrong," I replied with a smile, though a quiet heaviness settled in my chest like the soft glow of dusk.

For a long, tender moment, we sat in companionable silence, the ambient melody of the park weaving around us, the rustle of leaves whispering secrets, the jubilant laughter of children on the swings, and the distant, playful bark of a dog echoing among the trees. Caleb finished his ice cream, wiping his sticky hands on his shorts without a care in the world as if the mess was just another part of the adventure.

"Dad?" he said abruptly, his voice soft yet laden with meaning.

"Yes?" I responded, lowering my gaze to meet his bright, earnest eyes.

"You don't wanna mess it up with Jules. He's cool. Just remember to share," he advised, his words imbued with a simplicity and wisdom that cut deeper than any spoken philosophy.

The ache within me deepened, his candid observation mingling with the tender complexity of my feelings. "Thanks, buddy. I'll try," I murmured, my voice thick with unspoken emotion as I wrestled with my own internal storm.

He nodded, seemingly satisfied with my answer, and with an energetic leap, hopped off the bench. "Can we get fries now?" he requested, his eyes wide with anticipation as he looked up at me.

I chuckled, rising from the bench and casually tossing my empty coffee cup into a nearby trash can. "Yeah, let's go get fries."

As we ambled back toward the car, his small hand slipped into mine, sticky fingers lending a tangible reminder of our shared moment. It was one of those rare instances where time felt both fleeting and infinite. Caleb had a magical way of cutting through the noise of life with simple, clear truths sharper than any words I could muster. And as we headed toward the inviting glow of the nearest diner, his earnest wisdom lingered in my mind.

Maybe it was time I learned to share the sunlight, the space, and every small piece of joy in between. For Caleb, for Jules, and perhaps even for myself.

JULES

The Green Bean Café thrummed with its familiar afternoon energy, the air alive with the rhythmic clamor of baristas calling out drink orders, the gentle hiss of steaming milk, and the resonant clatter of mugs colliding with wooden tabletops. I sat secluded in a shadowed corner, my well-worn sketchbook unfurled before me like a whirlwind of ideas, while a half-drunk iced latte condensed droplets in its glass, tempting and cool. Across from me, Callie reclined leisurely in a chair, their bare feet casually propped up on a rickety metal seat that creaked in protest. Despite the oppressive summer heat, Callie's oversized knit sweater, an ensemble of vibrant yarns, provided a striking counterpoint, as if it were a deliberate act of sartorial rebellion.

"You're not even listening to me, Cal," I admonished, snapping my fingers sharply in the charged stillness between us.

Callie's response came in a lazy grin as they lowered their reflective sunglasses, peering at me with a mix of mischief and mild irritation. "Oh, I'm listening. You've been going on about interactive displays and touchscreens for a solid ten minutes. I just choose to process selectively. And, yes, we will follow up on that snapping shit later."

In a moment of exasperation, I crumpled a napkin in my hand and sent it sailing toward them. They dodged it with effortless grace, their laughter ringing out like a carefree melody amid the background din.

Before I could muster a retort, the melodic jingle of the café door ushered in new energy. Maya and Jayden strode in with an unmistakable vibrance that sliced through the ambient noise. Maya, with her signature precision, sported a bright, body-hugging crop-top and distressed jeans, her hair pulled back into a high, immaculate ponytail. In contrast, Jayden exuded a relaxed coolness, his backward-turned cap and Frappuccino creating an aura of nonchalant charm.

"Oh no," Callie muttered sotto voce, feigning a coy retreat behind their coffee cup. "It's the GSA dream team."

I waved them over with an eager smile. "Maya! Jayden! Over here!"

The two converged on our table with the energy of a well-rehearsed performance; Maya gracefully slid into the seat beside me, while Jayden settled into a chair snugly positioned between me and Callie.

"We come in peace," Jayden declared, brandishing his Frappuccino as if it were a white flag in a mock gesture of surrender.

Callie's eyes twinkled with amusement as they smirked. "I don't believe you for a second. What's up, troublemakers?"

Leaning forward, Maya's eyes, sharp and inquisitive, flickered toward my sketchbook. "We're just checking in on the event," she said softly, her tone laced with both lightness and a subtle urgency. "You know, the Queer History event that's supposed to blow everyone's minds?"

"Yeah," added Jayden, his words punctuated by the deliberate slurp of his drink. "The one where you and Mr. Brooks are supposed to be the ultimate co-planners."

A ripple of tension passed through me, and though I tensed, I maintained a neutral expression. "What about it?"

"Well," Maya began, deliberately drawing out the word as she folded her arms, her gaze both compassionate and challenging, "we just wanted to see how things are going. With you and Mr. Brooks so… busy."

Jayden leaned in conspiratorially, lowering his voice to an intimate murmur. "And by busy, we mean… ironing out all the kinks. Right?"

Callie's laughter, lively and warm, erupted as they nearly choked on their coffee, thoroughly relishing the unfolding banter. "Oh, this is going to be good," they chuckled.

Narrowing my eyes in playful exasperation, I retorted, "You two think you're subtle, huh?"

Jayden merely shrugged, his demeanor unruffled. "We're not saying anything, just checking in. Making sure everything's on track."

Maya's sly smile deepened as she nodded. "Because it's kind of important. To us. To the school. To, you know, everyone."

"And you two," Jayden added quickly, his tone earnest yet teasing, "are kind of the glue holding it all together. We just don't want the… vibe to get weird."

Leaning back in my chair, arms folding as if shielding myself from the candid critique, I mused, "So, what? You're saying this is all my fault?"

"Whoa," Maya interjected, raising her hands in a placating gesture. "Nobody said that. In fact, we didn't even know until now that something had indeed happened. We're just saying… maybe talk to him? Figure out whatever's going on before it derails everything."

Jayden offered a sheepish smile that softened his directness. "It'd be nice if the whole thing didn't crash and burn before it even starts, is all."

Ouch. Crash and burn. Again.

Callie's sneer returned, their tone laced with both humor and wisdom. "Wise words from our resident sages."

Maya and Jayden, their mission seemingly accomplished, rose from their seats. Maya shot me a knowing glance, her eyes glimmering with both encouragement and concern. "We're just saying, Jules. The event, and, well, everything else, needs you and Mr. Brooks to… work."

Jayden gave me a casual salute that danced on the edge of irony. "No pressure or anything."

As they strolled away, their departure leaving an echo of friendly responsibility in their wake, Callie finally broke the charged silence. "Well, they're not wrong."

I let out a heavy sigh, my fingers absentmindedly tracing the rim of my coffee cup as if seeking solace. "Don't you start."

With a nonchalant shrug, Callie mused, "I'm just saying… maybe those two kids have a point."

I remained silent, lost in a labyrinth of thoughts, their words weaving into the messy ball of anxieties I'd been trying desperately to ignore since the argument began.

ELLIOTT

The staff lounge at Havenwood High wasn't exactly a sanctuary of creativity, yet it offered its own modest comforts, a well-worn coffee machine that still managed to brew something decent, chairs that cradled your tired back without excessive punishment, and a battered table that somehow resisted years of daily misuse. The space was imbued with the faint aroma of stale coffee and dry-erase markers as the afternoon sun spilled in generously through the expansive windows, casting long, warm beams on the worn linoleum. I found myself perched on the edge of one of these tired chairs, enveloped in thought while nursing a cup of lukewarm tea, struggling to silence the persistent, gnawing sensation gripping my chest.

Across the table, Sam lounged comfortably in his habitual relaxed sprawl, one elbow casually resting on the scarred wooden surface as he stirred sugar into his steaming coffee. He lifted his eyes, those sharp green orbs narrowing with a blend of teasing amusement and genuine concern. "Alright, Brooks," he declared, his tone laced with both mockery and firm insistence, "this brooding 'lonely poet' act isn't fooling anyone. Spill it."

I exhaled a slow, resigned sigh, my fingers idly tapping against the cool ceramic of my mug. "I'm not brooding," I muttered, though even as the words left my lips, I doubted their truth.

Sam chuckled softly, a sound laced with disbelief, as he leaned back and crossed his arms. "Please. I've known you since our crazy college days. You still have that same haunted look you had when you completely botched your conference speech and then barricaded yourself in the library for what felt like an eternity."

A reluctant smile pulled at the corner of my mouth as I replied, "It wasn't an eternity. It was just three days."

"Two and a half," he quipped, his grin widening. "But who's counting?"

We shared a laugh, one that flowed easily after years of shared memories. Sam had always been my grounding force, the friend who not only remembered the intricate details of my past but also had an uncanny knack for yanking me out of my tangled thoughts when I needed it most.

Yet today even Sam's buoyant levity couldn't slice through the dense fog of thoughts weighing me down. I hesitated, clutching the warm ceramic of my mug as if it were a lifeline. "It's about Jules," I admitted, the words emerging hesitantly, slower than I had intended.

Sam leaned forward, his mischievous grin softening into earnest concern. "Yeah, I figured. What's got you so wound up now?"

I sighed deeply, resting my elbows on the table while my gaze fixated on the swirling remnants of tea. "It's everything," I said. "We haven't spoken since that night, and I can't stop replaying every moment. I know you said to 'just show up.' But part of me wonders if I should reach out, mend things… but another part is paralyzed by indecision."

Sam tilted his head, studying me with the kind of careful patience honed by years of understanding. "And the rest of you?" he prompted gently.

I lapsed into silence for a beat before my voice dropped to a whisper. "The rest of me is questioning why this matters so deeply. I've built my life around precision and predictability, every day mapped out like clockwork. And I like that. I thrive in that. Then Jules comes along, a dazzling mix of sparkle and chaos, and suddenly every certainty I had is thrown into disarray."

His lips twitched into a faint, knowing smile, though his eyes remained serious. "Sounds like Jules has managed to fully burrow under your skin."

I lifted my eyes to meet his, feeling the truth of his words resonate sharply. "Yeah," I admitted quietly but firmly. "He has."

"And that scares you," Sam observed, his tone less interrogative and more a statement of undeniable fact.

Frustration bubbled beneath my composed exterior as I ran a hand through my disheveled hair. "It terrifies me," I confessed, the words heavy with raw vulnerability. "I've methodically structured my life around control, a life where every outcome was predictable. With Jules… nothing about him fits into that neatly ordered plan."

Sam reclined once more, his arms loosely crossed and his gaze thoughtful. "Maybe that kind of disruption isn't such a bad thing," he mused after a moment's pause. "When's the last time someone made you feel this profoundly off-balance?"

"Never," I admitted, the simple word slipping out before I could catch it.

Sam's eyes held a knowing glint as he nodded. "Then maybe it's time to figure out why."

His words struck me with an unexpected intensity, the elegance of his simplicity peeling back layers I wasn't entirely sure I was ready to confront. I nodded slowly, my gaze drifting to the bright window as Sam offered a reassuring pat on my shoulder. His footsteps mutedly echoed on the linoleum as he departed, leaving me alone with my swirling thoughts and the cool, silent presence of my tea.

The sunlight felt overly intrusive now, as if highlighting every jittery nuance of my internal disarray. I sat there, attempting to unravel exactly what it was about Jules that left me feeling so disoriented. I recalled the fierce passion that had ignited during our argument, clashing with the effortless warmth of his laughter, his ability to command a room with chaotic energy, making everything around him pulse with unbridled life rather than overwhelm it. With mid-May ushering in the restless promise of the school year's end and each day crawling slowly toward the inevitable finish line, the looming GSA event only deepened the weight of my thoughts. The mingling anticipation of endings and fresh starts swirled around me, magnifying both the disquiet and the exhilaration that Jules seemed to effortlessly evoke.

Perhaps, as Sam suggested, the real conundrum wasn't Jules at all. Perhaps it was me.

16

ELLIOTT

The Havenwood Farmers' Market was alive with the sounds of approaching summer, children's laughter mingled with the hum of conversation, the clink of jars and produce crates, and the occasional bark of a dog. The scent of freshly baked bread wafted through the air, mingling with the earthiness of ripe tomatoes and the tang of herbs. I navigated the bustling aisles, my hands carefully cradling pots of basil and thyme for the backyard garden I barely had time to tend.

The mid-May sunlight was warm on my face, though not oppressively so, its golden rays filtering through the budding canopy of trees that lined the cobblestone streets. The air carried a hint of humidity, a gentle reminder of the approaching summer, mingled with the faint floral notes of blooming dogwoods and azaleas. The chatter of the crowd was oddly soothing, a blend of laughter, casual conversation, and the occasional bark of a leashed dog from the nearby park, even if my thoughts were anything but. The argument with Jules still lingered like a dull ache, even weeks later. It was easier to focus on the practical things: finding the best produce, avoiding bruised fruit, and sidestepping the occasional rogue child darting through the market.

I paused before a stall displaying neat rows of amber honey in clear glass jars, each one glinting softly in the afternoon light. As my fingers traced the cool surface of the container, a sudden flash of vibrant color caught my eye, Jules. He was about ten feet away, gracefully

weaving through the throng with a signature blend of confidence and chaotic energy. His oversized shirt and brightly colored scarf created a striking contrast against the market's earth-toned backdrop. His arms were laden with an assortment of freshly picked vegetables, and bundles of aromatic herbs tumbled out of his well-worn tote bag, marking him as a master of this lively environment, as if he were born from its very soil.

Accompanying him, laughing merrily at something only Jules could evoke, was Liam. With his solid, comforting presence clad in a well-fitted Henley and dark jeans, Liam stood out in his own quiet way. His warm brown eyes sparkled with mischief as he ambled through the crowd, a small carton of gleaming fresh berries held casually in one hand, a berry popping into his mouth as if to punctuate the moment. Jules hadn't noticed me yet, but Liam's observant gaze quickly shifted in my direction, a knowing smile spreading across his face just as Jules finally looked up. Our eyes met in an unexpected collision of awareness, an encounter that made the surrounding noise and rapid motion blur into the background, leaving us suspended in a soft, almost magical moment. Jules' eyes widened in brief surprise before softening into a small, hesitant smile.

Liam, ever the playful instigator, let out a low chuckle. "Well, well. Look who it is," he said, his voice light and teasing. He glanced between us, clapping a friendly hand on Jules' shoulder before turning with an easy grin to face me. "Hey there, Elliott."

"Hey, Liam," I replied, my tone casually warm though edged with reserve.

Liam's smirk deepened as he alternated his glance between us. "I'll let you have your moment, you've got plenty to talk about," he teased, prompting a half-annoyed, half-appreciative look from Jules before Liam winked and slipped away into the maze of market stalls, already engaging someone in animated conversation with a nearby vendor.

Jules then turned back toward me, shifting the weight of his overfilled tote bag on his shoulder with a gentle, self-aware chuckle. "Hey," he said softly as he closed the narrowing gap between us.

"Hey," I responded, my tone neutral but not unkind.

We stood for a moment in the thick air of the market, the unspoken awkwardness intermingling with a flicker of possibility. My eyes drifted down to the precarious pile of produce in his arms, a visual echo of his unguarded clumsiness.

"You need help with that?" I asked, tilting my head in the direction of his precariously laden tote.

Jules huffed a soft laugh and shifted his bag, his voice light as he replied, "Says the guy trying to juggle plants and honey. I think you're the one who needs help."

Despite the lingering sting of past discord, the corners of my mouth lifted in involuntary amusement. "Fair point," I admitted.

His laughter, warm and easy, reverberated around us, coaxing us into synchrony as we began maneuvering through the market together. With every step, the initial tension began to unravel, and our conversation embarked on tentative, healing notes.

"I, uh, wasn't expecting to see you here," I confessed, clutching the basil and thyme with a tender possessiveness.

"Yeah, I'm gathering supplies for a Playhouse potluck," Jules replied with a casual shrug, a sprig of rosemary playfully peeking out of his bag like a small secret. "I'm in charge of some kind of… rustic, herby thing." His hand waved vaguely, a sheepish smile tugging at his lips. "What about you? Planning a garden?"

"Something like that," I said after a thoughtful pause, then added, "It's nice here. Peaceful."

Jules' gaze softened visibly. "Yeah. I come here when I need a reset," he shared as if confessing a small personal ritual.

We walked in silence for a few measured moments, the ambient hum of the market enveloping us in a cocoon of sound. Jules adjusted his bag again, stealing a tentative glance my way. "So, um… things have been a little… off since the meeting," he admitted, his voice carrying the weight of unsaid regrets.

I stopped and turned to face him, my tone gentle yet forthright. "You weren't the only one avoiding a conversation," I said quietly.

His brow furrowed, and his usual vibrant energy dimmed perceptibly. "Look, I'm sorry. For pushing too hard. I get impatient sometimes, like if I don't keep everything moving, it will all eventually fall apart," he confessed, his voice trembling slightly with vulnerability.

I studied his face, noting how the sincerity in his eyes softened the remnants of our conflict. "I know," I replied carefully. "And I'm sorry too. I get so absorbed in making sure everything works perfectly that I sometimes forget to leave room for life's little surprises."

A faint smile played on his lips as he said, "I don't want to be impossible to work with. I just… care too much sometimes."

"That's not such a bad thing," I said softly, my voice a comforting declaration that even surprised me.

For a charged moment, we simply looked at each other, the heavy remnants of weeks of tension gradually lifting like morning mist. Jules let

out a small laugh, shaking his head in a rueful acknowledgment. "How do you always make me feel less of a disaster?" he asked, almost in awe.

"Maybe you're not as much of a disaster as you think," I replied, the simplicity of the truth warming the air between us.

We soon reached my modest sedan, parked carefully near the edge of the lot. With a theatrical groan, Jules dropped his bag onto the car's hood. "Next time, I'm bringing a wagon," he declared with a playful exaggeration.

"Or buying fewer vegetables," I teased back, unlocking the trunk with a gentle smile.

He gasped in mock offense. "Moderation? From you? I always thought you preferred order, not tyranny."

As I loaded my cherished plants into the car, his playful words lingered like a soft reminder of better times, lighter than our past quarrels, yet no less meaningful.

When I turned to face him once more, I found him leaning casually against the car, his expression a tender enigma.

"You know," he began with a thoughtful undertone that bridged the gap between apology and hope, "for someone so cautious, you're braver than you think."

I paused, hands still resting on the trunk. "Brave?" I echoed softly, as if testing the word.

"Yeah," he affirmed, his smile gentle and encouraging. "You show up. Even when it's difficult, even when everything feels like it's falling apart. That's a kind of courage, isn't it?"

I hesitated, moved by the unexpected truth of his words, and then replied, "You're fearless in ways I'm not. You dream big, that's… really inspiring."

A slight blush warmed his cheeks, and for a moment, he seemed momentarily lost for words. The silence stretched between us, not uncomfortable but charged with the promise of something unspoken yet hopeful.

After a quiet beat, Jules' gaze softened further. "How's Caleb doing, by the way?" he inquired gently.

My expression brightened at the mere mention of my son. "He's good. We caught up over the weekend, and he's completely absorbed in this robotics project at school, it's the only thing he talks about," I explained, warmth seeping into my tone.

"That's wonderful," Jules said, his smile genuine and unforced. "He sounds like an amazing kid."

An awkward pause followed, filled with the weight of unsaid words as Jules shifted his stance. Glancing at me with tentative sincerity, he offered in a low voice, "Well… thanks for letting me crash the party."

I nodded, and just as he hesitated before turning away, he spoke once more. "Hey, um… how's the planning for the event going?" His casual tone was laced with an unmistakable depth, a careful inquiry into things left unsettled.

I exhaled slowly, running a hand through my hair in weary resignation. "Honestly? I tried to keep working on it, but I'm stuck. It's not coming together the way I hoped."

Jules pursed his lips in thought, adjusting the strap of his bag as if weighing each word. "You know, I could… help," he offered, his tone treading the fine line between tentative and hopeful. "I mean, if you don't think it's weird, or too soon after… everything."

A faint smile crept over my face, as fragile hope mingled with understanding. "I was actually going to ask if you'd do that," I admitted softly. "It might be a bit tacky, considering we're just finding our way back to each other, but would you want to meet up and work on it together?"

His grin widened, and something familiar sparked in his eyes. "Sure. How about tomorrow? At the café? We can grab some coffee and hash it all out."

"That works," I said, feeling a subtle lightness in my chest that eased the lingering heaviness. "Thanks, Jules."

"Don't thank me just yet," he teased, his grin softening into something warmer and more genuine. "Just bring your timelines and prepare to have them completely reimagined."

I managed a small chuckle before adding, "I'll brace myself."

Jules turned back once, his eyes meeting mine again with a quiet, hopeful spark. In that brief exchange, I felt the promise of new beginnings, both for the event and, quietly, for our fragile reconciliation. As he melted back into the vibrant market crowd, I slid into my car's driver's seat, my thoughts swirling with the possibility of starting over, not just with the project ahead, but with Jules, too.

17

JULES

The Green Bean Café buzzed with the warmth of a bustling Sunday morning. I had claimed a secluded corner table where my sketchbook lay open, its pages alive with wild, half-formed ideas, and colorful sticky notes encircling it like a mismatched, yet chaotic halo. My iced latte sat within arm's reach, droplets forming along the rim of its glass and trickling onto the coaster below, as I absentmindedly drummed a pen against the table's edge. My foot tapped restlessly beneath the table, echoing the quickening pace of my thoughts, while frantic lines and doodles sprawled along the margins of the paper.

Across from me, Elliott occupied his space with a sleek laptop lying open, his fingers dancing steadily over the keys as if composing a silent symphony. The gentle clicking of his keystrokes blended harmoniously with the ambient noise of the café, yet I found my attention irresistibly drawn to him. His focus manifested almost tangibly, his brow slightly furrowed in concentration as though the rest of the world had faded away, leaving only him in his own quiet sphere. Dressed in a simple yet impeccably pressed light button-down with neatly rolled sleeves, Elliott exuded a composed confidence that set my heart racing every time I stole a glance.

"We'll need to finalize the tech specs for the projection mapping by Monday," he declared with calm authority, breaking the comfortable quiet without taking his eyes off his screen. His voice was smooth and

measured, each word meticulously chosen as if the sentence had been refined in his mind long before it left his lips.

I flipped eagerly to another page in my worn notebook, instantly met by a chaos of scribbled notes and frantic arrows pointing in every direction. "Agreed. I'll touch base with the Concert Hall's tech crew. They've pulled off miracles on tight schedules before, and they owe me a favor anyway," I replied, my tone carrying a mix of determination and humor.

A quiet lull fell over us once more, though this silence was filled with a sense of progress, like two interlocking puzzle pieces finally beginning to fit snugly together. Despite my best attempts to plunge into my own notes, my gaze betrayed me, drifting time and again to the steady rhythm of his typing hands, the slight set of his jaw in deep concentration, and the soft, rebellious curl of hair that refused to lie perfectly in place. With every stolen look, the tension in my chest deepened, pooling in my stomach until the sensation grew too overwhelming, forcing me to avert my eyes and swallow hard.

In a moment of absentminded clumsiness, I flipped a page with too much force; the sharp, echoing sound reverberated across the table. Instant regret washed over me as I saw Elliott glance up, one eyebrow arched in mild amusement at the unexpected noise.

"Sorry," I mumbled, warmth flushing across my cheeks while I fumbled with a sticky note to cover my embarrassment.

A subtle, almost imperceptible smile danced on Elliott's lips, a gesture so delicate yet electrifying, it sent a jolt of energy coursing through me. "How dare you?" he teased lightly before punctuating his playful reproach with a wink.

The space between us seemed to become charged, thick with an unspoken energy that had lingered since our last heated argument. I wasn't certain if it was the close proximity or the grounding effect of his unwavering presence that made my thoughts spiral into a storm of emotions. My eyes involuntarily traced the sharp contour of his jawline, and a sudden, insistent ache stirred within, prickling along my skin. Shifting uneasily in my seat, I adjusted my sketchbook, trying desperately to dispel the warmth that was steadily igniting within me.

"What if we added personal reflections from the audience at the end?" I ventured, my voice overly bright as I motioned toward a printout resting on the table. "Imagine a station where they could jot down notes or record messages, it'd imbue the event with a living, breathing pulse."

Elliott leaned back slightly, his penetrating gaze now softening as it met mine. "That could work," he mused, his lips curving into that rare,

contemplative smile that set my heart aflutter once more. "It would tie everything together, past, present, and future."

"Yes!" I grinned, scribbling a note in the margin of my sketchbook. The excitement of the moment made me lean forward without thinking, reaching for another printout just as Elliott's hand moved toward it.

Our fingers brushed, just for a moment. The contact was fleeting but electric, a spark that shot up my arm and sent another one directly to my groin. Heat coiled low in my stomach, sharp and immediate, and I had to fight the instinct to shift in my seat. I froze, my breath catching as my eyes darted to his. God, I was grateful we were sitting—any attempt to stand right now would have been an unintentional spectacle for both Elliott and the entire café. My pulse thudded in my ears, and I swallowed hard, willing myself to focus on something, anything, other than the sudden and very inconvenient rush of desire threatening to betray me.

His gaze met mine, steady but softer now, like he was trying to decipher something unspoken between us. The café seemed to dissolve, the sounds fading into a distant hum as the weight of the moment pressed into the space between us. My skin tingled where his fingers had grazed mine, and the heat that had been simmering under the surface flared into something I couldn't ignore.

"I've missed this," he said, his voice low, each word deliberate and laden with meaning.

The simplicity of the statement made my chest tighten. I swallowed; my throat suddenly dry. "Me too," I admitted softly, my voice barely above a whisper. "I've missed… working with you."

For the next hour, we worked together in a seamless, almost hypnotic rhythm, our creative energies interlacing with ease despite the lingering tension. A rare chuckle from Elliott at one of my sarcastic remarks felt like a small, precious victory, and our ideas cascaded into one another like notes in a well-rehearsed melody. In that moment, it felt as though we had rediscovered a lost rhythm, and for the first time in weeks, a glimmer of hope shimmered within me, hope not only for the project but also for us.

As the steady hum of the café began to dwindle, I stretched my arms overhead with a dramatic groan of both fatigue and satisfaction. "We've got a solid foundation," I proclaimed with a grin as I leaned back contentedly in my chair.

"We do," Elliott concurred, his tone gentle as he closed his laptop and offered me a warm, subtle smile. "Thanks for sticking with this."

Meeting his gaze, I softened my grin into a more heartfelt expression. "Thanks for… not giving up on me."

We gathered our scattered belongings, and as we stepped out into the embrace of the warm summer evening, I nudged him playfully with my shoulder. "You know, for someone who claims to hate chaos, you're remarkably adept at keeping up with mine."

His chuckle bubbled up, and his shoulders seemed to finally relax, exuding an ease that the night had scarcely seen. The sound of our shared laughter mingled with the soft hum of the evening and standing together on the sidewalk illuminated by the gentle glow of streetlights casting long, dancing shadows, I sensed that we were on the verge of a significant turning point, not merely for the event we were planning, but for us as well.

"Tomorrow, after school," I said with a wide grin, hoisting my bag onto my shoulder. "We'll tackle the next steps. Same place?"

"Same place," he confirmed, his voice steady yet warmly laced with promise. Then, almost as an aside, he added, "I've missed you."

His words halted me mid-step, a powerful surge of unanticipated emotions crashing into me like a tidal wave. I slowly turned back to face him, my expression softening as I endeavored to process the depth of his confession.

"I've missed you too," I replied quietly, the sincerity in my whisper laden with more truth than I had dared to hope. The unadorned honesty of the moment hung suspended between us, heavy, profound, yet somehow entirely comforting.

For a long, silent beat, neither of us moved, both of us caught in an implicit understanding that transcended the project we were constructing. It was about rediscovering the connection we once shared, a reconnection that reached far beyond the professional, whispering of a reconciliation long overdue.

Finally, I managed a tentative smile as I lifted my bag higher. "See you tomorrow, Teach," I said, the lightness in my tone belying the lingering weight of uncharted feelings.

He nodded, his steady gaze locking with mine just a moment longer before he offered a shy, genuine smile. "Tomorrow."

As I walked away into the warm embrace of the evening, I stole one last glance over my shoulder. Our eyes met once more, and his lingering smile, quiet and authentic, stirred a hopeful emotion within me.

For the first time in weeks, it wasn't just about moving forward, it felt like we were stepping toward something undeniably better.

18

ELLIOTT

A couple of weeks had passed, and now it was early June, Pride Month, and everything had fallen seamlessly into place. The school year had ended, giving me more time to devote to the event, and Jules had truly turned it out with his connections, donations, and amazing knack for making big things happen. The Harmony Concert Hall buzzed with activity, a symphony of clinking tools, overlapping conversations, and the hum of projectors coming to life. The late afternoon sun streamed through the large windows, casting a golden glow over the bustling scene, as if nature itself were celebrating the occasion. Outside, the June air was warm but not oppressive, carrying the faint scent of blooming wildflowers and freshly cut grass, with the promise of the long summer days Havenwood was known for.

Rows of plush seats waited to be filled, while the stage was a hive of activity, brimming with artifacts, screens, and banners, each detail a testament to the careful planning and collaboration that had gone into the event. It was the eve of the *Pride Month: Stories That Change Us* celebration, and the air carried a palpable mix of excitement and urgency, a fitting atmosphere for the longest days of the year when possibilities seemed endless.

I stood in the back at the audio booth, a clipboard clutched in my hand, my eyes darting over the meticulously updated checklist. The color-coded columns on the page were like safe beacons amidst the pandemonium, anchoring me in the midst of the whirlwind activity. Surrounding me, students and volunteer aides moved with a shared purpose, their energy creating an undercurrent of quiet determination.

Maya and Jayden were stationed near the entrance, huddled around a table strewn with an assortment of craft supplies. Jayden's gentle concentration showed in the careful way he cut bright strips of paper, while Maya's pencil danced across large poster boards, sketching intricate designs with a flourish that mirrored her bubbling enthusiasm.

"Mr. Brooks!" Maya's voice resonated cheerily across the hall as she waved, one hand clutching a marker as if it were a magic wand. "We've got an idea for the event!"

Setting my clipboard aside, I navigated through clusters of volunteers, each busily adjusting lights, fine-tuning displays, or double-checking tech setup, until I reached their lively table. With an excited flourish, Maya lifted a long strip of vivid orange paper that boldly declared, *What Does Pride Mean to You?* in flowing, elegant script.

"We're thinking of setting up a paper chain station," she explained, her excitement bright enough to illuminate the room. "Everyone can jot down their thoughts on a strip of paper, and by the night's end, we'll join them together into one living representation of our community's voice."

Jayden, still snipping away with his scissors, added, "It's going to be like a living installation, a testament to our united spirit."

I hesitated for just a moment, the thought of an unscheduled addition tugging at my mind. "But we hadn't…," I began, only to be swiftly reassured by the infectious sparkle in their eyes. I cleared my throat and softened, "That's a fantastic idea. Have you thought about where you'd like to set it up?"

Maya gestured toward a cleared-off corner near the interactive timeline. "There's plenty of space there, and it won't interfere with the main displays."

"Perfect," I replied. "Just let me know if you need any more supplies."

"Thanks, Mr. Brooks!" Maya beamed, before returning to her creative flurry, while Jayden flashed a confident thumbs-up that warmed my heart.

Not far from this creative corner, near the stage, Jules was a dynamo in motion, a flurry of energy coordinating a team of volunteers

as he wrangled the final adjustments on a set of projectors. His signature bright scarf billowed behind him like a triumphant banner as he moved deftly amongst the organized chaos.

"Shift that screen two inches to the left," Jules commanded with playful intensity, gesturing as though orchestrating a grand performance. "The projections need to fall in perfect harmony with the lettering."

Nearby, Callie was multi-tasking effortlessly, balancing a cup of steaming coffee in one hand and a clipboard in the other, and couldn't help but raise a teasing eyebrow. "You do realize you've adjusted that screen at least four times already? Not that I'd know, since my domain is hair and keeping things fabulously in place," they remarked with a wry smile, flipping an imaginary strand of hair over their shoulder like it was no big deal.

Jules shot them a playful glare. "And now it's perfect… just like you. Trust the process, Cal."

I then made my way toward the stage, carefully sidestepping cables and equipment scattered like hidden treasures. Spotting me, Jules waved me over with an exuberant grin that outshone even the stage lights.

"How's it looking back there, Teach?" he asked as he leaned casually on the edge of the stage.

"Everything's on track," I replied. "Maya and Jayden have conjured up an incredible paper chain station idea. I have a feeling it's going to resonate immensely."

"Of course they did," Jules replied, his voice laced with admiration. "Those two have an unstoppable spark."

"Wonder where they get it from," Callie teased lightly, eliciting a chorus of light laughter from the group as they sipped their coffee.

Jules's focus then returned to the projection screens, his playful banter giving way to a more measured concern. "What about the sound cues? Are we all synchronized?"

I nodded firmly. "Everything's been tested thoroughly. The transitions are seamless, and the microphones are all set."

Jules released an exaggerated, relieved sigh. "Thank you, Teach. I'd be completely lost without your steady hand."

"You'd figure it out," I replied with a teasing smirk. "But it's nice to know you're grateful."

His warm laugh washed over us like a calming tide, and for a fleeting moment, amidst the orchestrated chaos and buzzing energy, the world felt perfectly still.

As twilight began to nudge its way into the hall, the space itself metamorphosed into its final form. Softly glowing interactive displays began to illuminate the room, the screens cycling through vibrant images of queer history, marches, protests, celebrations, and tender everyday instances of resilience. Volunteers moved like busy fireflies, adding the final artistic touches to decorations and arranging seating with attentive care.

Maya and Jayden had positioned their paper chain station near the interactive timeline, and already the first few links hung proudly, each strip carrying heartfelt inscriptions like "Love is Love," "Visibility Saves Lives," and "Community Means Everything."

Just then, Sam breezed in, his perky energy slicing through any lingering tension like a burst of sunlight. He handed me a fresh cup of coffee, its aroma rich and comforting, and offered Jules a grand mock salute. "How are my favorite social justice warriors holding up?"

"Thriving," Jules declared with dramatic flair, twirling his clipboard as if it were a prized scepter. "We're on the verge of changing the world, Sam."

"And doing it all fabulously along the way," Callie chirped, drawing a round of hearty laughter from everyone.

The hall vibrated with the excited buzz of guests arriving; the sound of their footsteps and soft chatter formed a rhythmic undercurrent as Jules and I stood near the stage, our shoulders lightly brushing as we watched weeks of labor blossom into the magic of the moment. Vibrant banners fluttered from the walls, tables laden with colorful art projects and fresh resources dotted the space, and the excitement was as palpable as the warm hum of summer itself. In that moment, I felt a profound sense of pride, not only in the event we had all created, but also in the journey Jules and I had navigated together.

"Can you believe this?" Jules murmured softly as he rested his hand gently on the edge of the stage, his eyes brimming with a mix of anticipation and quiet awe.

I turned to meet his gaze. His warm, open expression reflected the shared wonder of our journey, and for the first time in what felt like ages, I allowed a genuine smile to tug at my lips. "It's incredible," I whispered, feeling the weight and beauty of the moment.

His grin widened, quick and incandescent, rekindling the spark that had carried us through every challenge. Just as I began to settle into this rare calm, a subtle movement at the entrance caught my eye. I paused, blinking in surprise as Anna and Caleb stepped cautiously inside. Caleb's face lit up with an exuberant grin that danced across his features,

while Anna's eyes, sharp yet kind, took in the bustling scene with quiet understanding. My heart skipped a beat; I had invited them in a hopeful, offhanded manner weeks ago, never truly expecting them to appear.

"Everything okay?" Jules inquired, tilting his head in concern as he studied me.

I fumbled with the edge of my jacket, my voice betraying a trace of nervous energy. "I, uh… I didn't think they'd show up." I motioned subtly toward the entrance. "That's Caleb and Anna, my son and his mom."

Jules straightened, his buoyant confidence flickering momentarily into surprise. "Oh."

Glancing back at him with a quickened pulse, I said, "Come with me. I want you to meet them."

Jules hesitated, his usually confident persona softening into genuine concern. "Elliott… are you sure? You don't have to do this if you're not ready."

In that tender pause, I realized this moment was about far more than just an introduction, it was a step toward sharing every part of who I was. Offering a small, reassuring smile, I replied, "I'm ready. I think it is time. If you are ok with that."

After a moment of quiet reflection as he searched my expression, Jules gave a slow, measured nod. "Alright," he said softly, a faint tremor of vulnerability coloring his tone. "Lead the way, Teach."

Together, we navigated through the throng, the background chatter of the hall softening into an indistinct hum as my nerves swirled with anticipation. My heart pounded a little faster when Caleb's bright face caught sight of me, his arms flung wide in an enthusiastic wave.

"Dad!" he called out, tugging gently on Anna's arm as they made their way closer.

"Hey, buddy," I greeted warmly, my voice gentle yet edged with nervous excitement. Bending slightly, I wrapped him in a quick hug, the lingering scent of peppermint gum and fresh air mingling around him like a familiar perfume. Straightening, I met Anna's gaze.

"Anna, Caleb," I began, gesturing toward Jules, "this is Jules. He's been a cornerstone in putting this event together with me."

Anna's smile was warm and genuine as she extended her hand in greeting. "It's so nice to meet you. This event is nothing short of incredible, I mean, wow."

Jules shook her hand with firm respect, even as his tone softened. "Thank you. We've had an amazing team behind this, but Elliott has been the heart and soul of it all."

Anna's eyes softened further, filled with quiet pride. "I can see that clearly. I'm really proud of you, Elliott."

Clearing my throat, I let the simple, heartfelt compliment sink in. "Thanks. That means a lot to me."

Meanwhile, Caleb's curiosity pulled him closer to Jules. "So, you're the theatre guy?" he asked bluntly, eyes wide with admiration. "Dad says you're really creative."

Jules chuckled warmly, crouching slightly to meet Caleb's earnest gaze. "I dabble a bit here and there. Your dad is the one who keeps everything on track, with his spreadsheets and all that."

Caleb grinned, nodding as if the explanation fit perfectly. "Yeah, that totally checks out. He's pretty much the GOAT."

Anna laughed softly, gently resting her hand on Caleb's shoulder as she remarked, "We should let you two continue getting settled. Caleb and I will grab some seats."

I nodded, feeling a tender mix of awkwardness and warmth at the unfolding scene. "Thanks for coming. It truly means a lot to have you here."

Anna's smile radiated warmth and understanding. "We wouldn't miss it for the world."

As they drifted toward the seating area, I turned to Jules, who regarded me with a thoughtful look. "So… that was them," I said, lightly scratching the back of my neck.

"They seem wonderful," Jules replied quietly, his voice tinged with genuine interest.

"They are," I agreed softly, pride threading through my tone. "And Caleb… well, he's simply everything."

Jules nodded, his expression softening in companionable understanding. "I can see that."

With the hall now brimming with the welcoming buzz of arriving attendees, Jules and I returned to our spot near the stage. For a few unspoken moments, we simply absorbed the evolving energy around us, watching with quiet satisfaction as the culmination of weeks of hard work unfurled before our eyes. The vibrant banners, art-filled tables, and carefully arranged seating all resonated with the spirit of the event, establishing me in a serene confidence amidst the remaining chaos.

"You ready for this?" Jules asked again, his tone gentler now.

I met his steady gaze and nodded. "I think we've got this."

His smile returned, quick, confident, and filled with the spark of unyielding hope. For the first time in a long while, I allowed myself to truly believe in the promise of the moment.

19

JULES

The glow of Harmony Concert Hall was a living, breathing thing, warm light spilling from the stained-glass windows and pooling on the sidewalk outside. The buzz of excitement hummed through the air, spilling out into the lobby where vibrant banners announced the Pride Month: Stories That Change Us Event. Tables were adorned with stacks of queer literature, handmade crafts, and memorabilia donated by local LGBTQ+ elders. Young children darted between the tables, their laughter blending with the chatter of parents, students, and community members of every age.

The room was alive with color, rainbow pins, pride flags draped over shoulders, and sequins glinting under the overhead lights. At one table, Maxie Glam, the larger-than-life drag queen trivia host from the Rainbow Taproom, stood like royalty, her family of queens and kings flanking her. Parents took pictures with her as she teased the children, slipping into an exaggerated Southern drawl. Noah Patel stood near the art station, chatting with Renzo Santiago about their shared love of queer Latinx poetry, Renzo's quiet nods matching Noah's animated gestures. At the queer literature table, Max O'Connor laughed with Tess Franklin and Avery Summers, who leaned in to debate the merits of a particularly colorful book. Callie Nguyen breezed by with coffee, tossing a playful remark to Harper Adebayo, whose calm presence anchored the lively

scene, while Liam Carter's booming voice at the mic kept the energy high with his quick wit. Administrators and teachers from Havenwood High, local business owners, and even a few curious older folks from the assisted living center had all shown up, filling the space with an energy I could only describe as electric.

I navigated eagerly between clusters of lively conversations, my outfit a vivid spectacle that mirrored my exploding personality, a flowing ensemble splashed with clashing, bold patterns of deep purples and vivid yellows. Clutched in my hand, a clipboard scribbled with frenzied notes was my talisman for the evening, a comforting distraction that kept my energy channeled. I paused at the GSA table, where Maya and Jayden had transformed the area into a pulsing hub of artistic creativity and heartfelt connection. Hovering above the table, the question "*What Does Pride Mean to You?*" was penned in grand, flowing script, beckoning curious onlookers to engage.

"This is amazing, you two," I marveled quietly, my eyes drinking in the living canvas before me. With a beaming smile, Maya motioned excitedly toward a continuously growing chain of vibrantly colored paper strips, her enthusiasm practically contagious. "We've been adding to the paper chain all night," she explained, each strip a fragment of shared hope. Jayden, deftly snipping through more paper with practiced ease, added, "It's a huge success." I laughed, though my gaze was constantly darting about to take in every exquisite detail. Suddenly, the sound of my name being called drew me toward Callie, who had claimed the queer literature table like a stage. Holding court with a fresh cup of coffee in one hand and their clipboard in the other, Callie beckoned, "Jules!" with an exuberant wave. "You've been glowing all night. Is it nerves or just an obscene amount of caffeine?"

"Both," I admitted with a self-deprecating chuckle, casually brushing back a rebellious strand of hair. "Also, a dash of sheer terror." Callie's gentle laugh and reassuring shake of the head brought instant comfort. "Relax. This is incredible, and you know it." I managed a smile, but before I could offer a full reply, my eyes drifted across the room and locked onto someone, or something, that seized my attention.

There, at the tech booth, stood Elliott, meticulously adjusting the controls on the soundboard. Dressed in a sharply tailored, dark suit that sculpted his physique perfectly, his striking appearance nearly made me drop my clipboard. He exuded a magnetism so potent that every inch of him appeared to whisper composed professionalism, even as my mind flirted wildly with unprofessional thoughts of sneaking him into a quiet supply closet for a secret rendezvous.

"Jules, focus," I muttered silently, shaking the daydream from my head. Too much depended on my attention tonight, and the event wasn't going to orchestrate itself.

The program unfurled with the students taking center stage. Maya's spoken word performance struck the room like a series of powerful, emotional drumbeats, each line a visceral punch of resilience and defiance. Soon after, Jayden moved through his monologue, causing the audience to alternate between hearty laughter and tear-streaked eyes. The air swelled with snapping fingers, heartfelt cheers, and standing ovations, as every performance built the momentum higher.

I flitted back and forth between the bustling audience and the organized controlled chaos backstage, ensuring that every transition shimmered with seamless precision. At one point, I ducked into an aisle near Elliott, where the soft glow of stage lights gently illuminated his focused face. "They're killing it out there," I whispered as I leaned in close. He turned, his gaze warm and soulful, and answered softly, "Because they had someone who believed in them." His tender words sent an unexpected flutter through my chest, momentarily stealing my breath away. I squeezed his arm lightly in grateful acknowledgment before slipping away backstage, my heart drumming in a wild, hopeful rhythm.

Bathed in the luminous warmth of the spotlight, I stepped to the center of the stage. The ambient hum in the room settled into an almost sacred stillness that was as exhilarating as it was terrifying. My eyes swept across a sea of diverse faces, students, parents, artists, teachers, business owners, and many others, each one a sparkling constellation in the night's vast sky. For a suspended moment, I allowed myself to breathe in the collective energy, feeling its unique gravity hold me in the significance of this night.

"Okay, funny story," I began with a playful smile curling at my lips, "I once tried to organize a protest without checking anyone else's schedule. Turns out, you can't march solo and call it a movement." A warm ripple of laughter cascaded over the room, softening the tension coiled in my chest. After letting that moment of levity settle, my tone deepened into something more reflective.

"But seriously," I declared, taking a deliberate step forward, "being vulnerable is like stepping onto a stage without a script. You never know how it will land, whether you'll evoke cheers or stumble flat on your face. And yet… you do it anyway, because the story, the raw truth, is worth the risk." The room hushed, every eye and ear fixed in rapt attention. My gaze flickered toward the tech booth once more, resting

on Elliott's steady, composed stillness. Even from afar, he exuded a softness that spoke directly to my soul, an ineffable quality felt in every beat of my heart.

"You know," I continued, my voice growing stronger with each word, "each of you is not just enough, you are magnificently, unabashedly more than enough. If anyone ever told you that you're too much, too loud, too passionate, too weird, too chaotic, remember this: it's not a shortcoming in you, but a limitation in them. They just couldn't handle your fabulousness." Genuine laughter and heartfelt sounds of agreement filled the space, but I pressed on, grounding the message in deep sincerity.

"This event, tonight, is about connection. It's about cherishing our past while constructing a future where every story, every truth, matters. Storytelling is not merely words, it's connection, community, courage. It's the steadfast declaration, 'We're here. We've always been here.' And we're not going anywhere." My eyes wandered over the audience, finding flickers of familiar joy, Callie's beaming grin, Max's encouraging nod, Tess's gentle hand in Avery's, each individual a vibrant thread in our collective tapestry.

"And despite all our differences, our varied histories, and even the world's attempts to pull us apart, hear this and hold it close: you are loved. Exactly as you are, right here, right now." The words hung heavily in the air, their weight an embodiment of shared truth. Locking eyes with Elliott one final time, the rest of the world blurred into insignificance. This message was for him as much as for the room, perhaps especially for him.

"Because when we come together, with all our differences and even our conflicts, we forge something far greater than ourselves. We create belonging. And tonight, you're not just etched into history, you're woven into a family. A family that sees you, a family that cherishes you." As the applause began as a gentle rumble, swelling into a roar that cascaded through the hall, I stepped back and bowed my head, overwhelmed by a surge of profound emotion. In that fleeting moment, as I looked back toward Elliott, who was clapping with quiet, warm intensity and the faintest crescent of a smile, I dared to hope he understood. That the message wasn't solely for the crowd, but for him, for us. In every contrast and obstacle, there was love found in the nuanced space between.

Thunderous applause filled the hall once again. Backstage, Callie enveloped me in a bear hug before I could even draw a breath. "You crushed it," they said softly, their voice a tender reprieve from the night's

chaos. "Thanks, Cal," I whispered, my voice trembling with a blend of relief and wonder. As the echoes of applause reverberated through the building, I found a small, quiet corner to catch my breath. My heart thumped wildly, not with fear, but with hope. A hope that, at long last, I was stepping into the full, radiant version of myself that I was meant to be.

20

ELLIOTT

The applause still echoed faintly in my ears as I stepped outside into the warm night air. The energy inside Harmony Concert Hall was electric, conversations buzzing, congratulations exchanged, laughter rippling through the space. It was the kind of atmosphere that could buoy anyone's spirits, but I needed a break from the noise. I wasn't ready to join in the post-event revelry. Instead, I found myself drawn to the quiet of the parking lot, where my car sat under the glow of a single streetlamp.

As the crowd slowly dispersed, I lingered at the edge of the lot, watching familiar faces drift away in clusters, their voices laced with snippets of excitement and farewell. A few school administrators passed by each offering firm handshakes accompanied by warm, sincere smiles.

"Mr. Brooks, that was an incredible event," said the principal, his tone laced with genuine admiration. "You've set a new standard for what the GSA can achieve. Congratulations."

"Thank you," I replied as I shook his hand, a flicker of pride igniting inside me. His words were a tribute to the countless hours of planning and dedication that had made the evening possible.

Praises continued to flow in from colleagues and community members as they passed by, their kind words forming a steady stream of affirmation. In the distance, I spotted Callie waving her arms in an exaggerated manner. "See you at the Taproom, Teach! Don't keep us waiting!" she called out, her voice playful and bright.

I couldn't help but smile, recalling how Jules would tease me about that very smile. My gaze shifted as Anna and Caleb emerged, their faces glowing with unmistakable pride. Caleb reached me first, enveloping me in a spontaneous hug that tightened my chest with the warmth of his affection. "That was awesome, Dad. Like, really awesome," he exclaimed.

"Thanks, buddy," I replied, squeezing him back before releasing him. Anna then approached with measured steps, her eyes shimmering with unshed tears as she drew me into a brief but heartfelt embrace.

"You should be so proud of yourself," she whispered, her voice thick with sincerity. "Elliott, tonight was incredible. The way you pulled everything together, the way you moved people, it was beautiful."

I nodded, swallowing hard against the unexpected lump in my throat. "Thank you," I managed in a softer voice than intended. "It means so much that you were here." Her hand lingered on my arm for a moment longer before she stepped back, smiling through the tears. Caleb hesitated a moment as he followed her, then looked back at me with a grin full of warmth.

"Dad?" he called, edging forward.

"Yeah?"

"I'll see you soon, right?"

"Soon," I replied, pulling him into another, tighter hug. I rested my chin briefly on the top of his head before looking him in the eyes. "I love you, Caleb. Always."

"I love you too, Dad," he answered, his voice light but sincere, before jogging off to catch up with Anna.

I stood there watching them leave, the quiet night wrapping around me like a soft blanket. In the rearview mirror, I saw Caleb turn to wave through the window, and I lifted my hand in return until his car rounded the corner and faded from view.

Turning back toward my car, I still heard the faint echoes of laughter and applause drifting from the hall, a reminder of how much the evening had meant, not simply for the students or community, but for each of us. Resting against the hood, I gazed out at the dimly lit trees bordering the lot. The crisp night air provided a welcome contrast to the enduring warmth of the auditorium, while my fingers idly toyed with the edges of my coat pockets. A nervous churn twisted in my stomach as I shifted my weight from one foot to the other.

I wasn't ready to leave yet. Somewhere between the crescendo of Jules' speech and the quiet close of the program, I knew I had to speak

with him. There was something unspoken that I could no longer hold back.

The door to the hall creaked open softly, and I instinctively straightened. There he was. Jules stepped out, his colorful scarf catching the streetlight's glow like a beacon of vibrancy in the night. His movements, usually so fluid and self-assured, were now slowed by a palpable hesitation. For a moment, he didn't notice me; his eyes scanned the lot until they fell on mine.

"Hey, Teach," he called, his voice light yet edged with exhaustion. "Hiding from the crowds?"

A quiet chuckle escaped me as I pushed off the car. "Something like that," I admitted in a subdued tone. "I just… I need to say something."

His playful smile softened into a more attentive expression, and as he stepped closer, his scarf slipped slightly from his shoulder, revealing his hands twisting the fabric anxiously. Jules was not one to exhibit nerves openly, yet tonight his usual spark was replaced by a tender vulnerability.

"What's on your mind?" he asked cautiously, as if unsure if he wanted the answer.

I hesitated, the words catching in my throat. For so long, I had been adept at keeping things inside, at remaining silent. But Jules had a way of coaxing hidden truths into the open, and tonight was no exception.

"What you said tonight," I began, my voice faltering slightly, "about vulnerability, about stepping on stage without a script, it hit me harder than I expected." I paused to gather my thoughts, meeting his gaze steadily.

"I've spent so much of my life hiding, Jules, afraid to take risks, afraid to be seen for who I truly am. And you… you make it seem so effortless."

He blinked, his features softening as he regarded me. "It isn't easy," he admitted, his voice trembling with honesty. "I've been running my whole life, both toward and away from things, because the thought of getting close and then losing someone terrifies me."

His words struck like a solid blow, and I clenched my hands in my pockets. "I know that feeling," I muttered in a quiet, layered tone. "When I came out to my wife, to my son, I convinced myself that I didn't deserve something like this. Like us. I wanted it so dearly, but after everything I put them through, I thought it wasn't mine to claim."

Jules edged closer, his eyes glistening in the soft light, his bravado giving way to raw emotion. He tilted his head, his voice taking on a gentle, deliberate cadence. "Elliott," he began, "what are we?"

The question hung heavy between us, laden with both uncertainty and possibility. I opened my mouth to respond, but he continued, his voice shaking yet resolute.

"I can be patient," he said. "I'll wait as long as it takes. But I need to know, because I'm really into you. Despite all my fears of you leaving, there's something about you I can't shake. Something essential."

I stared at him, my throat tightening as his words sank in. For a heartbeat, I could not speak, lost in the intensity of our connection. Then, slowly, I stepped forward, closing the distance between us.

"I want this too," I declared, my voice steady despite the swirling maelstrom inside me. "Labels don't matter. What matters is that we figure it out together. Wherever this leads… I want to go with it."

Jules' breath caught as his eyes searched mine, the anticipation thick in the cool air. Almost instinctively, I reached out, gently brushing a stray strand of hair from his face. My fingers trembled as they caressed his skin, lingering in a moment stretched by unsaid promises. He leaned in, his gaze unwavering.

"You don't have to run anymore," I whispered, my voice nearly drowned out by the pounding of my heart.

A small, genuine smile broke across his face as he responded in silence, and before I could overthink further, I leaned in and our lips met in a kiss that began as soft and tentative, a cautious exploration of shared vulnerability. As we deepened the kiss, it became a profound release of all that had been left unspoken, our passion unfurling like a long-held secret finally set free. His hands rested lightly upon my chest, anchoring me as the world blurred around us. I felt his warmth seep into me, igniting a slow-burning fire that had long been smoldering beneath layers of fear.

When we finally pulled apart, our foreheads still pressed together, our breaths mingling in the cool night air, Jules let out a soft, shaky laugh, a sound of pure relief.

"So," he teased in a gentle voice, "does this mean I'm officially on your spreadsheet?"

I chuckled, the sound light and sincere. "You've always been on it," I replied, my tone filled with warmth. "I just hadn't figured out which column you belonged in yet."

His grin widened, the spark returning to his eyes as he looked at me with quiet certainty. "I think we'll figure it out together."

Unable to resist, I leaned in once more through our laughter. Our lips met in another soft, tentative kiss, a delicate conversation of desire and promise. The kiss deepened with each passing heartbeat, our lips pressing together more firmly as Jules' hands swept up to cradle my face. His thumbs traced the lines of my jaw, sending delightful shivers down my spine. Our tongues met in a slow, sensual dance as his fingers explored the contours of my skin, pulling me ever closer. I wrapped my arms around his waist, and in the charged space between us, the undeniable heat of our arousal intertwined, provoking a surge of desire that coursed through me. My hands traveled lower, exploring the firm curve of his body beneath the fabric, the sensation intensifying the flame burning within us both.

When we finally broke apart, our breaths ragged and our foreheads still touching, I exhaled softly, "I want this. I want you. No more holding back."

His response was a soft, breathless laugh: "Then stop holding back."

Jules' laughter softened further into something warm and serene as he rested his forehead against mine for a lingering moment before stepping back just enough to meet my eyes. His playful smile was accompanied by a slight blush, and I could tell he was still catching his breath, just as I was.

"As tempting as this is," he said in a low, teasing tone, "we did promise everyone we'd be at the Taproom tonight."

I groaned theatrically, tilting my head back in mock despair. "Do we have to? What if we just… skipped it? My house isn't far."

Jules burst into a hearty laugh, the sound echoing softly in the still night. "Oh, believe me, that idea is very tempting," he admitted, his eyes sparkling mischievously. He reached out and adjusted the lapel of my coat where his fingers had lingered earlier. "But no. If we don't show up, Callie will have half the town tracking us down, and I'm not in the mood for that kind of scandal."

I sighed, leaning comfortably against the car's hood. "Fine. But don't expect me to be sociable."

With a knowing smirk, Jules glanced downward briefly before his eyes flicked back up to mine with a playful glint. "Seems like we both need a moment to savor this before heading in," he quipped, his grin hinting at a mischievous secret as he made a subtle adjustment beneath his pants.

My own laughter bubbled up in response, mirroring his playful awkwardness as I tucked my own erection up into my waist. "You're not making this easy, you know."

"I'm not supposed to," he shot back in a tone developing into flirtatious warmth. Leaning in deliberately once more, he kissed me again, this time softer, yet no less intoxicating. His lips lingered against mine with a gentle insistence, leaving me craving more even as he drew back.

I exhaled sharply as the space between us suddenly expanded, the temporary absence of his warmth leaving me momentarily unsteady. Jules grinned at my dazed expression, his head tilting in that infuriatingly charming manner of his.

"You're REALLY not making this easy," I admitted, my voice rough with emotion even as a smile tugged at the corners of my lips.

Jules winked playfully, his laughter trailing behind him as he stepped toward the hall. "Come on, Teach. Let's not keep everyone waiting. I'm sure Callie's already halfway through a karaoke rendition of 'Vogue.'"

I followed after him, my heart still racing with both anticipation and contentment. For the first time, being off my usual schedule felt perfectly right, whatever tonight had in store, I was ready to embrace it, as long as it was with Jules by my side.

The taproom pulsed with an infectious energy as we crossed the threshold, every corner filled with the low buzz of lively conversation blending with the bubbly rhythm and synthesizers of Madonna's *Holiday*. The Rainbow Taproom was in full, exuberant swing; its walls boasted a riot of neon signs, and the colorful flare of pride flags draped luxuriously over every available surface. Maxie Glam, the undeniable queen of the town's drag scene, commanded attention by the intimate karaoke stage. In a dazzling sequined gown that shimmered under every light, she radiated her signature charisma, warming up the eager crowd with every animated gesture and flamboyant smile.

Jules, the epitome of vibrant energy, was already a step ahead of me. His presence drew admiring glances even before I had fully witnessed his every move. He waved exuberantly at Callie, who sat regally at a spacious corner table, surrounded by our familiar friends. Just

watching Jules caused my heart to race; every laugh and every confident stride seemed to have a magnetic pull that I found irresistible.

Seated around a table that overflowed with familiar, friendly faces, each one brightened by the shimmering glow of the neon lights, I felt at home. Callie, ever graceful, slid a cocktail toward me as soon as we sat, her wink punctuating the clink of our glasses. Nearby, Tess and Max delved deep into conversation with Sam, while Renzo leaned intimately close to Ezra, his hand resting with a tender familiarity upon Ezra's arm. On the far side of the table, Liam captivated Harper and Avery with a story so funny that it sent bursts of laughter across the room. When Liam locked eyes with me and winked knowingly, a smile tugged at my lips as he greeted me with, "Hey there, Teach!"

Jules gracefully slipped into the seat beside me, our legs meeting under the table with a subtle, electrifying brush of knees. That slight contact sent a jolt through me, and I caught his sly, knowing smile before he turned his attention to the animated tale Callie was spinning. My pulse quickened, and I took a long, steady sip of my drink, silently pleading for the alcohol to steady my fraying nerves.

Throughout the evening, Jules found every opportunity to lean close. He'd touch my arm when he spoke, his fingers lingering just a beat too long. At one point, he laughed at something I said and rested his hand on my thigh under the table, his fingers brushing dangerously close to my cock. I swallowed hard, my cheeks burning, and Jules smirked knowingly.

"Having fun, Teach?" he said, his tone low and intimate, ensuring his words were meant only for my ears.

I cleared my throat, desperate to regain focus on the surrounding chatter, yet his hand remained, a constant, delicious distraction. When Callie burst into an enthusiastic suggestion about karaoke, Jules leaned in once more, his breath warm and inviting against my ear.

"You should sing something," he teased with a playful lilt. "Something sexy. Maybe 'Careless Whisper.'"

I couldn't help but roll my eyes, even as my heart pounded wildly. "Not happening," I retorted.

Jules pouted dramatically, his lips brushing teasingly against my ear. "You're no fun."

At one point, Max asked if I could walk with him to the bar to grab another round of drinks. Jules shot me a mischievous glance as I hesitated, my mind racing. The tenting in my pants had only worsened thanks to Jules' relentless teasing, and standing up wasn't an option without giving the whole table a very clear view of my predicament.

"Uh, I think I'll stay put," I stammered, awkwardly shifting in my seat. "Maybe Callie can go instead?"

Jules bit his lip in suppressed laughter. As soon as Max departed with Callie, Jules leaned in closer, his voice a husky whisper meant solely for me. "What's the matter, Teach? Can't stand up?"

I glared at him, though a small, reluctant grin betrayed my amusement. "You know exactly why."

He stifled a laugh, his hand drifting back to my thigh with a slow, deliberate touch that sent shivers coursing through me. "I do," he replied, his voice rich with amusement and desire. "And I'm loving it."

As the table erupted into laughter over one of Liam's jokes, Jules' hand slipped higher, his fingers tracing the outline of my erection through my pants. The movement was bold, concealed only by the thin tablecloth, and I felt a jolt of electricity run through me. I inhaled sharply, my drink teetering on the edge of the table as I set it down, trying not to draw attention to myself.

"Jules," I warned under my breath, my voice low and tinged with strain.

But he only smiled, his eyes locking on mine with a daring glint that promised more mischief. He didn't withdraw his hand; instead, he applied a gentle, teasing pressure that sent tremors of pleasure down my spine. "You're not going to make a scene, are you?" he whispered, his warm breath tickling my ear.

I shifted uncomfortably in my seat, trying to maintain some semblance of composure, but it was no use. The heat between us was palpable, and I could feel myself getting harder by the second. Jules' hand remained in place, a constant reminder of the thrill and danger of what we were doing.

Just when I believed I might reach my limit, Jules leaned closer still, his lips softly brushing against my ear once more. "I love watching you squirm," he uttered in a sultry tone. "It appears Mr. Brooks has been keeping a big secret down there," he teased, his voice low and dripping with playful intrigue. And with that provocative remark, he gave my cock a firm, confident squeeze before finally retracting his hand, leaving me breathless, flushed, and achingly wanting more.

By the time the evening began to wind down, I felt utterly spent. Jules' relentless teasing, his lingering touches, and the weight of his provocative glances had driven me past my limit. When Maxie Glam finally announced last call, I rose abruptly, smoothing my jacket with a determined finality.

"Well," I announced to the table, "this has been a night full of delights, but I believe I'm calling it a night."

Jules raised an eyebrow, his smirk resurfacing as he noticed the tension in my posture. "Already, Teach? The night's still young," he teased gently.

I brushed off his words, turning towards Callie and the others to offer my goodbyes. "I'll see you all soon. Have a great night," I said softly.

Jules followed me out into the cool embrace of the night, his grin widening as we stepped away from the warmth and clamor of the Taproom. I said nothing; each step toward my car was measured and resolute.

"What's the rush?" Jules called after me, his voice laced with playful curiosity.

I paused and turned to face him, an impish smile breaking through as I replied, "You know exactly what the rush is."

His laughter, rich and genuine, filled the space between us as he stepped closer, his hand resting lightly on my chest, a tender balance of mischief and affection. "You're too easy, Elliott," he whispered.

"And you're impossible," I muttered, though I couldn't hide the warmth of my smile.

Jules leaned in once more, planting a quick yet deeply lingering kiss on my lips, his hand trailing up to cradle the back of my neck. When he pulled away, I was left breathless, each heartbeat a reminder of the night's passionate promises. "Ready to head home?" he asked in a softened tone that contrasted with the earlier sparks of electricity.

"More than ready," I replied, opening my car door for him.

"Good," Jules replied, his voice rougher than I expected, thick with want.

My gaze dragged over him, drinking him in. "Because I'm ready to fuck you."

The way his fingers tightened on the car door sent a fresh wave of heat straight to my cock. I knew exactly what I was doing to him, and fuck, if that didn't make it worse, make me need him more. The cool air was useless against the fire under my skin.

I stepped closer, just enough to let my breath warm the space between us. My fingers ghosted over his wrist, then trailed up his forearm, slow, deliberate. "Get in," I said, smirking as I watched his throat bob with a swallow. "Before I decide we're not making it home." Tonight was far from over.

21

JULES

The night air was thick and sultry, the kind of intoxicating summer evening that crackled with untamed possibilities. Elliott's car screeched into the driveway, the stark glow of the porch light slicing through the darkness, casting long, ominous shadows across the yard. My heart thundered in my chest as I stepped out of the car, each step toward his door igniting a fiery heat within me that I hadn't felt in an eternity.

Elliott strode ahead, the keys in his hand jingling like a distant alarm as he ascended the porch steps. My eyes were riveted, tracing the way his shirt clung to his muscular back, how the dim light accentuated the chiseled line of his jaw. My feet moved of their own accord, closing the gap between us with a hunger that couldn't be denied. Before he could even slide the key into the lock, I pressed myself against him, my body burning against his back, my cock hard and insistent, pressing firmly against him through the layers of our clothes.

"Jules," he warned, his voice a low growl, thick with desire despite his attempt to remain composed.

I rose up, letting my lips graze the back of his neck before trailing a line of fevered kisses down to his collarbone. His breath caught; his hand frozen on the doorknob. My hands slipped around his waist, sliding beneath the hem of his shirt to caress the scorching skin beneath.

"Having trouble there, Teach?" I teased, my voice a sultry whisper against his neck.

He turned his head slightly, his blue-grey eyes blazing with heat. "You're not exactly helping."

My laugh was deep, provocative, as I nipped sharply at his earlobe. "What can I say? You make me impatient."

In the haze of our fevered kisses and the wild, desperate way my hands roamed over his torso, he unlatched the door as if unlocking some forbidden secret. The moment we crashed inside, the door slammed shut behind us, and Elliott's restraint shattered like brittle glass. He spun me around with an urgency that pinned me against the door, sending shivers cascading over my skin in a trail of electrified desire that ignited every inch of me. His mouth collided with mine in a forceful, all-consuming kiss, where our tongues intertwined like burning flames. I could feel his hardness pressing insistently against me, a promise of raw, unbridled passion that left me aching to devour him completely.

My trembling fingers fumbled eagerly with the buttons on his shirt, each touch matching the mounting intensity of his searing kisses. "Let's get this off," I gasped, pulling back just enough to yank the fabric down his arms, exposing more of the man beneath. He shrugged off the barrier with a devilish grin, letting the shirt drop to the floor as his hands claimed my waist with unrelenting hunger. "You're unbearably impatient," he teased, his voice thick with desire and barely restrained need.

I grinned wickedly, my hands trailing sensuously over the newly revealed terrain of his chiseled chest. "Can you blame me?"

We surged through the house like a wild storm, shedding clothes in our wake. Elliott's belt clattered to the floor in the hallway, swiftly followed by my shirt, while his hands roamed every inch of my skin with an intensity that bordered on feral, as if he couldn't get enough. My lips sought his over and over, each kiss diving deeper into the depths of our shared hunger.

We pulled apart only for a heartbeat, gasping for breath, before Elliott's hands yanked me close again. "I need you," he growled, his voice raw and desperate, vibrating with an unquenchable need.

I grinned, my hands mapping the contours of his bare chest as I whispered in a low, husky tone, "I'm going to make you cum so hard." My hand slid down with fervor, cupping him through his unzipped pants, feeling the throbbing hardness that sent shockwaves of desire through my body. "I want you in my mouth," I declared, my teeth playfully nipping at his lower lip with burning anticipation.

"Jules," he breathed, his voice a tantalizing mix of warning and surrender.

“Are you a top or a bottom?” I challenged, my lips trailing provocatively down to his jawline.

“I like both,” he admitted, his voice faltering as I showered his neck with heated kisses. “But tonight… I want you to take the lead.”

I pressed him harder against the wall, confidence surging as his body yielded with explosive intensity. By the time we stormed into his bedroom, nearly naked and fueled by raw desire, the only obstacles between us were a stray pair of boxers and the ever-growing, burning heat neither of us could ignore. I shoved him onto the bed, climbing over him as my lips crashed onto his. My hands roamed his body, greedily learning every hard line and tense curve. He groaned as I bit his neck and tore down his chest, my tongue flicking over his nipple before continuing my descent.

"God, I've been craving this," I growled.

My eyes locked onto Elliott’s. The first touch was electric, a spark of hunger as I brushed my lips against the head of his throbbing cock. It was a tantalizing promise of what was to come. I deepened the kiss, opening wider as I took him in, my tongue swirling around the sensitive skin.

When I took him into my mouth, he bucked beneath me, his hands gripping my hair. "Jules," he rasped, his voice hoarse with need.

Elliott's eyes rolled back, his head falling away as he released a ragged breath. His hands guided me deeper, the movement slow but relentless, each inch a fierce claim.

I feasted on his pleasure, taking him deeper into my mouth as he groaned and arched beneath me. His taste was addictive, and I couldn't get enough. "Mmm, you taste so fucking good," I growled.

As he slid in and out of my hungry mouth, I gripped his balls, heavy and full. I pulled back slowly, my lips releasing him with a wet pop. I looked up, meeting Elliott’s gaze with a wicked smile that spoke volumes about my hunger for his cock and my delight in teasing him. I leaned forward again, taking him back in with a slow, intense movement.

This time I went deeper still; until my nose pressed into his pubic hair. He smelled incredible. A heady mix of musk and sweat that drove me wild. Each stroke built upon the last; slower but more intense, pushing him closer to the edge.

"You're fucking killing me," Elliott gasped. "This feels too good. I'm close," he warned. "I don't want to cum yet."

He yanked me upward, sending a surge of heat through my veins as his mouth descended on mine, his lips merging with an untamed ferocity while his hands devoured the last vestiges of my clothing.

"I want you to fuck me," I declared bluntly, unashamed and raw.

He trailed scorching, deliberate kisses down my body, his tongue dancing and teasing until I writhed beneath his relentless attentions. "You're beautiful," he said, his eyes locking with mine and igniting a fierce, unspoken promise.

Lying back, I felt Elliott's warm, pulsing breath cascade over my skin, rippling shivers along my spine. His lips clung to me as his tongue embarked on a sultry journey, swirling in slow, tantalizing circles that overwhelmed my senses with each lapping stroke. I surrendered to the cascade of sensations, my body hardening with mounting desire.

Then, Elliott's focus shifted with carnal precision. With a soft pop, his lips broke apart as his tongue traced a deliberate, igniting path down my shaft, exploring every vein and ridge until it reached my balls. He cupped one in his mouth, his tongue rolling it languidly with such tender intensity that I moaned in sheer need.

The sensations were almost unbearably intense, the soft suction, the rhythmic lapping of his tongue against my hyper-sensitive skin, as he caressed each ball methodically until I squirmed uncontrollably under him.

He ventured further, his tongue skimming across the sensitive skin behind my balls, sparking fiery currents through my body as he nuzzled against my exposed ass cheeks, his breath scorching my skin.

"Elliott," I gasped urgently.

"Shh," he whispered, his tone commanding yet reassuring. "Just relax."

His skilled tongue circled slowly at my most intimate entrance, tracing deliberate paths around my rim. The sensation was nothing short of transcendent, a mingling of exquisite pleasure and unyielding surrender that banished every remnant of tension from my body.

As he continued his relentless, delicious onslaught, I melted into him. Elliott's fingers joined the exquisite torment, probing my entrance with practiced precision before slipping inside and igniting a fierce, consuming heat.

"Okay?" he asked, his voice thick with desire.

"Yeah," I managed in a breathless whisper. "More."

A low, throaty chuckle escaped him as he slid another finger inside me. "You're so tight," he groaned, intensity dripping from every syllable. "I love it."

I groaned as he stretched me slowly, first employing the slick warmth of his saliva and then the silken glide of lube that made every thrust feel impossibly smooth and raw. With every deliberate movement,

I opened further, baring myself to an unforgettable blend of agony and ecstasy.

"You're doing so good," Elliott said, his voice a dark promise. "Just relax, let me get you ready for me."

"I am relaxed," I protested, though it came out as a sensuous moan laden with need.

He laughed softly, a sound full of dangerous promise. "Not yet, darling," he teased. "But you will be."

The brutal combination of his expert rimming, stretching fingers, and the other hand clutching my throbbing cock escalated every sensation into a frenzy of raw anticipation. My entire body vibrated with desire, each touch and thrust building the intensity until it seemed I could hardly bear to wait for the moment when he would finally thrust into me with that insatiable cock.

"Almost there," Elliott whispered, his fingers still dancing inside me. "Just a little more ..."

When his fingers finally withdrew, a sudden void of emptiness coursed through me, quickly overtaken by a fierce, overwhelming anticipation. I watched as he reached for a condom, his hands deliberate and confidently slow, each movement sending my heart spiraling into a frenzy of expectation.

"Yes," I whispered, my voice a trembling confession barely reaching him. Elliott's eyes locked with mine as he tore open the packet with deliberate hunger, smoothly unrolling the condom down his throbbing length. The sight was intoxicating, his hardness a promise of the fervor that awaited us. With his other hand, he reached for the lube; every movement was charged with raw intent. As he prepared me, his kiss deepened, fierce and unyielding, his whispered reassurances igniting a burning ache in my chest.

He positioned himself between my legs, his tip teasing the edge of my desire, a whisper of what's to come. "Ready?" he asked, his voice low and husky, vibrating with anticipation. My heart pounded in response as I nodded, surrendering to the magnetic pull of his touch. Elliott began to push inside me slowly, the deliberate movement stretching me wide. An initial sting of pain flared as he entered, swiftly overtaken by an explosive wave of pleasure that surged through every fiber of my being.

"Ah," I exhaled, my eyes fluttering shut as ecstasy claimed me. His hands gripped my hips, holding me steady as he inched forward. "Okay?" he asked, genuine concern threading through his commanding tone. I could only nod again, my voice lost to the overwhelming intensity.

The fleeting pain was dissolving, replaced by an ever-growing conflagration of pleasure that engulfed me entirely.

As Elliott continued his slow, deliberate rhythm, my body began to unfurl, opening up to him with a hunger that burned like wildfire. The moment his full length was inside me, reality shifted, filled with overwhelming fullness, searing intimacy, and an almost unbearable delicious intensity. We moved together in a primal, synchronized dance, each thrust pushing us further into the depths of passion.

"Yes," I moaned, my eyes snapping open with unrestrained desire. "More." Elliott's expression ignited with a wild smile as he quickened his pace, his thrusts growing harder, faster, more demanding. My body arched upward, surrendering to the relentless, scorching rhythm that drove us both to the brink.

"Oh God," I gasped, every word punctuated by the raw sensation that consumed me. "You feel so damn good." In response, Elliott growled, a deep, feral sound, as he pounded into me with a fervor that spoke of desperate, reclaimed time. His movements were fierce, inescapably intense, perfectly executed to shatter all lingering inhibitions.

Our voices escalated into a roiling crescendo of need, echoing the promise of an ecstatic climax. "I'm close," I warned breathlessly, as my body tightened in a desperate, electrifying plea around him. Instantly, his voice roared, "Me too. Come with me, Jules," and we surged together into a singular force of pure, unrelenting passion. I clung to him, nails digging deep into his back as we neared the edge, each of us hurtling towards our breaking point.

In an eruption of shared desire, I came in thick, explosive ropes that rained down on my chest and stomach. Almost immediately after, Elliott's own climax surged through him; his cock pulsated powerfully within me as he filled the condom with his release. Every drop was a declaration, a tidal wave of pleasure washing over us, leaving us momentarily suspended in the aftermath of our passion.

For a fleeting moment, our bodies locked in that perfect, incandescent union, we remained poised on the edge of rapture before collapsing back onto the bed. Exhaustion and satisfaction mingled as Elliott fell atop me, his full weight a reminder of the intensity of our encounter. Our lips collided in a fevered, sloppy kiss, tongues intertwining as we struggled to reclaim our breath.

We lay there, entangled in crumpled sheets, bodies slick with sweat and hearts still hammering with residual ecstasy. I rested my head on his chest, listening to the steady, insistent beat of his heart as his fingers traced lazy, soothing patterns along my back.

Softly, his voice broke the post-coital quiet, laden with exhaustion and profound vulnerability. "I hope you know… you've completely ruined me for anyone else." I laughed, a sound raw with satisfaction, pressing a tender kiss to his chest. "Good. Because I'm not planning on letting you go."

He tightened his arms around me as if to etch this moment into our very souls, his lips grazing the top of my head. "I think I could get used to this," he said, his tone both possessive and hopeful.

"Me too," I whispered back, our voices merging into a promise as sleep beckoned, drawing us together into the lingering aftermath of our intense, all-consuming passion.

22

ELLIOTT

The early sun cascaded gently through the sheer curtains of my little kitchen, drenching the room in a soft wash of golden light. The inviting aroma of freshly brewed coffee intertwined with the savory scent of sizzling eggs, filling every corner with warmth and possibility. As I moved gracefully between the counter and the stove, a tender smile played upon my lips, a quiet recognition of a morning so peaceful, so grounded, that it felt like a long-forgotten treasure finally found.

A soft hum, unconfined and genuine, emerged from me, a melody of liberation that had been absent for far too long. I stirred the eggs with a well-worn spatula, the sound of sizzling a gentle accompaniment to the quiet symphony of my solitude. My eyes flicked to the door leading to the hall, half anticipating the familiar energetic burst of Jules making his entrance. Yet, for now, the house remained serenely silent; only the melodious crunch of the skillet and the distant whispers of birdsong punctuated the calm.

A delicate shuffle of bare feet skimming across the cool tiled floor reached my ears from behind. A knowing smile tugged at my heart even before I turned, fully aware of the playful spirit that had arrived.

"Morning, Teach," Jules mumbled, his voice thick with the remnants of sleep.

Leaning casually in the doorway, he appeared clad in nothing but form-fitting black boxers, his lazy grin radiating mischief. His hair was a

delightful composition of tousled strands, defying gravity and styling with its own charm, while his eyes, still heavy with sleep's drowsy allure, held a spark of mischief. The snug fabric clinging to his hips made it all the more difficult to divert my gaze, capturing me in a moment of shared intimacy.

"You're up early," he remarked with a playful arch of his brow as he sauntered into the kitchen and leaned against the counter. "What are we making?"

With a sweeping gesture toward the bubbling frying pan, I replied in mock formality, "Eggs. Toast. Coffee. A breakfast as respectable as it is comforting."

Jules yawned indulgently before seizing the coffee pot, pouring himself a carefully measured mug. Settling onto a stool at the kitchen island, he added with a teasing lilt, "Respectable, huh? Seems fitting after last night."

A blush warmed my cheeks, though I continued my culinary dance at the stove. "You mean after you insisted on proving you could make me lose control?"

A low, throaty chuckle escaped him, broadening his smile as he sipped his coffee. "I'd say mission accomplished. You weren't exactly reserved yourself, Teach."

I turned slowly, arching a knowing eyebrow. "Careful now. If you keep this up, you're not getting any breakfast."

His laughter, a soft, contagious melody, filled the room and made my heart swell in response.

"You wouldn't dare," he teased, a humorous glimmer in his eyes. "I earned this breakfast."

"You earned something," I teased, my focus briefly shifting from the stove to the mischievous sparkle in his gaze as I concealed my smile.

Jules padded closer, his bare feet whispering against the cool tiles. As he wrapped his arms around my waist in a relaxed, affectionate embrace, his chin rested gently on my shoulder while I continued to work. "You're happy," he noted softly, his voice laced with sincere wonder.

I leaned into his touch, nodding gently. "I truly am."

He pressed a tender kiss onto my shoulder, a touch both delicate and grounding. "Good. You deserve every bit of it."

"This is nice," Jules whispered, his warm breath drifting against my ear like a gentle caress.

I lowered the burner and shifted deeper into his embrace. As his arms relaxed around me, I turned completely to face him, my hands

naturally finding the contour of his waist. His sleepy grin deepened as his eyes, still burning with a playful sheen, locked with mine, igniting that familiar, thrilling tenderness within me.

"You look stunning like this," he whispered, his voice softening as his hand brushed lightly against my chest.

I leaned forward, our lips meeting in a slow, unhurried kiss that started as a whisper of promise. Jules responded immediately, his fingers curling into the hem of my t-shirt as he pulled me closer. The kiss deepened gradually, our mouths finding a rhythmic harmony that was both instinctual and natural. His hands wandered, tenderly exploring from my shoulders to my lower back, each touch sending sparks of desire racing across my skin.

In that moment, as Jules' fingers slid under the fabric of my shirt, I tilted my head and allowed the kiss to swell with an insatiable hunger. His quiet hum of approval resonated against my skin, and every touch fanned the flicker of passion between us.

Abruptly, I broke the kiss, my breathing uneven as I pressed my forehead against his. "Jules," I rasped, the rough edge of my voice blending with desire, "if you want breakfast, let me finish cooking."

He chuckled softly, his lips brushing mine one last time as he pulled back with a twinkling, playful defiance. "Cooking can wait," he teased, though the gleam in his eyes made it clear that he fully anticipated my inevitable surrender.

Reluctantly, I stepped back to readjust my shirt and refocus on the sizzling eggs. Jules remained by the counter, arms folded, and eyes locked on me with an intensity that almost tempted me to forgo breakfast altogether.

"You're impossible," I muttered, determined to concentrate on my culinary creation.

"And you love it," he shot back, his smile mischievously radiant, sealing the morning with a promise of more delightful chaos to come.

We sat on the back porch beneath a sky painted in soft morning hues, the rising sun spilling golden warmth over the aged, wooden deck. We balanced our plates on our laps like treasured relics of a quiet ritual. Jules lounged in only his boxers, his long legs stretched out carelessly as the

sunlight traced gentle lines on his skin, while I was clothed in a plain t-shirt and well-worn sweatpants. It wasn't an extravagant affair, but in its simplicity, there bloomed an intimacy that no upscale brunch could ever replicate.

Jules reached for a slice of toast and proceeded to butter it with an exaggerated, almost artful precision. His eyes shone mischievously as he broke the comfortable silence with, "So, about last night…"

I responded with a playful groan, feigning exasperation: "Jules."

His tone was gentle yet teasing. "What? I was just going to say it was… spectacular."

A soft chuckle escaped me as I shook my head, amused by his peculiar charm. "You're impossible," I said, the words laced with affectionate reproach.

"Impossible to resist, apparently," he countered with a cheeky grin, taking a deliberate bite of toast as if punctuating his point.

I rolled my eyes, though beneath my playful scorn lay the undeniable truth: he was, indeed, impossible to resist, and I was beginning to relish that truth.

Jules reclined further, the sun caressing his skin as if sealing our secret connection. "You know, this weather's perfect," he remarked. "We should do something outside."

I arched a brow, sensing the widening ripple of his intentions. "Define 'something,'" I challenged gently.

A spark ignited in his eyes as he sat up straighter, brimming with sudden enthusiasm. "Hiking," he declared simply, his tone rich with promise.

I couldn't help but roll my eyes once more, half amused, half resigned.

He leaned forward, his smile widening into an invitation. "C'mon, Teach. Havenwood Hills is practically begging us to visit. The trails, the rustle of squirrels in the treetops, the wild, unbridled sense of adventure..."

I muttered under my breath, "You mean the uphill vertical climb," my tone blending humor with slight reluctance.

Jules dismissed my protest with a languid rollover of his eyes. "Details. Besides, you didn't complain too much last time."

"Didn't I?" I replied dryly, a hint of a smile tugging at my lips.

Then, as if punctuating life's unscripted moments, he stood up and stretched with the languid elegance of a cat awakening from a sun-drenched nap. In that fluid movement, the fly of his boxers shifted just enough to reveal a brief and tantalizing glimpse of his magnificent cock.

For a mere, breath-stealing instant, I caught sight of its smooth, taut skin, a subtle flash of dark pubic hair trailing along the edge, before the fabric draped itself back in modesty, leaving behind only the ghost of a delightful memory.

Catching me in the act, Jules chuckled lightly and teased, "Look, I'll make it easy for you, no weird boots, no ticking time limit, and you can even pack your spreadsheets if that makes you feel better."

Despite my better judgment, laughter bubbled out as I shook my head in playful exasperation. "You're relentless."

Drawing closer, Jules bent down until our eyes met at the level of the chair's armrest. His gentle hands rested on my thigh and gradually trailed upward toward my cock. The tender assured pressure of his fingers stirred a reaction in me that was both physical and deeply emotional. "And you love it," he replied in a quiet, mischievous tone, his words wrapping around us like a secret as his hand wrapped around me.

I held his gaze for a long, lingering moment before sighing in acquiescence. "Fine. But I'm not carrying you back down if you twist your ankle."

He pressed a soft kiss to my cheek before one final squeeze of my cock then beginning the walk back into the house, his voice echoing with playful determination, "Deal. Now hurry up, we've got trails to conquer."

As he led me inside to change, I couldn't suppress a smile and called after him, "Tease." In that fleeting moment, a deeper realization anchored itself within me, this wasn't merely a fresh chapter for us as a couple; it was the dawning of a new perspective for me, a reawakening to the vibrant possibilities of life, and an emergence into the person I aspired to be. And with Jules woven so intricately into that vision, I knew I was ready to embrace the journey ahead.

The trails at Havenwood Hills pulsed with life, alive with the vibrant chatter of birds perched high in the dense canopy and the soft, constant rustling of leaves underfoot. The air carried the deep, rich aroma of damp earth and decaying foliage, infusing a wild, grounding energy into every breath, while the filtered sunlight danced through gaps in the foliage, scattering gentle, warm beams along our path. Jules led the way with an

unhurried confidence, his sturdy boots audibly crunching over the uneven, gravel-and-dirt trail.

Every so often, he stole a glance over his shoulder, a wide, mischievous grin lighting up his face as his boundless energy radiated in the interplay of shadow and light. "You're doing great, Teach," he called out cheerfully, now sauntering backward with the casual ease of someone who probably spent his childhood effortlessly climbing trees. His hands were tucked deep in the pockets of his well-worn hiking shorts, and the tousled cascade of his hair, unkempt yet charming, lent him a roguish air of adventure that I silently admired.

I, on the other hand, was less sure about "doing great." My breaths came heavier with every step, and the incline of the path seemed to grow more daunting, each forward push sending searing burns through my calves. I refused to voice my discomfort outright, though I couldn't hide a note of playful exasperation as I spoke. "This trail's steeper than I remembered, and it's blazing much warmer than the last time we did this," I remarked, leaning forward to steady myself against the rugged incline and dabbing at the trickle of sweat that glistened on my brow.

Jules chuckled, his laughter echoing softly among the towering trees. "Details, details," he said with a dismissive wave of his hand, executing a dramatic spin on his heel before resuming our upward journey. "Think of it as a metaphor, climbing out of your comfort zone!"

I raised an amused eyebrow even as a small smile tugged at the corners of my lips. "That's quite the spin," I teased.

"Spinning is what I do best," Jules quipped back, adding a theatrical flourish that made me laugh despite the persistent ache in my legs.

As we ambled onward, Jules suddenly reached out and seized my arm, leading me off the well-trodden path into a secluded nook hidden by thick undergrowth. With an impulsive urgency, he pressed me against the rough, bark-covered trunk of a massive tree. His eyes locked onto mine, intense and inviting, as he leaned in to capture my lips with a heated kiss.

In that secluded glade, our hands began to explore with a fervor fueled by desire. My fingers traced the contours of Jules' back, reverently mapping out the curve of his spine and the defined planes of his muscles. The warmth radiating from his skin beckoned me forward, and a primal urge compelled me to dig my fingers into the firm lines of his hips, drawing him even closer as I could feel the undeniable hardness of his cock pressed insistently against mine.

Jules' own hands were equally adventurous as he wandered over my chest and shoulders. His fingertips, light and teasing, traced patterns under my shirt, igniting shivers as he brushed against my sensitive skin and teasingly circled the hardened peaks at my nipples before sliding down to the curve of my waist. With a deliberate, slow motion, he slipped his hand beneath the waistband of my pants, and I felt a sudden jolt of electric anticipation as his fingers grazed against the burgeoning heat of my cock, still confined within my boxers.

Our movements became a synchronized dance of exploration, each gesture sparking new waves of desire. Jules' fingers wrapped around my shaft, giving it a gentle squeeze before releasing it again. I groaned into his mouth, deepening our kiss as our bodies pressed together. I nipped his bottom lip just enough to hear him moan into my mouth. The air was electric with tension, and I could feel ourselves getting lost in the moment, our passion building with every passing second.

When we finally broke apart for a fleeting moment of breath, Jules' eyes burned into mine with a fierce, almost desperate intensity that left me momentarily breathless. His lips curved into a sly smile as he whispered, "I want you." In that instant, his eyes danced with mischief as he slowly sank to his knees, his gaze never wavering from mine, and with deliberate intent pulled my cock out. He looked up at me, our eyes meeting as he took me into his mouth.

Looking up at me, he took me into his mouth with an eager determination. "Jules, wait," I warned nervously, the adrenaline mingling with a hint of anxiety. "What if someone sees us?" But Jules only smiled, his voice filled with playful assurance. "There's no one else here today, Teach. And even if someone did wander by, they wouldn't be able to see us. Now it's up to you to keep quiet so they can't hear what's going on." He went back down on my cock, taking my full length down his throat. He inhaled deeply as he took in the sweaty musk of my crotch. "Fuck! You smell so good, Elliott." His mouth was warm and wet, and I felt myself getting closer and closer to climax.

I tried to warn him that I was about to cum, but Jules just kept going, his eyes never leaving mine. That sent me over the edge. "Jules...I'm going to..." I whispered urgently, but he just shook his head slightly and continued sucking. Finally, I couldn't hold back, and I shot my load into his mouth, making noises that I tried to keep quiet despite the intensity of the sensation. Jules swallowed everything, then nonchalantly wiped his mouth with the back of his hand before standing up with an evil grin still plastered on his face.

Our eyes met once again, and in a spontaneous moment of shared passion, I pulled him in for a fiercely passionate kiss, savoring the lingering taste of myself on his lips and tongue. Without missing a beat, he spun around and began retracing his steps up the trail, leaving my still hard cock exposed in the open air, though our isolation in the dense forest rendered the risk of discovery remote.

"I think you're trying to get us caught," I teased with a breathless, playful lilt.

"Maybe just a little," Jules replied mischievously over his shoulder, his voice dripping with playful challenge.

I quickly gathered myself, put my dick away, and I followed him back onto the trail. Jules continued his march ahead, his energy undiminished and his stride full of exuberance.

Soon enough, as we began to ascend a gentler, leveled section of the trail, the dense woods gave way to a small clearing where nature stretched out in a painterly display. Amidst the soft, sunlit carpet of fallen leaves and sporadic shafts of light, Jules crouched by a vibrant patch of wildflowers. The delicate blooms exploded in bright yellows and deep purples against the rich background of greens and earthy browns of the forest floor. Each petal was kissed by golden sunlight, rendering them as if aglow from within.

"Look at these beauties," Jules said in a hushed tone of reverence as he gently brushed his fingers over the fragile petals. "You can't get this kind of wonder in a classroom."

I paused, momentarily caught in the delicate magic of the moment, not wanting to disturb his awe. Then, curiosity drew me closer. Kneeling awkwardly beside him, I studied the meticulous details of the flowers, the intricate pattern of each petal, the delicate network of veins, and the sublime, almost velvety softness of their curves. "They're… intricate," I finally managed, my voice filled with wonder as I struggled to articulate the marvel before me.

Jules tilted his head, his gaze softening as he looked at me, and the gentle warmth in his eyes made my heart tighten with unspoken emotion. "Yeah," he said, his voice imbued with a quiet reverence. Before I could probe further into his thoughts, he casually pulled out his phone and snapped a fleeting photo of me amidst the natural splendor.

"What are you doing?" I asked, glancing up at him with playful curiosity.

"For the scrapbook," he replied with an exuberant grin, his eyes sparkling mischievously. "You'll thank me later."

I shook my head, chuckling softly as I stood up. "Highly doubtful," I retorted.

With a wink, Jules slid his phone back into his pocket and bounded cheerfully back onto the trail.

When at last we reached the summit, the late afternoon sun draped the rolling hills in a surreal, golden radiance, bathing the entire landscape in soft, ambrosial light. The endless, rolling green fields stretched before us, punctuated here and there by clusters of trees that appeared like wild, painterly brushstrokes upon an expansive canvas. A gentle breeze tugged at my shirt, cool and invigorating, as I stood transfixed on the edge of the overlook, lost in the harmonious beauty of the scene.

For a timeless moment, I was oblivious to the arduous climb and the chaotic world beyond, only the majestic view and the soothing serenity of nature mattered.

I was so enraptured by the scene that I barely noticed Jules approaching silently from behind. Suddenly, his strong arms enveloped my waist, and he rested his chin softly on my shoulder, his warm breath tenderly teasing my ear. "Pretty incredible, huh?" he mused, his tone a quiet blend of awe and intimacy.

"Yeah," I replied softly, my eyes never leaving the endless horizon that beckoned with serene promise. "It really is."

Jules shifted slightly, producing his phone as if by magic, angling it just right to capture our shared joy against the sprawling vista. "Hold still," he directed with a broad, infectious grin. "We need a selfie for the scrapbook."

I couldn't help but laugh as he snapped the picture, capturing a candid moment of us framed by the awe-inspiring landscape. Jules glanced at the image on his screen, a spark of genuine pleasure lighting his features. "Perfect," he exclaimed. "Now you can't complain about being a solo subject in every photo."

I shook my head, laughing softly in agreement. "I wouldn't dream of it."

We lingered there for a few more enchanted moments, our shoulders gently touching, his hand still resting lightly on my waist. The silence between us was steeped in an unspoken intimacy, filled with the kind of quiet understanding that I longed to hold onto.

The journey downhill proved easier, even as Jules' unquenchable energy persisted unabated. He chattered animatedly about potential adventures waiting just around the bend, his hands flitting expressive gestures into the crisp air as he described each new possibility. I listened,

bemused yet indulgent, nodding in quiet agreement as he pointed out notable trees, curious rock formations, and even paused to capture amusing snapshots along the way. At one point, a bushy-tailed squirrel darted across our path, pausing just long enough to regard us with inquisitive eyes before scampering upward into a nearby tree. Jules gasped dramatically, pointing after the little creature. "I'm telling you, that one's the ringleader. Look at those shifty eyes!"

I smiled, shaking my head in loving disbelief. "I'll be sure to add that to my lesson plans. 'The Secret History of Squirrel Uprisings.'"

Jules laughed, playfully bumping into me as we continued along. "You joke, but one day you'll thank me for this groundbreaking discovery," he teased, his laughter ringing light and infectious. I couldn't help but smile more than I had in weeks, his vibrant energy perfectly balancing my more reflective, subdued nature.

By the time we reached the car, the sun had begun its gradual descent toward the horizon, casting long, languid shadows across the parking lot. I unlocked the doors and tossed my jacket into the backseat, while Jules stretched dramatically beside me, his body language radiating post adventure exuberance.

"Not bad for a Saturday," he remarked, his grin bright and unrepentant, echoing the warmth of the fading sunlight.

I glanced at him, my expression softening in quiet contentment. "Not bad at all," I replied.

As he climbed into the passenger seat, already brainstorming our next outdoor escapade, I couldn't help but reflect on how immeasurably bigger my world had become since Jules had breezed into it. For the first time in a long, weary while, I felt ready and eager to see where this adventurous, winding path would lead.

23

JULES

The rush of cool air conditioning hit me like a refreshing wave as we stepped inside from the warm, enveloping summer night, The Rainbow Taproom buzzed with energy and promise. Neon lights danced erratically off the sleek, metallic walls while the air pulsed with a symphony of music and laughter. The mingling scents of spilled beer and a subtle trace of cologne wove together, creating an intoxicating combination that anchored the space in the kind of unpredictable frenzy I adored.

I found myself drifting toward the dance floor the moment we arrived, irresistibly drawn by the pulsing beat that vibrated through the room and the magnetic mass of bodies moving under the ever-changing lights. It was my element, a place where rhythm and energy intertwined, allowing me to lose myself completely to the music.

Yet tonight, I wasn't alone.

From the periphery of my vision, I caught sight of Elliott near the bar, casually seated at a high table amidst a small circle of his friends: Tess, whose calming presence radiated warmth, and Harper, who couldn't help but burst into laughter at one of Elliott's witty remarks. Clutching a drink in hand, Elliott appeared both composed and delicately poised, yet a subtle stiffness in his posture made me grin. Always impeccably polished and inherently reserved, Elliott in a place like this

seemed as out of place as a historian suddenly transplanted into a wild, pulsating rave.

I navigated the dense crowd with purpose, pausing briefly to exchange a few words with Max and Callie, who were effortlessly carving out their own space and dancing along the fringes of the floor. Max flashed me a look filled with hidden amusement and a wide, knowing smile.

"You're going to drag him out here, aren't you?" they teased, nodding in the direction of the bar.

"Of course," I replied with a mischievous glint in my eye, already imagining the subtle flush that would dance across Elliott's cheeks.

Callie chimed in with a lighthearted laugh, giving me an encouraging nudge. "Don't let him off the hook too easily."

"Oh, I won't," I promised confidently as I weaved through clusters of dancing bodies toward him.

When I finally reached Elliott, he was caught mid-laugh, his previously tense shoulders relaxing into a rare moment of genuine ease. Tess noticed me instantly, his smile radiating a welcoming warmth as he beckoned me over to join their little gathering.

"There you are," he said softly. "We were just mentioning how delightful it is to see you both out together."

Harper's voice, light as if floating on a summer breeze, added, "The town's newest power couple graces us with their presence tonight."

Elliott's ears tinged a delicate shade of red, yet he couldn't help but smile as his gaze found mine and I casually leaned against his chair.

"Power couple, huh?" I teased, placing a tender hand on his shoulder.

"You better believe it," Harper replied with a playful raise of his drink in a mock toast.

Elliott cleared his throat, his tone tinged with wry affection. "They're certainly exaggerating."

I leaned closer, my lips brushing softly against his ear as I whispered, "Are they, though?"

He shot me a look that mixed amusement with a hint of challenge, and I couldn't resist breaking into a broad grin. Straightening up, I extended my hand toward him.

"Come on, Teach. The dance floor awaits."

He hesitated for a split second, glancing around at the swirling mass of revelers. "I was just getting comfortable…"

"And now you're about to get even more comfortable," I declared, tugging him gently by the hand. "You're with me. There's nothing left to worry about."

Tess's laughter mingled with the beat of the music as Harper waved us along with an encouraging cheer. "Go on, Elliott. Let loose. Jules always gets his way, anyway."

"That's not true," I replied playful over my shoulder as we made our way toward the vibrant throb of the dance floor.

"It's completely true," Elliott muttered under his breath, yet he followed willingly.

The dance floor was awash in an otherworldly glow, the lights bouncing off the walls in bursts of pink, blue, and green that bathed everything in a dreamlike radiance. I immediately surrendered to the rhythm, drawing Elliott closer with every step.

"Just follow my lead," I said with a bright grin as he attempted to mirror my movements.

At first, his steps were hesitant and awkward, a stark contrast to the fluidity of the music, but I wasn't about to let him retreat into his shell. I looped my arms around his neck, guiding us in a gentle, swaying rhythm that left no space for uncertainty.

"You're doing great," I teased, pressing my forehead briefly against his in an intimate moment of connection.

His laughter, low and genuine, resonated through the air. "You're lying, but I appreciate it," he admitted with a chuckle.

All around us, the crowd seemed to surge and sway, the music intensifying as if to celebrate our union. I could feel the heat of his body and the way his hands initially hesitated on my waist before becoming more assured and supportive. It wasn't merely dancing, it was a declaration, clear as day: we were here, together, and it was impossible for anyone to miss.

From the edge of the floor, Callie and Max cheered, their voices slicing through the soundscape. "Look at you two!" Callie shouted, raising a glass high in our direction.

Elliot's cheeks flushed even deeper, but he didn't pull away. Instead, he held me even closer, his smile softening into an expression that sent a comforting ache through my chest.

"See?" I exclaimed as I leaned in near him. "You're a natural on the floor."

He returned a warm smile, his tone imbued with quiet affection. "You're impossible, you know that?"

"And yet, here you are," I shot back playfully, spinning him around unexpectedly.

He stumbled slightly, a burst of laughter escaping him as I caught him before he could falter. For an enchanted moment, the cacophony of the club melted away, leaving just the two of us in a cocoon of shared joy where the music and lights faded into a distant hum.

"I wouldn't want to be anywhere else," he said softly, his voice steady despite the intimate vulnerability.

My heart did a little flip, and I masked the sudden flutter with a bright grin while leaning in to plant a quick, affectionate kiss on his cheek. "Good answer, Teach."

By the time we meandered back to the bar, both of us were breathless and grinning like school kids, completely lost in the magic of the night. Harper greeted us with raised glass, eyes sparkling as he inquired, "How was it?"

"Not bad," Elliott replied in his trademark casual tone, though his smile betrayed the exhilaration of the moment.

"Not bad?" I nudged him with a playful elbow. "You were absolutely incredible."

He responded with a knowing look, yet his hand found mine under the bar, his fingers intertwining with mine in a quietly reassuring gesture that spoke volumes.

Max tilted his head, watching us with an amused, knowing smile. "You two are disgustingly cute, you know that?"

Elliott arched an eyebrow, his tone tinged with dry humor. "That's quite the compliment."

"It is," Max declared, lifting his drink high. "Own it."

As the night wore on, the drinks flowed like liquid joy, the music pulsated with relentless energy, and laughter filled every pause. Elliott's hand remained securely in mine, and every now and then, he would steal a glance my way with eyes that made my knees grow weak. In that moment, we were learning how to exist together in each other's worlds, and for the first time, I wasn't afraid of facing what came next.

ELLIOTT

A few days later, as the late afternoon sunlight slanted softly through the trembling leaves of my garden, a rich golden glow draped over the meticulously organized rows of herbs and vegetables. The air was alive with the aromatic duet of basil and rosemary, their fragrances intermingling with the deep, loamy scent of freshly churned soil. In the midst of this sensory pallet, Jules sat cross-legged on the cool, smooth stone path. His dirt-stained hands moved deliberately as he placed a small sprig of mint into the nurturing earth.

Gone was his usual burst of lively energy, replaced instead by a serene focus. With his head tilted in quiet concentration, Jules listened intently as I explained how to gently tease apart the tangled roots before easing the plant into its new home. His hair was pulled back in a charming, imperfect knot, and a streak of dirt adorned one cheek like nature's badge, yet in the soft, filtering light he seemed nothing short of radiant.

"Patience is the secret to gardening, huh?" Jules quipped with a teasing smile that crinkled the corners of his eyes as he glanced up at me.

"It's certainly one of the secrets," I replied, crouching beside him to demonstrate the careful process once more. "Gardening's all about tuning in to the needs of each plant, learning its language."

Mimicking my deliberate motions, Jules dipped his fingers into the soil and tenderly loosened the roots before cradling the mint sprig and lowering it into place. His hands moved with a surprising deliberateness, as if his habitual restlessness had surrendered to the noble art of gardening.

"I can see why you're so drawn to this," he uttered softly, patting the soil down with a gentle touch. "It's… peaceful."

His reflective tone caused me to pause, to lean back on my heels and take in the quiet dedication mirrored in his eyes. I smiled, offering soft encouragement. "You're really good at this."

Jules' eyes shone with a quiet, proud light as he returned my smile. "I've got a great teacher."

Before I could offer another word, he leaned in and brushed a delicate kiss across my cheek, a brief, tender gesture that sent a rush of

warmth through me. "Careful," I teased in a low voice, "or I might begin to think you secretly enjoy these little moments."

His laugh, soft and filled with affection, was like the rustling of leaves in a gentle breeze. "Don't push your luck, Teach," he replied playfully.

As the sun dipped further, casting the garden in a dramatic palette of amber and crimson, we continued our work side by side. A quiet camaraderie settled between us like the night's first stars. Every so often, Jules stole glances in my direction, his eyes twinkling with mischievous undertones.

At one point, his tone turned light and playful. "You know, this would be a lot more fun with some music in the background."

"Music?" I inquired, raising an eyebrow in amused curiosity.

"Yeah. Something upbeat, maybe a bit of Madonna?" he suggested with a cheeky grin.

I smirked and shook my head. "This isn't exactly a 'Like a Prayer' moment."

Jules leaned in with a conspiratorial smile. "Every moment can be a 'Like a Prayer' moment if you just believe hard enough."

I rolled my eyes, yet I couldn't help but feel the warmth in my chest swell a little more.

By the time we finished, the garden was bathed in the gentle, enchanting glow of string lights draped artfully between the trees. Jules and I sat together on an old wooden bench near the garden's edge, the cool evening air soft against our skin. Jules absentmindedly twirled a tiny mint sprig between his fingers as he leaned back, exhaling contentedly.

"Alright," he admitted with a relaxed sigh, "I'll say it. Gardening isn't terrible at all."

I chuckled, tilting my head to study his expression. "High praise coming from you."

"Don't get too comfortable," he teased, playfully bumping his knee against mine.

For a long, comfortable while, we sat wrapped in a shared silence, the stillness of the garden enveloping us like a warm, familiar blanket. Jules shifted and turned to face me fully, his eyes alight with that familiar mischief, softened by a tender vulnerability beneath.

"You know," he said, voice dropping to a gentle murmur, "this is really nice. I mean, I'd still rather be dancing, but… I can appreciate it."

I smiled and reached out to take his hand. "And I'd rather be immersed in a good book, but I get that too."

Jules' grin widened as he leaned closer. "We're really figuring this out, aren't we?"

"Slowly but surely," I replied, my tone warm and earnest.

He tilted his head, studying the lines of my face for a moment before our lips met in a soft, teasing kiss that gradually deepened. My hand caressed his cheek tenderly, and in that instant the rest of the world seemed to fade away, leaving just us under the gentle glow of the lights.

When we finally pulled apart, Jules wore a mischievous grin and flushed cheeks. "Careful, Teach. You're starting to really like this whole impulsive thing."

I laughed softly, brushing a loose strand of hair from his face. "And you're beginning to enjoy the art of slowing down."

Resting his head on my shoulder, he let his hand softly find mine once more. In that quiet moment, the perfect balance between us felt natural, as if two scattered puzzle pieces had finally found their home.

"You're good for me," Jules said in a voice barely above a whisper.

"And you're good for me," I replied, my heart full as the last vestiges of sunlight melted into the tender embrace of the night.

24

JULES

A week later, the soft, constant hum of the dishwasher and the occasional creak of worn floorboards filled Elliott's house with an unexpected vibrancy. Though compact, the space overflowed with character, his character, each corner whispering hints of his personality. Above the stove, a mosaic of spice jars stood in neat formation, their labels penned in Elliott's meticulous handwriting. A row of well-loved cookbooks, their spines delicately cracked from years of enthusiastic use, rested on the counter, each one a memory of culinary adventures past. This was not merely a house, it was Elliott personified. Thoughtful. Deliberate. Incredibly inviting.

I sprawled on his couch, a book pilfered from one of his shelves resting loosely on my lap. I wasn't really absorbing its words, a treatise on the Bauhaus movement, but the rhythmic motion of flipping pages lent me an odd sense of purposeful distraction. My leg bounced impatiently as a restless energy built within me, my eyes darting toward the kitchen where Elliott was orchestrating his culinary domain.

Emerging from the doorway with an effortless grace, Elliott appeared, a dish towel casually draped over one shoulder. His hair, slightly tousled in a deliberate, messy way, sent a flutter through my stomach. He had rolled his shirt sleeves up neatly to his elbows, thereby revealing freckled forearms that seemed to hold their own quiet allure. A

warm, inviting smile gently curved his lips, as if he were extending an unspoken invitation to lean in just a little closer.

"So," he began, his voice calm and deliberate as he leaned against the doorframe with an air of casual authority, "change of plans for tonight. No Taproom. We're staying in."

I arched a brow and nonchalantly tossed the book onto the coffee table. "Staying in? On a Friday night? Do you even know who you're dating?"

Elliott's smile broadened into a playful smirk, a gesture that always sparked a jolt of excitement through me. "Someone who might actually enjoy making homemade pizza if he gives it a chance."

"Homemade pizza, huh?" I teased as I rose from the couch, drifting toward him with purpose, each step drawn out to relish the moment. "Alright, Teach, I'll bite. But if this turns into some sort of monotonous domestic trap, I'm summoning Callie to stage an intervention."

A deep, rich chuckle rumbled from Elliott, a sound that resonated like a secret reward. "Deal. Now, come help before you change your mind."

The kitchen was alive with a gentle, rhythmic buzz of quiet activity. Elliott moved with the practiced precision of someone who had performed this culinary dance countless times before. He kneaded the dough with steady, confident movements, sprinkling flour across the countertop in an orderly, almost artistic layer. In contrast, my efforts were delightfully chaotic. I found myself haphazardly flinging toppings onto the counter, not giving a second thought to their arrangement.

"Do we really need olives?" I inquired, holding up the offending jar with an exaggerated look of skepticism.

"Olives are fun," Elliott replied without missing a beat, his eyes briefly glancing in my direction before returning to his work with the dough. "You just haven't learned to appreciate their complexity."

I gasped theatrically, clutching the jar to my chest as though it were a prized possession. "Complexity? Teach, it's a pizza, not a master's thesis."

A small, knowing smile played at the corner of his lips, a look that always signaled a tiny victory. "And yet, here we are."

I couldn't help laughing, scooping up a generous handful of shredded cheese. "Fine. Let's get philosophical, then." With a playful toss, I sent the cheese arcing through the air in a clumsy attempt to catch a few pieces in my mouth. Most of the cheese, however, ended up adorning the countertop instead.

Elliott raised one arched brow in a deadpan expression. "And now we're out of cheese."

"Worth it," I grinned triumphantly, popping the last stray piece into my mouth.

Slowly, I found myself drawn into the rhythm of the process despite my earlier restlessness. The comforting aroma of freshly torn basil leaves, and subtly roasted garlic filled the space, mingling into an olfactory embrace that softened even my most untidy edges. At one point, Elliott circled around the counter to demonstrate how to shape the dough with care.

"You're folding it too much," he said gently, guiding my hands with a light, assuring pressure. His voice dropped to a near-whisper, and the warmth of his breath grazed my ear, sending a shiver down my spine.

"Maybe I'm just adding character," I retorted with a playful lilt, though my tone softened under the tender insistence of his touch.

Leaning closer, his chest brushed against my back, the proximity amplifying every shared sensation. His warmth seeped through the thin barrier of my shirt, and I could feel the slow, steady rise and fall of his breath. "Character doesn't make it bake evenly," he said softly. And then there it was. His groin pressing into my ass, unmistakable and impossible to ignore. Heat surged through me, my mind suddenly miles away from the dough beneath my fingers.

I turned to reply, but the words caught in my throat as I realized just how intimately close we'd become. Our eyes met, his blue-grey gaze steady and searching, making the noisy, bustling world of the kitchen fade away until it was just the two of us in that tender, suspended moment.

The space between us vanished. He tilted his head, and before I could second-guess it, his lips crashed into mine—urgent, hungry, tasting of warmth and longing. My hands found his waist, fingers curling into the fabric of his shirt as he pressed even closer, molding against me, his body speaking in ways words never could. His fingers slid up my arms, over my shoulders, before tangling in my hair, pulling me deeper into him. A quiet groan escaped between us, lost in the way our mouths moved together, desperate and searching.

The moment stretched, heady and electric, before reality nudged its way back in—the scent of flour, the low hum of the oven, the knowledge that we were still in the middle of making a damn pizza. Slowly, reluctantly, he pulled back just enough to let out a breathy laugh, his forehead resting against mine.

"Guess we should finish this before we get completely distracted," he said, his voice rough around the edges.

I exhaled a shaky chuckle, my lips tingling. "Yeah… probably."

Still, even as we turned back to the dough, the heat between us lingered, simmering beneath every touch, every stolen glance.

Hours later, the pizza had faded into a distant, almost surreal memory; its half-devoured slices lay abandoned on the aged coffee table, a silent testament to our earlier hunger. Beside the plate, two wine glasses rested at a lazy tilt, one marked with the faint smudge of my lips, the other nearly empty. An open bottle, drained of its last drops, stood nearby, catching the dim light in its dark glass. We had migrated to the couch, sinking deeply into its sumptuous cushions as a gentle cascade of warm, golden light streamed from the kitchen, bathing the room in a soft, inviting glow. I was draped against him, my head nestling comfortably on his broad, steady chest, while his arm encircled me with a secure, tender strength.

"This," I murmured softly, my fingers idly sketching slow, meandering patterns along his arm, "is one pretty solid Friday night."

Elliott's low hum of agreement filled the space as his hand played absentmindedly through my hair, each strand a silky caress. "Told you," he said, voice imbued with calm satisfaction. "Sometimes, when you slow down, you let the magic of the moment truly unfold."

I tilted my head up towards him, a teasing grin tugging at the corners of my lips. "Careful, Teach," I chided playfully, "you're starting to sound just like me."

And then, as our lips met in a tender, charged kiss, the soft intimacy between us sparked something fierce within, a flame of desire that slowly deepened our connection. Our mouths moved in perfect, languid sync, the heat of our embrace building steadily like a slow-burning fire. Elliott's hand cradled the back of my neck, drawing me ever closer, while my fingers delicately trailed along the worn hem of the old sweater, a sweater of his that I had borrowed and, in a moment of sweet defiance, never returned.

"Wait," he whispered breathily against my lips, his warm, uneven exhale sending thrilling shivers cascading down my spine. "Are we really doing this here?"

I smiled, locking eyes with him as I tugged at his t-shirt once more. "Unless you've got a better idea," I replied, my voice barely above a whisper.

Elliott's rich, unguarded laughter rang out, infusing the room with a liberated sense of fun. His hands, warm and assured, found my waist as he pulled me into his lap; our bodies interlaced as we sank further into the inviting couch. In that moment, the rest of the world seemed to vanish, leaving only the pulse of our shared passion and the magnetic gravity of our closeness.

As we paused to catch our breath, the intensity of our connection blossomed into an exploration of newfound desire. Elliott's hands began an intentional journey, roving slowly over my body as he tugged my t-shirt upward until it slipped off my shoulders, baring my skin to the ambient light. Each touch, every delicate stroke, sent ripples of heat and excitement deep within me. I watched, completely mesmerized, as he carelessly brushed off the discarded fabric, letting it fall onto the floor behind me.

"My turn," I said huskily, my voice dripping with anticipation as I reached for Elliott's belt. With deliberate slowness, I unbuckled it and unzipped his jeans, the sound echoing into the quiet room like the prelude to a symphony. Raising his hips just enough, he allowed me to pull his pants down, revealing the sleek, dark boxer briefs hidden beneath.

"I think these need to go too," I teased, meeting his eyes with a playful smile.

Elliott's gaze remained locked with mine as he nodded, his voice smooth and affirmative. "I think you're right."

I slid my fingertips expertly beneath the waistband of his underwear, tugging them down slowly to unveil him, every part of him, hard and unmistakably ready. The sight of his cock, long and thick, pulsed with unbridled desire, left me momentarily breathless.

Without missing a beat, Elliott's hands shifted their focus, working deftly to undo my own pants and push them down over my hips. One by one, my layers followed until we both lay exposed on the couch, skin against skin, every part of us laid bare in the soft glow of our private haven.

The air between us was charged with an electric tension, our bodies vulnerable and raw. Our lips met again in a fierce, consuming kiss that left us both gasping, lost in our own world of heat and yearning.

Then, as if stirred by a sudden command of desire, he pulled back, his eyes dark with longing. "I want to taste you," he purred, his voice thick with need. "I want your cock in my mouth."

I nodded eagerly, my heart pounding with the thrilling pulse of anticipation. Elliott's lips, warm and teasing, trailed a fiery path down my body until, finding my cock, he enveloped it gently at first, gradually increasing his pressure until every nerve in me came alight.

"Ah, God," I moaned softly, my hands tangling fervently in his hair as he worked his practiced magic over me.

Then it was my turn to return the favor. I pushed him back onto the couch, my eyes locked on his as hunger shimmered in them. Leaning forward, I whispered quietly, "My turn now."

He nodded, smiling, as I took him into my mouth. The sounds of my lips on his cock filled the room, raw and unbridled, mingling with the ragged cadence of our breathing.

After what seemed like an eternity of pleasure, Elliott pulled me up gently. "I need you now, Jules," he said, voice laden with desire and urgency. "I need to be inside you."

"Yes, please," I said, grinning mischievously. "I want you inside me."

Gazing deeply into his eyes, I sensed his unspoken longing, and as I straddled him, aligning our desires, reality intruded with one practical question: "Condom and lube?"

Elliott, calm and collected, pointed toward the bedroom. "In the nightstand drawer," he instructed lightly.

I released an exaggerated, frustrated sigh and bolted naked down the hallway, my bare skin catching the cool air as I embarked on an impromptu treasure hunt for protection. Bursting into the bedroom, I searched high and low, talking to myself in mounting exasperation, "Perhaps we should have a conversation about not using protection, but I still need the lube because that cock isn't sliding in with just spit. Fuck! WHERE IS IT?!" My voice rang out in disbelief as impatience threatened to boil over.

Just as I teetered on the edge of losing my mind, Elliott's playful voice echoed from the living room, his laughter teasing me. "Check the top drawer of the dresser! And hurry up!" His tone, light and spirited, only fanned my impatient energy.

Throwing open the top drawer, I finally spotted the condoms and lube cozily hidden amid Elliott's mismatched socks. "Yes!" I exclaimed in triumph.

But before I could make my way back to him, his taunting call reached my ears again: "Come on, Jules! What's taking so long? You're killing me over here!" I couldn't help but chuckle at his exaggerated whine. Rushing back into the living room, I caught sight of him, his hand still gripping his cock as he stroked himself slowly, his eyes daring me with an unspoken challenge.

The sight of his self-pleasure sent my desire spiking even higher. A look of raw, unadulterated lust flashed across my face as our eyes met; he raised an eyebrow knowingly, still clutching a condom packet in one hand and a lube bottle in the other, his smirk urging me on.

"Hurry up!" he teased once more, his voice laced with playful urgency.

"Shut up," I retorted breezily, my eyes rolling in affectionate exasperation.

Managing to steady my trembling hands, I carefully unrolled the condom onto his throbbing erection and squeezed a generous amount of lube onto it. Then, with a sly grin playing on my lips, I straddled his hips, positioning myself deliberately above him. I took a moment to trace my fingers along my own heated skin, preparing my entrance with silky lube, teasing him as I slowly worked myself into a heightened state. When he could bear the anticipation no longer, I aligned the head of his cock with my ready, waiting entrance.

As our bodies aligned, so did our eyes as we locked into each other's stare. He grasped my hips firmly and guided me down onto him slowly, allowing us both to savor the sensation and the connection between us. Slowly, he pushed inside, and we both groaned loudly. It had been a while since the last time we fucked, and the initial stretch was intense. His cock is perfect, and my body wanted him. But this was not a starter dick. He is quite blessed down there, so I took my time. He let me take all the time I needed to adjust and soon the shock subsided, and our bodies started to move together.

His cock slid in and out of me, our rhythm slow and sensual at first, but it quickly built in intensity as we found our pace. My hands, one braced against the couch cushion the other on my cock, my back arched, welcoming him deeper as we both groaned in response. I took my time to ride him as I used his cock to hit the spot inside me. His cock did this perfectly, so I didn't want this to end.

Elliott was clearly content with this because he said, “Fuck, yes! Use my cock, baby. You feel so damn good! Ride me!” His dirty talk only encouraged me, and I rode him for all I was worth. He picked up on the moment when my leg muscles were nearing exhaustion and couldn’t take it anymore, he said, “I want you on your knees. I want to watch my cock go inside you.”

I dismounted his hips and positioned myself on the couch. My hands on the arm of the couch while my face was buried in a pillow. Elliott said, “Don’t you muffle your sounds. I want to hear you as I watch you take my cock.” He applied a little more lube and then slid back inside. His hands gripped my hips, guiding me as his thrusts grew stronger. The rhythm was slow and sensual at first, but it quickly built in intensity as our bodies found their pace. I could feel his cock sliding in and out of me, the friction sending sparks of pleasure through my entire body.

I was lost in the sensation of it all, my mind consumed by the sheer pleasure of being filled by Elliott. My moans seemed to fuel his body. His thrusts were deep and powerful, hitting all the right spots and sending me soaring. I could feel my orgasm building and I wasn’t even touching my dick; a tidal wave of pleasure that threatened to consume me at any moment.

Elliott's hands were everywhere, touching and teasing me as we moved together. His fingers danced across my skin, sending shivers down my spine as he explored every inch of my body. His mouth was on my neck, his lips tracing patterns that made me shiver with delight. He nibbled at my ears as he whispered in my ear how good I felt. I grabbed my t-shirt as I knew I couldn’t last much longer. I was present enough to know I didn’t want my cum on the couch cushions.

As we moved closer to our climax, our movements became more frantic and desperate. We were both chasing the same thing, the ultimate release, and we were willing to do whatever it took to get there.

And then it happened.

Elliott's thrusts became faster and more intense, his cock pounding into me with a ferocity that left me breathless. I felt myself being lifted off the couch, my body weightless as he supported me with his strong arms and my feet on the floor.

My orgasm hit like a ton of bricks, a wave of pure pleasure that crashed over me like a tsunami. I felt myself contracting around Elliott's cock, milking him for every last drop as he came inside me.

The sensation was indescribable, a mix of heat and pressure that seemed to fill every inch of my body. I could feel Elliott shooting into me, filling the condom between us.

As we came together like this, two bodies united in perfect syncopation, for a moment, time seemed to stop. We were locked together, savoring the intimacy and connection of this shared moment. And when our breathing gradually slowed and the haze of our shared climax began to lift, we collapsed into each other, completely spent yet overwhelmingly fulfilled. In the quiet aftermath, with his chest still rising and falling beside me, I felt undeniably and completely his.

When reality gently crept back in and the remnants of our fervor began to settle, a deep, heart-stirring silence hung between us, a silence soon pierced by soft, vulnerable words. "I love you," Elliott whispered, his voice raw and trembling as it caressed my damp, sweat-slick skin.

I paused, feeling my breath catch in my throat as his words hovered in the air like a delicate promise, a vulnerability that could alter everything. My hand then reached up to brush away a stray lock of damp hair from his forehead, my eyes searching his for a truth reflected in their depths. "Are you sure?" I asked quietly, the low tone mingling hope and disbelief.

Without missing a beat, Elliott's steady gaze never wavered. "I've never been surer of anything," he said softly, the calm strength in his voice belying the intensity of his feelings. "You don't have to say it back if you're not ready, I just… needed you to know."

A warmth unfurled in my chest, coaxing away the last remnants of tension, replaced by the radiant glow of shared understanding. A soft, unbidden smile curved my lips as I leaned closer, resting my forehead against his in silent affirmation. "I love you too," I replied, my voice steady yet brimming with emotion.

Elliot's smile lit the room, his relief and joy evident as his body relaxed into mine. With a light, breathless laugh, his hands drifted back to the nape of my neck, pulling me in for a kiss that was unhurried and tender, a gentle celebration of the heartfelt truths we had finally shared. Outside, the world shrank to insignificance, time seemed to pause for us, and as our hearts beat in perfect unison, I realized that for the first time in a long while, I wasn't afraid of what tomorrow might bring. I felt seen, truly and completely loved, and it was a feeling I would never surrender.

After a long, contented silence, Elliott shifted slightly, his fingers idly drawing intricate, lazy patterns along my chest. Then, with a teasing glimmer in his eye, his voice broke the quiet once more. "Did I just see you use your shirt to catch your cum?"

I snorted softly, nestling my face against his warm shoulder. "Yeah, I wasn't about to ruin those couch cushions," I retorted with a playful laugh.

Elliott shook his head in amused disbelief, chuckling. "Jules, that's what Scotchgard is for. The couch is protected, for future reference."

I lifted my head to offer him a bright smile. "Good to know. Maybe next time I'll aim a little higher," I teased.

Rolling onto his back with an exaggerated groan of amusement, Elliott quipped, "Remind me why I put up with you?"

I grinned impishly and pressed a quick, affectionate kiss to his chest. "Because I'm charming, devastatingly attractive, and let's be real, you love it."

He sighed dramatically yet pulled me even closer, his warm breath and soft laughter mingling with the lingering aroma of our passion. "God help me, I really do."

The warm, velvet night had settled into a soft symphony of crickets chirping and the occasional gentle hum of wind threading through the trees. Elliott's back porch transformed into a secret haven, where the string lights draped gracefully between the posts shimmered with a warm, amber glow, mingling with the pale, enchanted silver light of the moon. The air embraced my skin with a comforting warmth, and I found myself draped in one of Elliott's oversized t-shirts, its fabric a cocoon of coziness that somehow carried the faint, soothing hint of lavender from his laundry detergent, a reminder of his gentle presence.

We reclined on the weathered wooden bench, our legs intertwined in a languid closeness that spoke of effortless connection. My legs, free of the constraints of anything more than boxer shorts, found their space upon his lap, while his fingers traced slow, wandering patterns on my knee. Each touch was delicate and soothing, laced with an irresistible allure that made every caress both maddening and exquisitely addictive.

A glass of wine rested in my hand, its deep red hue catching the light as I swirled it slowly, creating ripples of ruby reflections. Elliott held his own glass with a similar unhurried grace, sipping occasionally as if

savoring every moment. The complex, earthy aroma of the wine mingled with fresh, herbal whispers wafting from the garden below, a fragrant blend of mint, basil, and rosemary that imbued the evening with sensory delight. I absentmindedly twirled a sprig of mint between my fingers, the leaves cool and damp, grounding me in the present.

"You were right," I whispered, softly breaking the lull of our shared silence. Even as the words tumbled out in a gentle murmur, they carried the weight of soft certainty. "This whole domestic thing? Not terrible."

Elliott's eyes lit up with a small, knowing smile, a subtle arch of his lips that held secret promises. The light of the porch glowed in his eyes, casting them with a warmth that almost seemed tangible. "And I'll admit I didn't hate dancing," he replied, his voice low and steady, each syllable carefully measured, carrying a hint of playful amusement.

That admission coaxed a light, genuine laugh from me, the sound resonating like a soft chime in the evening air. Leaning into the familiar comfort of his shoulder, I felt anchored by the weight of his presence. The thin fabric of his shirt revealed the comforting warmth of his skin beneath, as I let my eyes wander up to the scattered stars, each one twinkling like a distant memory of wonder.

The wine had loosened the usual tension within me, allowing a serene calm to wash over my body. Every now and then, I could sense Elliott's gaze drifting towards me, a quiet flicker of warmth and unspoken depth that made my heart flutter in the most indescribable way.

"Do you ever think about how strange it is?" I asked as I rotated the mint sprig once more between my fingers, its coolness a counterpoint to the heat in the night. "That two people like us could make this work. You with your checklists and schedules, and me with…" I gestured vaguely, laughing at the absurdity of it all. "Whatever this is."

Elliott's chuckle rumbled low and rich, and he casually set his wine glass on the small side table. His hand reached out to rest gently on my ankle, fingers curling tenderly around it as he met my gaze. "I think about it all the time," he confessed softly. "And it doesn't feel strange. It feels... right."

His words lingered between us, a quiet promise more substantial than any overt declaration. Shifting slightly, I sat up just enough to fully capture the warmth in his eyes, eyes that were unreadable yet comforting, as though they held a secret meant only for me.

Leaning forward, I closed the gap between our lips, pressing a tender kiss that was soft and lingering, infused with the faint, rich taste

of wine. He responded with immediate warmth; his hand tightened just slightly on my ankle while the other gently cradled my face. The kiss was unhurried, a subtle dance of affection and longing, leaving an echo of tenderness in its wake. When I eventually pulled back, his gaze held mine a moment longer, and I couldn't help but smile in quiet contentment.

The silence around us needed no filling, it wrapped around us like Elliott's worn t-shirt, secure and safe. The stars above shone brighter than ever, or perhaps it was simply the way he looked at me, making me feel like I was the epicenter of his world. In that moment, for the first time in as long as I could remember, I felt truly at home, not merely in this secluded space, but within the shared sanctuary of his presence.

Every so often, his eyes would meet mine with a look that blended curiosity, admiration, and a depth I wasn't entirely able to label, yet couldn't ignore. Each glance made me smile in return, a silent acknowledgment that we were forging something real, something unique and undeniably ours.

25

ELLIOTT

The delicate jingle of the bell above the door announced our entrance as Jules and I stepped inside, his magnetic presence effortlessly filling the space with an undeniable allure that only he could command. He wore his casual elegance like an art form, a flowing, sun-bleached linen shirt casually tucked into perfectly cuffed jeans, with his signature scarf, a vibrant streak of color, adding a dash of irresistible flair. Standing there in my modest khaki shorts and a simple polo, I couldn't help but feel painfully ordinary in contrast, yet Jules's eyes sparkled with unspoken delight, welcoming the warmth and energy that the bustling bakery radiated. It was early July, and over the past few weeks, Jules had found himself spending more mornings at my house, and our shared routine was slowly evolving into a natural, unspoken rhythm that neither of us dared to disrupt.

Inside Sweet Haven Bakery, the hot morning sun spilled exuberantly through the expansive windows, casting liquid streaks of summer across the polished wooden floors and igniting a shimmering dance over the glass display case. The space was filled with the delightful aroma of freshly baked bread mingling with sweet cinnamon and a rich, buttery scent that teased my senses and made my stomach churn in anticipation despite the breakfast I'd already savored. The gentle hum of hushed conversations blended with the occasional, friendly clink of ceramic mugs, creating an atmosphere of coziness and quiet charm that

felt like stepping into an charming postcard of small-town life, familiar, comforting, and almost too perfectly orchestrated.

At that moment, Miss Audrey, the formidable owner of the bakery, raised her eyes from an artful arrangement of golden, flaky croissants. Her sharp, discerning gaze lit up as it fell upon us. With a presence as commanding as a summer storm, she exuded strength, her salt-and-pepper hair secured neatly into a no-nonsense bun and her flour-dusted apron telling stories of countless early mornings and diligent care.

"Well, well," she intoned, her voice carrying confidently over the soft hum of conversation. "If it isn't Havenwood's newest lovebirds."

Leaning casually against the counter, Jules's grin morphed into a mischievous grin as he replied, "Lovebirds, you say? Miss Audrey, I think we deserve a title upgrade. Power couple actually has a pretty enthralling ring to it."

I felt a flush of heat creep up my neck and quickly interjected, "What coffee flavors are featured today?" My voice carried both a nervous energy and a subtle plea to shift the teasing conversation away from our love story.

Undeterred, Miss Audrey leaned on the counter with a theatrical flourish, tapping her chin as if pondering a grand mystery. "Let's see," she drawled, "I've got hazelnut cream, caramel praline, cinnamon spice, and a house dark roast that'll knock your socks clean off."

Instantly, Jules's eyes lit up with excitement. "Caramel praline for me, please. And make it extra hot."

Adjusting my glasses with a small, grateful smile, I replied, "I'll have the cinnamon spice, black, thank you."

As Miss Audrey's knowing smile deepened, she proceeded to fill our order, her practiced eyes dancing between us with a mix of warmth and playful mischief. At that exact moment, the espresso machine burst into a satisfying mechanical hum, and she artfully slid a plate brimming with vibrant, rainbow macarons across the counter. "On the house, because you two are simply too cute," she declared with a twinkle in her eye.

Jules turned to me with a smirk that practically shouted, Told you so. "See? We're famous," he teased.

I couldn't help but shake my head while suppressing a laugh, adjusting my glasses once more. "Infamous, more like it," I quipped.

With a flourish befitting the moment, Miss Audrey returned, carefully setting down our coffee cups. Her wide grin conveyed genuine

happiness as she added affectionately, "Whatever you call it, I'm so happy for you two."

Jules's smile broadened as he accepted her words, "We'll take it."

Grasping the warm coffee cups in my hands, I felt the gentle heat seep through, grounding me in the moment. Jules picked up the plate of macarons with a theatrical flair, popping one into his mouth as he held the door open for me. His eyes danced with mischief and a lingering sense of pride, as if to say, I told you so.

"Caramel praline was an excellent choice," he remarked with a playful chuckle, his voice delightfully muffled by the sweet treat.

I rolled my eyes, a smile tugging at the corners of my lips despite my best efforts to appear modest. Jules's vibrant energy was utterly infectious, and even as Miss Audrey's teasing words echoed in my ears, I felt lighter, free, and, perhaps, a little more receptive to the affectionate spotlight than I cared to admit.

Stepping out onto the sun-kissed street, bathed in a soft, magical morning glow that made every mundane detail shimmer with life, I felt a subtle thrill. Jules strolled closely beside me, his arm brushing against mine with every step, a deliberately gentle reminder of his presence that sent a blush of warmth through me.

"You really enjoy this, don't you?" I asked softly, casting a sidelong glance at him as we walked, playful energy mingling with the morning light.

"Enjoy what?" he replied, his tone laced with a mock innocence, as he licked a lingering trace of macaron filling off his thumb with effortless charm.

Raising an eyebrow in feigned exasperation, I countered, "The attention. The teasing. All of it."

He laughed, a bright, contagious laugh that mingled perfectly with the shimmering sunlight filtering through the canopy of trees. "It wouldn't be half as fun without free macarons," he said with playful nudging. "Besides, I think you secretly delight in it too."

I opened my mouth to argue, but his unwavering confidence and infectious grin rendered my protest moot. And perhaps, in this small, wonderfully unexpected way, I did enjoy every moment, being seen, being part of something larger than myself, and simply, delighting in the presence of him.

Hand in hand, as we continued our leisurely stroll down the sun-dappled street, our fingers interlaced naturally and effortlessly, I allowed myself to lean fully into this day. The combined warmth of the coffee and his tender hand anchored me in a new kind of contentment, a

blissful, serene feeling that whispered promises of more beautiful mornings yet to come.

Later that evening, The Rainbow Taproom pulsed with an effervescent energy that breathed life into every corner of the room. Neon lights danced wildly across the aged brick walls, sending cascades of color that played over the cheerful crowd like flickering brushstrokes on a vivid canvas. Near the dartboard, Jules was already engrossed in a lively conversation with a few of our closest friends. His magnetic energy and effusive gestures drew people in, each laugh and animated story pulling them closer like moths attracted to a vibrant flame.

I lingered by the bar, cradling a glass of amber whiskey that glowed warmly in the dim light. Flanking me were Sam and Callie, comfortably stationed on high stools as if they presided over the establishment. Callie swirled their cocktail languidly, the liquid catching glints of neon as they spoke with a dramatic flair. "You know, Teach, you're kind of a big deal these days," they declared, their voice mingling mischief with genuine admiration.

Sam's smile widened into a conspiratorial grin as he leaned in, his tone imbued with playful mischief. "Power couple of Havenwood, you have to admit it. How does it feel to be basking in the spotlight?"

I took a measured sip of my drink, feeling the whiskey's bold warmth ignite a subtle fire as it burned its way down. "Honestly? Not as unbearable as I expected," I replied with a relaxed chuckle, letting the ambiance ease any lingering reservations.

Callie gasped dramatically, the theatrical shock almost causing their drink to tip over and spill a cascade of colors onto the bar. "Did I just hear Elliott Brooks confess he relishes attention?"

Suppressing a smile, I added with a smirk, "Let's not get too carried away. It certainly doesn't hurt when someone else takes most of the heat."

As my words faded into the ambient hum of chatter and clinking glasses, my gaze wandered to Jules. There he was, vividly animated as he described an anecdote to our group, his laughter light and echoing through the room like a melody of pure delight. Catching my admiring

glance, Jules winked mischievously before smoothly weaving through the swarm of patrons toward me.

"There you are," Jules said, his voice blending warmth and playfulness as his hand casually rested on the small of my back. "The whiskey isn't keeping you chained to the bar, is it?"

I chuckled in response, amusement dancing in my tone. "I'm pacing myself, Jules. Someone has to remain coherent in case you decide to outdo last week's infamous karaoke performance."

Jules' eyes sparkled with mischief as he grinned, his presence a beacon of carefree charm. "That's a bold assumption, Teach. But for now…" He gestured invitingly, extending a hand that promised both an escape and an adventure. "Dance with me."

For a brief moment, I hesitated. My natural instinct to blend into the backdrop wrestled with the enticing warmth of his touch and the promise of shared exhilaration. Just as I was about to place my glass down in answer, Callie interjected with impeccable timing, the sound of their voice slicing through the moment as they slid off their stool with exaggerated flair.

"Hold it right there," Callie declared, a mischievous grin tugging at their lips as they looped an arm affectionately around Jules' shoulder. "Don't wear him out too soon, I'm whisking you two away for a quieter soirée. My place awaits, with the comforts of good drinks, savory snacks, and absolutely no dance floor pressure."

An eyebrow arched in playful challenge as Jules looked at Callie, amusement clearly etched on his face. "Are you saving him or me?"

Callie's tone remained breezy and teasing as they replied, "Both, of course. Besides, I'm curious to see if the infamous Teach can hold his own in a conversation without the distraction of music, dazzling lights, and flamboyant drag queens."

Jules glanced back at me, his hand still resting on my back as if to offer silent support, then turned back to Callie with a grin that promised mischief. "Fine. But you owe me a dance later."

"Deal," Callie responded with a wink, their eyes twinkling like playful stars. "Now, let's make our escape before Jordy ropes you into another impromptu duet."

And with that, the three of us slipped out of the Taproom, the night air cool and refreshing as it greeted us. Jules' laughter trailed behind us like a lingering note, wrapping around our departure as we strolled toward Callie's place, a promise of a quieter, more intimate adventure shimmering in the moonlight.

Later, at Callie's apartment, the energy shifted from the frenetic energy of the Taproom to the cozy warmth of familiar camaraderie. Callie's apartment was exactly what you'd expect from them: vibrant, eclectic, and full of personality. String lights zigzagged across the ceiling, casting a soft glow over the mismatched furniture. A well-worn beanbag chair claimed the center of the room like a throne, while a low coffee table was cluttered with half-empty glasses, a few takeout containers, and an impressive array of cocktail ingredients.

Callie, lounging luxuriously on their throne-like beanbag, took command of the room with animated flair. They regaled us with the latest episode of romantic misadventure, a dating disaster fraught with tangled text messages, a thoroughly bewildered florist, and an awkward encounter at the gym that unfolded like a scene from a madcap comedy. Their expressive gestures, wide eyes and theatrical chuckles, had everyone bursting into gleeful laughter, myself included.

"I mean, who sends 'I had a great time last night' to their yoga instructor by mistake?" Callie proclaimed, their arms flailing in an exaggerated display. "I don't even do yoga!"

Perched on the arm of the sofa, drink in hand and exuding a playful nonchalance, Sam shook his head in feigned disbelief. "You're a magnet for madness, Callie. It's impressive, honestly."

Beside me on the cozy couch, Jules reclined with his legs casually draped over mine, a quiet yet tender smile playing on his lips. Though his voice was soft and measured, every now and then, he interjected a witty remark that kept the contagious energy flowing effortlessly throughout the room.

With a mischievous glint in their eye, Callie pointed a glass at Jules. "You two really are the talk of the town," they teased, a smile crossing their face as they gestured between us. "It's kind of disgusting, honestly."

Jules's response was as playful as it was endearing; he grinned and lobbed a pillow in my direction. "Careful, or I'll start charging you for this privilege."

The pillow sailed humorously off course, landing near Ezra, who was seated cross-legged with a cold beer in hand. With a dramatic raise

of his bottle in surrender, he remarked, "Collateral damage. I'm staying out of this."

"Smart man," Sam toasted, raising his drink high.

I shrugged, feeling the subtle shift of Jules' legs as he adjusted his position next to me. My hand found its way onto his knee, a gesture both new in its intimacy and comfortingly familiar. "Good company helps," I offered with a small, contented smile, meeting Callie's amused gaze.

Leaning his head against my shoulder, Jules said warmly, "See? I'm a good influence."

"Debatable," I replied lightly, my tone laced with fond teasing as I squeezed his knee gently.

"Well, Teach," Callie declared with a widening grin that lit up the room, "we've heard about Jules' infamous karaoke antics, but it's your turn. What's the most embarrassing thing you've ever done in public?"

The question caught me off guard, yet the infectious laughter ringing around the room and the reassuring presence of Jules eased my apprehension. I took a measured sip of my whiskey, its warmth spreading through me like a quiet, fiery embrace. Blushing slightly, I began, "There was an incident back in college… Let's just say I learned the hard way that debuting brand-new shoes for a presentation is a recipe for disaster."

"Oh no," interjected Ezra, his smile growing wider as he leaned forward, clearly relishing every detail. "What happened?"

"They squeaked," I admitted, shaking my head in exasperated amusement. "Every step I took sent out a loud, unmistakable squeak, like a series of comic farts reverberating through the lecture hall. By the time I reached the podium, half the class was doubled over in uncontrollable laughter."

The room exploded into a chorus of hearty laughter, even Jules joining in with that infectious mirth of his. "I would pay good money to see that," he quipped, his eyes sparkling with mischief.

"Don't give Callie any ideas," I shot back with a playful smirk, gesturing toward our ever-entertaining host.

Callie, pretending to scribble in an invisible notebook, announced with mock solemnity, "Elliott: squeaky shoes. Got it."

As the banter continued, the room became a blend of shared stories and teasing remarks, stitched together by the ease of friendship. Soon enough, Renzo and Avery joined our little circle, sliding onto the floor with freshly procured drinks. Quiet Renzo, ever the observant one, interjected occasionally with razor-sharp one-liners that left us all in peals of laughter, while the inquisitive Avery peppered me with rapid-fire questions about Jules, his tone half-serious, half-teasing.

"So, Teach," Avery said, his voice carrying a playful gravitas, "what's the most surprising thing you've learned about Jules since you two started dating?"

I glanced over at Jules, who raised a single, amused eyebrow in silent challenge. "That he can recite every single lyric from every ABBA song ever written," I deadpanned, the statement humorous in its absurdity.

Jules feigned shock, swatting my arm in playful protest. "That's not surprising, that's a life skill," he declared with a dramatic flourish.

Laughter swelled around the room once more, and I couldn't help but savor the sweet rediscovery of my own mirth. The sound of my laughter felt both strange and wonderfully liberating, a liberation of a part of myself long obscured by routine.

As the night gracefully slipped into its quieter phase, the raucous laughter softened into intimate conversations. Jules stayed near, letting me share the spotlight with our trusted friends, his smile both soft and proud as he watched me weave through the discussions. At one point, I caught him gazing at me with an expression layered in both affection and something deeper, a moment so tender it nearly took my breath away.

By the time we finally stepped out of Callie's apartment, the cool, crisp night air and the hushed serenity of the empty streets provided a quiet counterpoint to the warm glow inside. Jules slipped his hand into mine, his touch steady and reassuring. "You were great tonight," he said softly, the compliment lingering in the space between us.

"So were you," I replied in a nearly whispered tone, my voice carrying a gentle warmth.

In that quiet moment, beneath the soft glow of streetlights and the whisper of the night, I realized just how immeasurably important this little community, and especially Jules, had become in my life.

26

JULES

Later that week, dinner at my apartment wasn't the candlelit dreamscape I might have pictured in a quieter, simpler life, it was messy and erratic, yet full of its own comforting charm. The table I had cleared for us was in fact my cluttered desk, usually buried beneath stacks of handwritten notes, scripts, frayed costume sketches, and the ever-present evidence of late-night caffeine in the form of a lone coffee ring. Tonight, however, the surface was transformed: mismatched plates were arranged as if to celebrate the imperfect, a single, wavering candle stub flickered in a small glass holder, and the enticing aroma of roasted vegetables mingled with garlic bread that Elliott had insisted on preparing filled the room.

The apartment itself carried a medley of scents. The rich, herby fragrance of fresh basil from his perfectly roasted chicken intermingled with the lingering, faint musky scent of paint and sawdust, a constant reminder of the space's creative chaos. A solitary window, cracked open to let in the cool evening air, offered up the gentle hum of the city beyond, setting a quiet, rhythmic backdrop to our conversation.

I sat cross-legged in a somewhat improvised chair opposite him, mechanically moving carrots around my plate as if they held the answers to my frustrations. My body buzzed with exhaustion; every nerve from head to toe still thrummed with the remnants of tech and dress rehearsals. Yet even as fatigue overtook me, I hesitated to admit the full extent of my weariness.

"It's like… no matter how much I do, it never feels like enough," I confessed, a tremor of frustration threading through my voice. "The costumes are nearly perfect, but they're always missing something. The stage blocking is still clunky in parts. And honestly, the lights, either they blind or leave the stage shrouded in darkness like some forgotten crypt. It's a relentless barrage of imperfection, and I can't see where it all leads."

Elliott leaned back in his chair, his own nearly clean plate a quiet counterpoint to my scattered emotions. Watching me with that familiar, patient calm, he cradled a wine glass loosely between his fingers as he spoke. "You're trying to carry it all on your shoulders, aren't you?" he observed, his tone gentle and understanding.

I exhaled slowly as I set my fork down, the dull clink against the plate emphasizing my inner turmoil. "Of course, I am. It's my vision, Elliott. If I don't micromanage every detail, who will? It's tech week, every minute is consumed by chaos, but it's my chaos. Surrendering even a tiny piece of control isn't an option."

With his head tilted slightly and brows drawn in a faint expression of concern, Elliott's calm voice persisted. "Jules, you're just one person. You've got a whole team behind you. Let them shoulder some of the burden. And trust me, if things don't fall exactly into place, it isn't the downfall of the entire production."

Each word from him tightened and then gradually pried loose the knot in my chest. I leaned forward, resting my elbows on the table, meeting his steady gaze. "You don't understand," I insisted softly, "this isn't just about me. It's the entire production. Every element must mesh perfectly, or the whole thing comes apart."

He nodded slowly as though letting my words settle into the quiet hum of the evening. "I understand, Jules. More than you might believe. But sometimes, it's not about reaching flawlessness. Sometimes, it's the raw heart, the passion behind it, that makes something truly great, and you've got more heart than anyone I know."

His tenderness took me by surprise, softening the tension within me as his words cascaded gently over my frayed nerves. "It's really hard to let go," I admitted in a quieter tone, vulnerabilities laid bare in the flickering candlelight.

Elliott's smile was faint but sincere as he set his wine glass down and leaned forward. "I know it is," he shared. "But you taught me that sometimes, taking a leap of faith is the only way forward. Perhaps it's time to allow someone else to catch you, even if it's just for one night."

I sank back into my chair, feeling a gradual release of the pressure in my shoulders, and a small smile began to tug at the corners of my lips.

"You're annoyingly wise," I teased softly, amusement brightening my weary eyes.

A playful smile curved his lips in reply. "I try," he said lightly.

A burst of laughter, fragile yet liberating, escaped me, echoing against the apartment's brick walls and filling the space with warmth that contrasted the day's heaviness. Turning my attention back to the moment, I lifted my wine glass and took a measured sip as I watched him. His presence, calm and unwavering, seemed to still the small, cluttered room in a sense of stability.

After a quiet pause, Elliott tilted his head inquisitively. "What else is going on?" he asked softly, his eyes probing with care. "I mean, aside from the play. You've been a bit quieter than usual."

I hesitated, swirling the ruby liquid in my glass as if it could summon the right words. "Well, there's… life stuff," I finally offered. "The lease on this apartment is up in a few months, and honestly, I'm not sure I can keep up with it. Rent has skyrocketed, and with every dollar tied up in the Playhouse, finances have become scarcer than ever."

A flicker of concern crossed his face. "Do you have a plan?" he inquired gently.

"Sort of," I admitted, biting my lip in thought. "Callie mentioned that I could move in with her for a while. It would alleviate some of the monetary pressure, and truthfully, a change of scenery wouldn't be unwelcome. This place has its own peculiar charm, but…" I gestured vaguely at the room, its walls chipped with peeling paint and furniture mismatched in both style and era, "it feels like it's holding onto its past a bit too tightly."

Elliott nodded slowly, his thoughtful gaze unpressured as he allowed the conversation its space. I felt grateful for his silence on the matter; it was a topic I wasn't yet ready to unpack in full detail, even as his quiet support anchored me more steadily than I had realized.

After our meal, the dishes remained abandoned on the tiny counter as we lingered at the table, enveloped in an easy camaraderie that wandered from the trials of the Playhouse to tales of his week with Caleb, and even the humorous mishaps of my failed attempt at reupholstering the very chair he occupied. His laughter, light and sincere, danced between us and seemed to stitch together the frayed edges of my day. In sharing these moments, not only was I unraveling the knots of stress, but I was also revealing the parts of myself I usually guarded so fiercely, and he listened, every word a gentle affirmation.

When I finally rose to clear the plates, Elliott's hand rested softly on my wrist, halting me. "Leave them," he declared, his voice tender with unspoken care. "You've done enough for tonight."

I looked down at his hand, steady, warm, and reassuring, and nodded. For the first time that week, a real sense of calm flickered within me. Despite the relentless crazy of tech week and the weight of so many looming uncertainties, there was something profoundly grounding in knowing that Elliott was here, a constant beacon of stability amidst the storm. And for that evening, I allowed myself a long, measured exhale, embracing the moment of reprieve.

27

ELLIOTT

The late July evening air was warm and heavy, its humid embrace carrying the distant, rhythmic hum of cicadas as Caleb and I made our way to Sorella's, a quaint, family-owned Italian restaurant hidden just off Havenwood's main thoroughfare. The setting sun spilled a molten, golden glow across the storefronts, bathing the neighborhood in a soft, amber light, while the lingering heat of the day gradually softened into a more comfortable, soothing warmth. Stepping inside, we were immediately met by a chilled caress from the air-conditioning, a pleasant counterpoint to our flushed, sun-kissed faces, and the rich, intoxicating aroma of simmering garlic and freshly picked basil wrapped around us like a welcoming embrace. The interior exuded cozy charm, its warm lighting caressing every corner, while the gentle strains of a soft piano melody danced amid the delicate clinking of glasses and the low murmur of hushed, contented conversations.

Caleb tugged at the collar of his crisply pressed button-up shirt, his eyes darting around the room with childlike curiosity. "This place is fancy," he remarked, his voice blending exhilaration with a hint of mild unease.

"It's not too fancy," I replied with a light-hearted chuckle, expertly adjusting my tie. "But I thought we could make a night of it, a delicious dinner paired with an enchanting show. After all, it isn't every day that you get to witness a live Shakespeare production."

A playful grin spread across his face as he slid into the booth opposite me. "True. I've never seen one. We discussed *A Midsummer Night's Dream* in class last year, but all we got to do was read excerpts. It was kind of cool to imagine, though."

Our conversation was momentarily paused as a courteous server glided by, replenishing our water glasses with crystal-clear liquid as we placed our orders. Caleb chose a steaming plate of spaghetti and meatballs, the savory aroma promising a delightful meal, while I opted for the classic, comforting allure of chicken parmesan.

As the server retreated, Caleb leaned forward eagerly. "So, Jules is really calling the shots here, right? Basically, the big boss?"

"Pretty much," I affirmed with a nod. "He's the director, the heartbeat behind it all, running rigorous rehearsals, coordinating with the designers, and making sure every intricate detail comes together flawlessly."

"That has to be a lot of pressure," he observed, his eyes widening with genuine admiration. "But he seems incredibly good at it. You mention him all the time."

I paused, my thoughts fluttering as I searched for the right words. "It's a massive project, no doubt. And Jules… he's not just talented, there's something about him that's really special. I'm excited for you to see the show."

"Me too," Caleb said earnestly, his fingers absently twirling the rim of his water glass. After a moment, he leaned in with a mischievous smile. "So, tell me, are you two... I mean, are you guys going to be boyfriends?"

The question took me by surprise, and I blinked as I strove to mask my surprise with neutrality. "I… well…" I began, my voice honest yet tentative. "Would you be okay with that?"

"I like him," Caleb declared without hesitation, his tone sincere. "He's funny, kind, and it's obvious how happy you are when you talk about him. So, yeah, I'd love it if you two were together."

A warm, comforting glow spread through my chest at his words, though I maintained an even tone. "What would you think if… one day, Jules moved in with us? I mean, this is your home too. I'd want to make sure you're comfortable with that kind of change."

Caleb's eyes sparkled with excitement as he nodded enthusiastically. "Are you kidding? That would be so fun! Jules is awesome, he'd definitely bring a lot of personality and energy to the house."

I laughed, shaking my head in amusement. "He'd certainly add his own unique flair to everything. But right now, it's just an idea. Nothing has been set in stone."

"Still," he said with a wide grin, "I'd be cool with it."

Just then, our meals arrived, interrupting our conversation. We settled into a pleasant rhythm of easy chatter about Caleb's eventful week, the little highlights of our time together, and his excitement over the upcoming Marvel movie he was already planning to watch with his friends back home. The food was nothing short of exquisite, and in a playful mishap, Caleb managed to smudge marinara sauce onto his chin, a detail he only noticed when I extended a napkin toward him with a teasing, pointed look.

By the time we stepped out of the restaurant, the sinking sun had dipped behind the horizon, leaving the streets of Havenwood's Rivermere District bathed in the soft, warm glow of streetlights and emitting a noticeably cooler, crisper air than what we had left behind at dinner. As we strolled along the sidewalk, Caleb casually looped his arm around mine, his bubbling excitement clearly visible.

"Dad, this is going to be amazing," he exclaimed, his voice bubbling with anticipation as he practically bounced on his heels. "I can't wait to see how he brings all that magic to life with Puck and the fairies."

I smiled, giving his shoulder a reassuring squeeze. "You're going to love it. Jules has put his heart and soul into making it something truly special."

As we meandered toward the Playhouse, our conversation drifted effortlessly from the heavenly taste of the cannolis we savored for dessert to reminiscences of a fun-filled day at the pool earlier in the week, and even to a playful recount of the video game where Caleb had bested me this very morning. Yet, quietly echoing in the back of my mind were the gentle reverberations of Caleb's words about Jules, a small spark of hope kindling within me as I pondered the intriguing, unfolding possibilities that the future might hold for all of us.

The Havenwood Playhouse hummed with anticipation that night, its historic walls alive with the gentle rumble of animated conversation and the soft, deliberate rustle of freshly printed playbills. Overhead, the

chandeliers cast a warm, inviting glow that danced off the polished wooden beams, bathing the room in a cozy, intimate light that promised an evening of enchantment. It was an ideal evening for the opening night of *A Midsummer Night's Dream*, and for Caleb, it was his first foray into the magic of live theater.

As Caleb and I strolled through the ornate lobby, I couldn't help but notice how he positively stood out in the most endearing way. His crisp, white button-up shirt, sleeves casually rolled to just below the elbows, and his dark, neatly pressed slacks exuded an air of refined, polished confidence. I had chosen a light blue shirt layered under a tailored jacket paired with slacks, striking just the right balance between casual comfort and special occasion flair. Caleb, clearly wrestling with his own teenage awkwardness, tugged self-consciously at his collar.

"Do I really have to wear this?" he asked, giving me a sidelong glance as he fumbled with the button at his throat.

"You look great," I replied with a warm smile. "We both do. Besides, it's opening night; you've absolutely got to look the part."

A hesitant grin broke across his face. "You mean like someone who actually gets Shakespeare?"

"Exactly," I laughed softly, guiding him toward the grand entrance to the theater.

The massive wooden doors of the Playhouse stood proudly beneath a cascade of soft white lights that draped delicately over clusters of arriving patrons dressed in semi-formal attire. Caleb's pace quickened as we neared the threshold, his wide eyes absorbing every intricate detail of the building's architecture.

"This place is enormous," he whispered in awe, craning his neck to study the detailed carvings and historic flourishes that told stories of years past.

"It's one of Havenwood's gems," I said, resting a reassuring hand on his shoulder as I led him through the ornate doors. "You haven't even seen the inside yet."

Inside, the lobby was a feast for the senses, the rich, almost velvety aroma of polished wood mingled with the crisp scent of newly printed programs and delicate floral notes, all underscored by the excited hum of the gathering crowd. Caleb's gaze flitted from the glimmering crystal chandeliers overhead to the detailed posters adorning the walls, each poster a vibrant echo of past productions. Captivated, he breathed out in wonder.

"Whoa," he whispered, his voice filled with astonishment. "This is like a scene out of a movie."

"Told you it would be special," I said, handing him a playbill and carefully tucking mine into the pocket of my jacket.

Caleb's fingers traced the glossy pages as his expression shifted from curiosity to intense focus while he scanned the cast list. "Do you think he'll have real trees onstage for the enchanted forest?" he asked, his tone laced with wonder.

"Not actual trees," I chuckled lightly, "but knowing Jules, every bit of it will feel pure magic."

His grin broadened with excitement. "I can't wait."

We wandered over to a quaint side table that offered refreshments, where Caleb eagerly grabbed a glass filled with sparkling lemonade. As he sipped, his eyes caught sight of an elegantly dressed older couple, their attire impeccable and clearly formal. Nudging me gently with his elbow, he whispered, "Are we underdressed?"

I shook my head with a smile. "Not at all. We're perfectly at ease, comfortable yet polished. It's about the experience, not just the wardrobe."

A soft bell chimed to announce the opening of the auditorium doors, and as the crowd began to stir, a familiar, lively group made their entrance into the lobby. A large assembly of kids from the GSA, led by the ever-enthusiastic Maya and Jayden, burst in with radiant energy, their excited chatter creating a joyful backdrop. They wore vibrant pins and spirited shirts in support of the production, some even carrying small bouquets of fresh flowers. My heart swelled seeing them come together, united in their admiration for Jules.

Just then, as my attention was drawn back to Caleb, Anna appeared by the entrance, scanning the bustling room for us. Dressed simply yet elegantly in a navy dress that complimented her auburn hair pulled back loosely, her warm smile lit up her face at the sight of us.

"Mom!" Caleb called out, waving her over with uncontained delight.

Anna quickly joined us, her heels clicking softly on the polished floor as she wrapped Caleb in a quick, affectionate hug before turning toward me with genuine warmth in her eyes. "This place is stunning," she remarked, her gaze slowly drifting over the beautifully lit space.

"It truly is," I agreed softly. "Jules has poured so much heart into making this show something extraordinary."

With a playful raised brow and teasing smile, Anna replied, "I wouldn't expect anything less."

We then found our seats in the heart of the theater, perfectly positioned to command a full view of the stage. Caleb seated between

Anna and me, his excitement visibly bubbling as he bounced slightly in his seat while flipping through the program once more.

"Thanks for bringing me, Dad," he said, leaning in closer so his words might be heard, "This is really cool!"

I smiled, gently squeezing his shoulder. "I'm glad you're here, buddy."

Anna's eyes softened with unspoken gratitude as she glanced at me before we settled into our seats. The theater itself buzzed with the kind of anticipation that filled every historic nook of the venue, its worn wooden beams and ambient lighting exuding an intimate, almost magical warmth. Sam and Callie joined our group shortly thereafter. When I shifted in my seat, the creak of the wooden chair echoed softly as I tried to calm the nervous flutter in my chest. The air carried a delightful medley, the nostalgic aroma of old wood, the subtle scent of stage dust, and the sweet hint of lavender from a single flower tucked safely beneath my jacket, a quiet tribute to Jules' vibrant energy and his remarkable ability to transform chaos into art.

Sam leaned in, his voice low and tinged with playful mischief, "You look like you're about to take a final exam."

I laughed, adjusting my glasses with one hand while my other hand rested thoughtfully on the playbill. "Just hoping everything runs smoothly."

Callie swirled the cocktail they'd picked up in the lobby, the clinking of ice a soft musical note against the glass. With a knowing grin, they said, "Teach, have a little faith. Jules has been pouring his soul into this for months. It's going to be incredible."

I nodded silently, my eyes fixed on the stage where the curtains lay shrouded in darkness, even as my imagination leapt to visions of Jules backstage, a whirlwind of clipboard-clad determination, issuing final technical notes, rallying his cast with pep talks, and orchestrating last-minute adjustments with the precision of a maestro. He lived for these moments, the energy, the pressure, and the unbridled artistry that defined his very essence. It was one of the many things I adored about him, even as I wondered if I'd ever truly keep pace with his relentless passion.

As the house lights gradually dimmed, a hush of collective expectancy fell over the room, silencing the buzz of the audience. The deep crimson curtains parted to reveal a stage metamorphosed into an ethereal woodland; glowing hues, carefully suspended lights, and artful touches of painted magic turned the set into a shimmering dreamscape. The first tender notes of the music swelled, drawing us irrevocably into the world of *A Midsummer Night's Dream.*

My breath caught in awe as the palpable tension filled the room. My fingers clutched the playbill a little tighter as the first actor stepped boldly into the light, his voice clear, resonant, and inviting, wrapping the audience deeper into the unfolding tale.

Leaning in once more, Callie whispered, "I can spot Jules' touch in every detail of this scene. The lighting? It's undeniably pure Jules."

I beamed with pride as my heart swelled. As the actors gracefully danced through the opening scene, gentle laughter rippled through the audience at Puck's mischievous antics, and a soft tear of emotion threatened to escape during Titania's tender moments. I blinked rapidly, trying to quell the stir of emotions, yet it was impossible to disregard the overwhelming brilliance of the moment. Jules' vision had come alive on stage, inviting every visitor into a realm of enchantment and wonder.

As dialogue replaced the musical overture, the interplay among the performers grew wonderfully sharp and effortlessly fluid. The laughter, the spellbound silence during introspective moments, and the commanding presence of Oberon as he fully embodied the king of the fairies, all came together in perfect harmony. Jules had succeeded magnificently. He transformed the entire experience into something truly extraordinary.

At one point, I felt Caleb's hand brush mine gently on the armrest as he leaned forward, his eyes fiercely glued to the mesmerizing stage. Anna's tender smile, with her hand resting lightly on his shoulder, said it all. In that moment, for the first time in what felt like ages, everything was exactly as it should be.

The applause that erupted at the end of the show was like a rumbling storm, a thunderous ovation that could only be earned by the flawless enchantment of exquisite storytelling. The entire audience surged to their feet in a collective exultation, clapping and cheering as the cast took their bows, each gesture a testament to the magic woven on stage. The actors, radiant in the fading glow of stage lights, wore smiles that were as bright as the glittering stars above, their palpable joy mingling with the warm, lingering energy of the crowd. My hands ached from the relentless clapping, yet that minor sting was drowned out by the overwhelming swell of pride that filled my heart. Jules had truly done it.

I cast my gaze to the right and saw Anna and Caleb rising amidst the sea of fans. Caleb's face shone with unbridled excitement, his eyes sparkling like polished gems as he kept his unwavering focus on the stage. Beside him, Anna, usually a picture of composure, now had glistening tears dancing in her eyes, her smile tender and brimming with pride as if each drop carried a memory of hope and admiration.

"Wow," Caleb breathed, his voice trembling with awe. "That was… absolutely amazing."

Anna nodded slowly, her delicate fingers dabbing at her eyes with a crumpled tissue drawn from her bag, her tone warm and husky as she added, "Incredible." Turning to me, she rested a gentle hand on my arm as if to share the intimate intimacy of this moment. "You must be so proud of Jules. This was simply beautiful."

"I am," I said, my voice soft yet loaded with emotion, each word filled with the quiet resonance of heartfelt pride.

As the house lights gradually crept up, signaling that the night was drawing to a close, I remained seated, my eyes magnetically locked on the stage. Though Jules had vanished into the wings at the fall of the curtain, I could still catch the faint echo of his laughter mingling with the excited backstage chatter, each sound a warm caress that filled me with a cozy, lingering glow.

Callie sat beside me, their empty glass a silent witness to the night's exhilaration. Observing my rapt expression, they offered a teasing smile. "Proud of him, huh?" they quipped, their tone light but unmistakably infused with affection and genuine admiration.

I nodded, a small, almost involuntary smile gracing my lips as I confessed, "More than he probably realizes."

Nearby, Sam rose with a dramatic stretch, his movements theatrical as he scooped up his coat. "I'm heading for the exit before the lobby turns into a full-blown mob scene. You two on board?" he called out playfully.

Callie waved off Sam's departing figure, their attention still centered on me. "I'll catch up later," they replied, a glimmer of amusement dancing in their eyes. "Someone's got to make sure Teach doesn't spontaneously combust." Sam chuckled, throwing me a wink as he melted into the dispersing crowd.

Callie leaned in closer, their voice dropping to a softer, more confidential tone. "You know," they shared, sincerity sharpening their words, "Jules doesn't let just anyone into his world. He's truly lucky to have you."

Startled by the uncharacteristic earnestness, I glanced at them with a gentle laugh. "I'm the lucky one," I replied simply, the truth of the sentiment vibrating between us.

Before Callie could add more, my attention was snared by the stage. Jules had reappeared, pulled back into the limelight as the actor embodying Puck practically vibrated with uncontained excitement. The entire cast swarmed around him, their cheers and laughter resonating like a joyful symphony as they enfolded Jules in a raucous group hug.

Jules' smile was incandescent, his arms enwrapping his fellow actors as he exchanged high-fives and embracing hugs. He was unmistakably in his element, his brilliance radiating with every spontaneous laugh and every sincere gesture, all under the dazzle of the stage lights that bathed him in an ethereal glow. I found myself unable to tear my eyes away from the scene.

Then, as if conjured by a shift in the air, my gaze caught sight of a statuesque woman making her way toward Jules with an air of authoritative grace. With her silver-streaked dark hair impeccably styled into a sleek bob and a tailored emerald green suit that seemed to whisper confidence and professionalism, she was the embodiment of poise. A silk scarf, meticulously tied at her neck, added a touch of elegance to her commanding presence. Her piercing blue eyes, sharp and reflective, swept over the room with calculated precision before locking onto Jules.

Leaning in ever so slightly, her voice dropped to a low, smooth cadence, a private murmur meant to keep the conversation hidden from prying ears while still carrying a determined insistence. Jules nodded in response, his posture shifting in subtle acknowledgment, a mix of respectful attentiveness and a flicker of unease dancing in his demeanor as Margaret escorted him backstage. The encounter was brief, yet it weighed on the atmosphere like an unanswered question, stirring a flicker of curiosity and concern in my chest.

Ever observant, Callie leaned closer, their eyes narrowing as they whispered, "That's Margaret Caldwell, the board president of Havenwood Playhouse. I wonder what's brewing there." Their tone was casual, yet the intrigue was as palpable as the electric energy that still hummed in the air.

"I don't know," I said in reply, my voice barely above a whisper.

As the echoes of applause and laughter began to fade into the backdrop of the night, I continued to watch Jules and Margaret converse, the significance of the interaction settling around me like an inescapable shadow. Whatever the nature of their discussion, I had no doubt that Jules would confront it with the same grace and untamed passion he

brought to every performance. Still, the nagging curiosity within me yearned to understand every nuance of the moment.

Slowly, as the vibrant crowd began to disperse, Anna and Caleb turned their attention back to me. Caleb stepped forward and wrapped his arms around me in a heartfelt hug, his embrace warm and sincere as he said, "That was so cool, Dad. You need to tell Jules he did an amazing job!"

Anna moved in close, her eyes still shimmering with unshed tears, and enveloped me in a tender, brief embrace. "Elliott, tonight was incredible," she whispered softly, the excitement in her tone melding with a deep, resonating pride. "Jules is so talented, please send him our heartfelt congratulations."

"I will," I promised, my voice catching with emotion as I returned Caleb's hug one more time. "I'll see you soon, buddy. Love you."

"Love you too, Dad," he replied with a radiant smile before stepping back into the dimming throng of the exiting crowd.

With one final, lingering smile from Anna, they vanished into the receding crowd, their words echoing in my mind as I turned back toward the stage. I clutched a delicate lavender flower tightly in my hand, a small token that felt as symbolic as it was beautiful. Tonight was not merely a celebration of the play; it was a heartfelt tribute to Jules, whose brilliant, chaotic soul had, once again, lit up our worlds.

The Havenwood Playhouse began to empty at a slow pace, the vibrant buzz of opening night still clinging to the walls like a delicate veil, even as patrons and cast members emerged into the enveloping warmth of the night. I lingered just outside the stage door, leaning casually against the timeworn brick wall, a single lavender bloom cradled gently in my hand. The soft, soothing fragrance of the lavender intertwined gracefully with the crisp, cool evening air, and I found myself silently rehearsing the words I longed to share. I desperately wanted him to know the depth of my pride.

At last, the door creaked open, and there he was. Jules emerged, his presence still crackling with electric fervor despite traces of exhaustion etched around his eyes and on his face. His hair was artfully

tousled, and his cheeks bore a lingering flush from the exhilaration of the performance. There was an unmistakable aura about him, a vibrant, contagious confidence that had first captivated me from the moment we met.

"Hey, Teach," he greeted warmly, his voice carrying the softness of fatigue blended with genuine affection. "Been waiting long?"

"Not at all," I replied, straightening up and extending my hand to offer the lavender bloom. "This is for you."

At those words, his features softened further. His lips curled into a gentle, appreciative smile as he accepted the flower. "You're such a romantic," he teased, lightly twirling the stem between his fingers as if savoring each moment. "It's absolutely adorable."

I chuckled and felt the tension in my chest dissolve bit by bit. "I mean every word. You were simply mesmerizing tonight."

For a brief moment, Jules lowered his head, and I noticed a shy blush coloring his cheeks even in the dim glow of the exit. "Thanks," he said, his tone barely above a whisper, loaded with the weight of his gratitude. "Hearing that from you, it means more than you know."

Unable to keep the warmth from my voice, I added, "You're not the only one who was impressed. Caleb and Anna couldn't stop singing your praises. They had to leave to get on the road, but they insisted I tell you how utterly blown away they were by the performance."

His smile broadened and his eyes shimmered with grateful delight. "That truly means a lot. I'm glad they enjoyed it."

Just then, I hesitated, then gently inquired, "I couldn't help but notice that the board president pulled you aside after the show. Is everything alright?"

Jules's eyes met mine, and for a fleeting moment, his expression was unreadable, a blend of vulnerability and pride. Then, gradually, a broad grin unfolded, mixing disbelief with elation. "She asked me to consider becoming the Playhouse's artistic director."

Those words hung between us like a fragile, luminous promise. I blinked, absorbing the magnitude of what he had just shared. "Jules," I breathed, my voice imbued with wonder and heartfelt excitement, "that's... absolutely incredible."

He nodded slowly, his smile growing even wider as his gaze shifted down to the lavender still clutched in his hand. "It's a lot to think about, a huge step forward. But it feels right, like I'm finally on the path that matters."

"You are," I said without hesitation, conviction resonating in every syllable. "You absolutely are."

Stepping closer, Jules let his fingers casually brush against mine as our eyes locked in a silent exchange of understanding. "I couldn't have done this without you, you know," he confessed softly.

I shook my head, my steady voice carrying the truth of my feelings. "This was all you. I'm just incredibly lucky to witness it all."

His smile softened into something more intimate, as if veiling a secret promise, while he leaned in to press a lingering, tender kiss upon my cheek. The warmth of that kiss lingered long after he pulled away, leaving an indelible trace of affection. He held my gaze a little longer, his eyes revealing unspoken tenderness and shared dreams.

Then, with a sudden playful shift, his grin turned mischievous. "You know, I was thinking of saying we should head home, but Callie and Sam are already texting me about the after-party at the Taproom."

I laughed, shaking my head in mock exasperation. "Of course they are. Do we even have a choice in this matter?"

"Not really," Jules quipped, effortlessly slipping his hand into mine and interlocking our fingers. "But it promises to be a blast. And tonight, Teach, tonight is all about celebrating you, me, and everything we've built together."

With that, he gently tugged me toward the street, his laughter echoing into the night as we stepped into our shared future, a celebration not just of his success, but of the deep, unwavering foundation of trust and love that made moments like this extraordinarily unforgettable.

28

JULES

The town seemed to hold its collective breath as we left the afterparty behind, its vibrant, celebratory pulse slowly ebbing into the hushed embrace of the night. The cobblestone streets, still damp from a recent rain, shimmered under the soft, golden light of streetlamps, each stone echoing memories of centuries past. Nearby, the gentle murmur of the creek wove a delicate symphony with the rustling leaves, its watery notes merging with the quiet of the scene. Just moments earlier, we'd been enveloped by the raucous interplay of cheers and music, and now it felt as if the entire world had narrowed down to the two of us, walking side by side through Havenwood's tranquil, timeless avenues.

Almost instinctively, I reached for Elliott's hand. Without hesitation, his fingers entwined with mine, warm and reassuring. His jacket hung carelessly over one shoulder, and the slightest hint of a smile played on his lips as the cool night breeze playfully ruffled his hair. Beneath that calm exterior, the lingering spark of the evening's joy still danced in his eyes.

"That was some party," I said softly, my voice barely cutting through the gentle whispers of the night.

Elliott chuckled warmly, his thumb caressing the back of my hand. "I'm not sure I've ever seen the Taproom so packed before. They really know how to celebrate, especially you."

I couldn't help but roll my eyes, though the smile tugging at my lips betrayed my affection. "They weren't just celebrating me. It was about the performance, the whole cast, and the crew, the collective heartbeat of everyone involved."

"They were celebrating you," he replied, his tone firm yet tender, each word imbued with genuine pride. "You brought that entire magic to life, Jules. Every spotlight on you was well-deserved."

Glancing at him, my chest tightened with a mix of admiration and a quiet vulnerability. "You're biased," I teased lightly, my tone softer than usual, stripped of its usual playful deflection.

"I am," he confessed with a gentle smile that widened just a fraction. "But it doesn't make it any less true."

Our steps fell into a comfortable silence, accompanied only by the soft rustling of the trees and the bubbling creek. My thoughts drifted back to the Playhouse, the warm, embracing hugs from the cast after the show, the resonant applause that seemed to vibrate through my very bones, and the pivotal conversation with the board president that had sparked flickers of both hope and uncertainty.

Breaking the reflective silence, Elliott's voice, calm and measured, reached out. "You've been quiet since we left the theater," he observed, his tone laced with quiet concern. "What's going on in that brilliant head of yours?"

I hesitated for a moment, looking down at the timeworn cobblestones that had witnessed so many stories. "You know what," I said, giving his hand a reassuring squeeze, "it's the artistic director position."

His eyes softened as he nodded, a small furrow forming between his brows. "You've been thinking about it, haven't you?"

I exhaled slowly, the weight of the decision pressing gently against my heart. "Yeah," I admitted, each word laden with both excitement and apprehension. "We've talked about it before, but tonight… tonight made it feel so real. The Playhouse isn't just a building, it's the heartbeat of our community. Stepping into that role would be a monumental leap, a chance for permanence and deeper roots."

"Is that what's holding you back?" he asked tenderly. "The idea of staying put, of setting down roots?"

I shook my head, my voice softening to a near-whisper. "No, it's the opposite, really. I think I want that anchoring feeling, a reason to belong, to stay committed."

Elliott stopped walking and turned to face me fully, the soft glow of a streetlamp casting gentle shadows across his features. His expression

was a poignant blend of curiosity and deep affection. “More reason to stay?” he mused, his tone both light and searching.

I froze, suddenly aware of the vulnerability in my own words. Looking into his eyes, I found an unspoken understanding there. His hand tightened around mine, as if to silently promise that everything would be alright.

“Jules,” he said steadily, his voice resonating with emotion, “you don’t need a job title to have a reason to stay. You, in your entirety, are worth staying for. But I want more than that, I want us to continue building something real, something lasting. I want us to grow together.”

My breath caught as his words enveloped me in warmth, laden with unspoken dreams. “Elliott…” I began, but he wasn’t done.

“I’ve been thinking about this for a long time,” he continued, his voice gentle yet resolute. “I want us to take the next step. I want you to move in with me.”

A sudden rush of emotion left me momentarily speechless. “Move in?” I echoed, the phrase barely a whisper, heavy with hope and vulnerability.

He nodded, his lips curving into a tender smile. “Imagine making a space that’s truly ours, a place where you can have your own corner, a dedicated home office for your creative whirl, a sanctuary where your vibrant chaos can run free. More than that, I want you there, every day, sharing this life with me.”

After a brief pause, he added softly, “I even talked to Caleb about it. He’s excited at the thought of you being a part of our home. He gave his full blessing.”

I stared at him, a mix of relief, joy, and hope flooding through me, my throat tight with the swell of emotion. “You really want that?” I asked gently, almost afraid to sound too eager.

“I’ve never been surer of anything,” he confessed, his voice trembling ever so slightly with sincerity. “Jules, I’ve never felt this way before. I don’t want to let go of what we have. I don’t ever want to let you go.”

A tear slipped quietly down my cheek as I leaned into his comforting embrace, our foreheads touching in a silent communion of trust and affection. “Yes,” I whispered, my voice breaking tenderly, “Yes, I’ll move in. I want that too. I want you.”

In that profound moment, his face lit up with a radiant smile, pure and unguarded. He kissed me then, soft, lingering, and full of the promise of a shared future, his hands cradling my face with a tenderness that made my knees weak. Around us, the world seemed to dissolve into

a dreamlike tableau, where the only sounds were the gentle rush of the creek and the quiet, steady hum of the town.

When we finally pulled apart, a shaky laugh spilled from my lips, the weight in my heart lifting as I spoke. “So… home?”

“Home,” he replied, his voice equally soft, his hand finding mine once again as we resumed our leisurely walk.

As we continued down the moonlit path toward his house, something shifted deeply inside me, a profound sense of belonging and a newfound steadiness I hadn’t known I craved. With Elliott by my side, every step forward felt like a step into an expansive future where everything was not only possible but beautifully, irrevocably right.

EPILOGUE

ELLIOTT

Nine months into sharing a life with Jules, our home had transformed into a vibrant fusion of our shared journey, a place where every corner whispered tales of our union. My once meticulously ordered space now bore the beautiful chaos of Jules' presence: brightly colored fabric swatches draped casually over chairs, handwritten notes in flourishing script scattered across the coffee table, and an entire corner in the dining room overtaken by an eclectic vintage record player surrounded by stacks of cherished vinyl treasures unearthed from thrift shops. What had once seemed disorderly now felt like an artful expression of who we were together, and I couldn't imagine my life without it.

Tonight, that same delightful life was magnified by the warm embrace of our closest friends and family. In our backyard, twinkling string lights wove a fairy-tale canopy over mismatched chairs arranged lovingly around the space, each one cradling clusters of laughter and heartfelt conversation. Near the glowing firepit, faces were illuminated by its gentle, flickering radiance as guests roasted marshmallows or simply basked in the soothing crackle of the fire. The blend of vibrant chatter, punctuated by peals of laughter, mingled with the soft, mellifluous hum of background music, crafting an atmosphere that felt both exuberantly lively and intimately personal.

The early April Spring air was crisp and aromatic, carrying an alluring medley of scents: the smoky allure of roasted vegetables, the

savory trace of grilled chicken, and the lingering, sweet perfume of Jules' homemade sangria. Amidst this sensory banquet, Callie sat cross-legged on a rustic camping chair near the patio. They animatedly recounted their latest salon escapade, a glimmer of mischief in their eyes and a half-full wine glass in hand. "And then she says, 'I want bangs like Taylor Swift.' And I'm like, honey, Swift's bangs are a national treasure, and I'm just one person!" Their voice danced with humor as the group erupted into contagious laughter.

Perched on the worn arm of a patio chair, Jules added an exaggerated flourish, mimicking a theatrical recitation of Puck's monologue from *A Midsummer Night's Dream.* His performance was a burst of energy that carried effortlessly over the hum of conversation, drawing claps and cheers from everyone around. Callie raised their glass in a playful salute. "You're damn right I did," he declared with infectious pride.

Across the table, Sam and Avery engaged in a spirited debate about launching a podcast segment on local ghost stories. "I'm telling you, people love haunted history," Avery insisted, his tone sparkling with enthusiastic fervor. Sam, taking a measured sip of his drink, shot a wry smile. "Sure, because Havenwood really needs me recounting tales of the Taproom's infamous keg that apparently tapped itself once." The banter was as lively as it was endearing.

Meanwhile, Renzo and Liam lounged contentedly on the sun-warmed porch, beers in hand. They took turns hilariously recounting the intricate details of Liam's latest dating mishap, a fumble involving a clueless gym bro, an awkward lull that stretched into eternity, and an absurd attempt at dirty talk that had Renzo gasping with laughter. I manned the grill near the edge of the patio, flipping burgers with practiced care while keeping one ear attuned to the surrounding conversations.

Caleb, leaning casually against the counter beside me, sipped his soda with an air of quiet confidence. At 13, his lanky frame hinted at the promise of towering growth, and his easy demeanor was a striking, heartwarming contrast to the awkwardness I had known at his age. His inquisitive eyes twinkled as he broke the comfortable silence. "You're still gonna do it tonight, right?" he asked, his tone a blend of playful teasing and earnest curiosity as he popped a chip into his mouth.

I glanced his way, masking my eagerness with feigned innocence. "Do what?" I replied, a half-smile tugging at my lips.

He grinned mischievously, nodding toward the small velvet box hidden in my jacket pocket. "C'mon, Dad. You've been checking your pocket like it holds a secret every five minutes. It's not exactly subtle."

I chuckled, shaking my head in affectionate exasperation. "That obvious?" I mused.

"Painfully," he admitted with an impish pause, his grin evoking memories of his mother's warm humor. "It's cool, though. Jules is cool. You're… happier. I like it."

My throat tightened as I reached out to tousle his hair gently. "Thanks, bud. That means more than you know," I exhaled.

"Just don't get all mushy on me," Caleb teased, playfully shoving my hand away before breaking into a wide smile.

My eyes briefly left the sizzling grill to catch a glimpse of Jules. His voice soared clearly over the soft hum of conversation, eliciting bursts of laughter and spontaneous applause from those gathered. Watching from the periphery, my heart swelled with an overwhelming certainty and tender delight.

As twilight descended, painting the sky in ethereal hues of purple and gold, dinner began to wind down. Plates cleared away, making room for the delightful array of desserts that Callie had insisted on bringing tangy lemon bars, decadently rich chocolate tarts, and a fruit cobbler nearly devoured in anticipation. Jules took his place beside me on an old wooden bench, his hand resting lightly on my knee as his laughter mingled with the tale Sam spun aloud about his comically disastrous first (and only) roller skating experience.

Across the table, Callie's knowing eyes met mine, silently toasting with a raised glass in encouragement. My heart pounded mightily as I stood, drawing the attention of the entire gathering. Noticing the shift, Jules looked up with a playful yet curious expression. "What's up, Teach?" he asked, his tone laced with both jest and sincere interest.

In that electrifying moment, my hand dove into the inner pocket of my jacket, fingers grazing the cool velvet of the small box as the world around me seemed to decelerate. The joyful hum of conversation and the melodic clinking of glasses faded into a distant buzz, replaced by the deafening cadence of my own racing heartbeat.

"Jules," I began, my voice resonant and steady despite the tempest of nerves swirling within, "it's hard to fathom that it's been a year since our first date at the Bistro. I still recall the tremble in my voice, the nervous flutter, and how you made everything feel effortlessly serene. And look at Evan over there, laughing with Noah and Callie," I said, subtly gesturing toward our merry group. "He was the waiter that night.

It's wild, to think how much has changed in just one year, how much more vibrant and fuller our lives have become."

I paused for a heartbeat, glancing toward Caleb who offered me an encouraging nod that warmed me further. "These past nine months with you, Jules, have been the absolute best chapters of my life. You've flooded my world with light, joy, and colors I never knew existed." I let my voice soften, heavy with emotion. "Our world."

At that, Jules' eyes widened, and his lips parted in a silent gasp of understanding. "You've taught me to take leaps of faith, to embrace the beautiful chaos of life, and to find exquisite beauty in unexpected moments," I continued, my words pouring forth with both passion and vulnerability. "You've taught me to be brave, not only for myself but for us."

Then, with a reverent stillness that stole everyone's breath, I dropped to one knee. Holding up the small velvet box for all to see, the world seemed to hold a collective pause as gasps spread through the crowd. Jules clutched at his mouth in astonishment, his eyes glistening with unshed tears.

"Jules," I said, my voice thick with receding emotion yet brimming with hope, "will you marry me?"

For a suspended moment that stretched into eternity, the world around us faltered in anticipation. Then, like a beam of pure light, Jules nodded fervently, his voice trembling with joy as he whispered, "Yes. Of course, yes."

In that magical instant, the yard erupted into cheers, applause, and exuberant exclamations. Callie dramatically dabbed away tears, Sam clapping Caleb heartily on the back, and from the porch Liam bellowed, "Finally!" The joyous cacophony of celebration mingled with the lingering melodies of the night as I carefully slid a shining ring onto Jules' finger. Its silver band sparkled in the subdued glow of the evening, reflecting off Jules' beaming face as he pulled me gently to my feet. His arms enveloped me, and he kissed me with a passion so intense it seemed to dissolve the boundaries of time and space.

When we eventually drew apart, Jules leaned in close and whispered, "You're stuck with me now, Teach."

"Good," I declared, a smile curving my lips as I returned his kiss with a tenderness that mirrored the shared promise of our future.

Amid the reverberating cheers and the warm embrace of our loved ones, Caleb darted through the jubilant throng. His face was aglow with pure, unadulterated excitement as he raced toward us. Throwing his arms around me, he squeezed tightly and then quickly did the same for

Jules. "Congratulations, you guys! So, do I get to call you my dads now?" His exuberant declaration struck us both, drawing tears of joy to mine and glistening in Jules' eyes.

All around us, our friends and family joined in with warm hugs, heartfelt congratulations, and laughter that intertwined seamlessly with the sounds of celebration. The night stretched on into a symphony of music, merriment, and the unyielding warmth of community. Under a vast, starlit sky and the tender glow of the moon, surrounded by those who loved us most, Jules and I stepped courageously into the next chapter of our lives, side by side, exactly where we were meant to be.

ABOUT THE AUTHOR

Grafton Carter is a celebrated author of authentic, sexy, and gloriously queer storytelling, crafting heartfelt, captivating MM (male/male) romance novels that explore themes of love, identity, and self-discovery. With a unique ability to create multidimensional characters and deeply emotional narratives, Grafton is a rising star in the LGBTQ+ romance genre.

A native of the Midwest, Grafton grew up in a vibrant small-town community where he developed a love for storytelling through local theater and creative writing. After earning his degree in Education, he spent years as a high school drama teacher, bringing stories to life on stage and leading GSA clubs helping empower students to embrace their true selves. His transition to writing has solidified his place as a trusted voice in queer romance.

Grafton's work is known for its steamy, tender intimacy, witty dialogue, and heartfelt moments, always wrapped in a deep, authentic representation of the LGBTQ+ experience. His stories explore found family, the thrill of unexpected connections, and the beautiful, messy complexity of falling, and staying, in love. His books promise to leave readers swooning and reaching for the tissues with authentic, sexy, and gloriously queer storytelling.

When not writing, Grafton is a passionate advocate for queer representation in media and literature, frequently speaking at conferences and workshops about the importance of diverse storytelling. He's also an intimacy choreographer and theater consultant, ensuring safe and genuine portrayals of love, sex, and emotional connection on stage.

In his downtime, Grafton can be found curled up with a mug of tea and his three needy dogs, brainstorming his next novel while binge-watching trashy TV or organizing his ever-growing collection of Funko Pops. He lives in a charming suburban home in Illinois with his husband and their three stepchildren, whom he credits as his constant source of love and chaos.

Follow Grafton Carter on social media and visit his website to stay updated on upcoming releases, sneak peeks, and behind-the-scenes looks into his writing process.

www.graftoncarter.com

www.ingramcontent.com/pod-product-compliance
Ingram Content Group UK Ltd.
Pitfield, Milton Keynes, MK11 3LW, UK
UKHW021601280725
7106UKWH00042B/1531

9 798348 575540

SD - #0035 - 200623 - C0 - 178/111/10 - PB - 9781910942765 - Gloss Lamination